AFTER THE LAST DANCE

Sarra Manning

sphere

SPHERE

First published in Great Britain in 2015 by Sphere
This paperback edition published in 2016 by Sphere

1 3 5 7 9 10 8 6 4 2

A CIP catalogue record for this book is available from the British Library.

ISBN 978-0-7515-6115-9

Typeset in Baskerville by M Rules
Printed and bound in Great Britain by
Clays Ltd, St Ives plc

Papers used by Sphere are from well-managed forests and other responsible sources.

FSC
www.fsc.org
MIX
Paper from responsible sources
FSC® C104740

Sphere
An imprint of
Little, Brown Book Group
Carmelite House
50 Victoria Embankment
London EC4Y 0DZ

An Hachette UK Company
www.hachette.co.uk

www.littlebrown.co.uk

To all the men and women who passed through the doors of Rainbow Corner. Thank you for your inspiration, your courage and your sacrifice.

Acknowledgements

I bored so many people stupid talking about Rainbow Corner and how one day, I would write a novel about it. Thank you for bearing the brunt of it, Julie Mayhew, Anna Carey and Sarah Franklin. Sam Baker for our epic pizza and prosecco summits. Sophie Wilson and Sarah Bailey for general all-round loveliness. Lesley Lawson for TransPacific book talk.

A thousand thank yous to my agent Karolina Sutton for getting me there in the end and Norah Perkins, Lucy Morris, Melissa Pimentel and all at Curtis Brown.

Much thanks to my editor Manpreet Grewal for her incisive, tough love editing that really shaped this book into what I wanted it to be. (Let us never talk of the 20,000 words that she made me cut.)

And thank you to Kate Hodges. We'll always have our interest in the chapel.

Prologue

London, September 1943

King's Cross Station was cavernous, bigger than a cathedral, and filled with people.

It was eight o'clock, which probably wasn't that late in London where there were nightclubs and restaurants with fine linen tablecloths and silver champagne buckets where dark-suited men and women in fur stoles had supper after the theatre. In Durham, people didn't roam about at night, because there was nowhere to roam to, apart from pubs and well, she didn't know anyone who'd frequent a pub.

But here in London there were positively *hordes* of people hurrying about, heads down, faces grim and unsmiling. Soldiers. Sailors. Khaki and navy everywhere she looked. An older man with a suitcase lifted his hat as he saw her glance in his direction. A woman juggled assorted luggage, two small children, and a baby on her hip.

Next her attention was caught by two girls not *that* much older than herself in WAAF uniforms; hair rolled impeccably, arms linked as they marched smartly along. The blue serge was almost the same shade as her eyes and she thought that maybe she might join the WAAFs when she was old enough to volunteer, though they weren't allowed to fly planes, which was a shame because learning to fly a plane would be thrilling.

The longer she stood there, the more her eyes sought out the people who lingered, rather than rushed. Saying goodbye with embraces that went on too long: tense hands clutching at shoulders, sobs not quite swallowed up by the distant sound of a brass band and the cacophony of train doors slamming shut. She turned her head away from one young couple, the girl's face almost obscured by her handkerchief as she wept in the arms of her corporal.

She suddenly felt very small and very alone. Too scared to put one foot in front of the other, to choose a direction to go in. She had nowhere to hurry to, no one to linger with and the creeping suspicion that she'd made a terrible mistake. She was always getting scolded for being impetuous, though it was more than impetuosity that had made her jump on the London train with her mother's 'funeral' fur coat around her shoulders and her sister's two best dresses stuffed in her suitcase.

By now they'd have found the silly, spiteful note she'd stuck behind the clock on the mantelpiece.

I didn't kiss Cedric. He tried to kiss me. *I think it's beastly that you refused to give me a fair hearing and instead expect me to be happy that I'm being shipped off to the back of beyond to join the Land Girls as soon as I've taken my Highers.*

Well, I'm not going. By the time you read this I'll be in London having all sorts of adventures rather than seeing out the war shovelling pig muck, hoeing fields and wearing corduroy knickerbockers and horrid, clumpy boots.

It might have been her rashest, most impetuous act. Oh, if only she stopped to think about the consequences of her actions . . .

'Hey! Watch where you swing that thing,' exclaimed a loud voice to the left of her.

She whirled round to see two men carrying duffel bags. They were in uniform, but their khakis were crisper, sharper, and they wore their caps at a jaunty angle. One was fair, one was dark, but they were both strapping specimens of masculinity who didn't look the least bit like their raw-skinned, pasty-faced British comrades.

They were drawing level with her now as she stood there, mouth agape, because they were from that magical land of movie stars and Broadway and dancing girls in sparkling costumes and everything that was good and great and in glorious Technicolor.

Then they walked right past her, joking in loud, breezy voices, and the fact that she was alone, without purpose and in the most terrible trouble didn't matter any more. She rushed after them, suitcase banging against her legs. 'Please! Oh, please!' she cried, catching up so she could tug on a khaki-covered arm. 'Please! I need you to take me to Rainbow Corner!'

London, September 2003

The girl stumbled down from the train at King's Cross station, and stood there, eyes cast down.

Somehow she was in London, though London might just as well be Africa or somewhere to the left of Mars. None of this could be real.

The only thing that was real was the roll of money so thick she could barely clasp her fingers around it. She'd been holding on to it for so long that her hand had cramped up and sweat had reduced the outer notes to pulp. It didn't even feel like money any more. It never had. From the moment she'd picked it up, it had been a ticking time bomb.

There was a noise behind her and she shuffled just far enough that the man in the suit could get off the train too. Her eyes came to rest on the tips of his polished black shoes, holes punched into the leather to make a pattern. They were so shiny that if she looked hard enough she'd be able to see her reflection. She looked away.

'Do you know where you're going?' She'd never heard anyone talk like that. As if each word mattered, not just things to be screamed or shouted.

Words never worked for her. She stayed silent.

She didn't know what he wanted from her. Him with his beautiful voice and shoes and the suit – nothing good ever came from a man in a suit, she knew that much.

'Where do you want to go?' This time the words were sharp enough that she took one step away from him. She wrapped an arm round her midriff. Noticed the streaks of blood on her T-shirt, not red any more but dried to a dark, rusty brown. 'Do you know anyone in London? Do you understand what I'm saying?' There was a pause. 'Do you speak English?'

She shrugged.

'God help me,' he muttered. His hand almost came to rest on her shoulder. Almost, but not quite. 'You'd better come with me, then.'

She hadn't 'better' do anything. She could take care of herself – except taking care of herself meant keeping as still and quiet as possible.

She'd never thought about what the world might be like. Could hardly think about life outside that house, in that room, under that bed where she'd woken up this morning. But somehow she was in London with no idea of how she'd even got here.

All she had was this man not quite touching her, talking to her like she meant something.

'We'll get a taxi,' he said, and the hand that wasn't quite on her shoulder flexed and she was moving her feet in time with his, even as her fingers twitched around the roll of notes again.

1

Present Day

Even in Las Vegas, when a girl in a wedding dress walked into a bar, people turned to stare. The bride, minus groom, seemed unaware of the attention. She walked right up to the bar, put down her suitcase and hauled herself up on the stool next to Leo's.

It was then he realised that the gawping was less to do with the big, foofy white dress and everything to do with her beauty. Leo liked to think he was immune to beauty. He'd spent the last year in LA where you couldn't even pick up a carton of milk from the neighbourhood bodega without seeing at least one woman who'd spent thousands of dollars on her appearance. A little nip here, a hell of a lot of tucking there.

But this woman was so breathtaking that he was grateful she'd sat down next to him so he could gaze at each perfect feature on her face and marvel at the way they came together to form an impeccable whole. She'd had some work done, but it was very discreet. A few injectables, just enough Botox that she could still show emotion.

Her honey-blonde hair was swept up in a fancy plaited arrangement and topped with a tiara. Leo could tell by the smug glint of the stones even in the dimly lit bar that the tiara was adorned with proper, honest-to-goodness diamonds.

There were more diamonds sparkling on her ring finger, but no wedding band, which could explain why her cupid-bow mouth drooped at the corners. Though, when Leo caught her eye, she acknowledged his interest with a half-hearted twist of her lips.

'Hello,' she said in an English accent far more precise than his, as she settled herself more comfortably so the full white skirts of her dress floated around her like petals.

'Hello,' Leo said and before he could say anything else, the surly bartender who'd taken his sweet time before he served Leo was breaking the land-speed record to stand in front of her and wait expectantly for her to order.

The woman eyed the collection of bottles behind the bar doubtfully.

'Walked out on your husband already, did you?' the bartender asked and she blinked.

'I'm not married.' Her voice was so neutral, it was beige. She gestured at the acres of tulle and silk taffeta around her. 'Appearances can be deceiving.'

'Runaway bride, then? You got cold feet at the last minute?'

The woman set her shoulders back as if she were about to bristle and shut the man down, but then she smiled.

Before she smiled, she was beautiful. But once she smiled properly so her blue eyes twinkled like her diamonds, she was *absolutely fucking beautiful*. It was all Leo could do not to drool.

'Oh, darling,' she said to the barman, who'd now stopped pretending to polish the glass he'd been holding. 'Really, it's too boring to talk about.'

Though she seemed self-possessed as she sat there, her shoulders were so stiff that Leo's ached in sympathy – as if it were a superhuman effort to hold herself upright when all she wanted to do was wilt.

'So, did you break it off or . . . '

She held up her hand in protest. 'Please, no more questions. Not until I've had a drink.'

'What are you having? On the house,' the barman said as if he really thought he was in with a chance, despite his greasy, sparse hair coaxed into a sad little quiff, quivering chin and the fact that he was polishing glasses and serving drinks in a dive bar. Still, you couldn't blame a guy for trying.

'A glass of champagne, please.'

He stared at her like she was speaking Martian. 'We don't serve champagne by the glass. We don't got no champagne.'

'Really? How extraordinary!' She turned to Leo and shook her head, inviting him to share her disbelief. He shrugged and this time she rewarded him with a conspiratorial grin, before she turned back to the barman. 'Well, what do you have, then, darling?'

She made do with a dirty martini. She wrinkled her nose as she took the first sip and it was then that the barman realised that he was batting way, way, *way* out of his league because he started fussing over his bowls of tired-looking bar snacks and left her alone.

They sat there, Leo and the woman, in silence and it wasn't until she'd almost finished her drink that she turned to him. 'I'll be twenty-seven tomorrow,' she said.

He wasn't sure where she was going with this or if he wanted to find out. Women who looked like her, women wearing that calibre of diamond, had to be nothing but trouble, but since when had that ever stopped him? 'Happy birthday for tomorrow.' He lifted his tumbler of scotch and gently clinked it against the side of her glass.

She leaned in closer so Leo thought he might drown in the warm, sweet-scented nearness of her. 'The thing is, darling, I made a vow I'd get married before I turned twenty-seven.'

'Twenty-seven isn't that old,' he said. 'I managed to survive being twenty-seven without getting married.'

'It's different for men,' she insisted, glancing down at her engagement ring. 'For women, twenty-seven is . . . well, it's hard to explain.'

Leo waited for her to at least try but she was twisting the huge rock on her finger so it shimmered in the spotlight above her and stars clouded his vision. 'Look, you're obviously having a bad day but . . . '

'The baddest of all bad days.' She held her hand in front of her and stared at her engagement ring as if it were responsible for all her current woes. 'The baddest day since records began.'

He hardly had to think about it at all. 'You know, I could marry you. If you wanted?'

This vision, this goddess, choked on a mouthful of martini. 'You'd marry me?' she asked once she'd recovered. 'Why on earth would you do that?'

Leo shrugged. 'I used to be a boy scout. I still like to do a good deed every day.'

She shifted on her stool so she was facing him, the whipped white froth of her dress brushing against the knee of his jeans. 'You're not married already, are you?'

'No.' He smiled at her confusion; tremulously she smiled back and he was starting to like this game he was playing even if he didn't know the rules.

'Do you have a fiancée or some girl who you have an understanding with?'

'No.'

'Are you gay? Not that it really matters but . . . '

'No!'

She spread her hands wide. 'Still, darling, this is all quite sudden. Give me one good reason why I should marry you.'

There were a million and one lousy reasons – except being

married was about the only thing he hadn't tried. And this had to be fate – a gorgeous girl walks into a bar all ready to say 'I do' and the only thing she's missing is the groom. He summoned the bartender with a lazy finger and ordered another whisky and a vodka tonic for her, as the dirty martini hadn't been a great success. 'Give me one good reason why not?'

She shook her head as the barman placed a fresh drink in front of her. 'Where to start?'

'It'll be midnight in a few hours. I thought you were on a clock.'

She pouted a little, her gaze darting round for a more likely candidate. There wasn't one. Only a couple of old men who'd been nursing a bottle of beer apiece for the last hour and a man in the far corner staring disconsolately at his empty glass like he'd just put his life savings on black and red had come up. Still, her eyes narrowed as she considered her options.

'You don't have to marry me,' Leo said and he had her attention again. 'But let's have a little drink and a chat and see how we both feel about it in an hour or so. Deal?'

She picked up her glass and gave him another one of those smiles that made Leo want to find a puddle so he could drape his jacket over it for her. 'Deal.'

2

September 1943

The two GIs took some convincing. 'Why do you need to go to Rainbow Corner?' one of them asked. 'One of our guys done you wrong and you got your dad waiting in the wings with a shotgun?'

'I beg your pardon?' She stared up at him. He had olive skin and dark eyes, and at any other time she might have thought him quite dashing but not when she had the sneaking feeling he was mocking her as she stood there in her mother's fur coat, with sturdy lace-ups and ankle socks, her vampy red lipstick all but chewed off now. Still, there was no reason for him to look at her as if he thought she was up to no good. 'Oh! Oh! It's absolutely nothing like that. It's just, well . . . I've come all this way, from Durham . . . Do you know Durham?'

They both shook their heads and smiled at her indulgently as if she'd been brought downstairs to say goodnight to the grown-ups.

'Of course you don't know Durham because it's the most pitiful, boring place in England and I . . . I . . . we got bombed out and now I have no family and no home and so I decided that if

I had to be destitute then I might just as well be destitute in London and I saw Rainbow Corner on a newsreel and the announcer said that it never closed, that they'd thrown away the key to the front door so they were always open for anyone who needed a place to go.'

She was slightly ashamed at the fibs that tripped so readily from her mouth. But if someone didn't know all the circumstances leading up to her flight from Durham, then it might show her in a very poor light. Certainly, the taller, ganglier GI with the shock of wheat-blond hair wouldn't be looking quite so concerned.

'You poor kid. That's awful,' he said, though she wasn't a kid. As of two weeks ago, she was seventeen. 'There's no other family you could stay with?'

She shook her head. 'No. I'm all on my own now.' She sighed and imagined she must look very forlorn. 'I'll simply have to learn how to fend for myself.'

Meanwhile, his friend had a glint in his eye that she didn't like. 'You'd be better off finding the nearest YWCA than hotfooting it to Rainbow Corner.'

Her face fell. 'But the YWCA will be too much C and not enough Y.'

This time they both laughed then the blond one said, 'Come on, Danny. Been ages since we helped a damsel in distress.'

'How old are you anyway?' Danny asked.

'Nineteen,' she replied immediately, as if she didn't have to think about it at all because she'd been nineteen for months and months, but he scoffed like he didn't believe that either.

'OK, we'll take you to Rainbow Corner, but any more lies, then I'm going to start thinking you're an enemy agent. Might take you to the nearest police station instead.'

'Ignore him,' the other one said as she huffed indignantly. 'Got bawled out by our company commander last week. Been in a funk ever since. I'm Phillip, but everyone calls me Phil.'

'I'm Rosem— Rose,' she amended. He shot her a dazzling white smile and picked up her suitcase. Once they'd descended into the Underground, he paid for her ticket and found her a seat and didn't even mind that her attention wavered between him and the brightly lit Tube carriage, the girl sitting opposite with a covetable, extravagant hat perched on her head, the grab handles swinging with the motion of the train, even the advertisements – so many new things to marvel at.

It would all have been thrilling if she could only stop looking at her watch and imagining what was happening back in Durham. By now, they would have read her note. Shirley would say something hateful like, 'Even when she's not here, she manages to make an absolute nuisance of herself!' Mother had probably gone to bed with one of her heads and Father would have locked himself in his study. They'd also realise she'd taken the fur coat and borrowed Shirley's black crêpe de Chine and her pale blue taffeta, which would just compound matters.

'What's the matter? You're too pretty to look so sad.'

Rose blushed. No one had ever called her pretty before, though if she held her face a certain way and half-squinted, she thought she looked a little like Hedy Lamarr. Still, it didn't do for people to think that you thought you were pretty. 'That's very kind but I'm not . . . '

'You'd be even prettier if you smiled,' Phil said, and she did smile then and he pretended he was about to faint though Danny grunted. Rose decided that it was best to ignore him.

The next station was Piccadilly Circus.

Simply walking up the steps that led from station to street was exhilarating. Of course, they'd turned off the lights and she couldn't see Eros or the famous advertisement hoardings, but it took only seconds for the shapes and outlines in the murky night to shift into focus and become people hustling and bustling. Waiting for friends or sheltering in doorways as they lit cigarettes, queuing outside restaurants and nightclubs; there was an electric hum to their laughter and chatter.

The lemonade-fizz of anticipation made Rose's fingers twitch and her toes curl in her lace-ups. It was as if everything that was good and glamorous had converged on this one spot, including the gaggle of girls, all primped and preened, who were gathered on a street corner. 'Hey, GI, need someone to jive with?' one of the girls called out as she caught sight of Phil and Danny.

'Give you a kiss if you get me into Rainbow Corner,' another girl promised, checking Rose with her hip so she stumbled but before Rose could raise her foot or employ a sharp elbow, Danny had her arm in a firm hold and guided her forward.

'You and trouble are on first-name terms, aren't you? Here's some advice, kid: have your night on Uncle Sam, then go back home.'

'But I told you already, I was bombed out. I don't actually have a ho—'

'Yeah, yeah. Tell it to the Marines,' he drawled as he hauled her through the thickening crowd, their progress becoming a slow crawl. 'Go home or end up like them.'

Rose followed his gaze to another group of girls standing on the opposite corner. They seemed harmless enough. Pretty, even, though there was a word for the sort of girl who hung about on street corners calling out to men she patently didn't know. To think that *she'd* been accused of being fast for daring to attract the unwelcome attentions of fat Cedric, the bank manager's son. 'They don't seem so bad. What's wrong with them?'

'The Piccadilly Commandos?' he replied with a dry snicker that was a distant cousin to a laugh. 'You'll find out soon enough if you keep propositioning GIs at railway stations.'

'Well, I like that! That not what I did!'

'Cut it out, Danny,' Phil said sharply as he pulled open a large glass-set door. 'After you, ma'am.'

Rose had dreamt about this moment for so long, but now she was preoccupied with bickering with that hateful man, then squeezing past a noisy group of American soldiers on their way out, then suddenly here she was . . .

She'd left the drab, humdrum world behind – all that making-do and saving things for a best that never came. She'd lied and stolen and snatched herself away and accosted strange men to walk through a door and find herself in heaven on earth.

Rainbow Corner.

There was absolutely no point in having dreams if you didn't do everything in your power to make them come true, Rose decided, as she gazed around her. Truthfully, she felt a little disappointed as she took in the huge foyer. There were the same official-looking signs pinned to the noticeboard in front of her that she saw everywhere she went. But there was also an arrow pointing east with BERLIN – 600 MILES inscribed on it. Another arrow pointing in the opposite direction that bore the words NEW YORK – 3271 MILES and an American flag hanging proudly from the balcony above, reached by a sweeping staircase. If Rose stood very still and tried to block out the sound of people talking and calling out to each other in that smooth easy way that Americans seemed to have, then she could hear the distant strains of a band playing something swingy and infectious. That was where she wanted to be . . .

'Rosie?'

Phil tugged gently at her sleeve to pull her to the reception desk manned by two women in dark grey uniforms. She hung back as Phil and Danny signed in and asked if the rumours of hot showers were true. Rose could still hear the band; she swayed on the spot, one foot tapping out the rhythm, until she became aware of the two women looking at her quizzically.

'Hello,' she said in what she hoped was a confident voice. 'I'm with them.'

'Would you believe this is Phil's kid sis come all the way from Des Moines?' Danny treated both women to a look Rose couldn't see but one of them, an officious-looking brunette, smiled.

'I won't be any trouble,' Rose said. 'Honestly, I won't.'

The other woman, who looked even more officious, seemed unconvinced. 'She sure has a funny accent for that part of the world,' she said drily.

'Yeah, she's kind of pretentious.' Rose hissed through tightly clenched teeth. How dare he? 'She's hoping to bag a duke while she's here.'

Suddenly getting into Rainbow Corner didn't seem nearly as important as punching Danny hard between his shoulder blades, but both women laughed. 'I think there's an earl playing billiards – best keep your sister away from him.'

'Thank you. Thank you ever, ever so much. You won't even know I'm here,' Rose promised, as Phil led her away. She grinned up at him. 'That was touch and go for a minute.' She turned to Danny. 'Thank you for your help,' she added stiffly.

'Don't mention it, kid,' he said, touching his cap in mock salute. 'See you later.'

It was a relief when he shouldered his way past them. Phil was hoisting up his duffel bag too. Rose would be fine on her own because everyone said that the Yanks were very friendly and never stood on ceremony, and besides she was here under the protection of the American Red Cross so nothing bad would happen to her.

'Well, it's been very nice to meet you and thanks again,' she said brightly but briskly. 'I'm sure I'll be perfectly all right now.'

'It's like that, is it,' Phil said, his kind, open face closing off a little. 'I thought we were becoming buddies.'

'We were – we are. Really, you've been a brick, but you needn't worry about me,' Rose assured him with an airiness that she didn't believe herself. 'I'm sure you have lots of friends here you'd like to spend time with and I'd hate to cramp your style.'

'More like you don't want me to cramp your style,' he said, shifting his bag. 'Back home, we have a name for girls like you.'

'I'm not trying to get rid of you. I'm helping you get rid of me,' she explained. 'So you're free to, um, talk to other girls.'

He flushed bright red. 'I'd rather talk to you,' he said in a rush. 'I'd rather spend the whole eighteen hours before I go back to base with you.'

'You would?'

He nodded, a clumsy grin on his face. 'Yeah, I would,' he declared and he held out his arm so she could take it and led her up the stairs which, on closer inspection, weren't as sweeping as Rose would have liked them to be.

They danced to a swing band on the huge dancefloor, both of them dazzled by the lights bouncing off the brass section and trying not to bump into anyone, because there had to be at least two hundred other couples moving in four-four time.

'Have you ever jived?' Phil asked.

'Not really, but I want to more than anything,' Rose said, but there wasn't room to do much more than a fast foxtrot. Phil danced with her until her feet were sore and her throat was dry but when he ground to a halt and stood there panting, she didn't want to stop. 'Do let's stay for one more dance,' she begged but Phil laughed and shook his head.

'I heard a rumour about this place,' he said. 'If it's true, it's even better than dancing.'

'I can't believe that anything's better than dancing,' Rose said as he took her hand and hurried out of the ballroom and down the stairs. 'What is it?'

'I can't tell you. It's a surprise.'

'I love surprises!' In fact, Rose loved everything that had happened to her in Rainbow Corner. Even the contretemps in gaining entry, because those few fearful moments when she'd thought she was going to be tossed back to the cruel, unforgiving night made her appreciate being here all the more. 'Shall I shut my eyes so the surprise is extra surprising?'

'That's a grand idea,' Phil agreed and he was one of those people that you instinctively trusted and Rose knew that he'd lead her down the stairs and ensure that no one bumped into her. 'Two more steps. Careful, Rosie. Then we just head down here and hey! Watch it, pal, lady coming through . . . you can open your eyes when I say . . . now!'

Rose didn't open her eyes immediately because she wanted to let the anticipation build just a little while longer and then she couldn't wait and she opened them and, 'Oh my . . .' She thought she might faint or burst into tears or some heady combination of both. 'Goodness me, I must be dreaming.'

Like everywhere else in Rainbow Corner, the basement was packed to the rafters. There were people squeezed around small tables, more people crowded round the edges of the room, even lining the stairs as they clutched mugs and nodded along to the record playing on a jukebox and in the centre of the huge room was a soda fountain. A genuine soda fountain.

Phil visibly puffed with pride at her reaction. 'We have one just like it in Des Moines. More than one.'

'It's absolutely beautiful,' Rose gasped, and Phil chuckled as if she was joking but she'd never been more deadly serious in her whole life.

'Hey! Let's grab that table.' Phil was already pushing her down onto a chair, which had suddenly become vacant.

Mindful that the money in her purse had to last until . . . golly, until she found a job, Rose decided to make do with a cup of tea and a bun. Surely that couldn't cost more than a shilling?

'What shall we have?' Phil looked round for a waitress.

'I'm really not that hungry,' she lied. 'I eat like a bird.'

'You'll be hungry once our food arrives, you'll see,' Phil promised. His hand closed over Rose's as she reached for her bag. 'What kind of guy dances with a girl for hours, then expects her to pay for her own chow? It's my treat.'

'That's very kind of you,' Rose murmured as the waitress approached.

Once the waitress left, Rose wasn't sure what they were going to talk about. Boys never had much to say, though in her limited experience that never stopped them talking one's ear off.

Phil fished for a packet of cigarettes from the breast pocket of his uniform. 'Want one?'

'Yes, please.' She'd never smoked before but Rose let Phil light the cigarette for her then concentrated very hard on breathing the smoke out of the corner of her mouth in an insouciant fashion. How she longed to be insouciant! 'So . . . '

'You're the prettiest girl I've seen in England,' Phil suddenly blurted out. 'I'm not saying it so you'll put out, it's the truth.'

It was hard to be insouciant when you were blushing. The hand that was awkwardly holding the cigarette aloft started to nervously twirl a lock of hair until Rose heard a hissing sound before she even smelt the singeing. 'Well, I don't know if I'm *that* pretty,' she said doubtfully. Also, she wasn't entirely sure what *putting out* was or if she wanted to do it. 'My hairbrush is in my suitcase and I'm sure I must look an absolute state.'

Phil shook his head. 'You don't. You look pretty. Real pretty.'

He was staring at her so unashamedly that she didn't know what to say. 'You look very nice too,' she managed, which wasn't altogether true. He was tall and strapping but also rather homely-looking and had an alarming gap between his front teeth, but he was one of the nicest people Rose had ever met. He reminded her of the golden retriever her best friend Patience had owned before the war. Prince had had the same look of happy devotion when you called him a 'good boy' or patted his head. 'And you've been so sweet. Gone above and beyond anything I expected when I accosted you at King's Cross.'

Thankfully Phil didn't have a chance to say how pretty Rose was again because the waitress was back. 'There you are,' she said, whipping a laden plate off her tray. 'House special.'

The house special was a mound of misshapen hot doughnuts. 'The guys back at base call this place Dunker's Den,' Phil told her. He pushed the plate nearer. 'Go on. Have one.'

Rose was scared to touch them in case they weren't real but when she reached out to take one of the deep-fried, sugar-coated apparitions, it was hot enough that she snatched back her hand and sucked her injured fingers into her mouth. She closed her eyes as the sweet, sweet, sweet crystals coated her tongue.

Then she didn't care what she looked like as she tore one of the doughnuts in half and crammed it into her mouth. It was hot and greasy and she closed her eyes again in a moment of still, quiet bliss and when she opened them again, Phil was beaming.

'Have as many as you like,' he said munificently. 'Do you want something to wash it down with?' Phil gestured at the two glasses that she hadn't even noticed. They were full of an unappetising, effervescent brown liquid.

'Is that root beer?' she ventured.

'No.' Phil grinned, all teeth and gums. 'Guess again.'

'I haven't a clue. May I?'

'Knock yourself out.'

Rose picked up one of the glasses and took a cautious sniff. The carbonated bubbles leapt out of the glass to tickle her nostrils. She sipped hesitantly and then it took every ounce of willpower she possessed not to screw up her face and spit it out. It tasted *vile*, like the most hateful kind of expectorant. 'It's lovely,' she said and she must have sounded convincing because Phil let out a deep breath as if he'd been scared that she wouldn't like it. 'Delicious. What is it?'

'It's Coca-Cola,' he exclaimed. 'It's going to help us win the war.'

Maybe the US Army planned to spray it on the Nazi hordes instead of dropping bombs on them. 'Do Americans drink this a lot? How extraordinary.' Rose picked up her glass and tried to gulp down as much as possible, interspersed with bites of doughnut to get rid of the taste. It was a waste of perfectly good doughnuts.

After she'd eaten all but one of the doughnuts and drunk the entire glass of Coca-Cola, which now sloshed around in her belly, Rose felt as if she was getting her energy back even though it had been such a long, eventful day. There was a restlessness that she couldn't quell, which made her fingers drum on the table, and her teeth wouldn't stop chattering even though she was as warm as anything.

'Let's go and dance some more,' she said standing up so she could take off her cardigan and tie it around her shoulders. 'That's if you want to.'

Many, many dances later, the band stopped playing and couples drifted off the dancefloor arm in arm. Phil said it was too late for him to find digs and so they floated like ghosts up the stairs and through the club until they found an empty sofa tucked away in a corner. It was hard to remember to sit stiff-backed with legs elegantly crossed at the ankle when Rose also couldn't remember ever being so tired or staying up so late.

As Phil described Des Moines, Iowa to Rose, which seemed to contain a lot of cows and cornfields and a department store, improbably called Younkers, it was a terrible effort to stifle her yawns and open her eyes again each time she blinked. His voice sounded as if it were coming from further and further away and it was harder to smile and say, 'Gosh, that sounds interesting,' at appropriate intervals, but it was important that she tried.

She rested her head on Phil's shoulder and she didn't even

care when he gingerly put his arm around her. 'You can go to sleep if you like,' he said. 'I don't mind. I'm feeling kind of beat myself.'

Rose had to clench her jaw to stop herself from yawning. 'Well, perhaps we could have a little nap,' she suggested. 'But only a little one, because I really do want to hear more about Des Moines. It sounds charming.'

'It's the finest place I know,' Phil agreed, but he didn't sound quite so perky as he had done and when he shifted on the sofa so they could both slump, it was a lot more comfortable. Then he shut his eyes and he fell asleep even before Rose did.

3

After they struck their deal, became maybe engaged, they introduced themselves. 'Leo,' he said. He had a firm handshake – she liked that in a man.

'Jane,' she said and once they'd got that out of the way, they could get to know each other.

Although Jane already knew everything she needed to know from the thirty minutes she'd spent sitting next to him. Under the bar spotlights, she could clearly see the lines starting to creep around his eyes and his pretty, almost girlish mouth, which always seemed to be on the verge of a lazy grin, like smiling properly was too much of an effort.

Even slouched on a very uncomfortable barstool Leo was tall and rangy, though Jane would bet that underneath his Ramones T-shirt there was the beginnings of a paunch from too much alcohol and takeaway food snatched from whatever place was still open when he was kicked out of whichever bar he'd been holed up in. Still, there *was* something sexy about him. Maybe it was to do with the way he looked as if he'd been round the block a few too many times but was still ready for the next adventure. If you got rid of the shaggy hair (the bleached ends were begging to be cut off), spruced him up and put him in a suit, it would make all the difference. There was darkness to him, but an uncomplicated darkness; back in the day he'd have been described as louche, and he was flirting shamelessly with her.

'I'm not prying, that's not my style, but whoever it was that you didn't get married to ... he's a dick,' he told her. 'Obviously he didn't deserve you.'

'You don't know that,' she said. Her voice sounded muddied. They'd been drinking for an hour. Or rather he kept buying her drinks and she kept drinking them, though he was still nursing his second whisky. 'I could be on the FBI's Most Wanted List for all you know.'

'You're too beautiful to be a career criminal,' Leo said.

'How many career criminals have you met?'

'Oh, loads and loads. You're also too beautiful to look so sad,' he told her quietly, but he had a way of looking at her as if she wasn't just another beautiful woman, as if her heart were as beautiful as her face, that made Jane want to share all the sorrow festering inside her. Well, that and the four vodka tonics.

'I spent three years with him. Three years! Then, in the space of five minutes, none of that matters any more.' Jane was dangerously close to ranting. She pushed her glass away, straightened her shoulders and took a couple of deep breaths. 'All because of a bloody patent application.'

Leo frowned. 'Come again?'

'It's too boring,' Jane demurred, but she needed to give him some context. 'He, Andrew, my ... I always hated the word fiancé or intended, or betrothed. They all sound so ... ' She couldn't find her words today.

'Naff?' Leo suggested 'Shall we just call him Mr Ex? Seems appropriate.'

Jane nodded. 'He was designing this face and voice recognition software that had all sorts of people excited: Google, Apple, the Chinese government – don't even ask me to go into details because I couldn't. He had venture capitalists chomping at the bit. Millions in seed capital. Then today, when we had fifty of his closest family and friends waiting on one of the terraces at THEHotel at Mandalay Bay, he gets a phone call to say he's filed his patent applications wrong. Missed out a couple of circuit boards or chips or lines of code. Or forgot to write down his full name. Who knows?'

'Hardly the end of the world though, is it?' Leo obviously had no idea how catastrophic a bad patent application was.

'Oh, it is. It couldn't even wait a couple of hours for us to get married. He had to leave there and then. I'm a very understanding person.' Jane put a hand to her heart, which wasn't thrumming as frantically as it had been. Before, it had felt as if it wanted to burst free from her chest, worm its way out of the boned bodice of her dress and lie on the ground, limply beating. 'But I have my limits and he was so cold, uncaring of my feelings . . .'

'I told you that he didn't deserve you,' Leo chimed in. He was still staring at her with those soulful blue eyes, though generally she didn't think that blue eyes could be soulful. 'I can't believe he cared more about Google or the Chinese government than he did about you.'

'I didn't mind him being driven. I quite liked it. Being the sole focus of someone's life . . . well, it's just too much pressure, but I never expected him to leave me at the altar, or as near as damn it. Said he had to go to New York to sort it all out and that getting married was no longer a priority. Then he left without even saying goodbye.' She picked up her discarded glass and drained the contents. 'It's not a very nice feeling to know that you don't matter to someone you were planning to spend the rest of your life with.'

'Oh, now you're looking sad again. I'll get you another drink,' Leo said. He signalled the barman and pulled out another wrinkled ten-dollar bill from his back pocket. Jane wasn't even sure that he was listening to her, really listening, or if he just liked the way her lips made shapes as she spoke.

But then he turned back to her, looked at her again and his mouth hung slightly open, like he'd forgotten that by some fluke of nature and the attentions of two very good plastic surgeons her features – eyes, nose, mouth and the rest – were arranged in a very pleasing fashion. 'God, you are *so* beautiful. I'd love to paint you.'

'Really? Why would you want to do that?'

'Because I'm an artist,' Leo said and he held out his hands so she could see the speckled blobs of blue and yellow paint. 'An impoverished artist. I mean, is there any other kind?'

Jane hadn't the heart to tell him that there was. That she knew artists who got paid millions and millions of pounds for pickling dead animals or spray-painting graffiti tags on the walls of the homes of rap stars, so she nodded. 'Does that involve lots of starving in garrets?'

'Yeah. I have to sell my body to buy paint,' he said and he leaned in closer. 'Problem is that my body isn't up to much and paint is so expensive. See! I knew I could make you smile.'

'You keep going and I might be able to muster up a giggle,' Jane said, and then she did giggle, because it was impossible not to. She glanced at the sliver of platinum around her wrist. The hour was up. While Leo wouldn't be her first choice, or her second, or even a choice at all if her circumstances hadn't changed quite so drastically, she could do a lot worse.

He had a sense of humour. That counted for a lot. He was easy going. He was also unreliable. Shiftless. Feckless, but he didn't have what it took to hurt someone like her.

'There is another way you could make me smile,' she said.

Leo leaned in close enough that her skin prickled and she could smell the faint tang of whisky. 'And what would that be?'

His voice was smoky and low and he had a way of looking at you as if you were the only girl in the world. Jane was sure he'd left quite a lot of women sobbing into their pillows. She'd never been much of a crier though. 'I think I would still like to get married. Are you game, darling?'

For one moment, Leo looked utterly panic-stricken, as if they'd been dating since high school and living together for at least five years and she'd hit him with a positive pregnancy test and an ultimatum. He took a couple of deep breaths. 'OK. Yeah. I did offer, didn't I?' His words, which started hesitantly, ended with a lot more conviction and freed Jane from her fretting. 'Got to try everything at least once, right?'

'Oh, definitely.' She clasped her hands together. She'd be his Vegas anecdote. The crazy tale he'd tell about the wife he met in a bar and married an hour later. That was fine with her. She'd been worse things than a cautionary tale against marrying in haste. 'You do have your passport on you, don't you?'

Leo said he did and he even paid for the cab to the Cook County Marriage License Bureau. As they waited in line with the other couples – some drunk, some unlikely and a pair of teenagers who looked like they'd just skipped out on their senior prom – Leo solicited opinions about the best wedding chapels.

'How do you feel about an Elvis impersonator?' he asked once the special licence had been tucked away in her handbag.

Jane shook her head. 'Nothing that clichéd,' she said firmly. 'Nothing tacky. No hula girls. No neon. Absolutely no Elvis impersonators. Somewhere tasteful.'

Leo googled 'tasteful Las Vegas wedding chapels' on his phone and eventually they found a chapel with a gazebo – 'apparently they replace the lilies every day' – and a cancellation.

When they got to the chapel, although they hadn't even discussed tactics, they marched straight up to the gum-snapping, middle-aged receptionist and Jane started to haggle, because *everyone* knew that you never paid the ticket price. After she'd gently explained that in a way, a rather large way, she and Leo were doing them a favour by taking the empty spot, Leo moved in for the kill. 'Sorry that we've just rocked up at the very last minute,' he said. 'I bet you're sick of looking at girls in white dresses all day long.' He leaned over the desk so he could drop his voice; let his eyes linger on her crêpey cleavage displayed in plunging leopard print. 'Listen, I'll let you into a secret – if I hadn't already promised myself to this one, I'd be getting down on one knee right about now.' He gave the receptionist just a mere flicker of the insinuating smile that he'd given Jane and she knocked another fifty dollars off the price, handed them a ring binder and told them to pick their vows.

Moments later they were standing in front of a glib man with an orange tan, alarmingly white teeth and a rusty brown comb-over who asked them to hold hands.

Two hours ago they hadn't even met and now they were about to promise to love and cherish each other for better for worse, for richer for poorer. I should have made them take that part out, Jane thought as she parroted the vows back to the officiate. Then Leo took her hands in his, and her eyes, which had been fixed on the lilies interwoven through the rails of the gazebo, focused on him.

He smiled at her and raised his eyebrows as if to say, *Well, here we are.*

Jane gave him the smile she'd promised him earlier, gently squeezed his hands, and maybe, for this moment at least, they both felt some slight connection; a little pull towards each other.

'Repeat after me: "I, Leo William Hurst, take you, Jane Audrey Monroe . . ." '

They'd chosen the traditional vows, as the laminated cards in the ring binder had veered heavily towards talk of souls entwining and completing each other. Getting married was one thing, but souls entwining wasn't part of the deal. However now, as this stranger promised to honour her with his body, the sentiment behind the words touched something in her. Not for very long, but fleetingly, the words mattered.

'Repeat after me: "I, Jane Audrey Monroe, take you, Leo William Hurst . . ." '

Leo hadn't expected her voice to tremble. Jane turned her pristine, perfect profile away from him, swallowed, and after that her words were as clear and crisp as drops of champagne. When she smiled at him, it wasn't because this was a huge joke, a crazy Vegas night that he'd bore people with for decades to come, but because in this moment, in this tasteful gazebo, they understood each other. Two bruised people looking for a little comfort, some kind of distraction, and they'd found it with each other.

For an extra ten dollars, the chapel had provided rings. Leo slid the thin band of silver-coloured metal onto Jane's finger so it could nestle against her huge art deco diamond engagement ring.

Then it was her turn to slide a matching ring onto his finger and they were still holding hands as they were pronounced husband and wife.

'You can kiss now,' the officiate reminded them. 'You're legal.'

'We don't have to kiss,' Jane whispered at Leo. 'Not if you don't want to.'

'Why? Don't you want me to kiss you?' he whispered back.

They heard shouting from behind the gazebo. 'I don't want to harsh your special moment, but if you two could move things along . . .'

'Let's do this,' Jane decided while Leo was still dithering. She tugged at the sweetheart neckline of her dress with one hand and primped her hair with the other. 'Unless you really don't want to.'

He could hear doubt in her voice; see it clouding her eyes. 'Well, we've come this far. Shouldn't skimp on the final details.' Leo very gently placed his hands on the curve of her waist. Jane looked up at him. He'd thought her eyes were blue, but they were green, maybe only blue in a certain light. She bit her lip like she'd been waiting all her life for him to kiss her.

'You two really need to make this quick.'

Leo turned to the man to tell him that they still had a minute on the clock and it was a pretty important minute, but Jane's hand was on Leo's chin so she could turn his face back towards her and it was simple enough to bend his head and kiss her.

He was aware of the scrape of his stubble on her peony-soft skin, the firm press of her mouth on his. There was no time for it to be a good kiss or a bad kiss, but simply a kiss.

'I don't care if you are his mom, shut the fuck up! I'm marrying him, not you!'

Jane and Leo broke apart so they could be hustled through a concealed door in the gazebo's greenery. After a long walk down a corridor, the plush carpet designed to look as if it was strewn with red rose petals, and through another set of double doors, they were on the street.

It was cold now because Vegas was a beautiful illusion: a glittering town hidden in the middle of the desert. The bitter, brutal heat of the day had given way to the callous chill of night. Jane crouched down and opened her suitcase to gently unwrap a Chanel jacket nestled between several layers of tissue paper.

'Married in black, you'll wish you were back,' Leo said as she slipped it on.

She grinned. 'Bit too soon for the regret to kick in, darling.' She straightened up on her perilously high spindly shoes. 'I think it's only fitting that we toast our union with a glass of champagne, don't you?'

'I do, but I spent all my money on cocktails and cabs and our marriage licence.' Leo didn't want to be that guy but he didn't know how to be anything else. 'Unless you . . . '

'Not a bean. I was meant to be getting married today; I didn't really think I'd need much cash and I don't believe in credit cards.'

'You don't believe in them?'

She shook her head. 'Cash or charge every time.'

All sorts of bells and whistles were going off in his head. He should have listened harder when she was talking about her ex. About the millions in seed capital. What else had she said? He couldn't remember; he'd been too busy staring at her, but trying hard not to look as if he was staring. But now he remembered what she hadn't said; she hadn't talked about love or a broken heart, which you'd expect from someone who'd been jilted minutes before her wedding, but Leo couldn't find it in himself to care that much when Jane was suddenly beaming at him. 'Paying for my own drinks sets a dangerous precedent, but I desperately need a glass of champagne so we're going to find someone who'll buy me one. In fact, let's make it a bottle.'

The wedding chapel was on the main strip and she was already heading for a shimmering beacon of glass and neon in the near distance at a speed Leo wouldn't have thought possible. He had custody of her vintage Louis Vuitton suitcase and quickly caught up with her. Oh, this one was trouble. Caps-lock trouble. The tech-genius fiancé and the venture capitalists and the guff about patent applications could all be bullshit and he might well wake up hours from now in a bathtub packed with ice and minus his kidneys. All he really knew about her was that she was going to be twenty-seven in less than two hours, unless that was a line too. She smelt sharp but sweet like blackcurrants and he really wished he could afford to get her a bottle of vintage champagne.

'Darling, please don't look like you're having buyer's remorse.'

Jane managed to look reproachful even as she strode with a wobbling gait. 'I'm going to be an exemplary wife.'

Even if she did end up taking his kidneys, she was beautiful and funny and had what his great-aunt would call *gumption*. 'Are you going to make me breakfast every morning and iron my shirts and talk me up at the annual Rotary Club dinner dance?'

She shook her head. 'I think we can do a little better than the local Rotary Club . . . Why is it that building doesn't seem to get any closer, no matter how long we keep walking?'

'It's perspective,' Leo said and he told her about the effects of the reflection of the neighbouring buildings on the glass tiles and Jane listened, kept him talking, until they reached the monolithic temple of steel and mirrors. It was a casino with its own eco-system: hotel, several fine-dining restaurants, two of them Michelin-starred, high-end boutiques and row upon row of slot machines flashing and whirring as people sat glassy-eyed in front of them, feeding handfuls of coins into their gaping maws from huge plastic cups.

Jane did a slow circle, eyes narrowed. Then her nose twitched like she could actually smell the money. 'Platinum Bar,' she announced, grabbing Leo's hand and dragging him towards the bank of escalators. There was a gleam in her eye that hadn't been there before. 'I'll do the talking, darling. You just watch for my cues.'

Yeah, this was going down in the annals of all the wild nights that Leo had ever known. Number one with a bullet, eclipsing even the night he'd found himself on stage in front of fifty thousand screaming fans in Tokyo to introduce his best mate from art college's band. The aftershow had turned into the kind of drug-fuelled orgy that Leo thought only happened to members of poodle-haired cock-rock bands of the late eighties.

Or the night he'd flirted with a French girl in the Williamsburg bar where he was working between commissions. After closing, they'd nicked two bottles of vodka, walked all the way to Central Park and talked about life, love and what made them cry. Watched the sun rise. Kissed like it was the end of the world. He'd woken up the next morning on a bench, one of New York's finest shaking him back to bleary consciousness. The French girl had stolen all his money, except a ten-dollar bill on which she'd scrawled *Je t'aimerai toujours* in lipstick.

This night was shaping up to be beyond all those other nights, and all because he'd had nothing better to do than get married to a beautiful woman because it would make a great story.

If you didn't have great stories, then you were living half a life.

And the story Jane was spinning to Tom and Paula, Barbara and Hank was a tale of triumph over adversity, laughing through the tears, love over the barricades.

'I can't believe the airline lost *all* your luggage,' Barbara gushed. She and her husband, tubby, silver-haired Hank who looked as if he'd been shoehorned into his tuxedo, were in Vegas with their best friends Tom and Paula to celebrate their thirtieth wedding anniversaries. Within five minutes, Jane had gleaned that the four of them had been best friends since high school, had even got married together – 'that's one of the most adorable things I've ever heard' – and Tom and Hank owned a very successful chain of winter sports shops.

Barbara and Paula, who never missed an episode of *Downton Abbey*, were enthralled as Jane told them Leo had been cut off by his family, who were such old money that his grandfather had been an equerry to one of the King Georges, for marrying Jane, who was a nobody. 'My folks think that if your family aren't listed in *Burke's Peerage*, then you're beyond the pale,' Leo admitted cheerfully, because he was her straight man. The Ernie to Jane's Eric. The Desi to her Lucy. 'Love is more important than being heir to a dukedom, right?'

The two older women sighed and even Tom looked a little

misty-eyed. Barbara patted Leo's hand. 'It's like something out of a novel. You nearly a duke, Jane an orphan . . . '

'Oh, orphan is such a dramatic word. Honestly, the car crash happened years ago,' Jane said, but then she stared off into the middle distance and held it for three long beats until a waiter approached with a huge bottle of champagne. It wasn't a Methuselah but it might have been the next size down. A Nebuchadnezzar? 'Oh no, you mustn't. It's terribly, terribly sweet of you, but really we can't, can we, baby?'

Leo shook his head. 'Couldn't possibly accept this,' he said stuffily. 'We appreciate the gesture, but absolutely not.'

Jane cast her eyes down, shoulders drooping ever so slightly, and sighed.

'Now, you listen,' Hank said rather forcefully. 'We're going to toast you two kids and you're going to have a drink with us whether you like it or not.'

'Darling, what do you think?' Jane asked Leo as if she deferred to him in all matters, when no one had ever deferred to him in his life. She turned to Barbara. 'He gets so proud and British.'

Leo squirmed under their collective, condemning gaze. 'I do. I can't help it but I refuse to argue with my beautiful bride when the ink's still wet on the marriage contract.'

There were smiles and glasses of champagne all round. They even ordered another smaller bottle just before they left and insisted that Jane and Leo stay and drink it.

'It's still an awfully big bottle of champagne.' Jane stared at it with some trepidation. 'What on earth should we do with it all?'

'Get good and drunk,' Leo said as he poured more champagne into their glasses. 'Sound like a plan?'

Jane wrinkled her nose. 'I've never been good and drunk. Maybe the good bit . . . '

'I've definitely been drunk. I can give you pointers.' He'd been waiting to touch her again ever since they'd sealed the deal with a kiss. Now he gently nudged her with his elbow. 'I bet you're a fast learner.'

She nudged him back hard enough that he spilled half his glass over his jeans. 'Maybe I could teach you a thing or two as well.'

It turned out that the only things Jane could teach him were the kinds of things she must have picked up at an expensive Swiss finishing school. She knew how to address a baronet, the correct way to serve oysters and how to buy the perfect thank you gift. 'It's very important to include a handwritten note. Very important. I'd be absolutely no use in a plane crash but if you get invited to lunch with a baronet and he serves oysters, then I really come into my own.'

She was slumped against him, his arm comfortably around her shoulders. 'Being drunk is a lot more fun than being good, isn't it?' he said.

'Ask me that tomorrow when the hangover kicks in,' Jane said and whatever she was, gold-digger or scam artist or even an orphaned almost-tech-wife, Leo liked her. He liked her a lot.

But despite the amount he'd drunk, his jaw was tight and clenched. He could feel the itch starting. With difficulty, he extricated himself. 'Just got to go and powder my nose,' he said.

Jane pouted. 'Promise you won't be long,' she said, but she waved him off with a smile and soon Leo was resting his fogged, pounding head on cool marble tile. Then he locked himself in one of the cubicles – nothing as plebeian as urinals in here.

He still had the little baggie he'd managed to scoop up, along with his clothes, when Melissa's husband had come home unexpectedly. He must have had his suspicions, suspicions that were entirely founded as Leo had had his cock halfway down Melissa's throat when they'd heard Norman clomping up the stairs and jawing on his mobile.

He was too old to climb out of windows, shimmy down drainpipes and leap over security gates. He was also too old for chopping out lines on a spotless toilet cistern with a credit card that had been cancelled three years ago. *Too old* never seemed like a good enough reason to stop.

Leo rolled up his last ten-dollar bill with the skill of a virtuoso. Two hard sniffs and he could feel the coke cut through the fog, the champagne haze. Feel the acrid, acid taste at the back of his throat which he tried to swallow away. He straightened up, shook his head twice, blinked and exhaled.

That was a whole world of better. He felt more like himself, but sharper, smarter, funnier. Like he could go back to Jane and dazzle her with his wit and charm because what she'd had up until now was a fraction of what he'd got to offer. She might even fall in love with him.

He ran the tip of his index finger over the white porcelain, to gather up what he'd missed. Then ran his powder-coated finger over his gums, winced at the bitter taste.

As Leo ran a cursory eye over the cubicle, he saw something in the corner. Something orange and Leo might not believe in karma, but a one-thousand-dollar gaming chip had to be a sign that at some point in his life he must have done something good.

4

Leo was gone ages – long enough that a couple of men began to circle like sharks.

Even her wedding dress and just-married glow wasn't enough to put them off. 'I'm just waiting for my husband to come back,' she'd say if one of them got too close but even in her head, she got stuck on the word 'husband'. Because Leo wasn't the husband she'd thought she'd be married to when she'd woken up this morning.

Also, the word 'husband' sounded wrong. Clunky. Unwieldy. But then she was drunk. Drunker than she'd ever been before, because before she'd only ever been the tiniest bit tipsy.

Being drunk was quite nice; it made the huge chandeliers above her head sparkle even brighter and for a while she was content to hold up her hand to the light so her engagement ring got caught in the crossbeam and glittered as brightly as it had the first time she'd seen it. It had been displayed under a single spotlight and reflected all her hopes and dreams back at her. But the trouble with hopes and dreams was that they always—

'You've got that sad look on your face again. Please don't be a maudlin drunk.'

Jane blinked up at Leo. 'I'm not maudlin. I'm just thinking.'

He was too tall, too loud, but then he sat down and said, 'Thinking's not allowed,' in that drawly dream of a voice and he was all she had to cling to on this strange night. She had a wedding ring on her finger and a marriage certificate in her bag, but she should have been with Andrew, gliding across the floor of a ballroom at a hotel across town. Andrew's mother, Jackie, had insisted they take ballroom lessons so they could have a choreographed first dance. With the lessons, a spreadsheet and an app Andrew had designed one Sunday afternoon so he wouldn't have to count the beats under his breath, he'd been able to muster a passable foxtrot.

'Do you foxtrot?' she asked Leo.

'I'm totally up for it if you want to go dancing.' He smiled like he'd just thought of the funniest joke. 'I think I've got my second wind.'

'I wish I had. Do you think anyone would mind if I lay down and took my shoes off?' She leaned heavily against him, but this time when he put his arm around her, his fingers beat out a restless tattoo against her upper arm.

'Poor baby.' Leo kissed her forehead. 'We'll sort it out later. Because right now . . . well, I've got a surprise for you.'

Jane struggled to sit up straight. 'What kind of surprise?'

'It's in my pocket. Go on, have a feel.'

'Oh, darling, if I had a dollar for every time a man asked me to root around in his pocket for my surprise, I'd be independently wealthy by now,' she said in a prim voice.

Leo laughed. 'Does that mean you've already heard all my best lines?'

'Probably.' She held out her hand. 'Is it the kind of surprise that you could just show me?'

He dug into his pocket and pulled out an orange disc, which

he held between his thumb and forefinger. 'It's my wedding present to you. Or ... hang on? What's the time? Happy Birthday. It's can be your birthday present as well. Sorry I didn't have a chance to wrap it.'

Maybe Jane was getting her second wind too because suddenly she felt much better. 'Well, this changes everything,' she said but when she reached out to take the chip, Leo closed his hand around it.

'Everything,' he agreed, standing up so quickly that she almost landed face down on the sofa without him there to prop her up. He held out his other hand. 'Double or quits, at least. Yeah?'

She let him haul her out of the sofa's depths so she was standing up too, which made her head swim and the room revolve around her. 'Oh, goodness ... '

'The headrush is a bitch, isn't it? Come on. I've got your suitcase. Let's go!'

He was already striding out of the bar so she had to scamper after him. Her shoes weren't made for scampering. 'What do you mean, double or quits?'

'Actually, we can do better than double or quits,' Leo called over his shoulder. 'What do you fancy? Blackjack? Craps? Roulette?'

'You're not gambling with it!' He was heading for the escalators now with a long-limbed stride, bouncing on the balls of his feet, so there was distance between them and Jane had to screech like a wronged wife. It was a bit too soon for that.

Leo waited for her to catch up. 'Let's play roulette. You think of a number and I'll—'

'Are you crazy? That's a thousand dollars. It's money in the bank. Better than money in the bank and you want to throw it away? And where did you get it from anyway? I thought you were out of funds?'

It was hard to step onto a escalator when your brain and your legs weren't in agreement and you were trying to reason with a man who didn't even have a passing acquaintance with reason; the kind of man who'd marry a complete stranger just for the thrill of it.

Leo grinned. 'I found it. It's a sign. It'll be fun.'

They reached the roulette tables and she was still trying to reason with him. 'Darling, life isn't even a little bit like the movies. I know that you're imagining the moment when you kiss the chip, like you're in a Martin Scorsese film, and place it on the table with a little flourish. Then your number comes up even though all the odds were stacked against you and everyone cheers and claps and you feel you're invincible, but your number's not going to come up. Newsflash: the house always wins.'

'Not always.' Leo shook his head. 'What about if I don't kiss the chip first and I just place it on the table quietly? With decorum.'

The croupier stared right at them. 'Place your bets.'

'Come on, Jane. Ten minutes ago we had nothing. Now we have something. It's a sign.' He actually fluttered his eyelashes at her and she honestly couldn't tell if she wanted to ruffle his hair or smack him. 'We've got nothing to lose.'

'We've got a thousand dollars to lose.'

'It's a night for taking chances. Don't be so boring,' Leo said cajolingly. 'Never had you down as the boring type.'

'One thing I have never been is boring,' Jane said grandly, though she was bored with arguing about this when Leo held all the cards. Or rather he held that orange chip. 'Oh, if you must,' she capitulated with a weary sigh. 'But double or nothing. Better odds. Black or red. Put it on black.'

'What's the fun in that?'

'Put it on black,' Jane said and Leo did with a muttered aside to the man sitting next to him about 'the old ball and chain'. The man shook his head and smiled sympathetically.

'Final bets,' the croupier said and Leo moved so fast that Jane was still blinking as he flicked the chip to rest on twenty-seven, in the time it took to call no more bets.

'What have you done?' Jane wailed. Leo shrugged but looked immensely pleased with himself.

'Nothing ventured and all that,' he said and Jane turned away and closed her eyes as she heard the wheel spin. There was a deathly hush around the table, despite the chatter and clink of glasses and expectant hum in the huge room that seemed to stretch for miles.

'I can't look,' Jane said rather unnecessarily. She heard the ball settle into its final resting place. There was a moment of silence then Leo said, under his breath, 'Fucking hell.'

It served him right, she thought. 'Well, that's that.'

'Too fucking right it is.' He had to force the words out past the lump in his throat. 'Too fucking right. Thirty six thousand dollars, Jane! We're rich!'

It was just as well that Jane was beautiful because she didn't know *shit.* The house didn't always win and the people gathered round their tables were cheering and clapping and Leo couldn't help himself. He turned her round, saw her eyes gleam as realisation dawned, and then he picked her up and spun her round.

'Luck be a lady tonight,' he boomed and she laughed out loud and he had never seen anyone, not in real life, not even in his dreams, look as heartbreakingly beautiful as she did in that moment. So he kissed her for the sheer hell of it and for the delight of their audience, although the cheering was starting to peter out because it was only thirty-six thousand dollars. There were people here who'd won and lost ten times that much in the course of an evening and it hadn't even mattered to them. But thirty-six thousand dollars mattered to Leo.

'Oh God, if you keep twirling me, I'm going to be sick,' Jane suddenly said and Leo put her down just in time for the croupier to push a pleasingly substantial pile of orange chips towards her. 'Hello, my pretties. Come to Mummy.'

Even the croupier managed to crack an indulgent smile. 'Place your bets,' she said.

'Let's go again!'

'Let's not,' Jane said as she hurriedly scooped up the chips. 'For the first time in your life, you're going to quit while you're ahead.'

That was something he wasn't wired to do. 'But Jane, I'm feeling lucky. It's you. You're my good luck charm.'

'I'm really not. I'm your better half,' she said firmly, though that Park Lane diction was a lot less crisp than it had been. 'We had a thousand dollars, now we have thirty-six thousand dollars. Do you really want to risk that on the turn of a wheel? You can't be *that* drunk?'

'Final bets?' the croupier said and she looked at them. Jane shook her head.

When you had money, everything fell into place. A man from the casino suddenly appeared and for one heart-stopping moment Leo thought he was going to ask them where they'd got that first orange chip from, but he only wanted to help them cash in the chips. Even though they weren't high-stepping high rollers, there was every chance that with the right kind of coddling they might give the casino back their thirty-six thousand dollars. Besides, they'd just got married and everyone loved lovers as much as they loved winners, so while another casino employee was charged with organising a hotel room for them, a beaming hostess presented them with a complimentary bottle of champagne.

Jane said she couldn't touch another drop. 'I'm not sure that I like being *this* drunk and there's still a chance that I might throw up.'

But Leo wanted her to be drunk, because he was drunk and the coke high had become a winning high and he didn't want to come down just yet. 'Food. You need food,' he decided. 'Something to mop up the alcohol. Don't worry, I'll take care of you.'

'Aren't you sweet?'

Leo didn't think that he was particularly sweet. Not when he left her on a sofa in the lobby, picking at a club sandwich, so he could go to the nearest bathroom and snort two more lines.

Once he returned, he sat much closer to Jane than he had before, couldn't stop jiggling his leg as he watched her slowly nibble one half of the sandwich then push the plate away. 'I don't feel like I'm going to be sick any more,' she said. 'Now I feel quite giddy. You make everything so much fun. I haven't had any fun in the longest time.'

'Not even with Mr Ex?' he asked, his leg knocking against hers until she put her hand on his knee to still him.

'Don't get me wrong, darling, he has lots of admirable qualities, but knowing how to have fun isn't one of them. Not like you. You're very good at having fun.'

'I'm good at all sorts of things,' he said and he deliberately lowered his voice, made it as dark and insinuating as he could and Jane couldn't quite arch an eyebrow, not with the Botox, but she could still feign surprise.

'Oh, my! What sort of things?'

Leo moved in close enough to see that her complexion was soft and flawless like vellum, and so was the upper curve of her breasts. He was horny as well as high and all he could think about was what it would feel like to unhook her dress and shape the soft weight of them. Just had to be certain Jane was on the same page. 'I'm the sort of man your mother warned you about.'

Her laugh was a gorgeous, throaty, plughole gurgle. 'Somehow, I doubt that.'

'You'd better believe it,' he said and he lowered his head and pressed his lips along her collarbone, her perfume faded and powdery now but he could still smell the lingering scent of blackcurrants. He reached the corner of her mouth and her breath hitched and that was his cue to pull away.

Leo knew this game of old. Advance, retreat. Advance, retreat. Let them get used to it, like it, start to want it, withdraw. Make them panic that you were going to leave them high and dry, then press your advantage home.

So, as a porter took them to their room, an upgraded presidential suite, Leo danced Jane around the elevator and down a long, long corridor, halting every now and again so he could lean into her and kiss her cheekbone, her ear, her shoulder. Each time, Jane would giggle, then the giggle would become a sigh because he'd stopped. Then he'd take her back in his arms and the dance could start again.

When they came to their suite, at the very end of the corridor, the porter opened the door, ushered them inside and put down Jane's case. Then Leo took Jane's handbag, which was stuffed full of hundred-dollar bills, and gave one to the porter, who left them with a wink and a knowing look.

'I think there's a special hell reserved for people who don't tip well,' Jane said approvingly.

'See, I told you I was good at lots of things,' Leo said and she was standing by the door, looking maybe a little uncertain and unsure. She breathed in and exhaled, which did wonderful things to her already wonderful breasts.

Leo danced towards her with a little quickstep that even Gene Kelly would have been proud of. She didn't resist when he wrapped his arm round her waist and danced her the few steps that had her pressed up against a wall.

Leo didn't even have to think of his next moves, because he *was* good at this. He always got the girl, even if he didn't want to keep her afterwards. He peppered kisses along her shoulder, lifted up her arm and kissed her there where her skin was so soft.

'You're scratchy,' she murmured and he kissed her better. Kissed her neck, nuzzled against her pulse point, which was beating out its own frantic little rhythm, along her jaw, to her mouth, which curved into a tiny smile.

Jane was breathing heavier now. Her lips parted and he stopped. Body still pressed against her, but he wasn't kissing her any more and she pouted.

'You're so beautiful,' he said and for once, it wasn't just a line. 'I know I keep saying it, but you are and I want you so badly. I'm hard just looking at you.'

'Are you, darling?' She bit her lip. 'Just from looking?'

'Yeah, imagine that.' Even though he'd been working her, teasing her, building her up for the last half-hour, and her dress was wilting, wisps of hair escaping from that tightly wound, honey-blonde coronet, her make-up practically a memory, there was still something untouchable about her.

Leo took Jane's hand, which was warm and a little sweaty, and kissed her palm before he placed it on his crotch. Her fingers clutched convulsively and her tongue crept out to moisten her lips.

She wasn't *that* untouchable.

He lowered his head, so his mouth was against her ear and he could whisper, 'Can you feel how much I want you? Do you want me too?'

She shut her eyes, her fingers clutched once more and his dick got harder, throbbed against her touch. Then she took her hand away and his heart skipped one painful beat until she threw her arms round him.

'Yes! Oh, yes!'

Leo didn't bother teasing her any more, but kissed her hard and Jane kissed him right back. He walked her over to the huge bed, mounted on a dais, swathed in swagging and tiny pillows and didn't stop kissing her, so she wouldn't have time to think.

But she was right there with him, happy to fall back on the bed, twisting underneath him as he fucked her mouth with his tongue. Leo wanted his mouth on her breasts next, but he'd seen the impossible number of tiny silk-covered buttons that held the bodice of her dress together and it would take too long to undo them. Long enough that Jane might change her mind, and he needed this. On a day of a week of a month that melted into all the other months and became years when he never got what he wanted, never achieved anything much, some strange twist of fate had let him get *this* girl.

'You're fucking perfect,' he breathed into her skin as he mouthed the top of her breasts and he started to tug down the bodice of her dress. Jane froze.

'No, don't, darling,' she said. 'It's vintage. You might tear it.'

'I really want to get you naked.'

'And I really want you to kiss me again,' she said and he could do that and she didn't mind when he pulled up all those yards of silk tulle and taffeta and settled himself between her legs.

Jane hummed as he ground against her, lifted herself up so he could pull down the wisp of white satin and lace that covered her. He pressed his palm against her, she was bare and smooth; not quite wet enough, but he worked her with his hand. One finger inside her, thumb rubbing against her clit and she whimpered a little, eyes screwed tight shut.

'You really *are* good at this, aren't you?' she said, her voice thick.

She tasted like blackcurrants too when he sucked the finger that had been inside her into his mouth. He thought about going down on her, he never minded that, quite liked it, sometimes he even loved it, but she was wet now. She didn't need it and he really needed to get some.

'I'll die if I don't get inside you,' he said, as he placed his thumb just shy of her clit so she wriggled to try to get him where she wanted him. 'I can't wait to fuck you.'

'I don't want you to die.' She arched her hips. 'God, I think *I* might die.'

'Do you want it? Do you want me?' Leo said but Jane didn't answer, because she'd arched her back to a point where it looked painful.

He pressed his thumb against her clit again, let her ride it a little, but when she arched her back again, whimpered again, as if she was going to go without him, he stopped.

'Yes. I want you! Please. I do want it.'

He could do this with his eyes shut, one hand tied behind his back. Could keep her right up there, teetering but not going over the edge, as he fucked her with two fingers now, while his other hand groped in his back pocket for a condom, tore the foil with his teeth, unbuttoned and unzipped. He took her limp hand and put on his cock, closed his fingers around hers as she jacked him off. Then the condom was on and he was so hard that he hurt from it, could feel the ache deep in his balls, and sliding deep into her was the only thing able to save him.

She was tight. Even tighter when she gripped him, wrapped her legs around him. Leo hadn't even taken his jeans off and she deserved someone who'd do it sweet and slow, make love to her. But he couldn't be that guy.

So he pulled out then slammed back in and she shut her eyes

and gripped him even tighter though he hadn't thought that was possible.

Then her eyes opened. 'Oh, darling, is fucking me into the mattress another one of those things you're really good at?' she purred with a cat-like smile. 'Go on, then. Show me what you've got.'

5

October 1943

Rose thought about going back to Durham many, many times. When she had telephoned home on that first uncertain grey London morning a month ago, everyone had been out except Shirley, who'd screamed at Rose for borrowing her dresses. She'd said that if Rose did come back, she was going to be confined to her bedroom knitting balaclavas until they could ship her off to the Land Girls, if Father didn't have her arrested first.

Rose hadn't called home since. She was managing perfectly fine on her own. She'd found a job in a café in Soho, owned and run by a Mr and Mrs Fisher. She did everything from waiting tables to battling with the cantankerous hot water urn to make tea, peeling vegetables and washing up. By lunchtime her feet ached and her hands were now red raw and split in places from scrubbing at pots and pans.

Every day Rose enquired about vacancies at the Lyons Corner House on Tottenham Court Road. She'd much rather be a Nippy in a neat black dress instead of wearing a stained pinny over an old summer frock and cardigan. She was paid two pounds a week plus tips, which were so scarce as to be nonexistent, and rented a shared room with half board in a house just off the Edgware Road for one pound and ten shillings a week, which didn't leave much for her to live on.

Her landlady Mrs Cannon was thin and mean-looking and had commandeered Rose's ration book. She had to be at the café for seven every morning and Mrs Cannon left her out one measly slice of bread with a scraping of margarine for breakfast. When she got home from work at five, there'd be a bowl of stew with a lot of cabbage floating in it and a few pieces of something grey and both gelatinous and gristly. Rose was never sure if it was meat or fish.

But she got a decent lunch every day and the girl she shared her room with, Olive, volunteered as a roof spotter. The two of them would set the alarm for eight o'clock in the evening and go straight to bed, after their bowl of tasteless, indeterminate stew, for a nap.

At eight-thirty Olive would jump on the trolleybus to the City for her shift and Rose would head back into town. After two weeks, she'd stopped trying to get into Rainbow Corner. It was impossible without finding a GI willing to sign you in and those sharp-looking girls thronging the spider's web of streets around Piccadilly Circus didn't take kindly to newcomers trying to queer their pitch.

Those girls all had flashlights they shone on their ankles every time a man in uniform passed. They did things in doorways with soldiers too. Even though the doorways were in shadow, the noises from the couples, a hint of a bare leg braced, made Rose hurry past, eyes averted, and on the evening she saw two girls fall to the ground kicking, spitting and hair-pulling as they fought over the attentions of a skinny GI with a huge nose and buck teeth, she'd wondered if maybe one glorious night in Rainbow Corner was all she was ever meant to have.

Rose had even gone all the way back to King's Cross to see if she could find a GI at the source, but the ones she shyly approached either weren't going to Rainbow Corner or got completely the wrong idea about her. One of them had suddenly produced a nylon stocking like a magician pulling scarves out of a seemingly empty pocket. 'You want the other one, honey, then why don't you and me take a little walk?'

But at least there were still places, lots of them, where she could dance. Rose had become quite adept at jiving under the tutelage of the men she danced with at the Paramount or at Frisco's when she ventured back to Piccadilly. She'd also got awfully good at fending off advances from spotty young men who told her they were going off to fight for her. It was no wonder that she preferred to dance with negroes.

The negroes that Rose danced with all called her 'ma'am' and when they weren't dipping and twirling her – and on one glorious occasion actually lifting her over a pomaded head – would only touch her elbow to guide Rose off a sprung dancefloor, which sagged and groaned with the weight of all the spinning couples.

Tonight, with Kathy, who worked in the tobacconist's two doors down from the café, Rose was going to the Bouillabaisse Club in New Compton Street. 'They play jazz all night,' Kathy told Rose as they queued to get in. 'Do you love jazz? I do.'

'It's my most absolute favourite thing in the world,' Rose assured her, though she didn't really care what they played as long as the music had a beat that she could dance to. Soon she was in the arms of a strapping Jamaican called Cuthbert.

When she was dancing, the horrors of Rose's new life – the hunger, the what-was-to-become-of-her, and the fear of being dragged back to her old life and the terrible retribution that awaited – all receded.

Her feet stopped hurting and did all sorts of tricksy, quicksilver things that she didn't know they could do and Cuthbert had gleaming white teeth and told her that she was pretty as he spun her round again and again. Shirley's pale blue taffeta dress was growing limper by the day.

After an hour of dancing, Cuthbert said he'd 'be happy to procure the finest ginger beer money can buy' while Rose went to the Ladies' to do something with her hair.

The tiny cloakroom was heaving with girls either queuing for the one lavatory or fighting for space in front of a mirror. Rose got trapped between two girls debating the merits of gravy browning versus cold tea as make-do stockings 'if you can't find a Yank'.

'I'd rather use gravy browning than get a pair of nylons off a Yank and a dose of the clap,' one of the girls muttered darkly. Rose tried not to look shocked. She was a doctor's daughter, after all. There'd been two books in her father's study that were kept locked in his desk drawer, but he always put the key in his brass pen tidy and when he was at one of his Rotary Club or Freemason's meetings, Mother always went to bed early, so Rose wasn't entirely ignorant of the ways of flesh. Still, there were things one simply didn't say in public.

She gave both of them a wide berth until they vacated the space in front of the mirror. Her poker-straight hair was, as usual, escaping from the four pins that were all she had left. It was no less manageable for being washed under the cold tap because Mrs Cannon charged an extra shilling a week for access to barely lukewarm water for an hour every day.

Rose patted down her red cheeks and her sweaty forehead with powder from the gilt and paste compact Shirley had given her for her sixteenth birthday even though Mother had said she was too young and that the compact looked common. She was still flushed and glowing and there were damp patches on the pale blue taffeta from where she'd—

'I say, could I possibly beg just a smidge of your lippy?'

Rose looked up to see a girl standing behind her. She had china-blue eyes in a pretty doll-like face and hair like Jean Harlow, which Rose was sure was bleached. Women who bleached their hair were also common, but this girl certainly didn't sound like the brassy girls who came into the café or regularly blocked Rose's view of the mirror in the dancehalls of London.

When Rose tentatively smiled at her, she smiled back. 'Be my guest,' Rose said and she handed over her precious tube of Max Factor Tru-Color in pillar-box red. As soon as she gave it to the other girl, Rose wanted to snatch it back. Instead she watched anxiously as it was sparingly applied to a mouth that would be described in a novel as bee-stung.

'You're an angel.' The girl pressed her lips together to spread the colour. 'So, what did you do to get a tube of Max Factor?'

'What did I do? Oh! Well, nothing really. My friend Patience, her sister Prudence works in a munitions factory. All the girls were given a tube as a thank-you for doing their bit but Prudence has religious objections to wearing make-up and their parents said Patience was too young, so they gave it to me.'

'What rot. I can't imagine God caring whether a girl wears a little powder and paint. Surely He has more important things to worry about.'

Rose nodded. 'You'd think, wouldn't you?'

They smiled at each other again. 'It's awfully hard having a conversation with someone's reflection,' the other girl said, 'and we're creating a terrible bottleneck.'

'How annoying!' Rose shoved comb, compact and lipstick back in her handbag and turned away from the mirror to follow the girl out into the little antechamber that led back into the club. 'I'm Rose, by the way.'

'Sylvia!' It was a shriek, as a burly man in sailor's uniform had come up behind Sylvia and lifted her off her feet. 'Lovely to meet you. Thanks for the lippy!' Her words were swallowed up as she was carried off.

Cuthbert was waiting patiently for Rose by the bar with the promised ginger beer and as soon as she'd gulped it down, she was back in his arms.

They only had time for one fast jive before Sylvia tapped Cuthbert on the shoulder. 'Mind if I cut in?' she shouted, her arms already around Rose's waist. 'We need another girl to make up the numbers.'

'Make sure you bring my Rosie back in one piece,' Cuthbert said but he was already eyeing the girls lining the edge of the dancefloor, shifting their weight from foot to foot as they looked for a spare man. Rose didn't think that Cuthbert would wait for her again.

'Not sure if you needed rescuing but I've got a GI, six foot four inches, who's getting a crick in his neck from having to dance with so many short girls. Also some of the girls here are funny about dancing with a negro.'

Kathy had been funny about dancing with negroes. She'd said none of them washed properly, which wasn't true, because every one that Rose had danced with had been immaculately turned out, but Kathy had disappeared with a gum-chewing lance corporal within five minutes of them arriving, which had left Rose free to dance with whomever she chose.

Now she was introduced to a grinning, debonair GI called Ray, who kissed her hand, told her she looked like Hedy Lamarr, asked if she could jive then pulled her onto the dancefloor where he lifted Rose up as if she was as light as thistledown and swung her over his head. She just had time and the presence of mind to tuck her legs in so she didn't kick his ears.

By the time the band decided to take a break, the bodice of

the pale blue taffeta was soaked through, the ends of Rose's hair sopping wet. It was so hot and humid in the tiny club that condensation dripped from the ceiling and most of the soldiers had removed their jackets. The place reeked of mildew and sweat.

'Over here!' Sylvia waved frantically from a far corner. 'Rose! Ray!'

She let Ray lead her through the mass of resting dancers; girls with their hands on their knees as they tried to catch their breath, men mopping at their foreheads with handkerchiefs.

'Billy got you a drink,' Sylvia said to Rose as soon as they reached her table. Rose didn't know who Billy was and the glass thrust at her contained a lukewarm liquid that tasted even viler than the Coca-Cola she'd had at Rainbow Corner. 'Gin and French. Divine, isn't it?'

'Oh, it's my absolute favourite,' Rose said. She let Ray light a cigarette for her and find her a chair and it wasn't until she was sitting down and taking cautious sips of her drink and hesitant puffs of her cigarette that she noticed the other two girls. One was blonde, though not as blonde as Sylvia, and had a jutting bosom displayed in all its glory in an emerald satin frock and the other one was thinner, darker; she was dressed all in black and looked terribly chic.

'Phyllis.' Sylvia gestured at the blonde, then at the dark-haired girl. 'Maggie. This is Rose. She let me have a dab of lipstick and she knows how to jive.'

Rose resisted the urge to wriggle her shoulders as Phyllis and Maggie looked her over. 'It's very nice to meet you,' she said.

'How old are you?' Maggie said. Rose thought she had an accent but it was hard to know for certain as the band had started playing again.

'I'm nineteen.'

Maggie looked at Rose's sweat-stained dress, the hair that had once again broken free of its moorings and didn't say anything, but glanced at Phyllis, her eyebrows raised.

'So have you decided what you'll do when you get drafted next year?' Phyllis asked. Rose hadn't because she was still three years off twenty, and the war couldn't last another three years, though often it seemed as if it would last for ever.

'Anything but the Land Girls,' she said fervently but she didn't want them to think that the only thing she was doing for the war effort was dancing with soldiers on leave. 'I've only been in London for a few weeks but now I've settled in, I'm looking for some volunteer work.' Phyllis and Maggie still had pursed lips, which wasn't very encouraging. 'Olive, the girl I room with, spends three nights on duty as a roof spotter. She says it was quiet for ages, but it's got quite lively recently.'

In Durham, the bombing had become so sporadic that Rose's father even stored his bicycle in their air raid shelter, which would have been unthinkable two years ago. But in the few weeks that she'd been in London, Rose had got used to the whine of the siren again and having to feel her way down three flights of stairs in the dark to the damp cellar. She still wasn't used to the terrifying crackle and pop of the anti-aircraft guns, though, or seeing the sky lit up so brightly. Not just from the city blazing with fire from the bombs that rained down, but from the ghostly glowing beams of the searchlights picking out the German planes.

There was something to be said for spending most of her nights in dimly lit basements where the band and the thud of feet drowned out the sound of the world outside. Most times, when they let off the sirens, they were a distant wail and everyone carried on dancing.

But that wasn't important now, when Phyllis was glaring at her as if she'd confessed to something awful like having a secret Nazi lover or trading on the black market. Maggie wasn't looking too thrilled either and Sylvia wasn't any help as she had her back to the three of them while she talked to two airmen. 'Have I said something to offend you?' Rose asked timidly.

'No, of course you haven't,' Phyllis said but her massive bosom heaved. 'Though if London isn't lively enough for you then it's a pity you weren't here a couple of years back. Then it was *very* lively, let me tell you.'

'I'm sorry, I didn't mean it like that.'

Maggie picked up her glass, almost took a sip from it, and then put it down on the slick-wet table with some force. 'Have you any idea of what . . . everyone I know . . . *everyone* lost someone during the Blitz.'

'I'm sorry. I'm so sorry.' She was sorry from the absolute bottom of her heart, but even so Rose had noticed that Londoners had a tendency to go on and on about the Blitz as if not a single bomb had dropped anywhere else. As if no one else had ever experienced what it was like to suddenly have people *gone,* like Janet and Susan from her class at school and Timothy McFarlane who'd once taken Shirley to the fair and had been killed on his first RAF mission, but it was very hard to explain that to these two imperious girls who thought they had the monopoly on loss just because they lived in London. It was far better to apologise again, make her excuses, then leave. 'So, I take it you two don't volunteer, then?'

Or she could stay and dig herself in even deeper.

This time the look that Phyllis and Maggie shared was less sceptical, more smug. 'We do volunteer,' Phyllis said. 'For the American Red Cross.'

'But we're entitled to a night off,' Maggie added and though Rose's hair was sodden and heavy, Rose fancied that it was suddenly standing on end.

'Oh.' She tried to sound matter-of-fact, but that one syllable was so high-pitched, it rivalled any note that the band's saxophonist had played that night. 'At Rainbow Corner?'

They nodded. Sylvia, who'd caught the last part of the conversation, leaned over Phyllis's shoulder. 'I sometimes think we should pay them for the privilege of volunteering. It's such fun, everyone is so nice and the perks . . . I have bars of chocolate and packets of cigarettes coming out of my ears.'

'Do shut up, Sylv. Loose lips and all that,' Phyllis said, reaching behind to dig Sylvia in the ribs. 'Not that we accept any of the perks.'

Rose didn't care whether they did or not. 'You volunteer at Rainbow Corner? That's an actual thing that one could do?'

'Only if one was over eighteen,' Maggie told her. 'Anyway, there's a waiting list. It's very long. There's also a list of girls who are never allowed through the door.'

She made it sound as if she was going to personally make sure that Rose's name was added to the blacklist just because she had the audacity not to have been in London for the Blitz. Maggie and Phyllis were utterly objectionable and though Sylvia seemed friendly enough, Rose wasn't sure she could trust someone who was pally with such rude girls.

'Oh, look! There's Cordelia! I haven't seen her in *ages*!' Sylvia was suddenly gone and Rose sat there with Phyllis and Maggie, who ignored her for a good two minutes until Cuthbert thankfully reappeared and asked if he could have the pleasure of the next dance.

6

It could have been any one of a multitude of different agonies which forced Jane out of sleep.

She was face down, her head wedged at an uncomfortable angle because she was still wearing her tiara, which now felt like an instrument of torture. She still had her clothes on. Her wedding dress . . . she paused to remember why she was still wearing her wedding dress, and as she recalled all the horrors and indignities of the last twenty-four hours, Jane wished she were still comatose. All of her was sore; from her feet, which ached from too much walking in limo shoes, to her head, which felt like it had pincers crushing her skull, and all points in between. Especially in between.

Fuck me into the mattress.

Leo had taken her at her word. Fucked her long enough for Jane to realise that despite all the foreplay, all the build-up, she wasn't going to come. It didn't seem like he was going to come either, not even after she'd faked an orgasm. Two orgasms! Then at last he'd come and Jane had pretended to fall asleep while he crashed around their suite doing God knows what.

He was asleep now. Jane sat up very slowly, very carefully,

biting her lip because simply sitting up made her clasp her hands to her head to make it stop pounding.

Leo was sprawled next to her, paunchy and pale in his boxer shorts, mouth hanging open, which would explain why he was making that horrendous noise, like a waterlogged machine gun firing rounds. He hadn't looked like that last night. Or maybe her pique and all that champagne had clouded her judgement.

Jane stood up on wobbly legs, grabbed her phone out of her bag and crept towards the bathroom. She avoided the mirror, sat down on the edge of the tub and stretched out her left hand. The diamonds on her ring glittered, but she no longer took pleasure in them.

When the engagement was as new and shiny as the ring and she'd realised that she'd pulled it off, that her disco days were over, Jane would recite the ring's credentials like poetry. It *was* poetry. Art deco, Asscher-cut 6.10-carat diamond, flanked by two baguette diamonds and fourteen round-cut diamonds with a combined weight of 4.44 carats in a claw setting on a platinum shank. Ker-fucking-ching, darling.

It was her reward for all the time she'd spent searching for that pot of gold at the end of the rainbow. All the different men she'd tried on for size. The three years spent reeling Andrew in, very slowly, very subtly, so that he always thought he was the one doing all the reeling.

Three years since those awful two days locked in a Moscow hotel room by a Russian oil trader who'd done terrible . . . there was never any point in dwelling on the past. She'd known then that the party was over; she needed to settle down by the time she was twenty-seven because twenty-seven was the thin but deadly line that separated a good-time girl from a good time had by all.

Plus, being locked in that hotel room with that psychopath . . .

no, still not going there. Suffice to say, Jane was tired. So very tired of hotel bars in foreign cities, scanning the room for a man who wouldn't flinch when she asked for a glass of Louis Roederer Cristal Rosé 2000 so he had to buy the whole bottle. Holding him off, making him wait for another date, playing it out for as long as she could. Besides, the girls coming up behind her were much, much younger and hungrier and the Eastern European girls had no respect for the way the game should be played.

Jane was done with Russian oligarchs. Done with Eurotrash. Done with the spoilt sons of oil and steel magnates. She needed someone who was up and coming but who hadn't quite up and come and she really needed a change of scene. Then, at a dinner party in Aspen, she'd been seated next to a venture capitalist who specialised in tech start-ups. She'd picked his brains, done some research, drawn up a shortlist and packed her bags for San Francisco.

She'd bumped into Andrew during one of the breakout sessions at a TED talk on artificial intelligence. He'd helped her with some iPad-related problem, blushing all the while and falling over his words. Then they'd just happened to keep bumping into each other all over town. No such thing as coincidence – not when Andrew kept tweeting his schedule.

Andrew was green enough and new enough that though he had millions in seed capital, he didn't have a huge team of people, of hangers-on yet. Just a room full of boys who looked a lot like him working on code and a girlfriend who'd been with him since sophomore year at Harvard who didn't stand a chance. Her most pressing problem had been Jackie, Andrew's WASP mother in Providence, Rhode Island but she'd come round soon enough when Jane had sought her advice on how to cook Andrew's favourite meals, gifted her tea couriered over from Fortnum & Mason and finally won her heart with a very embellished story about sitting next to Pippa Middleton at a polo match. The only other cloud was Andrew's sister, Stephanie, who styled herself as Andrew's business manager, though getting Andrew a business manager who actually knew how to manage a business had always been high on Jane's to-do list.

It sounded so cold, but even the most starry-eyed girl approached matrimony with some degree of calculation. There was so much more to Andrew than being a soft touch. He was kind, handsome in a clean-cut preppy way, would never, ever raise his fists or his voice and he'd created the face and voice recognition software that Google and Apple and NASA and the Chinese were all over, which meant that Andrew was going to be very rich. Obscenely, obsequiously, oligarch-ishly rich. So, even if she and Andrew had been spectacularly ill-suited, Jane could have waited it out for three years.

After three years of marriage, she'd have earned herself a big fat alimony cheque, and being a divorcee had a completely different vibe from being a superannuated party girl.

But yesterday morning it turned out that bloody Stephanie, for all her talk of graduating top of her class at Wharton, had filed incomplete versions of his patent applications. They were missing a vital number of components and ironically number four on the list of tech suitors that Jane had drawn up three years ago was working on something similar and now Google and Apple and the Chinese were going to give *him* billions of dollars instead. In sixty short minutes, Andrew was old news. Just another nearly-made-it. Surplus to requirements.

'You can still get married,' Jackie had insisted as the entire Hunnicot clan had gathered in the bridal suite of THEHotel At Mandalay Bay. It was meant to be bad luck for the groom to see the bride before the wedding but bad luck had already arrived, taken a seat and poured itself a large drink.

Andrew had looked like hell. His face was as grey as his silk brocade waistcoat, but at his mother's words he'd turned hopeful eyes to Jane, who'd been sitting on the bed wondering if anyone would notice if she put her head between her legs because she really thought she might pass out. 'Do you still want to marry me, Janey?'

'Of course I do,' she'd said because you couldn't kick a man while he was down. Not in front of his nearest and dearest.

Then Andrew had talked about the possibility of a job at Microsoft. Of moving to Seattle and maybe even stock options and Jane had nodded and smiled and squeezed his hand when he came and sat down next to her.

Even once the engagement ring had been bought and paid for, every now and again Jane would get a feeling as if icy fingers were clutching hold of her heart. That she was close, but not close enough and it could still all go wrong. Now the icy fingers were back and not letting go. Also, the one time that she'd been to Seattle, it had rained the entire time.

Finally, she'd persuaded Andrew that everything was going to be fine, just fine, and he'd left to wait for her on the terrace. Jackie and bloody Stephanie and Jane's bridesmaids, though they weren't friends so much as the girlfriends of Andrew's friends, had lingered but Jane had begged them to go too.

'I just need a minute.' She'd swallowed delicately. 'To think about my parents. I wish they could have been here today.'

They'd melted away and Jane hadn't wasted any time. She'd quickly packed her case, sneaked down the service stairs and out through the staff entrance, and got in a cab that was dropping someone off. She'd only had twenty dollars on her, enough to tip the girl in the powder room, and it was just enough to take her back to the city and drop her off in the not-so-nice part of town.

Jane wasn't cut out to be anything other than a trophy wife but a six-figure salary from Microsoft and even stock options weren't much of a prize. That wasn't what she'd signed up for, wasn't why she'd agreed so readily, when Andrew had asked her to marry him. Yes, she was avaricious, mercenary and materialistic but that was the shape that life had moulded her into. She couldn't be happy with what Andrew was offering her now and if Jane wasn't happy, then she wouldn't be able to make Andrew happy either.

Best to do them both a favour and get out now. When Andrew discovered that she'd bolted he might hate her for a while, but really she was doing him a kindness.

She didn't feel kind, though. She felt terrible. And with emotion clouding her judgement, Jane had walked into the first bar she found and, forgetting all her rules about settling for nothing less than untold riches, she'd married the first man who'd looked at her.

'Oh God, you stupid, stupid fool,' she said out loud and she put her hands to her head.

'Hangover's kicking in, then, is it?'

Leo was standing in the doorway. He'd put his T-shirt and jeans back on, thank God.

'Something like that,' she said and sat down in front of the vanity unit with her back to him, hoping that he'd get the message.

'His and her baths, I didn't know they existed.' He stepped into the room so he could collapse into one of two deep, overstuffed red velvet armchairs. 'I've lived in houses that had less square footage than this bathroom.'

'Have you, darling?' Jane began to slowly remove hairpin after hairpin, yet there were still more and the tiara was still firmly anchored to her head. 'That sounds rather grim.'

'Let me help.' Leo heaved himself up with a grunt. He stood over her, took a moment to assess the complicated arrangement of plaits and hardware then began to methodically work on one piece of hair.

It was quite disconcerting and before the silence got spiky, Jane caught his eye in the mirror. 'You do realise we can't stay married?'

There was no easy grin this morning, no twinkle in those bleary blue eyes. 'You sick of me already, then? It hasn't even been twenty-four hours. I think that's a personal best.'

'You have to understand that last night . . . well, I was at a very low ebb and you made everything better for a while and I thank you for that, I really do, but I don't need a husband. Well, I do, but . . . ' She trailed off. She didn't need to spell it out and hurt his feelings, not when she wanted another favour from him.

'Yeah, well, I'd be a lousy husband anyway.' Leo handed her the two falls of hair he'd unpinned. 'We could get an annulment on the grounds of non-consummation. I won't tell if you won't. How would they ever know otherwise?'

'It would be rather medieval if they wanted a medical examination.' Jane shuddered and Leo grinned for the first time that morning.

'So, you are going to get married to him, your Mr Ex? Has he called?'

'I haven't checked,' Jane said. Those icy fingers had a chokehold on her heart again. She'd turned her phone off before she'd walked out of the bridal suite. But it was past two in the afternoon; Andrew must have called by now. 'I will. Later.'

'You're not in any hurry, then?' Leo asked. His face gave nothing away as he began to unwind the last section of hair. 'Want to savour the last moments of freedom?'

'We should swap lawyers' details before we say goodbye,' Jane said. There was no freedom to savour until she unravelled the mess she'd made last night in much the same way that Leo had unravelled the coils of hair that had been killing her slowly.

'I don't have a lawyer,' Leo said and Jane wondered if it might be easier and quicker to find a courthouse and a sympathetic judge who would listen to their sorry tale in his chambers and grant them an annulment there and then. 'Do you want me to get you out of your dress now?'

Jane narrowed her eyes, which made her head hurt all over again. 'I thought we'd just agreed that last night was a terrible mistake.'

'Sweetheart, even if I wanted to, I doubt I could. I feel like I've been put through a mincer. Can't imagine you're feeling much better.'

'I don't,' Jane admitted. 'There's not one single bit of me that feels anything less than awful. I knew there was a reason why I'd never been drunk before.'

'It won't last. You'll feel better by lunchtime . . .'

'It's past lunchtime!'

Leo shrugged. 'The best cure is to just get drunk again. Shall I see if there's any more champagne in the minibar?'

Jane considered it for one moment. She'd never got drunk before because she was afraid she might be genetically programmed to not be able to stop drinking once she really started. But the thought of pouring more alcohol down her sandpaper throat made her clutch the side of the dressing table and her stomach clenched violently. 'God, no! I don't even want to think about it.'

'You don't mind if I do, though?' Leo didn't even sound a little bit ashamed that he'd only just woken up and he already needed a drink.

'Don't let me stop you, just as long as I don't have to watch.'

'You're sounding very judgemental. Like a proper wife.' He'd been so much more amenable last night. 'So, did you want help unhooking your dress?'

'Please.' She straightened up again, presented him with her back and all those tiny, silk-covered buttons. Jane kept her elbows clamped to her side as Leo slowly unbuttoned her, swearing under his breath when the task proved too onerous for his fumbling fingers and fogged brain.

She held her breath when he finished and ran a finger down her spine, because she was in a hotel room with a man that she knew precisely nothing about. Sometimes that didn't work out so well for her. 'Why don't you run a bath and have a soak while I have a drink?'

After he left, Jane locked the door, sank into silky soft water and assessed the damage. Seventeen missed calls and voicemails from Andrew. Fifty-two texts. Three emails.

Andrew had a tendency to get quite blinkered. Stephanie, blighted and bitter because Andrew was always going to be the golden child, had once confessed to Jane that Jackie had had Andrew tested when he was younger and that he was 'definitely on the autistic spectrum. At the lower end, but he's still on it, Janey'.

Talking of which, she had numerous missed calls from Jackie and Stephanie. Calls from the tech wives that she'd cultivated and called her friends. Even from Andrew's father, Richard, though he tended to leave most of the heavy lifting to his wife.

A tiny bit of Jane wished that she were still drunk as she called her voicemail to listen to Andrew's first message.

'Janey! Where are you? We've been waiting and waiting, then one of the busboys said they'd seen you get into a cab. I'm sorry, baby. So sorry I screwed up but I still love you and I know you love me too. Please come back so we can talk about this.'

All Andrew's voicemails were variations on the same theme. He wasn't even a little bit angry with her but by the tenth message he was crying and it was a relief that the next voicemail was from Jackie, who wasn't crying. Why cry, when you could scream?

'You little bitch! How dare you do this to Andrew? You come back right now, young lady. We have a goddamn ballroom full of family, guests, Richard's business associates ... you've humiliated this family ... '

There wasn't much point in listening to any more.

Jane sighed as one tear, then another one, trickled slowly down each cheek.

Andrew had been the man that she was going to share her life with. Not only for the billions of dollars that he was sure to be worth – Jane had had other criteria, had had other offers before Andrew came along. But Andrew never sulked, never shouted, never got violent when he was drunk. In fact, he never got drunk. He loved his mum and dad and even his annoying sister. He used to text her an 'I love you,' at least once a day. Buy her flowers. Buy her ice cream, though he always ended up eating it himself.

Already she missed him and he didn't even know for sure that she wasn't coming back.

Jane raised her head to look in the mirror and inspect the damage to her face. It wasn't much. She'd only been able to squeeze out those two tears.

'You are not a bad person,' she said out loud. 'Bad things have happened to you; they've turned you into what you are. It's not your fault.'

Andrew would be absolutely fine. He'd take the job at Microsoft so he could go to Seattle for a new beginning. He'd tell himself that his heart was broken but he'd soon meet another girl who'd fall in love with him because he was very easy to fall in love with. This new girl might not even care about his Microsoft stock options. Within a year, Andrew would be happy again. There really wasn't much for Jane to feel guilty about. A year was no time at all.

Jane had once been with a man who'd planted a GPS tracker in her phone and though Andrew trusted her implicitly, it was best not to take any chances. After a couple of false starts and the help of a hairpin, she managed to get the SIM card out of her phone. Jane rested it in her palm and stared at it for one moment.

But her mind was already made up. It wasn't a decision that she had to wrestle with any longer. The SIM card disappeared after two flushes. Then she deleted the email account that Andrew thought was her only email account.

Jane couldn't imagine how people disappeared fifty years ago but today it was as simple as destroying a SIM card and a few swipes of a touchscreen. You built a life with someone, made up of feelings and experiences, all the things you shared, all those days and nights together. But in the end, none of that was real. You were two separate beings. Now it took five minutes to kill Janey Monroe.

As soon as he heard Jane sink into the tub with an unhappy little sigh, Leo sprang into action.

It was more of a stagger than a spring, straight to the minibar for a bottle of fancy imported beer to wash the dark brown taste out of his mouth. The second bottle tasted better than the first and there were still a couple of toots left in his little baggie, which he sniffed up, like a gentleman partaking of snuff. It pierced the fug in his head.

Jane's handbag lay open on the bed. Last night's winnings were still there in seven neat little bundles. Five thousand dollars in each bundle. He wasn't a complete monster; he'd leave her one bundle. That was fair. Besides, she was carrying around at least a hundred thousand dollars in jewellery. Jane would be fine.

When Leo had woken this morning, he'd lain there thinking that Jane couldn't have been that beautiful. Wondered if there was such a thing as coke goggles. Then came the moment of sheer mortification when he remembered that he hadn't been able to come last night after Jane had begged him to fuck her into the mattress and he'd had to fake it.

He'd almost walked out then, but he hadn't. Thought he'd better confront his demons and he'd gone into the bathroom and even with her face pinched, her complexion muddy, body tensed against the pain of the morning after, she was still beautiful.

It didn't change anything. He had as much use for a wife, even a beautiful one, as he had for herpes. Leo did feel a tiny bit bad about skipping out on her without leaving a forwarding address or a phone number but it was the only way to leave with thirty thousand dollars and without an argument.

He couldn't stay in Vegas. Recently cuckolded Norman had all sorts of contacts with thuggish-looking men with Italian names. Couldn't go back to LA when both his landlord and his dealer had threatened to break his legs. There was also a string of bad debts and angry husbands in New York, but there was always Austin or Portland or Chicago, and America wasn't the world. Enough time had passed that he could go back to Berlin or Prague and live well for a year, get back into his painting, as long as he stuck to just beer and weed.

There was nothing for Leo to pack. So he stuffed the bundles into the pocket of his jacket, then tiptoed to the bathroom door to make sure that Jane wouldn't suddenly burst through it and demand to know where he was going.

He heard the loo flush, Jane swear, and then it flushed again.

Leo wondered if she'd been sick. Then he realised that he was about to leave without his phone, which he'd left charging overnight on silent as there was no one he'd wanted to talk to.

There were three missed calls from Melissa – he hadn't got round to deleting her number – and one missed call from an international number. An English number. A London number. A number that he hadn't dialled in over ten years, but he still knew it off by heart and as he picked up his phone, his touch brought it to life again. It vibrated. That number flashed up again and it didn't even occur to Leo to ignore it.

'Hello?'

'Leo! I've been trying to get hold of you for *days*. I must have rung at least ten different numbers in five different countries. Spoken to several bitter exes and one man who said he used to be your landlord and then subjected me to a torrent of abuse.'

Leo sagged with relief because it wasn't *her*. He sank down on the bed. 'Hello, Liddy, my one true love. How the devil are you?'

'Oh, you're still exactly the same, aren't you?' Lydia didn't sound too happy about that.

'Not really – I'm ten years older, for one thing.'

'It doesn't sound like you're ten years wiser,' she said tartly.

'Maybe about two or three years wiser,' Leo hedged. It was lovely to hear her voice: those hard London vowels that made him think of sitting in the kitchen while she cooked him breakfast and poured him endless mugs of tea. 'So, what's up?'

'You need to come home. She's not well and this has gone on long enough,' she said simply and not that surprisingly.

Sometimes he'd wondered . . . because biologically, at least, she was an old woman but she'd always seemed more fun, more youthful than his parents who were a good twenty-five years younger than her. But then Leo had often thought his parents had come out of the womb worrying about their pension plan and with a preference for neutral colours. Nevertheless, she was old and he knew that she wouldn't live for ever but . . .

'What do you mean, she's not well? How not well is she?'

'It's come back,' Lydia said.

Leo knew what she meant without asking. Because Lydia was practically family and though the family on his mother's side were riddled with cancer, no one could actually say the word. 'I didn't even know she'd had it before.'

'Well, you weren't here and that time the treatment worked. This time, she's not having any treatment.' In his head Leo could see Lydia's soft, round face creased and anxious. 'Please come home.'

'Well, maybe I'll swing by for Christmas,' Leo said, because when he thought about going home, which he never, ever did, it felt like hard, heavy stones settling in the pit of his stomach.

'Christmas is over two months away. You need to come before that.' He'd forgotten how dogged Lydia could be.

'I can't just rock up like nothing's happened, can I?' He had a few scars, a couple of tattoos, a suitcase full of stories, but that was all he had to show for the last ten years. She'd be expecting more than that. 'Did she ask you to call me?'

He could almost hear Lydia's lips tightening. 'She doesn't know I'm calling.'

'I can't see the point of coming home. It's not going to do any good, is it?'

'You can live with yourself knowing you never made amends when you had the chance? You're happy to carry that burden around for the rest of your life? You really haven't changed, have you?' Lydia demanded. She was the only person, the only *other* person, who could make him feel like some mouth-breathing primordial life form without even raising her voice.

He hadn't changed. Hadn't even tried to. Had decided that he was what he was and that he couldn't live up to *her* expectations so there was no point in even trying.

'Leo? Are you coming home or not?'

He looked up from as the bathroom door opened and Jane stood there swathed in a white fluffy robe and backlit by the lamp she'd left on in the bathroom.

At this moment he had the clothes he was wearing, thirty

thousand dollars courtesy of his one and only lucky streak and a wife who could have been imported from a Hollywood soundstage back in the days when movie stars looked like they'd been beamed down from Heaven. Something had to be going right in his life if he came home with a wife like that on his arm.

Jane might be a hard sell but she needed his name on the divorce papers, so he had leverage.

'Yeah,' he said slowly. 'All right. Yeah, I'll come home.'

7

November 1943

It had taken three weeks of going to the Bouillabaisse every night and being especially friendly to Phyllis and Maggie when she saw them before they stopped treating Rose with such disdain.

All the smiles and compliments and agreeing with everything they said had got Rose nothing but pained sighs. Every gin and French she'd been bought by her dance partners, she gave to them. Finally, and it couldn't have come soon enough, Phyllis had cornered her by the cloakroom. 'If I start being nice to you, do you promise to stop being such a tiresome creep?'

'I'm not being a creep, I'm being friendly!' Rose protested but after Phyllis had conceded defeat, Maggie unbent a little too. Not much, but Phyllis and Sylvia said that was just Maggie's way and that she was an émigré from Czechoslovakia and she'd had to leave her family to the tender mercies of the Nazis so one had to make allowances.

But with the three girls to vouch for her and Phyllis being an Honourable whose father was a viscount or a baronet or some such, getting an interview at Rainbow Corner had been easy.

'Tell them you're twenty-one,' Sylvia advised her when they'd met at Lyons beforehand.

Rose kept her eyes on her cup of tea. 'You know I'm not twenty-one,' she'd said carefully.

'Of course I do! We all know you're not nineteen either,' Sylvie snorted, even though Rose was wearing her roommate Olive's heather-blue suit so she didn't look the least bit school-girlish. 'Just explain that you've been bombed out, lay it on thick, and say that your papers are being processed, because they are, aren't they? Aren't they?'

'Well, I haven't had a chance and my landlady has my ration book and . . . ' It was very difficult to run away and forge a new life for oneself.

'Don't worry. I know a man who knows a man,' Sylvie said, then she'd told Rose to scrub off her lipstick and to pinch her cheeks because the American Red Cross preferred their voluntary hostesses to look wholesome rather than glamorous.

In the end, it wasn't so bad. Mrs Atkins, the nice middle-aged American woman who interviewed her, was very kind. She nodded and smiled as Rose told her about growing up with four older brothers so she was very easy about being in the company of men, but not *that* kind of easy. Rose hoped that her brothers would be made to feel welcome by the people whose freedom they were fighting for, as she hoped to make the GIs feel welcome if she became a hostess. She really did need to stop telling so many lies.

'I think you'd probably be happiest dancing, wouldn't you, dear? If you're already waitressing during the day.'

'Oh, I would . . . '

'But you're not just here to jitterbug; our boys need a sympathetic ear and a friendly smile.'

'I can do that too.'

'Let's see how you get on after a couple of weeks or so,' Mrs

Atkins said. 'Do you think you might have your papers in order by then?'

'It'll be fine,' Sylvia promised when Rose came out of her interview with an anxious frown and a Rainbow Corner membership card with TEMPORARY stamped on it in big red letters. 'Follow me.'

In the darkest, smokiest nook of Rainbow Corner's billiard room, Sylvia marched over to a man wearing a pinstripe suit and bright yellow tie and reading the *Sporting Life*. He looked up with a grin as they approached. He had a receding chin, gums and hairline. 'Sylvia, love of my life, don't often see you in my office.'

'Rose, this is Mickey Flynn, don't believe a word he says,' Sylvia warned. 'Mickey, this is Rose. She's been bombed out and lost *all* her papers. *All of them.* Doesn't even have a birth certificate. Can you imagine such a thing?'

Mickey, his eyes running over Rose like she was one of the painted girls from the Windmill Theatre across the road, agreed that he couldn't and said that Rose should go to the authorities to have new papers issued.

'But that takes ages and she'd have to go to so many different offices and departments, unless she knew someone who could do it for her.'

'For a fee?' Mickey asked and Rose didn't know how much this fee would be but it was probably best for Sylvia to carry out the negotiations – she was as sharp as a tack and Mickey didn't seem like a very trustworthy sort of person.

Between the two of them they agreed that Mickey would supply Rose with a new birth certificate, identity card and ration books for the princely sum of five guineas. It was a princely sum too – just about all that she had.

'That should cover it.' Mickey gestured at Rose. 'But now she owes me a favour.'

'Depends what kind of favour it is. You'd better run it past me first.' Sylvia didn't sound quite so top drawer any more. She sounded a lot like the shop girls who came into the café and said, 'ain't' instead of 'isn't'. 'Now, where's your notebook? You need to take down Rose's particulars.'

There was a sticky moment when Rose had to look at her temporary Rainbow Corner membership card so she could remember the year of her birth. It also had her new surname written on it. She'd chosen 'Beaumont' because Beaumont was the name of the cinema she and Shirley had gone to every afternoon of the two weeks each summer when they were shipped off to their Aunt Patricia in Aberdeen. Aunt Patricia was a staunch believer in little girls being neither seen nor heard so she'd always given them a shilling apiece each morning and told them not to come back until dinner time.

Rose Beaumont. It was everything a name should be. Sophisticated, elegant, exotic. Someone called Rose Beaumont would have adventures and get invited to dinner by rakish men. Those sorts of things simply didn't happen to girls called Rosemary Winthrop.

Rose also acquired a new address a week later when, with the help of Sylvia and Phyllis, she executed a sneaky daylight flit. Phyllis kept Mrs Cannon talking with tales of playing with the little princesses, Elizabeth and Margaret, when she was a girl, as Sylvia and Rose tripped down the stairs with Rose's suitcase and with Rose owing a week's rent.

'With what she was charging you and that business with your ration book . . . well, she's lucky we don't report her to the police,' Sylvia said as they walked the length of Oxford Street to Rose's new digs: the two-bedroom flat in Holborn on a tiny street near the British Museum that Sylvia shared with Phyllis and Maggie. 'You'll have to bunk down with me but as long as you don't fidget or snore we should be all right,' Sylvia told her and the rent was only fourteen shillings a week each and there was no landlady living on the premises to take away her ration book and complain about the noise she made going up and down the stairs.

There'd been another girl, Irene, but she'd completed her nurse training and was working in a hospital in Birmingham. 'Also she was tiny, barely came up to my shoulder,' Maggie said later that night as they toasted Rose's arrival with a Scotch egg cut into quarters and a bottle of peach wine. 'So we couldn't wear her clothes.'

All of Rose's clothes – and what a pitiful collection they were apart from Shirley's black crêpe de Chine dress and her mother's funeral fur – were put in the communal wardrobe, though Sylvia said there was no point in hanging up the pale blue taffeta as none of them would ever want to wear it.

Sylvia, Maggie and Phyllis were so welcoming that first night but they'd still been appalled when Rose had confessed after too much peach wine that she hadn't written to her parents since she'd run away. They hadn't been too shocked about the running away but as Sylvia said, 'Have a heart, Rosie. They must be imagining all sorts of terrible things – that you've been killed by a bomb or kidnapped by white slave traders.'

The next evening, Phyllis sat Rose down as soon as they'd both come home from work – Rose at the café, Phyllis at the Admiralty offices in Whitehall – and under her gentle but firm auspices, Rose wrote home.

'It's best to stick to the facts,' Phyllis said. Then she smiled mischievously. 'Though the facts are always open to interpretation.'

First, Rose apologised profusely for the spiteful words in that other letter she'd propped up against the clock on the mantelpiece, then turned to more pressing matters.

Please don't worry about me. I have found a job at a small business run by a kindly older couple, she wrote. *In the evenings, I volunteer for the Red Cross and I'm sharing a lovely flat near the British Museum with three girls from good families.*

There were also quite a few paragraphs about learning from her mistakes and how doing her bit for the war had made Rose see the errors of her selfish, impetuous ways. Phyllis was very good at helping to write letters. She often set up shop in the Reading Room at Rainbow Corner and helped GIs write to girlfriends and fiancées who had to be let down gently because the man they'd waved off at the docks was now married to a British girl he'd got in the family way.

Her mother wrote back to tell Rose that as far as everyone was concerned, she *was* up to her knees in mulch with the Land Girls rather than people knowing that she'd both shamed and disappointed her loving parents in equal measure. After that, it was never mentioned. Rose sent her mother chatty letters about life in London, focusing more on her efforts to find fruit, and her mother wrote back with news from the WRVS committee and the church social committee and the hospital committee and all the many other committees she was involved with as well as admonishments to be careful. The word 'careful' was always underlined several times and punctuated with an exclamation mark.

Those first weeks at Rainbow Corner, Rose was more carefree than careful. The nights all seemed to merge into one delightful whole of dancing with appreciative servicemen who all told her that she was beautiful. Then she'd go down to Dunker's Den in the basement and let them order her doughnuts, sometimes waffles, occasionally thick American-style pancakes and always Coca-Cola. Each time, Rose pretended that it was her absolute favourite thing in the world. It was a tiny sacrifice that seemed to delight each and every one of her dance partners. She couldn't help write letters home like Phyllis or listen quietly to their confessions, then offer soft words of comfort like Maggie did and Lord knows, she'd never be able to flirt like Sylvia, but after a few weeks Rose could jive like she'd been born to it and gratefully gulp down a glass of Coca-Cola like it was cold spring water on a parched summer's day.

The only dark spot was her lack of official papers. It took Mickey Flynn three long weeks to get them in order. During those three weeks, Rose lived in utter dread of being called into the office and handed over to the police for giving false information on her application form. Or worse – having her name added to the list of girls who were banned from Rainbow Corner!

Then, one evening, after she'd met Sylvia at Piccadilly Circus Tube and they were scurrying past the girls waiting on the corner of Shaftesbury Avenue who always called them the most *awful* names, Sylvia said, 'I bumped into Mickey Flynn today. You're to meet him in the billiard room at seven-thirty. Do you have your five guineas? I'd come with you, but I'm stuck behind the information desk this week.'

Sylvia was already in trouble with the ladies in the office after she'd been seen kissing a sailor on the stairs, though she'd protested: 'he was kissing *me* and it seemed unpatriotic to refuse.'

'I have the money,' Rose assured her as they signed in; she felt that delicious frisson of fear as she handed over her temporary membership card to be scrutinised, but dear old Joyce simply smiled and handed the card back.

'I've been told to tell you, once again, no jitterbugging,' she said sternly to Rose. 'Any more of those fancy lifts and twirls of yours, Rosie, and you'll have someone's eyes out.'

'I promise to keep my feet on the ground,' Rose said and Sylvia grumbled about having to spend all evening trying to find spare beds for GIs in any one of a number of the clubs and hostels they had on file, but just as they were preparing to part company she took Rose's arm.

'If Mickey starts talking about favours, you tell him that he has to go through me,' she warned, her pretty, animated face quite serious for once. 'I adore Mickey, but he always tries his luck. Though that's the only thing he ever tries. Don't make any promises, all right?'

'Oh, Sylvia, it will be fine. I can handle the likes of Mickey Flynn,' Rose said then hurried away because the sooner she got this over and done with, the better.

She was wearing Maggie's red velvet dress, which was a little short on her but not indecent, and her new black heels, which she'd bought from Kathy, the tobacconist's assistant, who'd got them just after clothes rationing started because she'd mistakenly thought her feet were still growing. Rose's hands were clammy as she pushed open the door of the billiard room, then with a furtive glance to make sure that there were no Red Cross ladies lurking, slipped inside. There really wasn't anything to be frightened about – it was a simple business transaction, an exchange of money for goods and services – but her heart thrummed frantically as she saw Mickey sitting at what appeared to be his usual table.

'Step into my office, love,' he called when he caught sight of her. 'No need to be nervous. Sit down.'

There weren't any women in the billiard room. It was all groups of men laughing, ribbing each other, even a little roughhousing around one of the tables, and there was Rose in her red dress feeling conspicuous as if all eyes were on her.

'So, um, I have the money,' she said to Mickey, who was wearing an emerald-green satin tie tonight. He had the softest, whitest hands, one of which he waved dismissively.

'Plenty of time for that,' he said. 'Let's get to know each other a little bit. How are you finding London, my darling?'

Rose was absolutely not his darling but it would be rude to point that out, especially when he had her future in his hands – or possibly in the buff-coloured envelope on the table in front of him. 'London's wonderful,' she said.

'I'm thinking it'd be nice if we could help each other out from time to time,' he told her.

She swallowed hard. 'Well, that's very kind of you. But I'm not sure that I'd ever be any help. Unless . . . well, I work in a café on Wardour Street; I could probably treat you to a free cup of tea every now and again. Not particularly nice tea, I'm afraid.'

Mickey laughed, even though Rose wasn't attempting to be amusing. 'I'm sure a pretty girl like you could be lots of help without even trying to . . .'

He was staring in the vicinity of her neckline and Rose squirmed. 'I'm awfully sorry, I don't mean to be rude, but I'm meant to be doing my volunteer work so if I could just pay you . . .'

She opened her handbag to pull out her purse. Mickey's hand shot out to grab her wrist. 'Jesus, Mary and Joseph, will you put that away?' All bluff and blarney disappeared. Then he looked around like a pantomime villain, decided that his reputation was safe and smiled at Rose like they were still going to be terrific pals. 'You should have had the money ready. Do it under the table.'

It was very hard to retrieve her purse and pull out five one-pound notes and five shillings and hand it to Mickey under cover. In one deft movement, he took the money, shoved it in his pocket and slid the envelope to her. He even managed to put a hand on her knee for one lingering moment that made Rose want to wriggle her shoulders again.

Instead she held herself very still, every muscle tensed, until Mickey removed his hand, then she crammed the envelope into her handbag.

'Steady now, my darling, don't want to tear all those valuable documents that your good friend Mickey Flynn sorted for you,' he said. He was leering now, which was nothing compared to staring at her décolletage or curling hot fingers round her knee.

She couldn't very well look inside the envelope, not here, so Rose stood up in a jerky motion. 'Well, I'd love to stay and chat, really I would, but I have to go,' she said, smoothing down her plush skirt with nervous hands.

Mickey doffed an imaginary hat. 'We'll meet again soon, lovely Rose,' he promised. 'And remember, you owe me a favour now.'

Rose nodded as she backed away. 'Oh yes, well, you know where to find me.' Then, not caring how it looked to the casual observer, she ran for the door.

But before she could get there, some stupid man was blocking her way and the two of them danced an awkward waltz of clumsy steps and 'I'm sorry', 'No, I'm sorry', 'No really, I wasn't looking where I was going'.

'It was my fault, let me get that for you,' the man said and Rose was so desperate to get out of there, away from Mickey Flynn and any favours she might owe him, that she barely glanced at the man who was holding the door open for her.

He was in a British officer's uniform, though she never knew how to distinguish the different ranks, and even in heels she still had to look up as she shot him a brief smile and a muttered thank-you. It was a look that lasted no longer than a second but still long enough to take in the severe lines of his face and the discomfited expression that she was sure was a perfect match for her own. As if he didn't truly belong there either.

Rose was all set to brush past him, red velvet against khaki wool, when he shifted so he was blocking her escape route and held out his hand. 'I'm Edward Abernathy,' he said. He had a lovely voice. It reminded Rose of stealing into the pantry when Cook wasn't looking to open the tin of Lyle's black treacle that was used for ginger cakes and parkin. Rose would dip in her index finger, then suck on it and marvel at how the thick syrup could be both dark and sweet at the same time. That was what he sounded like. He also sounded very important, so Rose shook his hand, felt the strength in his long, lean fingers, but he was staring at her even worse than Mickey had.

Not at her chest but at her face, deep into her eyes, as if he knew all her secrets, and she so desperately wanted to get away from him, from Mickey, from this whole sorry business, and back onto the dancefloor where she felt safe.

'It's awfully nice to meet you,' Rose said hurriedly. 'I'm sorry but I'm meant to be . . . I should be somewhere else.'

He stepped aside then, and Rose shot through the door, sped along the corridor, remembering the feel of Mickey Flynn's hand on her, then that man's eyes boring into her soul, and only then did she shudder.

It felt as if she'd let the darkness touch her, which was something that Rose never did. It was why she preferred to dance with the soldiers than have to talk to them. Maybe laugh at their jokes as they sat for ten minutes between dances, but nothing more than that. Sylvia had been very clear. 'Most of them aren't coming back,' she told Rose frequently. 'They'll die or else they already have sweethearts at home. Don't be like Phyllis. She never forgets a single GI then gets into a terrible state when she hears they've been killed. Honestly, Rosie, there's been times when she's cried every night for two weeks.'

It was far better to hold something of oneself back, not let the bad side of the war wear you down. So that night Rose locked away her bag, along with the echo of a stranger's eyes and Mickey Flynn's touch, then danced without pause until half past ten.

8

'Will you come home with me?' Leo asked, when Jane came out of the bathroom to find him sitting on the bed finishing what sounded like a very tense phone call. 'Not home home, but to London.'

Jane was immediately suspicious. 'What's in London?'

Leo stood up and ran his fingers through his sleep-rumpled hair. 'My . . . aunt . . . well, my great-aunt. She's ill.'

Jane folded her arms. A sick great-aunt sounded like the flimsiest of excuses. Very possibly a scam. 'And where exactly is home home?'

'Well, home *home* is actually Durham but I haven't been back there in ages. Must be fifteen years or something.'

'But this great-aunt of yours is in London, is she?'

'You don't need to say it like that, like it should have speech marks round it. She *is* my great-aunt and I haven't seen her in ages either so if I get a phone call saying she's not well, then it's serious.' There was an edge to his voice that made her turn around, because the edge hadn't been there last night. She didn't remember him being this jittery either. He was prowling about the room and it could have been because he'd just had bad news, but she was sure there was more to it than that. 'We should be able to catch an early evening flight. You get your stuff together while I have a shower, then let's get out of here.'

'Why on earth would I want to go to London to meet your ailing great-aunt?' she asked.

He stopped prowling and scowled. Then he must have realised that the scowl wasn't conducive to putting Jane in a conciliatory mood. 'Are you reconciling with Mr Ex?'

Jane shrugged. 'I haven't decided one way or another.'

Leo furrowed his brows and tried to look plaintive. It didn't suit him. 'We still need to get unwed and I really need to get to London, so what's the harm in coming with me?'

He did have a point. Jane needed to get out of Vegas immediately. And if she needed to regroup, plan, move on with her life, then London was the best place to do it. Then again, she didn't want to rush headfirst into another questionable course of action when she was still feeling so fragile after the excesses of the night before.

'Come on, time's a-wasting,' Leo barked and he actually dared to click his fingers at her like she was an underperforming flunky. 'I don't see a whole lot of packing going on.'

Jane had a bad feeling about this, but then she had bad feelings about a lot of things, which she trained herself to ignore. But it wasn't until they were at the airport trying to get seats on the next available flight to London that Jane opened her bag and discovered that there was only one bundle of hundred-dollar bills in there, when there should have been seven. The thieving bastard!

'Don't freak out, I've got the rest,' Leo said quickly as if it weren't a big deal, when actually it was. 'Just to be on the safe side. You know what Housekeeping is like at these big hotels.'

He gave her back three of the bundles and it was all the warning Jane needed to stay glued to his side until they could be legally and permanently separated.

Leo didn't even thank her when they got upgraded to first class because Jane held her Chanel 2.55 bag in a conspicuous position and flirted like mad with the camp check-in attendant. Then he kept wandering off, shoulders hunched, as they waited for their flight to be called, but it wasn't until she was seated next to him that she realised Leo was under the influence of something she was pretty sure he hadn't got with a doctor's prescription.

His jaw was clenched, a muscle in his cheek pounding away like a Mexican jumping bean, arms and legs twitching. Not respecting her personal space boundaries at all.

It was going to be a very long flight. Leo spurned the glass of champagne offered and asked for beer instead, then pulled a tiny bottle out of his jacket pocket. 'Want a Xanax?' he asked.

'I don't do pills,' Jane said thinly.

He grinned. 'Like you don't do credit cards? You're going to have to write me a list of all the things you don't do. God, I can't believe we're married.' It didn't sound malicious, but heartfelt. 'Are you sure that we didn't get so drunk that we *thought* we'd got married?'

'Sadly, the marriage certificate in my handbag says otherwise.'

'You were much more fun when you were drunk.' He nudged her arm, and Jane had never wanted to hit anyone as much as she wanted to slap Leo. She had a vague memory of wanting to slap him the night before too. 'Go on, have some champagne.'

She refused, but Leo had two more beers and another pill then fell asleep, head on her shoulder, and she had to give him a good hard shove so he landed back in his own seat.

They were already married (to be annulled as quickly as was humanly possible) so Jane didn't have to be appeasing or alluring or the least bit charming. That, at least, was a relief.

Leo didn't even stir on landing until Jane shook him. Once his eyes were open and he was upright, he was still useless. Jane had to take hold of his sleeve and tug and pull him along the endless corridors and walkways to baggage reclaim where he moaned about having to 'carry your suitcase *again.* Can't you use a trolley like everyone else?'

He was infuriating, but Jane was grateful for the distraction as it took her mind off the utter dread that seized hold of her every time she stood in line at passport control. It never had anything to do with the thousands of dollars in cash and jewels in her hand luggage.

Jane didn't relax until they were in the back of a black cab on their way to central London. She'd check into a hotel while Leo went to see the doddery 'great-aunt'. At this rate, their winnings would dwindle to nothing. Thirty-six thousand dollars seemed like a lot, but split between two, a couple of transatlantic flights, hotel rooms, cabs – it would soon go, even if Leo didn't try to steal her share again.

As they sped nearer to the Hanger Lane roundabout, passing row upon row of suburban houses with grimy frontages like white towels that had gone grey in the wash, Jane was reminded of the first time she'd taken a taxi ride through London.

It had been getting dark then too. She'd sat perched on the tip-up seat, ready to scrabble for the door handle and leap out at the first sign of trouble. She wasn't sure what she'd got herself into but she still hoped that where she was going couldn't be any worse than where she'd come from.

Could it?

Charles's house was in Notting Hill. Though Jane couldn't remember if he told her his name or where he lived that first night.

He'd paid the driver and still hadn't laid a finger on her, but guided her with a series of hand gestures across the street, up the path and through his front door.

Then they'd stood in the hall, everything light and clean, and he'd said, 'You can stay here tonight.'

For the first time in days, weeks, maybe even months, she found her voice. 'Are you going to fuck me?'

No one had ever looked at her like that before either. Like she was a real person and not just a thing, a useless thing. 'Do you want me to fuck you?' he asked as she stared at his shoes, because she still couldn't look at his face.

Maybe he was different from all the others because none of them had ever given her a choice before. 'No,' she said. It sounded good so she said it again. Louder. 'No. No, I don't.'

'Then we understand each other,' he said and she followed him along gleaming black and white tiles to a kitchen and stood in the middle of the room, too scared to touch anything in case she made it dirty and watched as he boiled the kettle, sliced bread, put it in a toaster.

It was as if he knew she couldn't make any more choices. A mug of tea, two pieces of toast on a plate so delicate she knew she'd break it just by pressing the tip of one grubby finger to it. She drank the tea and ate the toast with one hand, other hand still clutching the wad of notes, still on guard, still not trusting that worse horrors weren't on their way.

It was almost a relief when he walked around her to open a drawer and pulled out a big, wicked-looking knife that shone in the soft glow of the overhead lights. With food in her belly and warm from the tea, she didn't even care any more.

At least she'd had this one glimpse of something else. Wasn't going to be just another name sunk to the bottom of the 'at risk' register and forgotten about until she was found naked with stab wounds, spunk splattered all over her, on a patch of waste ground.

The hand that was holding the wad of notes twitched in expectation of that moment when he'd point the knife at her. Take aim. Thrust deep.

'I'll show you to a spare room. There's a bathroom next door if you want to freshen up,' he said. He offered her the knife. 'Sleep with this under your pillow; it will help you to feel safe.'

Not then, but later, much later, she wondered what had happened to Charles that he'd once slept with a knife under his pillow too.

So many incredible things had happened to Jane since then, but she always thought that the most incredible thing of all was meeting the one decent man in all of England on that train speeding her towards her future.

'Jane? Jane? We're here. Wake up!' Leo touched her arm.

She tensed so violently that Leo realised she hadn't been asleep, just lost in another world with eyes closed, head lolling back. Jane sat up and patted down her hair as she peered out of the taxi window. They were slowly driving around a garden square full of big Victorian houses, white as wedding cakes. 'Where exactly is "here"?' she asked.

'Kensington,' Leo had been thinking hard about what he should say but he still felt woefully unprepared. 'Look, Jane, I'm sorry I keep winding you up.'

'It's all been a wind-up? Oh, well, that makes me feel *so* much better.' She was still looking out of the window, not at him, as the cab pulled into the kerb.

It was hard to keep going in the face of zero encouragement but that had never stopped him before. 'I know that everything is a bit weird between us, like we're both coming down from a bad trip, but I need to ask you a massive favour.'

'Another one?' Jane asked drily as she paid the driver. She'd changed some money at the airport while Leo had slumped against a pillar. 'Should I start keeping a tally?'

'You could, or I could argue that offering to marry you was such a massive favour that it automatically makes us even,' Leo pointed out.

Jane made another of her not-quite-faces as she got out of the cab. 'I'm not agreeing to anything else until you give me the small print.'

Leo took hold of her case again, no bitching about it this time, so Jane had to follow him to the corner of the square. It was cold enough that she was shivering and pulled her Chanel jacket tight around her though it wasn't designed to keep out the chill. No lingering, lazy Indian summer halfway through October. At the centre of the square was a little garden, locked to keep out the hoi polloi and the homeless. The fresh green leaves of the sycamore trees that surrounded it were on the turn, yellowing at the edges and drooping towards the ground.

Leo stared down at his shuffling feet in their worn sneakers. 'It would really help me out if we could act like we're married for real,' he mumbled.

'Why would I want to do that?'

Leo resisted the urge to grind his teeth. It was a pity he'd slept so long on the plane because it was at least twelve hours now since he'd last had a drink and he really needed a drink. 'It's nothing bad or illegal, I promise,' he explained. 'It's just the last time I saw her we had a bit of a fight . . . '

Jane's eyes barely narrowed. 'Her? Who?'

'I told you who. My aunt . . . '

'You mean your "great-aunt", darling. And, no, you haven't told me anything about her because you've been practically catatonic for hours.' She hadn't sounded like this, so querulous and tart, that lost night in Vegas.

'It was a ten-hour flight. What else was I meant to do but sleep?' He remembered he was supposed to be playing nice. 'The last time I saw her, years ago, we had a huge argument about my lifestyle choices and obviously I've grown so much as a person since then . . . '

'Have you really, darling?'

'I have. I really have.' Jane didn't look like she belonged with a man who still dressed like an art student. She was wearing designer jeans and a stripy top with her Chanel jacket, and ballet flats but it wasn't the polished, pulled-togetherness of her outfit that intimidated Leo, only the remote, unimpressed look on her face. 'If I turn up with a wife who looks like you and talks the way you do and if you could flash that gigantic rock on your ring finger and smile at me adoringly every now and again, then she'll see I haven't done too badly for myself.'

Jane folded her arms. 'It's been ten years; I'm sure she'll be happy just to see you.'

'You really don't know what she's like.' Leo had a horrible feeling that if he tried to bluster about all the exhibitions he hadn't had she'd sniff him out in a minute flat, whereas Jane was an indisputable fact. 'Where's the lie? We *are* married. There's actual legal proof.'

'Where does this great-aunt of yours live, anyway?' Jane executed a slow three hundred and sixty degrees. 'Is she tucked up in some little rent-protected bedsit around here?'

'What? Hardly!' Leo pointed in front of them. 'She lives in that house. Technically it's two houses but you can't see the join.'

Jane's gaze followed his outstretched finger. Suddenly her shoulders straightened and she stopped huddling into her jacket. She didn't say anything, but looked at the house for so long that Leo wondered if she'd turned to stone. He could have sworn that her nose twitched like the moment in Las Vegas when she'd sniffed out the Platinum Bar. Then she spun around. 'OK, darling, against my better judgement, I'll play the devoted wife,' she said. He didn't trust her reasons for suddenly agreeing to his plan, but he was too relieved to care. 'Now, before we go in, is there anything I should know? I really don't like surprises.'

'Not even when they're in little boxes from Tiffany's?' Another thing that he hadn't learned how to do in the last ten years was to stop blurting out every single thought he had.

Jane looked slightly affronted. 'Well, apart from that kind of surprise.' She gestured at the house. 'I'm not sure how convincing we're going to be as love's young dream.'

Leo hadn't thought much beyond turning up with Jane as a totem of his successful life. But now, as he glanced at that imposing black door, knowing what lay behind it, the welcome he was likely to get, he felt nervous. Actually, nervous didn't come close to describing the way his throat unexpectedly constricted and his guts roiled.

'It'll be fine,' he told Jane doggedly. 'We'll have to wing it but we'll just do what we did in Vegas.' Then he thought about Jane's Little Orphan Annie shtick. They were going to be facing a tougher crowd than Barbara and Hank and the rest of the gang from Boulder, Colorado. 'Maybe dial it down just a notch, yeah?'

'Oh God, I really wish I'd walked into another bar yesterday,' Jane muttered, but she still followed him as he walked towards the house. Up the steps. Three long rings on the bell.

'It'll be fine,' he said again.

Jane had one hand pressed to her mouth as if she had to physically prevent herself from speaking. Her hair was gathered up in a loose ponytail. One strand had escaped and was hanging forlornly against her cheek.

'Your hair . . . ' She had to look perfect. That was part of his plan. In fact, it was his only plan. Jane shied away as he tried to tuck the offending piece of hair behind her ear.

'I can do it,' she said as the door opened.

Leo was ready with a rueful smile and an 'I swear, you look ten years younger, not ten years older,' but standing there was a young woman in uniform: a pale blue dress with white collar and cuffs.

This girl wasn't Lydia, who Leo was going to get onside first. Tenderise Liddy and beg her to put a good word in for him.

'Is Lydia in?' he asked hopefully.

The girl shook her head. 'Miss Lydia busy,' she said with a strong Eastern European accent. 'You want to leave a message?'

Leo dithered. 'Maybe we'll come back later.'

Jane sighed. 'We're not here to see Lydia. We're here to see his great-aunt. What did you say her name was again, darling?'

'We're here to see Rose.'

9

They were ushered into an imposing foyer. Two enormous vases as tall as Jane, possibly Chinese, flanked the front door – nothing as prosaic as a coat rack or a little table to dump keys and post on in this house. The maid led them up an impossibly grand, intricately carved staircase, the kind that women in ball gowns swept down as the assembled company below gazed up at them in awe.

This was not the domain of an old lady. No chintz, no stairlift, no knick knacks.

There was no time to adjust what Jane knew of this great-aunt, which wasn't much other than the fact that she was gravely ill, before a set of double doors were opened onto a drawing room where a drinks party was taking place, even though it was barely half past four on a Sunday afternoon.

Though it was barely a drinks party, only six people but they were making a hell of a racket. All talking and laughing over each other and then, one by one, they sensed there were interlopers in their midst and turned to stare at Leo and Jane standing in the doorway. It was tempting to hide behind Leo until she'd got her bearings, but that wasn't possible when Leo tugged her forward so he could hide behind her.

'Hey,' he said. 'Hi, Rose. Hello, everyone. Sorry to turn up like this.'

There were four women and one man arranged on two huge sofas, but Leo was talking to the woman who sat in a white leather cube-shaped armchair framed by two large windows at the other end of the room. Even sitting down, Jane could tell she was tall; long legs neatly crossed at the ankle. Sat there poised and elegant like a queen on a throne.

'Leo,' she said in a clipped but amused voice. 'Goodness, you could at least have phoned.' She paused. 'And shaved.'

This was dear Great-Aunt Rose? Supposedly at death's door? She looked very much alive and present in an elegantly draped navy blue dress with a diamond brooch pinned to her collar. Her snowy white hair was cut in a sharp and precise angled bob, lips and fingernails painted scarlet. She didn't even have varicose veins.

'We only just flew in from the States a couple of hours ago,' Leo said and he rested his hands on Jane's shoulders in a show of togetherness, though she wanted to wriggle free, because they weren't together. 'This is Jane, my wife,' Leo added. He sounded quite defiant.

All eyes were upon her now, but all Jane could see was Rose. She wasn't doing much, just sitting there with a tiny smile on her face, eyebrows slightly raised, but she had presence. She also had the look of someone who could sniff out bullshit at fifty paces.

Jane straightened, drew herself up and smiled wider. 'Hello. It's lovely to meet you at last. Leo never stops talking about you,' she said and she stepped forward, out from under Leo's tense fingers, and walked further into the room.

It felt a lot like walking onstage, but she kept on going until she was sucked right into Rose's gravitational pull. When she'd first met Jackie, Andrew's mother, they'd embraced, kissed, but after only two minutes in her presence she knew not to try that with Rose. Anyway, Jane had never been much of a hugger.

Instead she held out her hand and Rose received it like a tribute. 'Married? I didn't think anyone bothered getting married these days.'

'Well, we were in Vegas – it seemed like the thing to do,' Jane said as she stood by Rose's chair, uncertain of what to do next.

'Yeah,' Leo said from the doorway where he still cowered, because he was absolutely dickless. 'Would have been rude not to.'

'Oh, stop hovering, Leo,' Rose said sharply. 'Why don't you get your lovely wife – Jane, was it? – a drink.'

A corner of one of the sofas was found for Jane, where she sat next to a striking redhead called Connie wearing an original Zandra Rhodes kaftan in greens and pinks, who ran her own landscaping business.

There was Elaine 'from across the square' and Gudrun, a Swedish textile designer; Sarah who taught yoga to 'prisoners, bored housewives, dancers, all sorts really' and George, who was a curator at the V&A. They all introduced themselves to Jane jovially but perfunctorily, as if they were waiting to return to their scheduled programming. Jane sat there clutching a lime and soda. Even the smell of their martinis made her eyes water, and because anything less than a clear head could prove fatal.

Leo perched on the arm of the sofa opposite with a lime and soda too. 'I never drink this early. The sun's hardly over the yardarm,' he'd said, eyebrows waggling. 'And on the day of rest too? God, what a bunch of reprobates you are.'

Rose merely smiled in a tight, composed sort of way then looked at Jane. It felt a lot like being under a microscope, but Jane had learned how to appear as if she was at ease in a room full of strangers.

She always imagined herself sitting on a beach, the sun warming her face, waves gently lapping, genuflecting waiters ready to bring her whatever her heart desired. When Jane thought about that, it was easy to sit there with a slight smile on her face too, her posture relaxed. Like she belonged in this beautiful room with these clever, chattering people.

The walls were a dark, smoky grey, but the space wasn't dark because of the two huge sets of French windows behind Rose's chair and because everything else in the room was white, from floor to sofas to rugs to mantelpiece. Over the fireplace, there was a Warhol silkscreen of Rose. A younger Rose, face a little softer; her hair dark apart from a streak of white springing from her widow's peak, still the same arch smile.

Rose had style that Jane, for all her intensive grooming regimen, appointments with personal shoppers and outfits that were always either black, white or grey because she was scared of trying to match colours together and terrified of prints, could never hope to emulate.

'Leo, how did you and Jane meet?' Rose asked, cutting through a heated debate about the Turner Prize. 'I do love hearing how people got together.'

Leo smiled but his eyes darted round the room because he was a *terrible* liar. Someone who lived the way he did, hand to mouth, winging it with very occasional lucky breaks, should have been much better at faking it. 'You tell it, baby,' he said. 'You're much better at telling it than I am.'

Then again, he was really good at passing the buck. All eyes were on Jane again. She smiled again as if she were reliving all sorts of happy memories. 'Well, I was engaged to another man. Having dinner with him when we had one of those silly arguments about nothing that escalated into a full-blown row until he stood up, demanded his ring back and walked out.'

Really she was doing Leo a favour when she went on to

explain that he'd been their waiter, because Rose with her gimlet gaze was never going to believe that Leo was a successful artist. She had an iPad next to her on a side table. This was a woman who knew how to set up a Google alert.

Anyway, she said, Leo had kept a discreet distance to give Jane time to compose herself then placed a slice of chocolate cake and a glass of champagne in front of her. 'On the house, which was very sweet. I was close to tears anyway, and that pushed me over the edge.' Jane then went on to describe how Leo had pursued her relentlessly, though she wasn't interested in a rebound romance as her heart was 'not broken, but bruised. Definitely bruised. Leo wouldn't take no for an answer though and in the end he just wore me down.'

Rose seemed to buy it because she nodded. 'That sounds like Leo. How long have you been married?'

There was no point in fudging that particular detail. 'Just over a day,' Jane said to shocked and delighted gasps. 'We were in Vegas for work and I told Leo that I always planned to be married before I was twenty-seven, so we got married with a couple of hours to spare.'

'And you decided to honeymoon in London? I can think of better places to honeymoon than London in October,' Elaine said.

'We didn't really plan a honeymoon, what with . . . '

'Lydia called,' Leo said. He'd been silent up until then. Smiling bashfully in all the right places, but now he was still, his face set. 'She said . . . Insisted I came home. Made it seem like . . . you know . . . ' He shrugged and stared down at his glass.

Jane waited for a hush to creep over the room, but the atmosphere remained relaxed and convivial.

'Did she tell you I was on my deathbed?' Rose asked. 'Well, not quite.'

'But you are . . . you're not . . . I don't know . . . ' He couldn't get his words out. All his flash and swagger suddenly gone, as if someone had let his air out. Jane couldn't help but feel sorry for him. He'd come here expecting the worst and now that the worst didn't seem so bad, he was lost and floundering.

'Yes, I am,' Rose said gently. 'No point in being all cloak and dagger about it. This way I can have a lovely time saying goodbye to all my dear friends and do all the things I wouldn't normally do, like having two cocktails before dinner instead of just the one. There's no need to be upset and I really can't see why you felt the need to hotfoot it over the Atlantic.'

That seemed unnecessarily harsh. Whatever Leo had done to be banished couldn't have been so terrible that he deserved to be humiliated in front of Rose's friends.

Still, Rose was Leo's problem, not hers. 'I'm sorry that we turned up unannounced,' Jane said. 'We really should be going now anyway, but Leo was so worried that we wanted to pop over right away.'

Leo was already on his feet, a grateful look on his face. 'Yeah, we'll get out of your hair now. Need to sort out a hotel, anyway.'

'Don't be so ridiculous. I'm sure Lydia will have got your old rooms ready.' Rose picked up the iPad. 'Anna will show Jane where she can freshen up before dinner and Leo, you can make us some more drinks. You did always make a mean martini.'

Within a minute of Rose swiping at her touchscreen, the young woman who'd shown them in was back.

'Go on, dear,' Rose said kindly. 'We'll eat at seven. You and I can get properly acquainted later.'

It was a relief to be dismissed. To be taken up another flight of stairs and down a corridor to a set of rooms: dressing room, sitting room, bathroom and bedroom where her suitcase had already been set down at the foot of the bed. The bedroom was painted a soft, smudgy indigo: a blue room for a blue boy. There were a few framed pen and ink sketches on the walls, books about art on the shelves, but Jane was more interested in digging her own iPad out of her bag, switching it on and typing 'Rose Beaumont Kensington' into Google.

Rose pointedly ignored Leo after Jane left the room. She still gave excellent cold shoulder.

He'd expected that. Instead he talked to George about the latest gossip from the V&A and Connie about garden design.

Every now and again, he'd catch Rose's eye and she'd shoot him a pained look, then turn to Elaine or Gudrun, who were seated nearest to her.

It reminded him of being a very small boy and Rose descending on Durham a couple of times a year. She'd roar up in her scarlet MG with pretty parcels tied with ribbons for Linda, his mother, whisky for his father, and big boxes of Lego, which she'd thrust at Leo then ignore him.

That suited Leo fine because he hated Great-Aunt Rose. His mother spent the week before one of Rose's visits telling him to 'mind your Ps and Qs and only speak when you're spoken to'. He wasn't allowed to eat with the grown-ups either but was stuck in the kitchen with his younger brother, Alistair, who was just a baby while Leo was a big boy of three, then four, then five. Still Rose greeted him with a look of mild distaste, as if she knew that he hadn't washed his hands even though he'd promised his mother he had.

Then, Rose had come to visit, just after Leo's fifth birthday. He'd stood in the hall, ready to be presented to her like she was the Queen, and with the film that he'd just seen fresh in his mind and Rose sweeping in with that streak of white in her brown hair, he'd blurted out, 'Great-Aunt Rose, you look just like Cruella de Vil.'

There'd been a terrible silence. His mother had given him a Look, which promised no TV for at least a week, his father had started apologising profusely, 'Sorry, Rose. Never thinks before he opens his mouth,' and Rose had stared down at Leo, who'd stared back at her because she really did look like a cartoon villainess. Then Rose had laughed. Properly laughed, a belly-deep chuckle.

'Do I really?'

Leo had nodded.

Then she'd tousled his hair and squatted down. 'Do you want to know a secret?'

He'd nodded again.

'I'd much rather you call me Cruella than Great-Aunt Rose. It makes me feel very, very old.'

'You're not *that* old.' His mother had sucked in a breath but Rose had laughed again.

They became firm friends after that. Her next visit, she bought him a cuddly Dalmatian from Hamleys and he'd drawn her as Cruella. 'You'd never think he was only five,' Rose had said to Linda, who'd beamed proudly. Linda's proud smiles were usually reserved for Alistair when he walked a few steps without falling over or managed to navigate a spoon to his mouth without spilling anything – all things that Leo could already do.

After that, parcels would arrive regularly from Rose full of felt-tips and pencils in more colours than Leo had names for. Even better than the parcels were the endless, magical summers at Rose's house in Lullington Bay, Sussex. It was where he learned how to paint as he tried to capture the pink and orange glory of the evening skies and the way the sea would shimmer in the sun.

There wasn't any discussion about whether he should train to be a doctor like his father and both his grandfathers before him. Rose had decided that he'd do his Art Foundation at the Chelsea School of Art and Design and his path was set. His future mapped out. Not many eighteen-year-old boys would have wanted to go and live with a great-aunt in her early seventies but Rose had never seemed like an old woman to him. She'd been his mentor, confidante, friend. But before that, she'd ignored him.

Now, as Leo sat at the other end of the room, frozen out, he wondered what it would take, what he had to do, before he and Rose could become friends again.

10

January 1944

Rose couldn't believe that she'd been in London for four whole months.

It seemed much longer, and yet in other ways it seemed like no time at all. Rose felt older, but in the mirror she still looked annoyingly girlish.

Christmas had come and gone with no treats from Durham. Instead Mother had sent her a pair of Father's worn-thin pyjamas and suggested she make a summer skirt with them and Shirley some stockinette so Rose could replace the gussets in her knickers. It was pretty shoddy when Rose had sent them a big box of chocolates and several packs of cigarettes.

But it had still been a magical Christmas. Even though Phyllis had had to work in the morning and Sylvia had spent Christmas Eve night at her parents' house in Hoxton. Rose had slept in until a scarcely believable nine-thirty, then woken up to see Maggie, who'd been granted the day off from the BBC Overseas Service, perched on the windowsill in the lounge smoking. She'd looked so sad, even though it was Christmas. Then Rose had remembered that Maggie was an émigré and that one had to make allowances.

'Are you missing your family very much?' she'd asked and Maggie had turned to her and smiled. It wasn't a very happy smile.

'Maybe. Though missing them doesn't do much good,' she'd said, then she'd smiled properly and said that she had a couple of ounces of coffee and Rose had some slightly stale doughnuts that she'd stuffed into her handbag the night before at Rainbow Corner, which they'd feasted on as they huddled round the gas fire. Then Sylvia had arrived home with a tin of hot chocolate and four rashers of bacon 'courtesy of Henry and Edna Crapper who send their love and best wishes' followed by Phyllis who'd received a huge parcel from her family estate. There'd been a precious, tart pineapple from the greenhouse, plum cake, elderflower wine, and a chicken that Maggie had managed to cook on the Baby Belling.

They'd got quite merry on the elderflower wine and Rose had organised a game of charades, though Maggie complained bitterly that English wasn't her first language and the others had an unfair advantage. Then, bundled up and reeling from the sudden shock of a bitter December evening after being so cosy indoors, they'd hurried to Rainbow Corner to dance the night away, and so Rose's first Christmas in London had been rather wonderful in the end.

But then most things in London were wonderful. Rose had her girls and she had her evenings at Rainbow Corner and even if they were experiencing what the papers called the Little Blitz – the Luftwaffe redoubling its efforts and dropping bombs every night – and the weather was cold and foggy, Rose would still much rather be in London than anywhere else.

The days were an endless drudge of washing-up and reprimands from Mrs Fisher but the nights were full of endless possibilities. Like the night halfway through January when Rose had plans to meet Sylvia and some of the other hostesses at the

Paramount after her shift at Rainbow Corner ended. She was in the cloakroom putting on her coat and wondering if the Canadian airman she'd met the other night might be there, when her friend Pippa let her in on a little secret. The chippy round the corner (that was what all the girls called it, even the frightfully grand ones) had got fish in. 'You'd better hurry,' Pippa warned. 'The queue was out of the door when I walked past.'

Rose fairly skipped across the lobby and barrelled out of the door straight into a gang of GIs.

'I'm so sorry!' Rose reached down to pick up a cap that one of them had dropped, but the GI was already crouching down too and she banged her elbow into the side of his Brilliantined head. 'Gosh! Sorry again.'

'Never been knocked off my feet by such a knockout,' one of them said. 'Can't tempt you to come back in and dance with a poor old fella who could be dead this time next week?'

That plea, which she'd now heard countless times over the last few months, left Rose unmoved. She shook her head, smiled sadly but didn't feel the teensiest bit guilty. 'I'd love to, but if I don't get home soon, they'll call out a search party.'

No man wanted to know that he was second best to fish and chips wrapped in yesterday's newspaper. 'Just one dance!'

They were all gazing at Rose like she'd just stepped down from the screen at the Empire in Leicester Square. 'There are lots of lovely girls inside who'd be more than happy to dance with you,' she said and turned away reluctantly, even as one of them took hold of her arm and tried to kiss her hand. 'I really do have to go.'

Rose backed away with a rueful smile, secretly pleased at how disconsolate they looked because they hadn't been able to beg a dance from her. It would all have been too perfect if she hadn't forgotten about the step and would have fallen if two hands hadn't gripped her elbows to steady her.

'Careful there, darling, you don't want to break that pretty little neck,' said a pleasantly deep voice in her ear, which sounded familiar. Maybe a little like James Stewart. Some of the other girls said that he came to Rainbow Corner when he was in London.

Rose turned her head and her eyes widened, mouth open on a silent gasp. 'Oh. It's *you*!'

'Oh! It's *you*. How you doing, kid?' It was absolutely not Jimmy Stewart, but Danny whatever-his-surname-was, the hateful GI she'd met on her first night in London, with his knowing grin and that way of looking at Rose as if she was no better than she ought to be.

'I'm fine,' Rose said thinly. 'And you're well?'

'I'm not dead, so I guess I'm peachy,' he said. Now Rose remembered he was the type of person who always had to have a smart answer for everything. She was also remembering that he was quite handsome, if one liked dark men, which generally she didn't. 'You're a regular at the Rainbow now? Didn't I warn you about hanging around in places like this?'

Rose liked to think there was a look of icy disdain on her face. 'I'm an American Red Cross volunteer. You can ask at the reception desk if you don't believe me!'

'I'd forgotten how uppity you were—'

'I am not uppity—'

'But I hadn't forgotten how beautiful you are.'

She suspected he was laughing at her again, but he was quite still as he stood there, head cocked to one side as he stared at her quite brazenly as if her beauty was for him and him alone.

'Well, I hadn't forgotten how rude *you* are,' Rose said flatly. She was determined to squash down that little frisson of delight because he'd said she was beautiful. 'I'm sure you don't even remember my name. That entire night you just called me "kid" in a superior voice.'

'That's 'cause you were being a brat,' he said with a conspiratorial wink. He was impossible. 'A monumental brat.'

'Time I wasn't here, anyway. Nice to see you again, I'm sure,' Rose said and it was in a curious way. Not just because he'd flirted with her, but also because it made her feel like a proper Londoner who bumped into people she knew on the street.

She started to walk down Denham Street, squeezing her way past the hard-faced girls and the little groups of men who wanted to take them into dark doorways. 'What kind of guy would I be if I didn't walk you home?' Danny said, as he fell into step beside her. 'Did you ever make it to the YWCA?'

'No, and I don't need walking home. Besides, I'm not going home yet.' She darted across the street. Danny darted with her. 'I'm going to get fish and chips if there are any left.'

'Still haven't tried fish and chips, I'll tag along,' Danny said. 'What kind of fish is it?'

Improbably, they talked about fish for the three minutes it took to walk to the chippy and join the end of a queue. There was a rumour of cod, though not much of it and Rose would have been anxiously counting the heads in front of her but Danny distracted her by describing the lobster he'd eaten at the dog-end of long summer days spent at a place called Judith Point in Rhode Island.

'But I thought you were from New York. Wasn't that what you said when we first met?'

Danny shook his head impatiently. 'No one spends summer in New York. It's filthy hot. A man could lose his mind in weather like that.'

'I'd love to go to New York,' she said and they'd been so busy talking that she hadn't realised they were now they were at the head of the queue.

'One piece left. You going to give it to your girl?' the man behind the counter asked Danny.

Rose desperately wanted that piece of fish, even if it was huss, but at Rainbow Corner she had it drummed into her head night after night that the US soldiers were guests in their country and were laying down their lives to defend Britain against the Nazis so the least she could do was give up a piece of fish for the cause. 'He can—'

'Give it to my girl,' Danny said firmly and she certainly wasn't his girl, never would be, but she didn't even attempt to argue her case.

'Thank you.' Rose watched as a tiny tail piece that she was assured was cod was placed next to a small pile of chips, sprinkled with salt and vinegar and left open at her request.

They walked along Brewer Street. It was quieter though it was hard to walk and eat chips (which had been fried in what tasted like old engine oil) at the same time. Rose saved the fish for last in the way she'd always saved the cherry on her fairy cake. One bite and it was half gone.

'Here. You can have the rest,' she told Danny, who'd been silent too. 'But I feel obliged to tell you that fish and chips have been very poorly represented by what we've just had.'

'It was great. Best fish and chips I've ever eaten.' She could see the flash of his teeth as he grinned at her.

'Not that you've ever eaten fish and chips before,' Rose reminded him. They crossed onto Old Compton Street. 'If you're set on walking me home, it's best to stick to the side streets. There's less chance of a bomb dropping on you if you avoid the main roads.'

'You'd hear the siren before any bombs started dropping.' They were walking side by side along the narrow pavement, hands occasionally brushing. Danny was big without being bulky and it made Rose feel safe, or safer.

'Not if it was just one bomber who'd got separated from the rest of his bomber friends and it was a cloudy night so no one even knew that he was up there,' Rose insisted.

Danny huffed a little. 'It doesn't work like that.'

It was a perfectly plausible scenario, but probably not worth arguing about. 'So, um . . . oh! How's Phil? He was so kind that evening. I hope he hasn't been too homesick. He talked so much about Des Moines, as if he was missing it rather a lot.'

'He's dead,' Danny said so softly that Rose wasn't sure that she'd heard him properly. 'Didn't make it back from his first mission.'

'He can't be dead.' Not Phil with his big, gangly limbs that he didn't know how to contain. His shy but ready smile, the tips of his ears red from the hours spent dancing just to please her. 'He was going to be a vet after the war. He's probably been taken prisoner or he's being smuggled back to England by the Resistance or—'

'Kid, his plane went down in flames. He's not coming back.'

'My name is Rose, not Kid,' she managed to say and then inexplicably she was crying. Because Phil had got to her before Sylvia's well-meaning lectures about not losing your heart and your wits to every man you shared a dance and a doughnut with.

She turned away, her shoulders shaking in her mother's funeral fur. Then she was stumbling to the nearest doorway so she could hide her face in cold stone and cry.

'Rose . . . ' Danny put a hand on her arm. She shook it off. 'Listen, you gave him the best night of his life. He never stopped talking about you after we got back to base and he—'

'Shut up! I don't want to hear it. Oh God . . . don't touch me!'

But he was touching her, turning her back round to face him with a firm grip that couldn't be denied when you were crying and all you wanted to do was sink against someone else because you couldn't hold yourself up any longer.

Rose found herself melting into Danny's embrace, his arm tight around her waist, and when he cupped her chin she couldn't even jerk her head away.

He stole the next sob out of her mouth with a kiss.

Her first proper kiss.

Rose wasn't quite sure what to do. There were so many strange new feelings. Of being pressed so tight against a man that not even a whisper could have come between them. Danny was hard, strong; she could feel his muscles tensing and she felt so soft, so pliable, as if he could mould her into any shape he desired. And then there were her lips. How they tingled and moved of their own accord as if she had no control over them.

She sighed. Wriggled even closer, then reared back as Danny tried to slip his tongue into her mouth.

'What are you doing?'

'Kissing you properly,' he said. 'Haven't you ever been kissed before?'

Rose was about to claim that she'd been kissed lots and lots, when she thought about how that might sound. 'Not really,' she amended.

'Let me show you,' Danny said and his voice was so deep it made something quiver in the pit of her stomach. 'Open your mouth a little bit.'

She let him kiss her again. It was impossible to refuse him and now she could taste him as well as feel him. The quivering grew stronger and Rose thought her knees might buckle if Danny weren't holding her up.

Still he kissed her, tongue delving deep into her mouth, until her lips were sore and she could hardly catch her breath. If a bomb had fallen on them right then she'd have been happy to die in his arms. But when his hand slid underneath her coat, touched her breast for one fleeting moment, she gasped and it was actually rather easy to pull free.

'That's quite enough.' Her voice was so weak and breathless she hardly recognised it. 'I really should be getting home now.'

Danny stepped back. In the darkness, his face was all angles and shadows. She'd never thought a man could be beautiful, but he was.

'Enough for now,' he agreed. 'But you're going to let me see you again, aren't you?'

'Yes, if you'd like to.' She couldn't even pretend that she had a million and one things to do, that she wouldn't be waiting for him. 'When are you on leave again?'

Danny tucked his arm in hers. 'It's too cold to stand here shooting the breeze. Let's walk.'

She was in an agony of not knowing. Finally, as they were walking along Theobalds Road and Rose was already dreading saying goodbye, she could bear it no longer. 'You never said . . . when you're next on leave?'

'I didn't, did I?' She'd never think of his grin as sneery again. 'So, you want to see me again, then?'

Rose hated this kind of dance. She was terrified that she was going to miss her footing and trip. 'Only if you want to see me again. You do, don't you?'

Then Danny took her hand, and even through her mittens and his gloves, she felt comforted by his touch. 'Of course I do,' he said. 'I'll meet you outside Rainbow Corner same time tomorrow night. Guess I shouldn't be so keen, but I don't want you going off with some other guy just because I was too slow to state my intentions.'

Rose didn't even care if his intentions were honourable, she was just pleased that he had them. She beamed at him. 'I'll see you tomorrow, then.'

But Danny wasn't there the next night when she came out of Rainbow Corner with Sylvia and Maggie. As she waited for him for ten agonisingly long minutes, Rose thought that he'd stood her up. Sylvia and Maggie thought so too. 'Rosie, how many times do I have to tell you that all these Yanks are full of hot air and empty promises?' Sylvia said. 'Come on, we'll find you another one to take your mind off things.'

Reluctantly, Rose allowed them to lead her away. They'd just turned the corner onto Windmill Street to cut through Soho when someone sneaked up and caught her round the waist so she shrieked in alarm. Maggie didn't miss a beat but hit Danny so hard on the head with her handbag that he unhanded Rose with a shriek of his own.

It wasn't the most auspicious of introductions. Maggie didn't apologise for hitting him and Sylvia took Danny's hand in a limp grip, looked him up and down with a weary expression, then said, 'Charmed, I'm sure.' She sounded far from charmed.

'Can I walk you home, then?' Danny asked with a smile. He didn't seem the least put out at the frosty reception.

She smiled back and had got just as far as saying, 'Well, I'd like—' when Sylvia and Maggie linked arms with her and started walking so she had no choice but to walk with them.

'We don't let Rose walk home with any Tom, Dick or Harry,' Sylvia threw over her shoulder.

'What about a Danny? Is she allowed to walk home with a Danny?' he asked as he followed them through the darkened streets. 'Do I need to get my CO to write a letter of referral?'

'The jury's still out on Dannies,' Maggie said.

'I'm so sorry. I can't think why they're being like this!'

Sylvia shot Rose a pitying look. 'That's exactly why we're not letting you walk home with him.'

Instead Danny came with them to the Bouillabaisse and paid their admission.

'I don't dance,' he said once Rose had slipped off her coat and fluffed up her hair, and the band had begun to play something fast and jivey. He looked around the crowded room. 'You do know this is a negro club?'

'So? The negroes have better manners and better steps than

most of the white fellows we dance with,' Sylvia informed him haughtily but Danny simply shrugged as if he was used to dealing with haughty best friends.

'They're really awfully nice,' Rose said and she sat down next to him, because she just wanted to be near him. Close enough that if she leaned in, then Danny might kiss her, but Danny didn't seem inclined to kiss her, not even when she pursed her lips and gazed up at him. Finally, when the third man plucked up the courage to ask Rose to dance, Danny told her to go ahead.

In between dances, he bought Maggie and Sylvia a gin and French each and Rose a ginger beer because she had yet to find a palatable grown-up drink, then stood guard over their table while Rose danced with men who weren't him.

Rose was always pleased to dance, but she was less pleased that Danny didn't mind watching her dance with other men. Surely, if he was keen on her, he should mind very much?

Rose might even have begun to despair but then in the lull between tunes and partners, Danny was *there* behind her. Wrapping her up in her mother's coat and his arms, then hustling her up the stairs while Sylvia and Maggie were in the Ladies' with Rose's red lipstick.

When she tried to tell Danny that, he shushed her with a kiss. 'I'll buy you another lipstick,' he promised, when she tore her mouth away from his because she simply couldn't bear the violent fluttering of her heart any longer. 'I need to spend some time alone with you.'

It was a cold, soupy night. Tendrils of fog curled around them, though Rose would have sworn on a whole stack of bibles that she could see stars in the skies. 'I'm sorry about Maggie and Sylvia. They do tend to be rather over-protective.' Rose half expected them to suddenly come charging out of the door of the club and demand that Danny unhand her.

Rose didn't want to be unhanded, especially when Danny tightened his arms around her and his look became less fond and more determined. 'So, the place where you live, do you have your own room?'

'Oh no. I share a tiny room with Sylvia and she'll probably be home soon, I should think.'

'There's nowhere we can be alone?' Danny said in a low voice that tickled her ear and made Rose feel heavy and languorous. 'Just the two of us.'

Rose knew exactly what he was angling for. She'd heard Phyllis and Maggie whisper about someone called Brian who'd broken Phyllis's heart after she'd allowed him certain intimacies that would ensure Brian was horsewhipped if Phyllis's father ever found out.

Then there had been those white-faced, red-eyed girls at her father's surgery with their grim-looking mothers. They were sent off to a home on the outskirts of Newcastle and returned a few months later, fatter and even paler. And Rose had been in London for four whole months now, long enough to know exactly what those brassy-looking girls meant when they shouted 'Quick march! Marble Arch style!' at the GIs on their way to Rainbow Corner.

Besides, there was something frightening and unpredictable about kissing Danny – as if Rose no longer knew herself or could begin to guess at what she might say or do so he'd agree to never stop kissing her.

So Rose made sure her eyes were especially wide. 'There's nowhere.' She didn't even have to fake the tremble in her tone, because Danny might be the sort of fellow who only wanted to take liberties and if she didn't let him take them then he might just walk off into the fog and never be seen again.

'I guess it's just as well that you're so pretty,' Danny said at last. 'Though I have to tell you, kid, pashing in doorways isn't my style.'

'It's not mine, either,' Rose said with a little more conviction now she'd got her way. 'But it's just as well that you are jolly good at pashing in doorways because you don't even dance!'

No one, not Shirley or Sylvia, had ever suggested that making a man laugh might guarantee his devotion. But making Danny laugh seemed to be the magic trick that kept him coming back night after night.

Danny was a bomber pilot. Or rather he hadn't denied it when Rose asked him, but cocked an eyebrow and said he knew his way around a plane. Though currently he was grounded and temporarily stationed in London. Something to do with an old injury that he insisted was nothing and something official that he wasn't allowed to talk about, which meant he was billeted at the Columbia Club in Lancaster Gate for two weeks.

Fourteen nights. By her reckoning, Rose was in love with him by the sixth.

Danny never came into Rainbow Corner, but he'd be waiting for Rose outside when she appeared with one, or sometimes all three, of her chaperones, though Phyllis thought Danny was splendid. 'He looks like a younger, more rugged Ronald Colman,' she'd sighed after she'd been introduced, but that didn't mean that she was lax in her duties.

Each night, Danny followed them to the Paramount or the Bouillabaisse or if they could bear to walk that far, to the Royal Opera House in Covent Garden, where they now held dances. He'd pay their entrance fee, secure them a table, buy their drinks and watch Rose dance with other men. Phyllis, Maggie and especially Sylvia were ever-vigilant and never left the two of them alone so it got harder to sneak away for those fierce, drugging kisses. Harder, but not impossible: Rose would seek out the darkest corners of the club and wait, heart racing, for two hands to steal around her waist, lips to kiss her neck.

He'd touch her too. Sliding his hands down to rest on her hips or shape her breasts over whichever borrowed frock she was wearing and Rose would let him because for the first few seconds that his hands moved on her she could barely remember her own name. Then she'd come to her senses and push him away. 'You mustn't do that.' She never really sounded that firm. 'It's not right.'

Sometimes she thought that she didn't even say it for propriety's sake but because Danny would grin when she did. A slow, insolent grin that made her feel exactly the way his kisses did and when they finally stumbled out of the dancehall for the long, kiss-bitten walk home, she was so heated up that she never even noticed the bitter sting of the dark winter night.

11

Nothing could be further from the rent-protected garret Jane had imagined. Not this beautifully restored house with its double-height rooms, gleaming tessellated tiles and parquet flooring and all those period bits and bobs: architraves, ceiling roses and whatnot. Then there was the art – as Jane followed Anna back down the stairs before dinner, they passed a Pollock, three Mondrians and God knows what else.

Being guided through a stranger's house, her footsteps echoing as they crossed the hall, Jane felt as if she was being directed towards a doctor's office. No hope of a cure. Worse, she was remembering Charles again. Arriving at his house. The waif and stray that he took in, no questions asked, no answers given.

She never liked to dwell on those first few months in London – it now felt as if they'd happened to someone else, another girl – but when she did, the memories were unwelcome. She couldn't say how long it was before she'd been able to sleep in the bed in the charming mint-green and white guest room. At first, she'd slept under the bed, the floor pristine, the carpet soft, with the knife clutched in one hand and the grimy roll of banknotes in the other.

She'd only come out when she heard Charles leave and it

wasn't a Monday or a Thursday when his cleaning lady came. She'd head straight to the kitchen where there was so much food. Peanut butter, even if it was the crunchy, wholenut kind, tiny sweet apples, individual pots of yoghurt, foil triangles of soft cheese and square white bread that Charles must have bought solely for her. Jane ate it all.

Then she'd spend hours in the bath, door locked and a chair wedged under the handle. She'd never felt so clean before and when she slid under the water to see how long she could hold her breath, she always came up for air long before she needed to.

But it still felt as if she was on borrowed time. Because one night had turned into so many days – she'd counted more than one hundred – and she'd have to leave eventually and the world outside this house was waiting to hurt her. And if she stayed, well, he'd given her somewhere to stay, fed her, clothed her. Of course he was going to want something in return.

One night she was waiting in the hall when he got back from wherever he went all day. She'd hardly been able to look at him that first night and now she was surprised that he wasn't as tall or as grey as she thought he was.

He was a fair, slender man with a pink and white complexion, in his forties, though she hadn't known that then. 'In your forties' looked a lot different where she'd come from.

'Hello,' he'd said as if he wasn't surprised to see her standing there. She'd followed him into the kitchen and leaned against the door to watch as he took things, vegetables mostly, out of the fridge chopped and stirred, added spices, then served two plates of something he called stir fry but was nothing like the Chinese takeaway she'd had the one time.

She ate, head down, fork held like a weapon, arm shielding her plate, and when she was finished, she took their empty plates and washed them up because she could do that for him and she waited for Charles to tell her what else she could do, but he never did.

He simply indicated she should follow him into the huge lounge at the back of the house. There was a big, grey tweedy sofa and he sat on it and gestured at the space at the other end, so there was distance between them. She didn't even feel scared. That surprised her, because she couldn't ever remember a time that she hadn't felt scared. It was always there, a rusty, cold trickle at the back of her throat, skin shrinking away from her bones; and in wondering why she wasn't scared, she realised that she hadn't been scared for quite some time now.

'It's Friday,' he said, which meant nothing to her. 'I like to unwind by watching a film on Friday night. Do you have any favourite films?'

Films were either Disney cartoons or something with car chases and explosions, people getting smashed up. She looked at him like he might just be taking the piss, but he didn't notice, just got up, walked over to the shelves about the TV and selected a DVD.

Then they watched *Barefoot in the Park*. It was still one of her favourite films.

That was their new routine. Dinner and a movie. Three weeks it took her to say what she wanted to say but it was still completely inadequate. 'Thanks,' she said, before she washed their plates from the Sunday roast he'd cooked.

'You're welcome,' Charles said. 'There is a dishwasher under the counter to your left.'

'It's all right. I want to do this.'

It was baby steps all the way. The first time she got up before Charles left for work, so she could wash up his breakfast things. The first time she got up before him to make him breakfast because she now knew that every morning he had porridge with just a splash of honey in it and precisely nine fat flame raisins.

The first time she left the house with Charles to go to a fancy supermarket and dog his footsteps as he wheeled a trolley around.

Probably the biggest step was the night that she slept in the bed instead of underneath it, the knife still in her hand and the bundle of notes under her pillow. Or maybe the biggest step was the evening that Charles came home from work to find her in the kitchen chopping and stirring and adding spices, which wasn't unprecedented by this stage, but the wad of money placed where he always sat was.

But it had taken months to get there – before that there had been months of unease, of being an interloper, an intruder. How many times had she revisited that feeling over the years? How many times had she pretended that she felt right at home even when she was sure that it was all a dream and that she'd wake up on rotting carpet underneath a sagging single bed in a damp, dilapidated house on the worst street in the roughest estate in Gateshead?

That feeling was with her now as Jane paused outside the dining room. The table was laid with white linen; the heavy silver cutlery and lead-cut crystal gleamed dully in the soft candlelight. And there was Leo, leaning against a sideboard in the same mid-century modern style as the table and chairs. Still unwashed, still unshaven, still wearing the clothes he'd got married in. 'Ah, there she is!' he announced as if he'd spent hours combing the house trying to find her. 'I knew she had to be around here somewhere.'

He was talking to an older woman who was gazing down the length of the table to check that each piece of cutlery, every glass, every napkin was in perfect alignment. She was maybe late forties, early fifties – it was hard to tell – and had curly blonde hair cut short, her soft, pudding-like features arranged into a faintly harried expression as she smiled vaguely at Jane.

'Jane, this is Lydia, Rose's housekeeper, cook and general saint. See, Liddy? I said she was a looker.'

'And I said, in that case, you were obviously punching above your weight,' Lydia said in a flat, deadpan voice, which made Jane instinctively know she didn't suffer fools or Leo gladly. 'Hello. I won't shake hands, I'm in the middle of dinner, but it's very nice to meet you.'

'It's lovely to meet you too,' Jane said. She looked at Leo, then back at Lydia who wasn't wearing a neat staff uniform but a floral apron over a jumper and grey trousers.

'Liddy's the love of my life,' Leo said. He was still leaning against the sideboard as if it were the only thing keeping him upright. He looked grey and tired. Playing the prodigal son had to be quite a stretch.

Lydia must have thought so too, because she shot him an exasperated look, then turned to Jane. 'I forgot to ask, you're not a vegetarian, are you?'

'No, I eat most things. Except octopus. Too many legs,' Jane said and Lydia smiled again.

'No octopus, I promise. Did you want a drink?'

Jane, ever the perfect houseguest, shook her head. 'Water's fine. Still, preferably, but I'll wait for everyone else.'

'I really must get back to the kitchen. I did placecards, though. Jane, you're on Rose's right,' Lydia said and she hurried out.

'I'd love a drink,' Leo said plaintively. 'Seemed politic to say that I was on the wagon, you know.'

'I don't, darling, because you've thrown me in at the deep end without checking if I can swim. Your Rose, she's quite something, isn't she . . . ?'

Leo had his back to her and was staring at the decanters on the sideboard. 'You only got Rose at half-throttle. Can you imagine how intimidating she is when she's firing on all cylinders?'

Of all the bars in the world, she'd had to walk into that one. 'That was half-throttle, was it?'

'I really need a drink. Maybe a snifter of brandy.' Leo held one of the decanters aloft so the amber contents glowed in the candlelight. 'I've always wondered exactly what a snifter is.'

'It's one of those pear-shaped glasses to the left of you.' Jane winced as Leo pulled the stopper out of the decanter and took a sip. She sat down in front of her place card. 'So, are we still going to play this like we did in Vegas? You were a lot more help then than you were earlier.'

Leo smiled sheepishly. 'Sorry about that. Look, it will all be fine, I promise.'

'What will be fine?' Rose was standing in the doorway, heading up her procession of dinner guests. She was taller and more imposing standing up. Jane rose to her feet. 'No, you might as well stay seated, dear, and stop slouching, Leo. You'll end up with a hunch if you're not careful.'

Jane hadn't had time to change for dinner and was still wearing the jeans and Breton top she'd flown in because they were comfortable and she was aching all over. Now she was sure she was included in the disapproving look that Rose gave Leo as she sat down at the head of the table. George, Gudrun and the others dispersed themselves as directed while Rose adjusted one of the spoons, unfolded her napkin and placed it on her lap, then glanced up. 'Goodness, how serious you two look. Am I that frightening?'

'Of course you're not,' Leo said, as he sat down at Rose's left, opposite Jane. 'We're both jetlagged, that's all. Jane can't sleep on planes and I slept too much.'

'Do you think you'll be able to sleep tonight?' Rose asked Jane, as George started talking to Leo about the time he'd gone to Vegas in the eighties.

'I hope so, but I don't think my body knows what time zone it's meant to be in.'

'It's a horrible feeling, isn't it? Not to worry, I promise I won't grill you too hard,' Rose said.

Rose didn't even wait to break bread but immediately launched into Jane's interrogation. There was no need for Leo to feel guilty, because Jane was quite capable of looking after herself. She answered Rose's questions politely but in a flat, disinterested voice as if she'd answered the same questions again and again.

'My father was much, much older than my mother,' she said. 'He died when I was quite young but before that we moved around a lot for his work.'

'Army brat? Or was he in the diplomatic corps?' Rose asked.

Jane shook her head. 'He worked in aviation.' She smiled faintly. 'One year he flew me to Greenland to see Father Christmas. He died when I'd just turned five. Plane crash. Then it was just my mother and me.'

'Where did you settle?'

'Well, it was my mother and me and a variety of stepfathers.' Jane sniffed. 'We weren't really close. She had family in Australia, an aunt, so I was shipped off to boarding school in New South Wales. A religious boarding school.'

'That sounds quite grim,' said Elaine, as they were served sea bass in some kind of citrus reduction. 'I hated being sent away to school. Did you like yours?'

'A bit too much emphasis on praying and they made us go on these camping trips into the Bush, which were pretty horrific. Then my mother died just as I was doing my final exams and my aunt passed away a year later so I don't really have much in the way of family.' Jane wrinkled her nose as if not having much in the way of family had stopped bothering her a long time ago.

'Not even on your father's side?' Elaine appeared to be gripped by Jane's tragic biography. Leo was pretty gripped himself.

'Not as far as I know. From what my aunt told me, his family didn't exactly approve of the marriage. I think they were quite well-to-do and my mother wasn't. Always sounded a little Victorian to me.'

Rose neatly placed her knife and fork on her plate. In a room lit only by lamps and candles with shadows hovering, she looked older than she had done earlier. Leo thought that there was something already cadaverous about the way her face was arranged. He blinked to clear the image and it was gone. She was the same old Rose who was smiling at Jane.

'I must say, I was quite taken with the idea of being an orphan when I was a child. I'd have been quite happy to have been sisterless too, no disrespect to your late grandmother, Leo.'

'None taken,' Leo said; his maternal grandmother had died before he was born. 'I'd have been quite happy to have been brotherless too. At least you never had any annoying siblings constantly getting you into trouble,' he added to Jane.

'Oh, I'm sure you've never had any difficulty getting into trouble all by yourself,' she said sweetly, and everyone but Leo smiled.

'You seem to have Leo's measure,' George said as Rose murmured her agreement. 'That will come in handy.'

Leo didn't really mind a little light teasing – it was the Reckoning that he was really dreading, but Rose wouldn't do that in front of company. 'Anyway, you do have family,' he reminded Jane. 'I'm your family now.'

It sounded ridiculous. Like he was hankering for evenings spent in a farmhouse-style kitchen, a couple of tow-headed brats in attendance, Jane cooking homely fare on an Aga while he spent the days painting in a converted barn. Not a life he'd ever wanted.

'I've never missed having a family,' Jane said as if his husbandly comment wasn't even worth acknowledging. 'I've got lots of friends and work keeps me busy. I'm in hospitality.'

'Are you? I always wondered exactly what that was,' Rose said. 'Leo, will you go and tell Liddy we're ready for pudding and coffee?'

When he got back to the dining room after finally teasing a reluctant smile from an unforgiving Lydia, Jane was silent and seemed grateful to no longer be centre stage as the grown-ups talked politics.

Leo was pleased to be quiet too. He sat down and tried to catch Jane's eye so he could signal that everything was A-OK, but she was looking everywhere but at him.

'Where do the two of you live, then?' Rose asked, as Lydia came in with the coffee. 'You mentioned San Francisco, Jane, but, Liddy, didn't you say that Leo had been living in LA?'

It was a horrible feeling when your heart suddenly hurled itself against your chest wall.

'They're not that far apart – it's just over an hour's flight and I travel so much for work that it's never really been an issue,' Jane said smoothly. 'Once Christmas is out of the way, we'll make a decision about where we're going to live.'

'I can live pretty much anywhere,' Leo said. 'It's not like I have a commute to get to my job.'

'So, you do have a job, then, because—'

'Actually, talking of travelling, I know we've hardly had a chance to get to know each other, but I'm fading fast,' Jane said. 'I always seems to end up with a terrific headache after a long-haul flight. Would it be terribly rude if I excused myself?'

'Of course not,' Rose demurred. 'You poor girl, and there was I doing a good impersonation of the Spanish Inquisition.'

'You should have said,' Leo choked out. 'Shall I come up with you?'

Jane gifted him with another of those sweet, sweet smiles that Leo was learning not to trust. 'No need for that, darling. You stay. I know you and Rose have *so* much to catch up on.'

12

Dinner had gone well, Jane thought, as she got undressed. She'd faced down worse foes than Rose, even if Rose did have a grande-dame hauteur that made Jane think of a dowager duchess refusing to secede the family manse to her young upstart of a daughter-in-law.

Jane didn't know if Rose had believed her, but there was no reason why she shouldn't. She'd told that story so many times, to so many people, and familiarity and repetition had given it a degree of authenticity. Jane could easily imagine the glamorous, distinguished father who could pilot his own planes; the flighty and discontented mother still chasing the last vestiges of her own youth who didn't want to be saddled with a kid. She could even imagine the dormitory in that Australian boarding school: the giggling and whispers after lights-out, someone in the bed by the window crying because they were homesick.

It shouldn't really have mattered whether Rose believed her or not and Jane shouldn't have really cared. Jane was just meant to be passing through, that had been the plan, except it hadn't been a plan but a series of catastrophic events that had placed Jane in Rose's orbit.

But now she was here, there was no harm in trying to make

the best of it. The Google search she'd done earlier had been very interesting. Enough to make a girl quite giddy.

On first meeting her, Jane had imagined that Rose was a wealthy widow with all her equity tied up in the house and her art collection.

Not even close. Rose reigned over a property empire. She owned whole streets of houses, charging rent on mansion blocks, shops and offices from Kensington to Chelsea, Notting Hill and Ladbroke Grove to Westbourne Park. Not to mention three estate agents, a building maintenance company and an interior design business all run from her company offices in a converted stable block in a little road behind Kensington High Street.

And although her other business interests included a partnership with a Housing Association that provided affordable accommodation for essential workers and a right-to-buy scheme for her employees that had earned Rose a Queen's Award for Industry, it was obvious that Rose was no soft touch.

Jane had married into money after all. One thing was clear, though: she'd need to tread very carefully. Not just with Rose, but with Leo too. No point in killing the goose that laid the golden egg.

For the first time since she'd sat in that bridal suite in Las Vegas and wondered if she might faint, Jane felt hopeful. At least now that she had a husband, she had options.

She was expecting Leo to turn up imminently, so Jane rushed through her skincare routine then rummaged in the chest of drawers for a T-shirt she could sleep in. And in case Leo got the wrong idea, Jane shoved two pillows down the centre of the bed. She wasn't handing out freebies any more, not with so much at stake.

By the time Leo did come up, half an hour later, Jane was asleep. Or she was pretending to be asleep. She heard him approach the bed. 'Are you awake?' he whispered loud enough that she might well have woken up if she really had been asleep. 'Are we cool? Do we need to talk?'

Jane would be quite happy if she didn't have to say another word to anyone for at least a week.

'So, that story about your parents and the Australian boarding school, was any of that true?'

She could feel him coming nearer and she held her breath, until she remembered that she was meant to be asleep. She made her breathing slow and measured, threw in a snuffle for good measure and Leo took the hint.

Jane heard him move away, go into the bathroom, then come out of the bathroom. Heard him unscrew something, the clatter of pills, everything amplified in the dark. He took one, no, two tablets. Then toed off his sneakers, clothes falling on the floor, and she tried not to freeze again when he pulled back the covers and the mattress dipped as he got into bed.

'You've got to be fucking kidding me,' he muttered when he discovered their pillow chaperone, then he made a sound in the back of his throat like it was funny.

Five times Jane watched the second hand of the clock on her nightstand do a full sweep and that was all the time it took Leo to fall asleep.

Jane was still asleep when Leo woke up with a furry feeling in his mouth and rocks in his head. He lay there and was happy to watch her for a while, even though that was probably a little creepy. She even slept perfectly. Limbs curled up into a tight ball, her face a beautiful blank because Jane would never do anything as ungainly as sleep with her mouth wide open or dribble and snore.

Leo still felt guilty about throwing her to the lions the night before. Talking of which, it was time to head for the Coliseum.

It was eight o'clock. The house had come to life. He could hear the distant sound of someone vacuuming, a door being opened, voices.

Leo pulled on the same clothes as yesterday. And the day before that. He doubted there was anything in the house that still fitted him, but he didn't want to wake Jane by yanking out drawers and rattling hangers.

He walked down the stairs, smiling at Anna, who averted her eyes as she dragged the vacuum cleaner behind her, and hurried along the corridor to the heart of the house.

'Ah, Leo, we were just talking about that wife of yours,' Rose said jovially before he'd even made it in to the kitchen.

She and Lydia were having breakfast together. Pride of place on the scrubbed pine table was the big blue and white Cornishware teapot that Leo remembered so well from other breakfasts in this kitchen. The chunky china mugs, the silver rack full of toast and Lydia's homemade jams spooned into little mismatched bowls were old and familiar.

The cosy scene reminded Leo of sneaking home 'with the milk' as Rose called it, coming in through the back door, only to find Lydia and Rose already in the kitchen.

'Do come in, Leo. We won't bite,' Lydia said, and now he was remembering how they'd always used to tease him then, too. Calling him a dirty stop-out and telling him he needed to settle down with a nice girl. 'Do you even know any nice girls?' Rose would ask and she and Lydia would both giggle. It was a nice memory.

'You smell less than fresh,' Rose said now, as Leo sat down next to her. 'Weren't you wearing that rather grubby T-shirt yesterday?'

'Yeah. I didn't bring any luggage with me. Long story.'

It wasn't that long a story really. The last time he'd seen his luggage it was in Melissa and Norm's pool house.

Rose looked at him wearily as if everything was always a long story with him. 'Anyway, about your Jane . . . ' she said. 'We were just discussing how extraordinary-looking she is.'

'I've never seen anyone so beautiful in real life,' Lydia added. 'Did you want me to make you some eggs, Leo?'

He shook his head and grabbed a piece of toast.

'One wants to sit down opposite her and spend hours simply staring at her face,' Rose said with a wry smile. 'Do you ever get tired of looking at her?'

Leo took a bite of toast and jam and munched contemplatively. 'She's all right, I suppose,' he said at last. 'To tell you the truth, she looks a bit rough first thing in the morning.'

'I'm sure she doesn't, you rude boy.' Rose tapped him smartly on the arm and in the pitiless morning light, with no make-up on, her hair covered by a scarf, he could see the deeply ingrained purple circles around the blue eyes that had grown filmy and red-rimmed. Even her hand where it rested on the table had changed. Rose had had beautiful, long-fingered, elegant hands. Pianist's hands, Leo had always thought, but now he could see raised veins like fat blue worms and her fingers were crabbed and crooked.

It wasn't just the cruelty of ten extra years on her face, her thin body, or the new rasp to her voice. There was a new hesitation to her movements as if she had to think hard before she lifted her mug to her mouth or spooned a blob of jam onto her plate. To make each action an economy so she could save her strength for when she had to tense her muscles to ward off the pain.

She was doing it now. A tremor made her fingers twitch and she lowered her head, took two short breaths, then sighed in relief. 'Your Jane, she's quite the character, isn't she?'

'Well . . . '

'I can't imagine what the two of you actually have in common,' Rose said tartly and she hadn't lost any of her edge. That edge could cut him into slivers, but Leo was rather pleased it was still there. 'Are you really married?'

'I know it seems unbelievable but yeah, we really are. Way out of my league, isn't she?'

Lydia was putting more bread in the toaster but she looked over at Leo and grinned. 'Definitely. Have you got something on her that forced her to say "I do"? Do you know where all her bodies are buried?'

It seemed a pity to puncture the light atmosphere but he couldn't ignore Rose's careful stillness any more. Before he left, she'd always been so restless, in constant motion. Leo covered her beautiful, ruined fingers with his hand. She was cool to the touch. 'How are you? Really?' he asked.

She caught his eye, held it and the connection that they'd always had flickered hopefully back into life. 'Not bad, I suppose,' she replied. He was dimly aware of Lydia leaving the room, so it was just the two of them. Leo and Rose. 'All things considered.'

'Cancer?' He could barely say it. 'Lydia said it was. Said you'd had it before. Why aren't you fighting it this time?'

If Rose could give up, then what chance did he have?

Now it was Rose holding his hand, not the other way round. 'The first time, I put up one hell of a fight,' she said. 'But that was nine years ago. When you get to my age, nine more years wreaks all kinds of havoc on one. Besides, I knew it would come back. It *always* does. With more teeth and claws.'

'But you're tough,' Leo protested. 'You could fight it again.'

'Oh, my darling boy,' she said as if he still meant that much to her. 'I've cheated this too many times. My mother, your great-grandmother, died not that long after the war. She was only forty-three. And your grandmother, my sister Shirley, barely made it past fifty, so I've done very well to get this far.'

'But why aren't you having chemo or what is it? Radio-therapy?' he demanded. Rose rubbed her thumb against the back of his hand in a distracted way that did nothing to soothe him.

'Because I had them before, both of them, and I was so very tired and weak. I didn't want to do anything. Go anywhere. See anyone.' Rose's eyelids drooped down as if it were exhausting just remembering the treatment. 'Leo, I have stage four secondary liver cancer. I have a couple of months if I'm very, very lucky. Weeks, if I'm not . . . '

'But the chemo would definitely give you months . . . '

'I'd rather spend what time I have left not feeling like a worn-out dishrag. Quality of life, my doctor calls it. You shouldn't worry, I'm stuffed full of tablets.' Rose smiled valiantly, and swayed very carefully on her chair. 'If you listen very carefully, you can hear them rattling.'

She wanted him to smile, was waiting for it. Leo stretched his lips wide obediently. 'Are you in a lot of pain?'

'Not too much. Last week I even strapped on a hard hat to inspect a renovation project, though I thought it best not to climb up any ladders.' Rose's smile was more convincing than his had been. 'Pain-wise, I'm about a three when the tablets have kicked in. Sometimes I'm up to a six if I'm late with my dose. That's not so bad, is it?'

'I suppose not.' He nodded his head decisively. 'But if gets worse than a six, they can give you something stronger, right?'

Lydia had come back into the room and the mood shifted again. Rose took her hand away, reached up to adjust her scarf and when she glanced at him he was aware of all his failings. From the jam at the side of his mouth, to the days-old stubble, T-shirt straining over his gut, the sour, parched smell if he didn't keep his arms pinned to his sides.

'While we're being honest with each other . . . do I need to worry about having prescription painkillers in the house, if you're staying?' she asked him and it wasn't always a good thing that Rose was so candid. Sometimes, like now, it was like being cut open, sides pulled back, pinned down and displayed under a microscope.

'God, no. No! You don't need to worry about that. I would never . . . ' He could only breathe through his nose.

'Do you still take drugs?' Lydia asked him baldly. The pair of them were merciless.

'From time to time. Only weed.' A half-truth was better than trying to explain that you could have a gram of coke over a weekend and then not go near the stuff for ages. There were months, even longer, when he hadn't wanted it. Like the two years he spent in Sydney, when he'd painted houses, done a bit of bartending, surfed. He might even have stayed if his visa hadn't run out. 'I haven't got messed up again. Like I did that time.'

'Really? Because we watched a TV show about these two men who cooked up crystal meth,' Lydia said.

'We did,' Rose confirmed. 'I couldn't imagine why anyone would want to take *that*. It didn't look like any kind of fun.'

Leo snorted with laughter, then hid his face in his hands, his shoulders shaking. He might even have cried a little bit. 'If I did crystal, I wouldn't be as fat as I am now,' he managed to say once he'd stopped laughing.

'That's something, I suppose,' Rose said. 'Are you back for a while, then?'

'I hadn't thought that far ahead. Never do, do I?' There was still something else bothering her. Not just his complete inability to come up with even a half-arsed apology. Some people wouldn't look at you when they were about to tell you something unpleasant, but not Rose.

'You might as well know that your mother's in town,' she said.

'Right. OK.' The news was like a note pinned to your door that you could see as you climbed up the stairs and with every step you took, the dread deepened until it had almost swallowed you. 'She's not staying here, is she?'

Rose shook her head. 'No, she insists it would be an imposition, even though it's not. We have exactly the same argument every time she comes to London.' She sounded exasperated, but then his mother's self-deprecation was exhausting. 'She's staying in a vacant flat in that serviced block of mine on Kensington Church Street.'

'So, she's well, then, is she?' Leo asked, guilt washing over him now in cold, oily waves.

'She is, and she's coming round for lunch today so it's probably best if you make yourself scarce.' Rose sounded angry now. 'Ten years, Leo, and you didn't so much as call or send her a postcard. I find that unforgivably cruel.'

'If I'd have called, she'd only have got upset.' Staying out of his mother's life was the kindest thing he could have done. It was practically noble of him. 'Please, I thought we were making up, Rose. Don't give me a hard time about this.'

Rose seemed to wilt before his eyes. 'I am very, very fond of your mother. She goes back to Durham in a few days, I doubt we'll see each other again . . . ' She stopped, turned her head, but not before Leo saw the tear trickle down her creased cheek. But it couldn't be, because Rose didn't do things like cry. Even so, her hand reached up to her face to brush away the evidence and Leo turned his own head and found that he was blinking away tears too. All this rousing talk of pills and quality of life had obscured the simple fact that in a couple of months Rose might not be here. Wouldn't be sitting down to breakfast or touching the teapot to see how warm it was, as she was now. She'd be gone. 'I would like it, more than you know, if at some point you were to make things right with your mother, introduce her to Jane, build bridges, but not now. You'll only be in the way. Is that unreasonable of me?'

'It's not,' Leo said. 'You're right. Maybe I shouldn't have come back.'

Rose had both hands curved round the teapot. Her attention was not on him, but on the kitchen window, which looked out onto the mews at the back of the house, where two men were standing by a ladder. 'Well, yes, maybe you shouldn't have,' she agreed.

13

February 1944

'Darling Rose, just because Danny's gone there's no reason to go into mourning,' Sylvia told her as they walked the backstreets towards Rainbow Corner one frigid night in late February. It was so cold that Rose had asked her mother to put her thermal combinations in the post. 'No point putting all your eggs in one basket, so to speak.'

'I thought he'd have written by now. Even a postcard. It takes no time at all to write a postcard,' Rose complained. 'Unless something dreadful has happened to him. What if—'

'I refuse to listen to what-ifs. Let's talk about something more cheery.'

Sylvia was still talking about the new hat she planned to buy when they reached Rainbow Corner and prepared to part ways. 'I'll see you back here at ten-thirty,' Rose said. 'Do you want to go out dancing after? The Opera House, maybe?'

'I can't be fagged to go to all the way to Covent Garden,' Sylvia complained, but just as Rose was going to suggest they might try the Astoria, she felt a hand on her arm.

'Just the little lady I was looking for,' Mickey Flynn said, even though Rose was at least four inches taller than he was. 'About that favour you owe me . . .'

'You're meant to talk to me about any favours,' Sylvia said sharply.

'I only came to tell our Rosie that we're even.'

'Are we?' It was impossible to get Mickey Flynn to look one in the eye. His gaze was either fixed on one's chest or on some point in the middle distance, as if he were permanently on the alert for someone else who might owe him a favour. 'How did that happen?'

'This is how. Rose, Sylvia, meet Edward. He's top drawer. Prince among men. Salt of the earth. As much as your good pal Mickey Flynn can vouch for any man, I vouch for him.'

Sylvia and Rose shared a look of confusion, then turned back to discover that Mickey had melted away as if the walls were made of blancmange. In his place was a tall, thin man in a major's uniform with a slight stoop, fair hair brushed back to show off lean, patrician features and a slightly nervous smile. Rose was sure she'd seen him before, but couldn't think for the life of her where.

'I asked Mickey if he'd mind formally introducing us. He drove a very hard bargain so now I owe him a favour and you've discharged your debt,' he said to Rose. 'It's probably for the best that I owe Mickey, rather than you. Mickey's idea of a favour can be rather unsavoury.' He had a dark, treacly voice and then Rose remembered where she'd met him before. Coming out of the billiard room the night she'd got her papers – she'd been desperate to run away, not just from Mickey's lecherous gaze, but from this man too. 'And I did rather wonder if the pair of you would do me a favour, but it's a very nice sort of favour.'

'What is it, then?' asked Sylvia, even though he'd barely taken his eyes off Rose, who'd smiled briefly at him but now didn't know where to look. He did *stare* so.

'My sources tell me you're the prettiest two girls at Rainbow Corner and I hoped that you might agree to make up a foursome with me and a colleague this evening.' He leaned in close. 'He's a very big noise in the Service Corps but he's also very dull. I might not be able to stay awake past the hors d'oeuvres.'

It didn't sound a tempting prospect to go out with a dull man in charge of stationery plus Edward, who'd stared unnervingly at her for five minutes. 'We'd get into terrible trouble if we just upped and left,' Rose told him coolly. 'We might even be blacklisted.'

'Don't make jokes like that.' Sylvia put a hand to her forehead as if she might faint.

'I'm sure I could square it with Mrs Atkins. Isn't she in charge of the volunteers?' He was already backing away as if he was intent on hunting her down.

'It has to be better than three hours on the information desk,' Sylvia hissed. 'Three hours!'

'Yes, but . . . '

'Oh, by the way, I thought we'd go to the Criterion, if that meets with your approval.'

Fortunately, Rose was wearing Shirley's black crêpe de Chine. It was a little tight with her thermals on underneath, but now she was in the Criterion, being led to a table by a stiff-backed waiter who walked like a penguin, Rose was eternally grateful she wasn't in Shirley's limp pale blue taffeta.

A portly, middle-aged man stood as they approached the table, eyed up both girls, kissed their hands as Edward introduced them, and said something about the other man being a brigadier. Rose wasn't paying attention – she was far too busy rubbernecking the other diners.

It was the London she'd always dreamed of. Women in beautiful gowns, white necks emerging from clouds of silk tulle. The urbane hum of muted conversation. All the men looked so handsome; even the older ones looked distinguished, all except . . .

'You must call me Bertie,' the portly man said. His face was very red and he was cultivating a pencil moustache, which didn't suit him. He made a big show of pulling out Sylvia's chair and smiled approvingly as the waiter reverently placed a white napkin on her lap.

'I suppose this will do, won't it, Rose?' Sylvia said with a sly grin.

It was left to Edward to pull out Rose's chair, then he sat down next to her, Bertie on her other side and Sylvia opposite so Rose could pull an incredulous face at her when she opened her menu and glanced down. She must have slipped down a rabbit hole like Alice to a land where there was lobster and caviar, steak and duck.

'I suppose it would be more patriotic to ask for the other menu that doesn't have all the non-rationed luxury items on it,' Edward said earnestly to Rose. Then he smiled so she supposed he was making a joke and smiled uncertainly back at him. To her left Bertie *was* cracking an off-colour joke about the oysters, which made Sylvia hoot.

Rose had absolutely no desire to eat oysters anyway. 'I'll have the caviar,' she told the waiter decisively. She ordered Tournedos Rossini for her main course, which earned her an odd look from Bertie, and enthusiastically agreed that a bottle of champagne as an aperitif 'would be simply heavenly'.

In the meantime, Bertie regaled them with tales of his hunting, shooting and fishing and how he'd much rather 'hunt the Hun' instead of pushing paper in an office in Whitehall.

Rose couldn't imagine he'd be much good in open combat; he was far too fat. Not that Sylvia minded. She laughed at every single one of Bertie's jokes, of which there were many –

he was particularly fond of puns – and flattered him shamelessly. 'I've been trying to think who you remind me of for the last half-hour. Bertie has a look of Clark Gable, don't you think, Rosie?'

Rose didn't, but she nodded anyway. She tried hard to think of bright, witty things to say, but it was hard with Edward barely saying anything at all and still looking at her when he thought she wasn't looking at him. Whenever Rose had thought of the glamorous London life she hoped to experience she was always blasé and languid and saying, 'Oh, darling!' a lot. She was doing none of those things, but sitting there mute. She could positively *feel* the gormless expression on her own face.

It was a relief when another waiter arrived at their table with a bottle in a silver bucket full of ice. Rose watched, riveted, as he expertly pulled out the cork. It came away with a resounding pop that made her think of crackers and fireworks and other things she loved.

She was handed a glass, the pinprick fizz of the bubbles tickling her nose, then they raised their glasses and said 'Cheers!' and she took her first sip.

Rose thought she might cry because the champagne was just as vile as Coca-Cola. Worse. At least Coca-Cola was sweet. The champagne had a sour taste and it took everything she had not to screw up her face in revulsion.

'Do you not like it?' Edward whispered to her. All he'd done was gawp at her so he must have caught the faint flicker of disgust that she hadn't been able to disguise.

'Oh no, it's lovely. My absolute favourite thing in the world.' Rose steeled herself to take another sip.

'It's all right if you don't like it. I could ask if they'd make you a mimosa, which you might like better,' he said. 'It's worth a shot.'

Rose would have liked to think that Danny would be so kind,

but he never missed an opportunity to curb what he called her brattiness. Certainly, she couldn't picture Danny at the Criterion. He wouldn't have been impressed when Bertie had pointed out Winston Churchill's usual table and he'd call all the waiters 'pal' and slouch in his chair, legs akimbo. Even with the slight hunch to his shoulders, Edward's back was as straight as it could be as he waited expectantly for her reply.

'What's a mimosa?' she asked.

'Champagne mixed with freshly squeezed orange juice. They used to serve it at the Ritz in Paris before the war.'

'I can't believe that even the Criterion can get oranges and so many of them that they don't mind squeezing them for juice.' Rose shook her head sadly. 'It's very wasteful.'

'Maybe they use what's left to make marmalade?' Edward suggested.

'Or cake. Our cook, before the war, used to make a wonderful orange and almond cake,' Rose said wistfully.

'With buttercream?' Edward asked a little wistfully himself. He didn't seem so unsettling now they were having a proper conversation and Rose relaxed enough to look him in the eye.

She even smiled at him. 'I do so miss buttercream!' Before she could ask Edward what food he missed, two waiters arrived with Bertie's oysters on a silver stand, Sylvia's sardines (she said that all the fancy seafood in the world couldn't compare to grilled sardines), and Edward and Rose's caviar.

The tiny, glossy black eggs were heaped in a little silver bowl and came with a silver spoon so Rose could scoop out the caviar and arrange it on tiny points of toast. Like the champagne, it tasted horrible. Fishy and oily and even slimier than Bertie's oysters, which he slurped down with gusto. Then he ate the rest of Rose's caviar when she said she couldn't manage any more.

'Waste not, want not.' He was clearly happiest when he was eating. 'Patriotic duty and all.'

All Rose's hopes were resting on the Tournedos Rossini – she was sure that she'd read about them in a book. Probably one of Shirley's romance novels, which always featured impressionable young women being wined and dined by very suave, very rich men.

Her heart sank when what was placed in front of her, with some ceremony, was not at all what she'd been expecting. On her plate was a huge piece of dried bread with three steak medallions perched on top; resting on each one was a slab of pâté and some strange mushroom-like shavings. The whole kit and caboodle was slathered in a dark brown sauce.

Still, Rose had managed to get through half of the caviar by washing it down with gulps of water and she'd ask Edward to order jugs of the stuff if that was what it took to force down steak that was red and bloody in the middle. They'd always had it so well done at home that one had to saw at it.

But the Criterion's bloody steak was actually beautifully tender, the pâté rich and buttery and what Edward said were truffle shavings tasted 'unbelievably yummy', she explained to Sylvia in the pauses between eating as she took sips of the Châteauneuf-du-Pape that had taken Bertie and Edward five minutes to order because they couldn't make up their minds between the '33 and the '36.

It was as Rose was mopping up the Madeira sauce with the bread that she noticed the three of them staring at her. Sylvia pointed delicately at Rose's plate and she realised that she'd abandoned her cutlery in favour of her hands, as if she were some kind of street urchin that they'd found begging outside. 'I'm sorry,' she mumbled, mouth full, but even though she was blushing rosy red, a combination of embarrassment, the food and wine, and her thermals, Rose didn't stop until her plate was clean.

'Nothing better than a girl who likes her grub,' Bertie declared, raising his glass to Rose. 'Can't abide a woman who lives on leaves and plants. You got room for pudding?'

Rose swallowed the last divine crumb and nodded. 'I'll say.'

'I don't know where you put it,' Sylvia said. 'Our friend Phyllis – Bertie, you must know her people; they own half of Norfolk – says Rose has hollow legs. One night at Rainbow Corner, a GI challenged Rose to a doughnut—'

'Oh, Sylvia, nobody wants to hear about that,' Rose pleaded, though it was rather late to claim she had no gluttonous tendencies.

'I would,' Edward said. 'I'm intrigued to know what you do at Rainbow Corner when you're not dancing.'

'Break some hearts, eh?' Bertie nudged Sylvia, who threw him an arch look, which Rose knew full well she practised in front of the mirror. 'Bet there's a fair few fellows pining after the pair of you.'

'I don't think they're pining after Rose so much as telling their soldier pals about the girl they met who scoffed twenty-one doughnuts in a sitting,' Sylvia said with a wicked smile at Rose, who hid her face in her napkin. 'Rose set a new Rainbow Corner record.'

'They were very small doughnuts,' Rose insisted but Bertie was laughing too hard to hear her.

Edward simply smiled gravely and asked Rose what she'd like for pudding.

She finished her meal with a pavlova and a glass of dessert wine and by the time they left, Rose was grateful for the sudden blast of icy air as they walked along Haymarket towards Bertie's flat near St James's Park for a nightcap.

'We won't have to do anything, will we?' Rose asked Sylvia as they walked arm in arm, the two men slightly ahead of them. 'Do you think the meal was very, very expensive?'

'Very, especially as you ate twice as much as anyone else.'

Sylvia was at her most capricious. 'Edward seems quite smitten. I never thought he'd have a thing for ingénues . . .'

'Oh, so you know him, then?' Rose asked in surprise, though Sylvia was one of those people who knew everyone.

'I know of him,' Sylvia lowered her voice. 'He's half-American, frightfully rich and does something frightfully hush-hush.'

'But what exactly?' Rose persisted; she was curious to know what strange, silent Edward did.

Sylvia sighed. 'You're not meant to ask. Do remember that there's a war on.'

'I'm hardly likely to forget.' Rose nudged Sylvia. 'Does he push paper like Bertie?'

'Special Operations, probably,' Sylvia said shortly. 'We shouldn't even be talking about this.'

Further ahead, Bertie was jabbering away at Edward, who was silent. Giving nothing away. 'You mean, he's a *spy*?' she hissed.

'Spymaster, more like,' Sylvia muttered and then she took pity on Rose. 'Strictly off-book and you didn't hear it from me. I know he seems perfectly nice, but you know what they say about still waters. I imagine he could be quite ruthless if he had to interrogate enemy agents and that sort of thing.'

'Don't tease,' Rose said crossly. 'Of course he doesn't interrogate enemy agents. He's absolutely not the type.'

'Will you keep your voice down? Goodness, Rose, are you all right? Even in this light, you're looking a little peaky.'

'I feel quite peculiar.' Rose plucked at her mother's funeral fur. She could feel sweat beading on her forehead and top lip. One moment she felt as if she was being boiled alive, the next she was freezing despite thermals and fur coat. 'I might be going down with the flu.' Both Phyllis and Maggie had been laid low with a flu bug that had decimated the volunteers at Rainbow Corner.

'Well, you'll just have to wait until we get home to go down with it,' Sylvia told her unsympathetically, as they caught up with Bertie and Edward who had come to a halt outside a mansion block that loomed up out of the darkness. 'You can't skip out on a man after he's paid for three courses and wine. It's unspeakably rude.'

They all crammed into a tiny lift and when Bertie pulled the door shut with a crash, Rose felt it reverberate in her belly. The smell of Sylvia's perfume, heavy with the scent of lilies, and the cigar smoke that clung to Bertie's topcoat, had her lurching back against Edward.

He put a hand on Rose's shoulder to steady her. 'Are you all right?' he whispered so he wouldn't be heard over the clanging of the lift as it travelled between floors and Bertie's guffaws as Sylvia said something. 'You're rather pale.'

'I'm absolutely fine.' Maybe she would be if she could sit down in a dark corner of Bertie's flat and stay very, very still.

But as soon as they entered, the floor and the walls crowded in on Rose and she could smell stale cigars and the kippers Bertie had had for breakfast and her belly lurched again and . . .

'Oh dear!' Sylvia exclaimed when Rose clapped her hands over her mouth. 'Bertie, where's the bathroom?'

'Good God! Down the corridor, last door on the left.'

Rose took off at a gallop, flung the door open and threw herself onto her knees.

Ten minutes later, flushed and cringing, she crept into the lounge where Bertie and Sylvia were flicking through records and Edward was perched on the arm of a sofa holding a glass of fizzing white liquid. 'Come and sit down,' he said gently, gesturing at the couch. 'I liberated Bertie's last bottle of Bromo-Seltzer for you.'

She sat down on the sofa and took the glass, then cringed again. 'I'm so dreadfully sorry. I don't know what you must think.' Her cheeks blazed with yet more shameful heat. 'I couldn't even open the window because of the blackout.'

Bertie waved a hand. 'No worse than me after a regimental mess dinner. The char can sort it out in the morning.'

That made Rose feel ashamed all over again because she'd imagined Bertie to be a bumptious oaf when really he was an absolute darling: so full of relentless good cheer.

Sylvia shot her a sympathetic look. 'No doughnuts for you for a while.'

'I may never eat again.' Rose sipped at the Bromo-Seltzer. Like every other drink she'd had in London, it tasted awful. 'I really am sorry,' she said again but Bertie and Sylvia had put on a record and only Edward heard her.

'Please stop apologising. You haven't done anything so terrible in the grand scheme of things. Though I did think ordering the pavlova was rather foolhardy.' He smiled that grave smile, which meant it was a joke.

'Well you might have told me,' Rose grumbled. She finished the rest of the Bromo, pulling a face as the last powdery, bitter dregs coated her tongue, but she did feel a little better. Wrung out and fragile but she didn't think she was going to die any more.

'I would have if I'd thought you'd take my advice,' Edward said. 'Sometimes we have to learn from our mistakes. I'm sure you'll never order caviar and steak tournedos again.'

'Don't talk about food,' Rose begged and he smiled again. She was tired and her thoughts had become all jumbled up. She leant her head back against Edward's side and he stroked her hot forehead with cool fingers. It felt lovely. Soothing. Safe in that cosy room, curtains closed tight against the night, Sylvia singing, '*Oh, please have some pity I'm all alone in this big city I tell you I'm just a lonesome babe in the wood . . .*'

14

Jane didn't know what time she finally fell asleep but she woke the next morning as Leo came into the room with a breakfast tray. 'To make up for putting you in front of the firing squad last night,' he said with a rueful smile, which Jane was more than happy to return, then agree to Leo's suggestion that they spend the day like tourists.

What else could she do? Besides, spending the day, lots of days, with Leo didn't have to be an ordeal. He was funny, easy-going, charming when he could be bothered to make the effort and once they left the house and began to make their way through Kensington, he had a story about every street they walked down. Stories about a misspent youth of illegal raves in derelict warehouses, pining after Chelsea heiresses who wouldn't give him the time of day and soaking up his hangovers with a fry-up.

This morning, the late October sun was high and bright but with an autumn crispness to the air that made Jane think of bonfires and fireworks. They meandered down the back streets, stopping for coffee at a tiny Italian hole in the wall – Leo was crestfallen that they didn't remember him – and then to the V&A.

'We'll start at the bottom,' Leo said although the bottom was very boring: fiddly stone carvings and pots and ancient religious relics. Even the word 'artefact' made Jane want to yawn. Then, there were the galleries. Jane suffered in silence for Leo's sake, because he obviously cared more about art than she did, but he shuffled along without much enthusiasm, hands shoved into the pockets of an ancient black coat.

'God, this is dull,' he announced. 'Let's go and look at the pretty dresses.'

The pretty dresses were the part that Jane had liked best when she'd come here on Sunday afternoons with Charles. He'd start at the bottom too but they'd always save the best for last and end up at the fashion galleries. 'I'll have that one and that one, not that one, but definitely that one,' she'd say as she pointed at Schiaparelli ballgowns or a Balenciaga cocktail dress, as if she were walking through Selfridges with a personal shopper.

Then and now, they finished in the café. Leo ate cake. It was too early for a drink, though if he were on his own Jane was sure he'd have had one. Jane drank decaffeinated coffee.

'What shall we do now?' he asked. 'What's the time?'

It was only half past twelve, the café filling up with the early lunch crowd: vacant-looking teenagers wielding massive backpacks, mothers with babies wedged into Bugaboos and Björn slings and a frightening number of ladies up from the provinces in comfortable walking shoes and anoraks.

'We can't go back for at least another two hours,' Jane said. 'Didn't you say Rose was having people over for lunch?'

'Not people. My mother.' Leo scraped the side of his fork across his plate to gather up the last smears of cream cheese frosting. They were seated next to a window and it was the first time that Jane had seen him in such clear, unflinching daylight. Greying at the temples, grey in the face, the skin slack around his eyes and jawline. 'She's in town for the next few days so I have to keep a low profile.' He wouldn't look her in the eye. 'I'm not even fucked up in an interesting, romantic way. All my problems are white middle class problems.'

Jane had figured *that* out within five minutes of meeting him. 'You could choose not to be fucked up,' she suggested.

'Nah, everyone's fucked up. Even you. Like if your dad *did* die when you were a kid and then your mum dumped you in some boarding school full of religious nutters in the Australian Bush, then you're fucked up too.'

'You can rise above being fucked up. It's a matter of applying yourself.'

Leo waved his fork at her, swollen eyes narrowed. 'Unless none of that stuff is true, which means you're fucked up in a completely different way.'

'Darling, do we really have to spend the next two hours debating the finer points of being fucked up?' Jane asked. 'If so, I'd much rather go and look at some really boring religious artefacts.'

'I'm just saying that—'

'Well, hello! Fancy running into the two of you here!' They both turned in the direction of the enthusiastic, slightly camp voice.

It was George. Rose's George, arrived to save them from themselves. As he was a curator at the V&A, he whisked them off to the bowels of the building to show them all sorts of treasures. A collection of early-twentieth-century Scandinavian glassware, a pair of Vivienne Westwood bondage trousers, origami sculptures no bigger than Jane's finger that were so beautiful but so fragile, they made her feel sad just to look at them.

George insisted that they join him for lunch in the staff canteen so he could regale them with stories of Rose. How they'd met at the cheese counter in Harvey Nichols nearly forty years ago: nineteen-year-old George with his blue Mohican and leather shorts stopping to ask Rose if her polka dot dress was a vintage Claire McCardell 'though she didn't call it vintage. Still doesn't. Says there's no point in throwing away perfectly good clothes. Anyway, it was love at first sight. No, that's sheer hyperbole. It was best friends at first sight.' George suddenly crumbled. His bright, bird-like face looked as if someone had started to rub out the edges, owlish eyes tearing up behind his horn-rim glasses. 'I don't think a day's gone by since then that we haven't spoken. I can't imagine my life without Rose in it.'

He was crying. Right there at the table. Jane sat there in an agony of embarrassment because everyone, all of George's colleagues, were looking at them.

'Rose would hate it if I cried, but when I'm not with her, I can't seem to stop,' George said. His tears were staining the slim-cut lapels of his suit; one landed with a buoyant plop onto his bread plate, right in the middle of his pat of butter.

Jane turned her face away, made her body stiff and hard. She hated seeing anyone cry. She always wanted to tell them to man up. Grow a pair. Crying didn't solve anything – it just made people think you were weak.

'Hey, George, come on, buddy,' she heard Leo say softly, then he clumsily got to his feet, grabbed a handful of napkins and crouched down in front of the older man. 'You know Rose would kill you if she heard you were crying in the V and A staff canteen. She'd expect The Ritz at the very least.'

George gave a short phlegmy laugh and took the napkins Leo offered. He wiped his eyes. 'Thank you,' he said quietly. Then he blew his nose. 'Actually, Rose hates The Ritz. Refuses to go. Says it's full of tourists and people with more money than sense.'

Leo patted George's knee. Jane hadn't expected him to be so capable of kindness. To reach out to someone who was hurting with no ulterior motive. Leo was still crouched down in front of George and had taken the older man's hands in his own. 'One day, when you really need cheering up, I'll tell you about the only time I ever went to The Ritz. Blagged my way into a supermodel's twenty-first birthday party. Twelve hours later, I was escorted out through the kitchens wearing motorcycle boots and a gold dress I got given by another supermodel.' He stood up and puffed out his chest. 'I was banned for life from every Ritz in the world.'

George was still blowing his nose, but his face was sharp again, though a little pinker than it had been before. 'I've missed you, Leo,' he said, with one final sniff. 'We both have. It's good that you've come back.'

They didn't stay long after that. It was after three. 'Lunch will definitely be over by three,' Jane said. 'Half two is industry standard. Let's go back so I can change shoes.'

They walked back to the house in silence. Ever since they'd said goodbye to George, Leo had been quiet. He only came to when they reached the square. The sun was starting to drift, the light soft and diffused, the drooping leaves creating dancing shadows. Leo took Jane's arm. 'Let's go round the back,' he said. 'So there's no danger of any doorstep confrontations.'

Jane decided not to ask Leo why he was so determined to avoid his mother. Family stuff was always messy, fraught with real and imagined slights, and feuds that went back years. Hopefully she wouldn't have to stick around long enough to get involved.

'Liddy and Frank live there, the one with the red door,' Leo suddenly said, as he steered Jane down a little mews to the left of the house, the cobbles playing havoc with her ballet flats. He was pointing at a pretty little carriage house. 'Have you met Frank yet? Liddy's husband and Rose's driver. He's also very handy around the house. Changing light bulbs, sorting out—'

Jane hadn't really been listening until Leo cut off mid-sentence – his attention caught by Rose and another woman, as tall as she was, but younger, hair darker, stepping out of a doorway. They embraced, awkwardly but affectionately, as if the obvious regard they had for each other didn't normally extend to hugging.

'Well, that's done it,' Leo snapped as if Jane had taken him to the very edge of his nerves then pushed him over. 'I'm out of here.'

'Don't be so silly.' Whatever bad blood there might be between Leo and his mother was no reason to stalk off, coat billowing in the breeze. 'For goodness sake, darling, come back!'

Rose and the other woman – Leo's mother, because she couldn't be anyone else – turned to look.

Leo could have just sucked it up. Said *Hello, you're looking well, how's Dad, weather's chilly for this time of year, isn't it?* It would have been trite and a little painful but it wouldn't have killed him. It wouldn't kill Jane either. So she did what Leo didn't have the guts to do: painted on her bravest smile and walked towards the two women.

'Hello,' Jane said brightly. 'Hope I'm not interrupting anything.'

Standing there on the kitchen doorstep, Rose introduced them. 'Linda, I told you about Jane, Leo's wife. And Jane, I haven't had a chance to tell you a thing about Linda, my sister Shirley's youngest girl. Her coronation baby, Shirley used to call her.'

They shook hands. Murmured greetings. Linda shrank back as soon as the handshake was over. There was an echo of Rose on her face, the faintest trace of Leo. Maybe around the eyes or in the generous curve of her lips, which twisted anxiously in a polite smile.

'Sorry about Leo. I could run after him?' Jane suggested, in the hope of making a quick escape.

‘There’s not much point,’ Rose said. She looked up at the sky, which had turned from blue to grey as they’d been standing there. ‘It’s going to rain.’

‘You go in,’ Linda said to her. ‘It’s too cold to be standing here.’

‘Stop fussing. A little breeze isn’t going to kill me.’ But then Rose shivered and Jane thought she might go in without arguing. Instead she paused and looked at Linda, then Jane. ‘You might as well sit down and have a little chat about that boy of yours.’

Rose abandoned them once she’d shown them through the kitchen and down a half-flight of steps to what she called the morning room and Jane would have called a conservatory.

Linda perched on the edge of the duck-egg-blue sofa like she might bolt at any second. ‘Rose said you were very pretty.’ It sounded like an accusation and maybe she realised that because she sank back a little as if she was forcing herself to relax. ‘I’m sorry.’

‘There’s no need to be.’ Jane willed her beauty to dim a little. ‘I’m sure this visit is difficult enough without Leo and me turning up like this.’

Linda wasn’t really relevant, but she was Leo’s mother and Rose seemed to be fond of her, so she might prove useful. After three years of shopping trips, spa days and girls’ lunches with Jackie, she could play the part of the eager-to-please daughter-in-law to perfection.

So when Lydia came in with a laden tray and Linda looked longingly at the walnut cake, Jane said she’d have a slice because Linda had the hungry, desperate look of a woman who couldn’t bear to eat cake alone.

Trying to make conversation though was like wading through treacle in six-inch heels. It was only through dogged perseverance that Jane discovered that Linda had two more days in

London, then would catch the train back to Durham on Thursday morning, as she hated driving on the motorway. And that it was something of a tradition that on her last evening in London, she and Rose would see a show then have dinner at Joe Allen's.

'That sounds lovely,' Jane exclaimed. She'd played to tough crowds before, but Linda might have been the toughest yet. She was staring down at the floor, refusing to make eye contact and hadn't even taken off her beige trench coat, which was slightly too big for her as if she'd bought it expecting to grow into it. 'What are you going to see?'

'Was Leo in Australia three years ago?' Linda asked. She'd raised her head and there were patches of red dusted along her cheekbones. 'In Sydney?'

Jane and Leo hadn't got as far as discussing what they were doing three years ago. 'We had quite a whirlwind romance. You know how it is. And so . . . '

'Because Alistair, his brother, lives out there. He was working for Doctors Without Borders, met an Australian girl.' Linda stopped to visibly gather herself. She took three deep breaths, placed her hands on her knees and drew back her shoulders. It suddenly occurred to Jane that the other woman wasn't flustered or awkward but so angry she could hardly speak.

'Are you all right?' Jane tried to loosen and relax her own limbs so they weren't stiff and tense too. 'We don't have to talk about Leo if it's going to upset you. Obviously, I *adore* him, but he can be impossible sometimes.'

'Alistair saw Leo walking towards him and he called his name and Leo looked right at him, then carried on walking past like Alistair wasn't even there.' Linda looked at Jane incredulously. 'Who does that? To his own brother.'

Jane couldn't resist the urge for one really good squirm. 'Families are quite complicated, aren't they?'

'There was a time, when he was in rehab after his overdose, that I blamed myself,' Linda said haltingly, her hands not still any more but twisting, fingers worrying at her rings. 'He didn't tell you about that, did he?'

'That's all in the past,' Jane said firmly, though it wasn't. Leo's drug-taking was as recent as two days ago.

'Well, I don't blame myself any more, I blame him.' Linda's chin jutted out defiantly. She looked more like Rose than Leo now. 'Ten years, and even now there are some nights when I get so furious thinking about him that I can't sleep. I know it's silly, but Leo wasn't around so I've never had the chance to tell him how I really feel. How *bloody* cross I am with him. So I say it to the Leo in my head over and over again.'

Jane didn't have conversations with her ghosts. She simply didn't let them in. When all this were over, Jane wouldn't allow herself a single sleepless night thinking about Leo. It was easier that way. 'It's been ten years,' she said gently. 'You should have just let him go.'

'You can't with family,' Linda said. 'When it's family, it's never done.'

'He's not so bad.' It was hardly a ringing endorsement from a besotted bride. Jane could do much better than that, if only to reward Leo for those flashes of sweetness he'd let her see. 'He has lots of good qualities. He's kind and wonderful at cheering people up when they're feeling down. He's funny, not in a mean way either. I think you'd find that he's changed.'

'He's never given me that opportunity,' Linda bit out, then she gathered again. 'I'm sorry. I shouldn't be talking to you like this. It's rude and inappropriate. I am usually quite a sane, rational person.'

'I'm sure you are. Don't get me wrong, I think Leo is lovely, but he can be really annoying too.' Jane decided she could risk a small conspiratorial smile. 'When he dares show his face again, I'll give him a good clip round the ear, if it would help.'

'It might,' Linda agreed. She almost cracked a smile. 'You've got your work cut out for you.'

'I know. It keeps life interesting.' Jane uncrossed her legs and changed position, then crossed them again and it was that easy to shift the mood. Draw a line. Start again. 'So, you mentioned Alistair? Is he still in Sydney? Have you been out to visit him?'

Alistair was clearly the golden child. A doctor, like his father and grandfathers. A first in medicine from Dundee University, three years at St Bart's then he'd joined Doctors Without Borders and worked in Niger, then Bangladesh where he'd met Vicky. They were now settled on Sydney's Upper North Shore and expecting their first child in January.

'It's hard, both boys gone,' Linda said. Lydia had popped her head round the door five minutes earlier to ask if they wanted a glass of wine and Linda had nodded gratefully. 'Gavin, my husband, he's taken a six-month sabbatical and we were going to fly out to Australia. Spend Christmas there. Vicky's mum has MS so she'll need a hand when the baby comes. Not that I want to step on any toes.'

'Of course you don't, but it's your first grandchild. That's something very special.' Jackie had been positively skittish about the prospect of grandkids, though Jane had refused to be drawn in. 'It would be lovely to escape winter. Have Christmas on the beach, that sort of thing.'

'There's no way we can travel, not with Rose so ill,' Linda said flatly. 'She's quite adamant that I should go, but I really I don't see how I can.'

It was all Jane could do not to squirm again. 'Rose could still be going strong this time next year.'

'She won't,' Linda said in the same dull voice. 'I doubt she'll make it to the New Year. But she won't entertain the idea of hospices, says that if I don't go to Australia, she won't even let me in the house. I know that Lydia is as good as family, but it shouldn't fall on her.' She looked at Jane expectantly. 'So, how long are you and Leo planning to stay?'

This was far beyond what anyone, even the most dedicated of young wives, could be expected to put up with. 'I don't know. It was rather a spur-of-the-moment decision to come here.'

'Because it isn't as if Leo is going to step up and . . . oh God, it's all such a muddle.'

It was left unresolved because the situation was unresolvable. Such a pity that life didn't come with a handy set of arrows pointing you in the direction that you should go, Jane thought as she saw Linda out the front door this time.

'I don't really think Leo's a bad person. I still love him, but I wish he wasn't so careless. Doesn't ever think before he acts,' Linda said as she ruthlessly tightened the belt on her coat. The angry patches of red on her face had returned. 'Maybe he has changed. Don't they say that the love of a good woman can change a man?'

'I think he's *trying* to change,' Jane said, though she wasn't a good woman and he wasn't really doing any such thing. She might have talked him up to his mother, but she was seething that he'd dumped Linda on her in the first place.

Linda was lingering on the doorstep, neither in nor out. 'The thing is, Jane, I can't worry about that boy at the moment when Rose . . . she's my last link to my mother; the only person who knew her when she was young, before she got married and had me and my brothers. She's told me so many stories, Rose has, but I'm sure there's still more stories to tell.' Linda swallowed hard, then opened her handbag and tried to pull out a little packet of tissues but her hands were shaking too hard.

Jane took the packet and handed Linda a tissue. 'It'll all be fine. You'll have a lovely time with Rose while you're in town, then you can go back to Durham and take a couple of weeks to decide what you want to do. If there's any change with Rose, Lydia will call you.'

Gratitude made Linda hug Jane for one brief, awkward moment. 'It's been very nice to meet you. Leo is a very lucky boy.' She looked beyond Jane to the house. 'You'd better go in. All the heat's escaping. I dread to think what the energy bills are like for a place like this.'

Then she was gone: a hunched taupe figure crossing over the square, and Jane was left to drift back inside.

15

Despite the chill that crept in as the sun sank below the buildings and the persistent drizzle that had started almost as soon as he'd left the square, Leo walked.

Walked away. He knew he was a coward. He could have gone up to his mother, said hello, that he'd been meaning to get in touch now he was back in the country. Just as he could have sent her a postcard every now and again. Called her on her birthday. But he hadn't. It was easier not to, because then he didn't have to remember the disappointed look his mother had perfected when she was confronted with the worst examples of Leo's behaviour; it was a unique blend of reproach and bewilderment. From bad school reports to the time in sixth form when his girlfriend thought she might be pregnant to those sessions when he was in rehab. Family counselling. Except Rose wouldn't come, and his father thought the whole exercise completely self-indulgent, so it was just Linda sitting on a plastic orange chair with her disappointed look.

'I blame myself.' She'd said it an awful lot over those two weeks. 'It's not your fault. I know you're better than this.'

But he wasn't better than this. He was still a selfish little shit. Didn't know how to be anything else. So he kept on walking away.

He'd forgotten the simple pleasure of taking a walk. The trick was to stay vigilant and that way you got to see the good stuff: the carved lion on the keystone of a Victorian villa, the house with the grotesque gargoyle's heads on either side of the front door. Date stones and cornerstones. Leo experienced a quick, joyful tug of recognition with each one, like bumping into old friends. It was the same when he rediscovered the blue plaques for William and Evelyn de Morgan, Hablot Knight Browne and Alfred Hitchcock.

When he had a crick in his neck from looking up and the drizzle had upgraded to a downpour, Leo got on a bus, then another one until he was in Shoreditch; his old stomping ground.

The warehouses and factories were all tarted up now, home to designers, brand consultancies and trend-spotting agencies. People getting rich off bullshit. In that case, Leo should have been a millionaire several times over and as soon as he thought that, he heard a loud, grating voice behind him.

'Leo?' Leo turned round. 'Leo Hurst, as I live and breathe! How the devil are you?'

It was Scoffer. His old friend from his Chelsea art school days. Called Scoffer because he could hoover up lines of coke in the time it took everyone else to roll up a five pound note and stick it up one nostril.

'I'm fine,' Leo said. 'How the hell are you?'

'Better than fine.' Scoffer had the well-fed look of a man who was used to expense account lunches and ten-course tasting menus. 'God, it's been years. Let's have a drink.'

They found a bar that had been carefully restored to resemble the abattoir it had been a hundred years ago. Then there were many drinks and several helpings of artisanal triple-cooked chips as Scoffer regaled Leo with tales of models shagged, evil art dealers vanquished and collectors who paid him silly money to design installations for their houses. 'How much does it cost to make a fucking neon sign anyway? Tossers!'

When the bar started filling up with people younger and hipper and with better hair than them, Scoffer invited Leo back to his studio, which took up the top floor of an old printing works off Shoreditch High Street. Even though it was past eight, there were still a clutch of assistants rushing about like they'd been cast as very busy people in a play. Scoffer told a pretty girl with ridiculously long legs to bring them some beers and they sat in his office, the city lit up and spread out before them and Leo reeled off all the tales he'd reeled off many times before. About going on stage in Tokyo and the Hollywood actress who'd given him a blow job, oh, and the time he spent a night in jail in Mexico, which he really wouldn't recommend and yeah, sure, let's do a couple of lines.

They were both full of bluster and bravado, but the proof of Scoffer's success was as tangible as the bitter taste in the back of Leo's throat as he snorted then swallowed. The envy, the disappointment, must have shown on his face because Scoffer placed a meaty hand on Leo's knee. 'Look, mate, if it helps, if you need a job . . . '

'Oh no,' He could hardly get the words out. 'I'm lining up some big commissions. You know what it's like. Don't want to jinx anything.'

'Course you don't. But I always need someone to think of ideas that I can work up. I wouldn't rip you off, boy. Pay you a decent day rate.'

Leo looked around the carefully curated space. At the stupid neon signs that said THE FUTURE IS TOMORROW, and NOTHING IS INFINITE, ONLY DEATH. The controversial Mexican Day of the Dead masks decorated with real human skin and teeth. The portraits of families living on council estates, their plasma TVs and pit-bulls rendered as lovingly as Gainsborough painted ships and horses.

It wasn't art. It was commerce. Bullshit. Bullshit. Bullshit.

But Scoffer's bullshit paid for another couple of lines of coke and when they stumbled out onto the street and Leo fell to his knees on the rain-soaked pavement, Scoffer gave a cabbie fifty quid to take him home.

It was just like the old days. He threw up in the gutter, then staggered down the mews to bang on the door of Frank and Lydia's little cottage. They weren't very happy to see him, although it wasn't *that* late. Still the right side of midnight, so Leo didn't think there was any reason for Lydia to look like she'd spent all evening sucking on acid drops.

Frank turned off the alarm so Leo could get inside the house. He took the whisky decanter off the sideboard in the drawing room and all but crawled up the stairs.

Then he remembered Rose got angry when he came home like this. She wasn't well. Needed her sleep. He tried to tiptoe down the corridor but settled for walking quietly. It wasn't until he opened the door of his room, shut it behind him with exaggerated care then flung himself on the bed that Leo remembered he had a wife, who woke up with a muffled scream.

Jane lashed out and caught the side of Leo's face with her nails but he was already rolling off her. 'Sorry! Sorry! I forgot I had a little wifey warming my bed.'

His words slurred and ran together. Leo winced as Jane turned on the lamp. Hoped she'd think that it was the light that made his pupils so dilated. As it was, he knew his face was dusted with beads of sweat and as he stared at her blearily, he could feel his jaw working.

She sat up, folded her arms and stared at him. Even wearing his old, faded Motörhead T-shirt with rumpled hair and absolutely no make-up, she was still too good for him.

'Aren't you tired of this, darling?' she asked him and in that moment, as he sprawled half on and half off the bed, another old T-shirt stretched tight over his belly, he hated Jane for her pity.

'Of what?' Leo touched a hand to his lips. He couldn't quite believe that he was still able to make sounds come out of his mouth. 'Tired of what?'

'The party's over,' Jane said. 'About time you realised that everyone else has gone home.'

She'd obviously been taking lessons from Rose in how to make Leo feel so small that if it weren't for the slightly repulsed look on her face, which had circumvented the fillers and the Botox, he'd swear he was invisible to the naked eye.

'Yeah, well . . . I'm going through stuff. Forgive me if maybe I wanted to get a little lost.'

'A little lost?' She echoed incredulously. 'Oh, so you needed some time off for good behaviour? What good behaviour?' She pointed a rigid, *j'accuse* finger at Leo. 'You scuttled off and left me to deal with your poor mother. That was a real touch of class.'

'I don't want to talk about my mother.' Leo tried to sit up but only succeeded in sliding further off the bed. 'Let's not argue. I thought we were friends,' he added plaintively.

Jane rolled her eyes. The more he got to know her, the less sweet she became. It was simply sugar-coating.

'Lydia asked you to come back because she expected that in the ten years since *you were carted off to rehab*, thanks for filling me in on that little detail by the way, you would have grown up, but she was wrong. God, was she wrong!'

'You didn't have to come to London with me. You only came because it suited you.' Leo wasn't a mean drunk. He was a charming, witty, life-of-the-party, king-of-spontaneity kind of drunk, but not tonight apparently. 'Don't forget that I saw you in action on the night we met. What is this, really? Some kind of scam?'

Leo didn't know if the mottled rash that broke out on her upper chest exposed by the gaping T-shirt was guilt or anger.

'Don't judge me by your own standards, darling.'

It was Leo's turn to flush and he had the coke sweats now, so he didn't say anything but tried to stand up while Jane simply sat there and kept staring at him like he was lower down on the food chain than pond scum.

'Stop looking at me like that,' Leo muttered. He finally managed to stand up and stagger to the bathroom where he splashed cold water on his face, which did nothing to clear his mind or make him feel better. He only felt worse, especially when he looked up to see that Jane had followed him and sat down on a stool in front of the vanity unit.

'I'm sorry for being shrewish, darling. It's so silly the two of us arguing like this,' she said with a placating smile. 'We've been thrown together by circumstance. Who knows for how long? And it would be so much better if we didn't spend the time fighting.'

Leo turned round a little too quickly and swayed against the sudden nauseating rush of blood to his head. 'So you're staying?' There was no reason for her to stay with him. Not for his charm and good looks, certainly not for his money – unless this had become about Rose's money, in which case Jane was going to be bitterly disappointed. There was another thing niggling at him too. 'You're not pining for Mr Ex? Not even a little bit?'

'That's not really any of your business, darling.'

'You must still love him, though? You don't just suddenly stop loving someone. Love doesn't have an off-button.'

'Whether I love him or not is neither here nor there. Anyway, darling, we're getting off-message. We had a deal. I've met your great-aunt, I talked you up, tried to smooth things over as much as I could with your mother, but I really didn't appreciate you running off like that.'

She looked calm as she sat there, but her hands were clasped tightly together and she kept flexing her pink polished toes, which was very distracting when Leo had so much to process. He even opened his mouth and wondered what Jane would think of him if he confessed to the reason why he'd been banished, kicked out of the kingdom. Then he shut his mouth. He didn't need to explain anything to Jane. Anyway, she was hardly perfect herself.

'I bet you'd be pining for him if all those billions of dollars from Google or whoever had landed in his bank account,' Leo drawled. 'Yeah, you said that he was the one who jilted you, but I can't believe that if you'd really loved him you'd have let him go without a fight. So maybe it was you who did the jilting, because you didn't fancy slumming it.'

'I married you, didn't I?' She shook her head and made a shooing motion with one hand as if she were brushing away Leo's words. 'And don't be so naïve. There isn't a woman alive who actually wants to marry a poor man.'

'That's what you tell yourself to make you feel better, is it?' Leo snorted. 'No wonder you were in such a hurry to get married before your looks started to go.' He was determined to get a rise out of her – maybe as payback for judging him, for being so superior and aloof, or because it took his mind off needing another drink. Somehow his slurred words had hit a nerve because Jane gave a little start, an ungainly jerk, as if he'd managed to drunkenly stumble upon the fears that even she couldn't gloss over, that were there every time she looking in the mirror.

'Careful, darling,' she said tightly. 'People who live in glass houses and all that.'

It was a warning to back the hell off, but, as usual, he ignored it. 'The funny thing about being a trophy wife, *darling*, is that it looks a hell of a lot like being a hooker.'

'Says the man who couldn't get back to London quick enough

once he discovered his rich great-aunt was dying,' Jane snapped. 'What a pity she hasn't rolled out the welcome mat.'

Leo braced himself against the basin. He fancied that he could crush the porcelain with his bare hands. 'That's not why I came back!' He said it, snarled it really, with enough force that Jane jumped again. 'You don't know anything about it.'

She stood up, put her hands on her hips. 'I know plenty. Honestly, how stupid do you think I am? You weren't just drunk in Vegas; you'd done some coke too, hadn't you? You even took some before we got on the plane and it's what you're on now. It's why your pupils are bigger than dinner plates and you've turned into a belligerent prick.' She nodded, as if it was all falling into place, like a deck of cards being shuffled by a maestro. 'I also know that you were going to take the money we won. You'd gone into my bag, taken it out and you didn't even . . .'

'Not all of it . . . ' Leo protested and there was nothing like a fight to bring cold sobriety crashing down on his head, but it was too late now.

He could feel her anger as though it were the third person in the room, crouching there at her feet, ready to pounce on Leo. 'You think I'm desperate? Well, at least I'm not some drug-addled, geriatric Peter Pan figure who can't function on any real level.' Jane's beautifully modulated voice was steadily getting louder and sharper. 'I bet you spent most of your time in LA hanging out in coffee shops and hideous bars like that one in Vegas trying to score pot off college kids and asking them if they knew where the cool parties were happening.'

'Shut up.' It was an agonised whisper. 'Rose will hear you.'

'That's got you worried, hasn't it? That your precious Rose will find out that you're even more of a fuck-up than she ever suspected.'

He'd asked for this. Wanted to know what really lay beneath

Jane's sweetness and light and now he knew: it was something dark and scabrous.

'Stop it,' he said urgently. 'We both need to calm the fuck down.'

'I am bloody calm!'

Leo launched himself away from the basin, started walking towards Jane. His own anger dissipated further with each step that he took. His come-down was fast approaching and already he was sick and ashamed of what he'd said to her. The truth always hurt worse than anything else.

'This is stupid,' he said and he was close enough to take hold of Jane's arm, connect with her, bring her back down to earth, but he didn't. Never touch an angry woman; it was like baiting a bear, but he forced himself to stand in front of her, just on the edge of her personal space in the hope that Jane would look at him, really look at him, and see that he was sorry. That he could be better than this. 'Come on, you were right. We shouldn't be fighting.'

'This . . . this is never going to work,' she muttered, so quietly that Leo had to lean in even closer to hear her. 'What a mess.'

'It doesn't have to be a mess,' he said softly.

'Bit late for that,' she hissed, and tossed her head back. 'God, will you stop crowding me?'

'Please, Jane.' There had to be a way to get through to her. If Jane gave up on him, then Rose would too. He could just imagine her reaction to the news that he'd managed to alienate his wife of less than three days after pledging to love and protect her. 'Let me make it up to you.'

'How the hell do you think you're going to do that?' She flared her nostrils and tossed her head back again like she was challenging him to give it a go.

Well, it couldn't hurt.

Leo had some vague idea that he might kiss her – she'd liked it when he'd kissed her in Vegas – but his fingertips had barely brushed against her when Jane wrenched herself free from his clumsy overture.

'Don't fucking touch me!' She snatched up the art deco brass figurine sitting on the vanity unit that Leo used to hide his stash in, and threw it. It glanced across the side of his head, making Leo rear back and give a surprised grunt of pain as the statuette fell to the floor with a dull but deafening clunk.

Jane stood there panting, palms flat against the wall, eyes wild, mouth open. Leo took his hand away from his throbbing head, his fingers wet with blood. He was ready to bellow, rage welling up in him all over again but then he saw Jane. *Really* saw her. Bed-sheet-white face, chest rising and falling in time with her ragged breaths, hands knotted and knuckled.

He'd never seen anyone quite so terrified before and he'd never felt so sober in all his life.

'What the hell just happened?' he asked her. 'What did I do? I was going to—'

'You don't ever fucking touch me, do you hear me?' she shouted in a voice that was nothing, not a thing, like her voice. 'You don't fucking put your hands on me unless I give you permission. And don't even fucking think that you're sleeping anywhere near me tonight.'

16

March 1944

March came in like the proverbial lion but by the end of the month, crocuses and pansies were colonising every idle patch of grass. On Rose's Thursday afternoon off, the weather was positively balmy and she set out to walk to Bayswater as Sylvia had it on good authority that a greengrocer had had a delivery of bananas.

Then she planned to visit Whiteleys, because Pippa, one of the girls at Rainbow Corner, was adamant that the haberdashery department had some cheap remnants left over from last summer. Maybe a cheery lawn cotton or poplin and Maggie had said she'd help Rose sew a dress as Rose's skills tended towards mending rather than making.

Shirley had written that very morning to gleefully inform Rose that she'd requisitioned two of Rose's summer frocks and turned them into overalls for the baby *because even you agreed that they were far too short for you and wearing thin under the arms. Fair's fair when you ran off with my black crêpe de Chine and lovely blue taffeta.* Rose was quite tempted to parcel up Shirley's blue taffeta and send it back to Durham, but then Shirley would be angry all over again when she saw the lipstick stain on the bodice that even scrubbing with carbolic soap hadn't shifted. Indeed, it had only made it worse.

Rose walked the back roads that ran parallel to Oxford Street to avoid the crowds, mentally sketching a perfectly lovely crisp white dress with shiny red buttons on the yoke and the cuffs, so it took a while to notice that a man had fallen into step beside her.

For one glorious second, Rose thought it might be Danny. But Danny had written to her two weeks before. Scribbled four lines on a postcard. *Princess, hope to have 48-hour pass mid-April. Let's go away. Somewhere romantic. Just the two of us. D*

Anyway, mid-April was a fortnight away so the man shortening his long strides to her slower pace couldn't be Danny.

'Hello,' said Edward. 'Just the girl I was thinking about.'

'You were?' Rose asked doubtfully, because when she wasn't thinking that every dark-haired American serviceman might be Danny, she was still crippled with shame when she thought about that night at the Criterion and its bilious aftermath. Sylvia was forbidden to mention it under pain of death.

Now Edward was suddenly at her side. Despite the mild weather, he was wearing a dark grey wool overcoat and grey hat as if he could merge into the shadows at any moment. As if he wasn't just a spymaster but a spy himself. 'You might be just the person who could help me with a little project I'm working on,' he said. 'Except you seem to be going somewhere with a very determined look on your face.'

'Bayswater.' Rose resolved to be sparing with her words like Maggie, who had an air of mystery and sophistication. Besides, she didn't want to encourage Edward in any way. 'I heard a rumour about a delivery of bananas, then I want to get some fabric for a summer frock.'

Alas, Rose had no mystery. She even told Edward about Shirley's letter and how she'd finished it with a smug, *Typical of you to be so contrary, Rosie, and hit your growth spurt after clothes rationing was introduced.*

Edward shot her a startled glance. 'Just how old are you?'

Oh, *damn*. 'I was a very late bloomer,' she improvised. 'What little project? Is it to do with the war? Is it top secret?'

'I won't bore you with the details now.' Edward was vague where Danny was evasive. 'Could I tag along to Bayswater, then show you what I had in mind after that?'

There was no earthly reason why Rose would want to spend the afternoon with Edward. He was old, at least thirty, and she knew nothing about him, other than that he was involved in possibly clandestine *things*, and though he'd been kind that other night, he was still quite unsettling to be around. 'Surely you've better things to do than come to Bayswater on a fool's errand for some rumoured bananas?'

'We'll never win the war with that kind of attitude,' Edward said. Rose had forgotten about that serious smile of his. 'Shall we take the bus? My treat.'

There were no bananas. The greengrocer rumoured to have had a delivery said even if he did have some, they were for his regular customers and Rose needn't think she could swan in without a by-your-leave to buy bananas and deprive the good people of Bayswater of them.

Then Edward pointed out that it was illegal to refuse to sell Rose fruit, including bananas, because they weren't rationed, which simply exacerbated matters. The grocer picked up his broom and all but chased them out of the shop.

Rose would never have imagined that she and Edward, grave, serious, earnest Edward, would run down Queensway, hand in hand, winded with laughter.

She was still giggling when they reached Whiteleys. Parts

of the store were still scarred by the damage from the Blitz and one would have thought they'd have been grateful for the custom, but the haughty young woman in the haberdashery department refused to even look for any remnants of summer-weight fabric. When she pointedly turned her back on Rose to serve another customer, Edward whispered in her ear, 'Maybe she's the greengrocer's daughter? There's something of a family resemblance, perhaps? A certain pugnacious set to the chin?'

Rose snorted with laughter but once they were on the 27 bus to Kensington with her afternoon off wasted, she sighed. 'I'm never going to Bayswater ever again. Not even if they're giving away silk dresses. Horrid people.'

Edward said that she was possibly being a little unfair but then he asked after Sylvia and it might have been because it was daylight and they were on a bus, and then walking along the streets of Kensington, but it seemed to Rose that Edward wasn't staring at her at in that discomfiting way of his and it was easy to talk to him without falling over her words.

She found herself telling Edward about the two pork chops and runner beans that Phyllis's mother had sent and how Maggie had produced one of her magical feasts on the Baby Belling. They'd stopped walking by now. Or Edward had stopped and Rose's story came to an uncertain halt too. 'And the flat positively reeked of garlic for days afterwards but it was worth it. Are we near the project you're working on?'

'Right outside it, actually,' Edward said.

Rose didn't know this part of London – Kensington – at all. The big white houses were different from the red-brick terraces all crammed together in Holborn. But white stucco or red brick; everywhere in London was soot-stained and dust-streaked. Streets were incomplete, buildings ripped in half with their insides on display. House, house, then nothing but debris and dust to mark the place where people had eaten their breakfast and tea, read the papers, had a bath. Their absence made Rose think of teeth snapped out of an old comb.

In the small square where they were standing, there were no gaps, but the buildings were empty and shabby. On the far side of the square, a small patch of grass and rubble separating them, the once tall and elegant houses listed to one side.

Rose wondered what she was doing with a man she barely knew in a semi-derelict, deserted square far from the bustle of more inhabited streets where someone might hear her if she screamed.

'Outside what?' she asked, holding her handbag out in front of her.

'Well, all of it,' Edward said. He gestured at the building in front of them. Most of its windows were missing and instead of a roof it had a green canvas flapping forlornly in the breeze. 'I've bought it.'

'This house? I hope it didn't cost you very much.' Rose turned away. 'Goodness, it must be getting late.'

'I've bought the whole square. Well, apart from three houses on the other side that weren't for sale.'

'You've *what?*' She looked again at the broken, haphazard houses lurching crookedly against the deepening sky. 'Why on earth would you want to buy *this*?'

'I know it's on the wrong side of the Park, but I had my reasons. Good reasons,' Edward said and he opened his arms, held out his hands in supplication. 'However, I now find myself at something of a loss and in desperate need of help.'

'But I know absolutely nothing about buying houses.' Despite that, her curiosity was piqued so Rose followed Edward up the crumbling path, black and white tiles once arranged in a pretty geometric pattern now smashed beyond repair.

Inside it was quite a hive of industry. Men were hammering and sawing and sloshing distemper on walls.

There wasn't any bomb damage, just neglect and the determined attentions of the neighbourhood tomcats, Rose thought as Edward pointed out various features. 'I thought the stove could go there,' he said when they reached the last room on the ground floor that backed out onto a wilderness that must have once been a garden. 'This would do as a bathroom if there was a bedroom on either side, don't you think?' he asked after they'd climbed a rickety ladder to get to the first floor because the staircase was rotten.

'Are you going to live here? It's awfully big just for one person.' Now they were on the second floor where Edward was planning more bedrooms and even another bathroom, which seemed excessive.

'Some people are coming to stay. Hopefully,' he said and he crossed his fingers and smiled his grave smile. 'Refugees from Europe.'

'Refugees?' Rose frowned. 'How would they get out of Europe?'

'It can be done. It's difficult, dangerous, expensive, but there are ways.'

Rose gingerly walked across the floor – it seemed likely the boards were rotting too – to peer out of the window at the square. 'But you bought all these houses . . . it would need a lot of refugees to fill them all.'

She heard him sigh, then his careful tread as he came to stand behind her. Not touching, but close enough that it was almost as if he was touching her. He was taller than Danny but Rose didn't feel that frantic panic that she had when Danny was close. Of wanting his hands on her, his mouth, but then being terrified when she got her wish. Edward was a solid, steady presence. 'The war won't last for ever,' he said. 'When it ends, there'll be more refugees. People coming home. Families reunited. They'll all need places to live.'

Rose remembered Sylvia telling her that a lot of Edward's business was conducted off-book. 'You're not a profiteer, are you?'

He shrugged. 'Aren't we all?'

Rose drew herself up. 'No! Not all of us.'

'Are you sure about that? What about all those cigarettes and bars of chocolate bestowed on you each night by grateful servicemen?' He glanced fleetingly at her legs and suddenly Edward didn't seem quite so solid and steady and Rose's heart started that familiar flutter. 'What about those stockings?'

'They were a Christmas present from a girlfriend,' Rose said indignantly, because she had never done anything with any of the men from Rainbow Corner to warrant getting a pair of nylons in return. What she did with Danny, what she still might do, was different because they were in love. 'Anyway, that's hardly the same thing.'

Edward held up his hands in protest. He was quite clearly one of those annoying people who never got angry. It was always so much easier to know where one stood if people got angry with you. 'I refuse to argue,' he said mildly. 'If I hadn't bought these houses someone else would, and after the war I may make some money from them but presently I want them to be a safe place for people who have lost everything, and for that I need your help.'

Rose was somewhat mollified and let Edward guide her down the ladder. They decamped to the tea pavilion in Kensington Gardens. Edward produced a notebook and pencil and asked Rose what furniture he might need.

'You can't get furniture. You can get utility furniture if you've been bombed out and have a special form but I'm not sure being a refugee counts.' Rose shook her head at the sheer enormity of

Edward's undertaking. 'You can't even get sheets. One of the girls at Rainbow Corner – even Phyllis said her people are richer than God – paid six guineas for two sheets and the first time she put them on her bed, her foot went clean through one of them.'

Edward wasn't the least bit bothered. He asked her to write a list. 'There'll be children too. What sort of things do they like? Toys and such?'

Rose had seen on a newsreel that London's firemen were collecting scrap wood to make toys, then distributing them to needy children, but again she wasn't sure that refugee children would qualify. Still, she wrote down everything she could think of in her still alarmingly schoolgirlish script, then handed it back to Edward, who said it was late now and he'd best put her on a bus to Piccadilly because she'd have to go straight to Rainbow Corner.

It was kind and thoughtful of him and although as they reached the stop she could see the number 9 inching towards them, Rose caught hold of Edward's sleeve. 'I'll nag everyone I know to see if they have any old toys and things they don't need any more. If it would help.'

She got on the bus full of good intentions to ask everyone she knew to spare something, even if it were just a dishcloth, for the refugees. But like so many of Rose's good intentions, they were forgotten in the time it took to step onto the dancefloor at Rainbow Corner to foxtrot and jive and duck and dip. Then on to another club, then home to bed for too few hours, before she got up for work at six.

It was the rhythm of her days and nights and what with that and pining for Danny, she quite forgot about the refugees and the promises she'd made.

Besides it was hard to concentrate on anything when there a hum and crackle to the air that made Rose's skin tingle. Whispers on the dancefloor; talk of the Allies landing in France. Even odds that the war would be over by Christmas.

Rose wasn't sure on either count. If even she knew that there might be an Allied invasion, it seemed certain that Hitler must too and people had been saying that the war would be over by Christmas every year. But, every year, Christmas came and went and the war still trundled on.

Still, a change was coming, easy to determine simply from the sheer number of men passing through Rainbow Corner. Every night was a sea of eager yet anxious faces and Rose had no time between dances to share anything more meaningful than a name and a quick gulp of something cold.

Every night Phyllis claimed to have some inside information that she shared as they all got ready for bed, whispering fiercely in case Mr Bryce upstairs was a German agent as well as working in the accounts department at St Pancras Town Hall. 'They're going to wait for a full moon, bomb Berlin to pieces then parachute in as many men as they've got parachutes for,' was just one of the things she'd heard.

Rose would stuff her fingers in her ears because she didn't want to think of Danny flying his plane on a bright moonlit night so he could be easily picked up on radar and then . . . she couldn't bear to think of what might come after 'and then'. All she could think about was the Friday night to Sunday night, two whole days they'd spend together. Her and Danny. Rose thought about all the funny things she'd saved up to tell him; she'd put dibs on Maggie's dark green silk dress and Sylvia had marched her to the chemist in Soho, the one with the words 'Birth Control Specialists' in huge letters stuck onto its window.

Rose had darted across the road so she wouldn't even be seen standing outside the shop. Sylvia had gone in, then come out ten minutes later clutching a brown paper bag, which she'd thrust at Rose.

'A box of Volpar gels and three French letters, the good ones. I'd no sooner trust a johnny from a Yank than a Yank who said he had a johnny,' she hissed. When her blood was up, her language became quite ripe. 'You owe me nine and six.'

'Nine and six! But I was saving up for a perm!'

'A perm wouldn't take on your hair and you'd be forking out more than nine and six if you got saddled with a baby,' Sylvia said, but she never stayed angry or sulked for long. So three days later when a telegram arrived from Danny asking Rose to meet him at Paddington the following Friday night, Sylvia even agreed to lend Rose her crocodile skin attaché case.

17

Leo slept somewhere else. Jane didn't know where and she didn't care. She'd locked the door, tried to wedge a chair under the handle, but he left her alone. Not that Jane slept.

She was too rattled to sleep. The memory of Leo looming at her, invading her space, hot breath on her, then his hands . . . she shook from thinking about it.

Though once she'd stopped shaking, when she did finally calm down, force her tensed muscles to relax and replay the scene, doubt began to creep in. He hadn't really loomed but he was just so much taller than her and she'd felt boxed in. Jane hated being boxed in. There'd been nothing more than a light touch on her arm, just his fingers, not even hard enough to grip her, let alone make bruises or angry marks. It was hardly a capital offence.

She'd overreacted, and as soon as she realised that Jane felt . . . not repentant, but a bit ridiculous. When she'd first met Leo she'd instinctively known that, despite his many other failings, he wasn't the type to hurt a woman. Now she was seeing things rationally again, she knew that this was still the case.

It was just that she'd been hurt so many times before and the way that he'd cornered her, come at her, had triggered memories of bad times and bad men from Gateshead to Moscow, and that wasn't Leo's fault. It *was* Leo's fault though that he'd come home wired to his eyeballs and laid her bare as if he'd stripped her as ruthlessly as those other men. He'd seen beneath her carefully constructed shell to what lay beneath . . .

Now everything was fucked up, which was what happened when you were winging it rather than following a proper plan of action.

For one moment, as she lay there, Jane even considered calling Andrew, but it was only a temporary lapse in judgement and she'd been having far too many of them lately. She'd burned her bridges with Andrew. He'd probably forgive her, but Jackie was never going to welcome her back with open arms. Besides, Andrew was still minus his tech billions.

Jane had sat huddled and brooding on the bed for so long that without her noticing, the darkness had receded. It was morning.

A new day.

Time for yet another new beginning.

Leo spent the night in a cold bedroom on the other side of the house. Normally after he'd come down, the buzz worn off, he could sleep standing up. One time, at a party, he'd even fallen asleep on the draining board with his feet in the sink.

But that night, he didn't sleep. He lay on the un-made-up bed and stared at the shadows, the beams of light stretching across the ceiling every time a car passed by outside, and he thought of Jane's face. Her beautiful, unadorned face all twisted up. The way she'd lashed out. The words she'd spat at him.

She'd been angry at the barbed accusations he'd thrown at her, his clumsy attempts to make amends, but mostly she'd been frightened. Now that the drugs were no longer fogging his senses, he knew that. Angry and scared looked similar but they were very different animals. No one had ever been scared of Leo before. He was a lot of things that he didn't like, but being *that* guy, the kind of guy who women wouldn't want to be alone with unless they had a clear path to the door, was something that made him feel sick to his stomach.

It was gone nine. He was too full of self-loathing to sleep so he might just as well get up. Leo spent long moments hanging onto the basin in the en-suite staring at his face for clues. There were scratches on his right cheek from where he'd startled Jane awake and a cut just above his eye courtesy of her throwing arm. The cut was crusted with blood, a muddy purple bruise just below it, made even more shocking by the greyness of his face. He deserved it.

Deserved the bloodshot, puffy eyes that wouldn't open any wider than a slit, jowls thickening his jaw, the sagging belly which spilled over the top of his jeans.

Deserved more of Jane's wrath, which she'd had hours to bring to the boil so he walked down the corridor and into his bedroom with his shoulders hunched in dread and expectation.

It took a while for his sluggish brain to register that Jane wasn't there, which Leo was grateful about, though it felt like a temporary stay of execution. Then he realised that all her things had gone. Clothes, shoes, the prodigious number of potions and unguents all packed up in her Louis Vuitton case and spirited away by his days-old wife.

He should have been glad that there was no morning-after row, but all Leo felt was an overwhelming sense that once again, he'd spectacularly fucked up. Maybe a quick and painless death might be preferable to always disappointing anyone who got too close to him.

Death didn't come. Instead, when Leo stepped out onto the corridor again, it was at the same moment that Rose was walking past. She stopped and turned to face him. Leo stood there and wished he could shrink away to nothing so that all that was left of him was a small pile of soiled clothes that Lydia could give to the gardener to incinerate.

Rose was wearing all black and dark glasses. This morning, she was utterly terrifying. Leo was sure that if she took off her shades she could turn him to stone with her ice-blue glare.

'Hey, Rose,' he said as brightly as he could, like it was business as usual. 'About last night. If I disturbed you . . . we disturbed you . . . ' Leo scratched his head. 'We had a bit of a domestic. Me and Jane. So, yeah. Sorry.' His tongue had swollen to twice its normal size and he had to squeeze the words past their impediment. He smiled cringingly and still Rose stood there, silent, unmoved.

'I really am sorry. Not just for last night, but, you know, everything.' Leo said it again, not just for Rose's benefit as she stood there still absolutely frozen, but because if he said it often enough and loud enough, then maybe it would stick. 'Not going to happen again, I promise.'

Rose stepped past him and walked away, as if she hadn't even seen him or heard a single word.

He turned and watched her walk, her stride as strong and sure as it ever was, then she reached the stairs and was gone.

How many times had Leo walked away from old girlfriends? Girls who thought they were The One until they found out that Leo was screwing someone else behind their backs? He'd crossed over countless roads to avoid countless friends he owed money to. Ducked into fast food joints and drugstores and once even a beauty parlour to avoid someone who wanted to give him a hard time. He'd never thought about how it would make that person feel. Now he knew. You felt like a ghost. Like your words were nothing more than the meaningless movement of teeth and tongue and breath. Like you weren't even there. Then he thought about that one time in Sydney, walking through Bondi Park, nowhere to duck and cover, so he'd walked right past his own flesh . . .

Leo heard the click of the front door. Rose must have left for the office. She was in her eighties. Dying, so she said, and she was going to the office when it was all Leo could do to shower, shave with dangerously shaking hands, then stumble down to the kitchen.

Lydia was sitting on one of the stools around the central island, laptop open as she consulted her big kitchen diary.

'I'm sorry,' Leo said, because when you'd said it once, the next time you said it, it hardly took any effort at all. 'So sorry about last night, Lydia. About waking you and Frank up like that. I was a total arsehole. Please say we're cool.' He smiled and the cut above his eye pulled and throbbed. 'How about I put the kettle on and you find me some ibuprofen and maybe make me your famous scrambled eggs?'

Lydia checked something in her diary, tapped at her keyboard. Then she looked up. Leo wished that she hadn't.

'I don't forgive you.'

He waited for her to say something else, to qualify it, though it wasn't like he needed any clarification, but she sat there, chin now resting on her hands, her normally good-natured face set in hard, uncomfortable lines.

'Come on, Liddy, I've said I'm sorry,' he said falteringly, on unsteady ground now. 'I mean it. Rose isn't speaking to me. Jane's left me. Don't you stick the knife in too.'

Lydia stared off to the left, then turned back to him as if she'd come to some long drawn-out decision. 'I've spoken to Frank. He agrees. I should never have asked you to come home.'

She sounded like her mind was made up and there was nothing he could say in his defence. 'Look, I know I can be a bit of a dick. I'm trying to change that.'

'No, you're not. Not even a little. I thought we could be a team. Be there for Rose because she should have her family with her right now and you used to be her family.' Her voice was tightening and she was staring off to the left again, because she was close to tears and Leo knew that if Lydia started crying, then he would too.

'I still am,' he said a little desperately. 'I still could be.'

'No. You can't.' Lydia got up from the stool.

'When Rose gets back, I'll apologise properly, explain to her . . .'

Lydia walked over to where Leo standing in the doorway and looked up at him. 'You disturbed her last night. *Twice.*' Her eyes were moistening now and she blinked rapidly. 'You can't be here. You're no good. I can give you some money, if you need it, but there's absolutely no point in you staying.'

By now he should have been used to his failure to live up to the very low expectations that people had of him. 'I can help,' he whispered. 'I *will* help. I'll change. This is the kick up the arse that I need. You have to believe me, Liddy.'

'I've heard you make this speech so many times,' She gently touched the cut on his face. 'As soon as you've had a few drinks, it will all be forgotten. And what about Jane? She tore out of here without even a goodbye. Had a car waiting for her. You buggered that up, didn't you?'

'Oh God, don't even ask. I've screwed up everything.' Leo would have given anything to sink to the floor and hide his face. Turning over a new leaf wasn't meant to be this hard. 'I'll sort things out with Rose and you won't even know I'm here. I won't be any trouble.'

'It's a bit late for that,' Lydia muttered, but Leo thought she might be wavering, wondered how he could press home his advantage, when there was a knock at the back door.

They both turned, eager for the distraction. It was Mark,

Lydia's son-in-law, though he'd only been Lydia's daughter's boyfriend back when Leo had first known him. He looked older, crew-cut streaked with grey, but when he saw Leo standing there he grinned and he was instantly the same cocky lad that Leo had got into all kinds of scrapes with.

'Hello, mate. Heard you were back.' Mark was obviously still working on the maintenance team because he was wearing paint-encrusted coveralls and stayed by the door so he wouldn't track dirt on Lydia's gleaming slate tiles. 'Also heard you'd got married. She do that to you, then?'

Of all his current woes, the cut on his cheek was the least of it. 'Something like that, yeah. How are you? Still working for the firm, right? Is Bill still in charge?'

'No, he retired a couple of years ago. I'm the boss these days.' Mark pretended to puff up his pigeon chest. 'I run a tight ship. No slacking on the job any more.'

Back in the old days, Leo had sometimes gone out with the maintenance team. There had been games of football in the vast empty rooms of Rose's properties. Long lunches at the nearest greasy spoon while they debated the finer points of Saturday's big match and even longer evenings in the pub drinking pints and playing pool. But he'd also learned how to plaster, rewire a circuit board and countless other real-world skills that had always come in handy when he was between commissions. Sometimes it seemed as if most of his adult life had been spent between commissions, like an actor who only rested.

Mark was now asking Lydia if she and Frank were coming over for Sunday lunch. There were children, Lydia's grandchildren; she was beaming as Mark showed her a photo on his phone. 'Wait until I tell Rose that they're dressing up as suffragettes for Halloween,' she said as Leo turned away and started rummaging through the well-stocked fridge.

He'd grabbed everything he needed for a fried egg sandwich

when inspiration struck. There might just be a way to start to make amends. With Rose. With Lydia. A tiny step in the right direction. 'Mark, don't suppose you need a spare pair of hands on the work crew, do you?'

'Maybe.' Mark cocked his head. 'We are a couple of lads down. Are you up to putting in some hard graft or would the shock kill you?'

Lydia was leaning against the island, arms folded. 'It might do,' she said tartly. 'If the hangover doesn't get him first.'

'Probably a bit rusty,' Leo admitted. 'But I'm game, if you'll have me.'

He'd missed those months when slapping paint on a wall had been more enjoyable than applying it to a canvas and every Friday afternoon he'd got a little brown envelope full of banknotes that he'd earned.

'All right. I'll give you a day's trial.' Mark glanced at Lydia, who nodded.

'I don't care what you do with him,' she said. 'Just get him out of my hair.'

18

Jane had booked a room in a small boutique hotel in Mayfair that she'd stayed in before when she'd needed a bolthole, somewhere to lick wounds that wouldn't stop stinging. As soon as she was shown to her room, and the door closed behind her with a soft, discreet click, she sank down on the bed, heavy shoulders bowed.

'You are not a bad person,' she said out loud. The comforting words of her tired old mantra. 'Bad things have happened to you; they've shaped you into what you are.'

But who was she? She wasn't Andrew's Janey Monroe. Or Leo's Jane Hurst. After all these years, it was time to simply be Jane again.

The name still fitted her as perfectly as it had done when she'd first chosen it.

She'd been with Charles a year by then. They'd progressed beyond trips to the supermarket. He took her to art galleries, museums, the theatre. Charles especially loved to take her to restaurants and steer her through menus full of dishes spelt out in words that she was still learning how to read. In all that time he still never touched her and Jane was finally starting to believe he never would.

Then one Sunday after lunch, Charles had sat her down. 'You don't have to tell me who you are or where you're from,' he'd said, because Charles's particular and beautiful gift had always been for providing the solution, rather than focusing on the problem. 'But you don't have a name. You need a name. You need documents. A person can't exist without documents.'

'I don't have a name,' she'd said, because she'd cast it off as soon as she'd jumped on that train and would never sound it out again. 'And I don't have no documents.'

'Any documents. You don't have any documents,' Charles had corrected her gently and at first he'd thought she was lying when she said that she didn't know her exact date of birth. Then when it became clear that she was telling the truth and that she'd never even had a single birthday with cards and presents and blowing out the candles and making a wish, that she'd been only fifteen when he'd met her on that train, was only sixteen now though she felt older than the hills, he'd slid off the kitchen stool, walked into the downstairs cloakroom and hadn't come out for some time.

'Give me a rough idea of what your date and place of birth might be and I'll put someone on the trail,' he'd said when he emerged, his face red, eyes redder. 'How odd that we've managed all this time without you having a name. What would you like me to call you?'

After watching *Gentlemen Prefer Blondes* every afternoon for a week, she chose Jane.

Jane Audrey Monroe. Audrey, because Audrey Hepburn taught her how to speak like a lady. Monroe, because Marilyn knew how to make people treat her like a goddess. And Jane, because Jane Russell didn't take shit from no one. Anyone. She didn't take shit from anyone.

Charles was pleased. 'I like Jane,' he said when he produced the forms she needed to fill in to become a new person. 'It's a good honest name.'

People always thought they knew where they were with a Jane. Janes were a blank canvas; they could be anything anyone wanted them to be. And a Jane had no qualms about walking into a hotel bar at noon all by herself in a long-sleeved, high-necked Alexander McQueen black jersey dress. Hair twisted up in a chignon. Make-up minimal. She took a seat at a table tucked away in the corner.

Jane was going to drink one glass of champagne, though she'd vowed never to drink again, to mark the end of this chapter of her life. To toast the future, however uncertain it might be.

She looked around the room. It was very muted – pale grey and dark wood, everything softly curved, reassuringly expensive. The other patrons were male apart from one forlorn-looking middle-aged woman who sat with an elderly man and resolutely stared out of the window as he read the *Financial Times*.

Jane tried to catch the eye of the waiter but he was already bearing down on her with a glass of champagne. He discreetly offered her a business card as he placed the slender flute on the table in front of her. 'From the gentleman at the bar,' he murmured.

Jane didn't even deign to look at the card. 'Tell him thank you, but I'm waiting for someone.'

She still drank his champagne, though. It was raining outside, fat drops coursing down the window, the room reflected back at her so she could watch the man in the corner leave the bar.

He hadn't been gone two minutes when the waiter brought over another glass of champagne, another business card from an overweight, balding man a few tables along. Jane sent both champagne and business card back. He got up, brushed the waiter aside, mouthed the word 'bitch' at Jane as he shot her a furious, spiteful glance.

Five minutes after that, yet another glass of champagne, but no business card this time, just a note. *You're too beautiful to be on your own. I'd love to join you for a drink.*

Jane couldn't see her benefactor. 'He's round the corner,' the waiter said when she asked him. 'Looks all right. Not old. Think he's Russian. Ordered a one-and-a-half-grand bottle of champagne, then asked me to bring you a glass. What do you want me to tell him?'

It seemed easy but actually it was the hardest way for a girl to earn her fortune. She couldn't go back to this.

Jane stood up. 'Tell him thanks awfully, but no thanks,' she said, then walked out of the bar.

Leo had thrown up on the way to the flat in Chelsea where Mark and his crew were working. Then he could do nothing but fetch and carry very slowly while the others carefully took down a sagging ceiling, making sure not to damage the cornicing.

At five, he got the bus back to Kensington and loitered in the square. Not wanting to face Rose or Lydia, but knowing that he had to. As he dithered, a taxi pulled up almost alongside him, he glimpsed honey-blonde hair and as he crept closer, the driver got out, opened the boot and hefted out a familiar suitcase.

'What the hell are you doing here?' he asked Jane, as she opened the door in time for Leo to hand her out of the cab. 'I thought you'd gone, that you'd left me.'

'Change of plan, darling.' She stood on the pavement next to him, suitcase by her side. Their own version of groundhog day. Only the rain was new. Jane looked up at Leo from under her lashes. He looked down at her. Her bottom lip was trembling. It could have been the cold or it might have been because she was remembering last night . . .

'I'm sorry, Jane.' Leo was getting so much better at saying it. 'Sorry about coming home in that state and I'm so sorry that I said all those terrible things but you have to know I wasn't going to hurt you when I came towards you. Everything had got out of hand and I thought that if I could hold you, connect with—'

He stopped when Jane put her hand on his arm, in much the same way as he'd tried to touch her the night before. 'I know, darling,' she said softly. 'I'm sorry too. I overreacted. I don't usually make a habit of hitting people with heavy objects. Is your face very sore?'

'Yeah, but I've had worse,' Leo said quickly before they could get sidetracked. 'You really don't have anything to be sorry about. It was me, wasn't it? Off my head again and all grabby hands and I scared you. That's what I feel really bad about – that I made you so frightened.'

Jane smiled and shook her head. 'Darling, it was late, I was tired, you caught me off guard. I wouldn't say I was scared so much as I just got a bad attack of déjà vu.'

'Someone hurt you before?' It didn't make Leo feel the least bit better, but even more wretched that Jane, who barely came up to his chin and had to weigh half of what he did, had suffered at the hands of another man. 'Did I trigger some—'

'Look, you've said you're sorry, I've said I'm sorry, we're both sorry.' Jane gave his arm another squeeze. 'All the sorries have been said, darling. Let's just move on, shall we?'

Leo had expected to fight much harder for forgiveness. It was a relief that he didn't have to. 'Fine by me. So, now you can get on with telling me why you came back.'

'Well, darling,' she said slowly. 'The thing is that we are married, you and I, and it does rather complicate things. And I had a life with my ex and now he's gone and I don't know who I am without him, where I should be, what to do next. So, I thought that maybe we should just stay married for a while and see where we end up.' Jane's bottom lip trembled again and it seemed to Leo that she'd angled her head in the perfect position to allow a raindrop to cling to her eyelashes then begin a slow descent down her cheek.

'Oh, Jane, please don't bullshit a bullshitter,' he said kindly. 'Why don't you try again?'

For one split second she looked utterly furious but then she pressed her lips tightly together as if she were trying to smother a laugh. 'Darling,' she said reproachfully, as if it was bad form on Leo's part that he wouldn't let her place the tip of one finger on his shoulder and push him right over.

'Do you want to try it again without the theatrics?' he asked.

They stood there in the rain, both of them waiting for the other one to blink. It wasn't until Jane shivered that Leo unbent, unfolded his arms. 'Come on,' he said, and picked up her case. 'Let's get a drink.'

The pub was a couple of streets away and empty, apart from a few stragglers in work clothes, lingering over pints rather than heading home.

He drank beer, she had a glass of Viognier and Leo talked about how he missed that warm fuggy scent of flat beer and stale smoke there used to be before the smoking ban. He talked of pubs in the East End he'd gone to as an art student 'because they were authentic and full of old men nodding off over their pints and copies of the *Sun* and we thought they were authentic too. They hated us for being pretentious, class tourists. Always used to shark us when we played pool.'

He grinned. She grinned back. 'Did you try to drink pints of bitter even though you really hated the taste?'

'How do you even know what pints of bitter are?' Leo pretended to choke on his lager and Jane giggled. 'Didn't you cut your teeth on champagne and canapés?'

'After a while a girl can get bored of living off vintage champagne and gull's eggs.'

The pizza they'd ordered arrived and she ate two pieces. Leo ate the rest and when his belly was full and he was on his second beer he felt mellow, expansive; that must have been why she decided to confess. 'I thought that Andrew, my ex, would take me back like a shot, but when I called him I had to tell him that I'd got married to you in Vegas. I had to. He was already talking about whisking me off to City Hall at soon as I landed at JFK.'

Leo looked at her curiously. He still couldn't tell when she was lying. 'What did he say?'

'There was quite a lot of name-calling, accusations; things said that are quite hard to come back from – again, I saw quite a different side to him. Not a side that I liked, so I decided that it was probably better to cut our losses.' Jane sat back and wriggled her shoulders, as if she was relaxed and supine, but her fingers clasped around the stem of her glass were so white-knuckled and tense that Leo wondered if they might snap. 'There you have it, darling. Honesty isn't always the best policy.'

'I didn't come back for Rose's money,' he said quietly. 'I came back because I did some things before I left, really shitty things, betrayed her trust, and I'm not going to tell you what I did but I want . . . *need* Rose to forgive me and yeah, I haven't got off to a good start with that.'

'I could help you,' Jane said. 'I do have rather a unique skillset when it comes to—'

'Stop trying to play me,' he said, sharply enough that Jane's fingers tightened again. She put her glass down. 'Why does it always feel like you have a secret agenda?'

'Darling . . . '

'No more darlings, no more bullshit,' Leo decided. After last night, after whatever had happened with Mr Ex, she still had no reason to come back to him unless . . . 'You did some digging on Rose, didn't you? Shouldn't have been too hard. All you had to do was type her name into Google or Wikipedia.'

He'd done it himself, over the years. When the loneliness and the homesickness were a physical ache and he wanted to be close to Rose again. The handful of dry facts on a computer screen didn't even begin to capture what Leo missed, but to a woman like Jane, used to a certain standard of living, they must have made for some interesting reading.

'It's no use,' he told Jane, who dipped her head as if admitting that she'd been rumbled. Maybe that was why she wouldn't meet his eye. 'Rose isn't going to leave me a penny, so if that was what you were banking on, then I might just as well call you another cab. Maybe you can still make it to New York tonight.'

Leo placed his hands, palm, up, on the table, as if he were a magician wanting her to search him for concealed keys, hidden feints, before he pulled out his next trick. Jane placed her hands on the table too. 'So, neither of us are the best people that we can be; well, tell me, who is?' she said. 'There's no reason why we couldn't make this marriage work.'

'Why would you want to be stuck with me?' Leo asked, because it seemed to him that the world was hers for the taking. That another rich man would soon come along to make everything better. 'What's in it for you?'

'I had a very brief chat with my lawyer this afternoon, before I meet with him next week,' Jane didn't even attempt to answer his question. 'It turns out we can't get an annulment. Not for non-consummation, even if we had the Pope vouch for us. Neither of us are already married or related by blood and we can't prove insanity either. Or temporary insanity.'

'That's a bummer.'

'My thoughts exactly. It has to be divorce, darling.' Jane leaned forward so she could rest her hands on his, palm to palm. It felt like a dare, even though they'd already kissed, even though he'd been inside her. 'I know you don't trust me, that I've given you no reason to, but I have nowhere to go. Apart from what we won in Vegas, I don't have anything. Andrew was quite insistent I FedEx my engagement ring and jewellery back to him right away so I can't even sell them.' She took a deep breath. 'That's why I was really hoping you might still need a wife.'

'I don't want to lie to Rose any more. I'm sick of lying to everyone, myself included,' Leo said, even though it was nice to pretend that Jane had picked him, chosen him.

'But it's not a lie. We are married and I just thought, hoped, that we could go back to those two people that we were when we first met,' Jane suggested.

'All those days ago?'

'Feels like years ago!' Jane traced the length of his middle finger slowly and Leo could feel his cock hardening just from that fleeting gesture. He was a hopeless case. 'Before we got married. When we sat in that bar. You, the charming stranger, and me, the damsel in distress.'

'Was I really that charming?' Leo's eyes felt so heavy-lidded that he was amazed he could still see out of them.

'You were devastating,' Jane told him. 'If I hadn't just been jilted and if we'd been somewhere more private, I think you could have had me naked in about five minutes.'

She was still stroking his middle finger up and down, slowly. So slowly. 'I think you're being too flattering,' Leo said and this game he knew how to play. 'Ten minutes probably. Ten minutes to get you naked, fifteen minutes to get you wet, twenty minutes to have you begging for it.' Leo laughed when Jane snatched her hands away and put her finger to better use by wagging at it him, but she was laughing too. 'Oh, Jane, Jane, Jane, please stop trying to play me, it's not going to work any more.'

The problem was that when she played him it was so much fun, and though Jane said that their new détente didn't extend to her getting naked for him, they walked back to the house hand in hand. They were just in time to catch Rose as she came back from her night out with his mother.

Rose looked tired, a little sad, and maybe it wasn't the right time, but Leo had to try.

Jane got there first. 'Did you have a nice time with Linda? Dinner and a show, wasn't it? What did you see, anything good?'

Good manners took precedence with Rose. 'A revival of *Anything Goes*. We weren't in the mood for anything too challenging,' she said and as she started to walk up the stairs, with the two of them trailing in her wake, her steps were slow and laboured. So different from how she'd marched along this morning. But it was late. She'd gone to the office and his mother was always hard work; no wonder Rose was exhausted.

It was apparent that Rose needed all her breath for the climb up two flights of stairs but when they'd reached the top and were about to go their separate ways, Jane touched Rose's arm. She was so much braver than Leo was.

'We're both so sorry about last night. I'm sure you must have heard me screeching like a Billingsgate fishwife,' Jane said, getting straight down to it. 'When Leo comes home in that state, it's how I tend to react.'

Rose's smile was wintry at best. 'And yet you still married him.'

Jane squeezed Leo's hand. 'I had drunk rather a lot of champagne,' she said as if she was confessing to a terrible crime, and a miracle happened. Rose grinned. It took fifty years, even sixty years, off her. She looked younger than Jane, more wicked than Leo, in that split second.

'If I hadn't drunk as much champagne as I have, then made some very questionable decisions as a result, I would have ended up leading a very boring, very quiet life,' she said.

'I am sorry.' Leo couldn't say any more than that, no matter how much he wanted to. There were things he didn't want Jane to know, some things he wasn't ready to remember himself.

Jane tucked her arm into Leo's. He thought about putting an arm round her shoulder but decided against it. 'We had a fight. Not our first. Not our last and it's not the end of the world, but if you're fed up with us then we can easily stay in a hotel.' Jane said.

'Don't be ridiculous,' Rose snapped. That she wasn't too tired to be annoyed had to be a good thing. 'Of course you must both stay here. It's a big enough house, but next time you feel the need to have a row maybe you can wait until you're off the premises.'

And with that, Rose tottered off down the corridor without even wishing them goodnight.

19

April 1944

If King's Cross station had heaved with people that September day when Rose first stepped off the train, it was nothing to Paddington on that Friday afternoon. The khaki and navy blue forces had swelled in number and were now converging with office and shop workers leaving the dreary nine to five behind them until Monday morning.

It was all Rose could do not to get swallowed up in the crowd's slipstream, but then she saw Danny. Even in a seething mass of people, she'd always be able to spot him. He saw her too, waved and smiled. If Rose got lost in his kisses then his smile always found her again.

A tiny pocket opened up, big enough for Rose to hurl herself into Danny's arms. Her feet left the ground as he picked her up and spun her round then set her down again.

'How did you get even more beautiful since I last saw you?' Nobody at MGM could have come up with a better line.

'I missed you,' Rose said because that was all that she could say. 'I've missed you so much.'

'Missed you too, Rosie.' He put an arm round her shoulders

to guide Rose through the crowd, which had receded to a distant place because all she could see was Danny. The tiny cut where he must have nicked himself shaving, the tender back of his neck; that soft, vulnerable space between the collar of his flying jacket and the brutally shaved hair at his nape, and his eyes all crinkled up and sparkling every time he glanced down at her.

There were no spare seats on the train and they had to wedge themselves into a tiny gap in a packed corridor. Danny kept his arm round Rose and fed her chocolate and stole tiny kisses that she was happy to give.

They got off the train at Henley-on-Thames. 'I booked a room,' he told Rose. She'd been feeling so cosy, so cherished, but now panic knifed through her. She tried not to let it show but she could never hide anything from Danny. 'No need to look so frightened, Rosie. Everything will be all right.'

'You mustn't think I'm like that and you're not to get angry with me but . . . ' It was hard to talk about these things, even with Sylvia, much less with Danny who was the one who wanted to do those things to her. Rose couldn't help thinking of Prudence and Patience's father and how he was very fond of saying in his sermons that 'our ability not to give in to our basest impulses is what raises us above the animals and the savages'. 'I don't want to be a savage!'

'I've never seen a savage wear red lipstick.' He was laughing at her but when Rose pouted, his expression softened. 'I got you a little present, but don't be getting any fancy ideas. Not yet anyway.'

'What sort of fancy ideas?' He didn't answer but slipped a ring on the third finger of her left hand. It was too big. Rose had to make a fist to stop it sliding off. 'Oh . . . '

Danny playfully cuffed her chin. 'No fancy ideas, I said. It's just a cheap ring from Woolworths but after the war . . . Well, let's see what happens at the end of the war.'

He promised everything, but gave her nothing – only a ring that Rose worried with her fingers as they walked the dusky streets away from the station and towards the river.

The hotel had seen grander days. The carpet and curtains were shabby and wearing thin, paintwork scraped, floral wallpaper faded. There was a collective lowering of newspapers in the lounge as Rose stood at the reception desk with a weak smile, clutching Sylvia's crocodile attaché case as Danny signed them in as Mr and Mrs Smith.

The room, *their* room, 'the nicest one in the house' according to the pimply-faced youth who took up their luggage and was rewarded with sixpence and a bar of chocolate from Danny, looked out onto the Thames. The water rippled darkly outside the window before Rose pulled down the blackout blind, then closed the curtains.

Danny turned on the light and the bed and its blue candlewick cover was all she could see. She averted her eyes to the pretty Delftware jug and basin perched on the dressing table. The lip of the jug was chipped. Danny sighed. 'Let's go and get something to eat.'

'Not downstairs. All those old ladies twittered when we walked in.' If they went out, left the hotel, then it wouldn't be a simple and quick matter to finish their meal and come back upstairs to a room with a bed in it.

Danny sighed again but they soon found a little pub that served food and after she managed to force down a couple of pink gins Rose felt better. Her left hand was still clenched so the ring wouldn't fall off but she could smile and nod and listen as Danny told her what it was like to fly at night over the unfamiliar British fields and valleys. Sometimes, he said, he wanted to keep on flying until he ran out of sky.

They'd never spent so long in each other's company with nothing to do but simply talk. Not that Rose had much to say because all she could think about was that bed and the dry words in the forbidden books in her father's study. It wasn't until they were served their steak and kidney pudding, which was more kidney than steak and more gristle than kidney, that she was able to look at him properly. Not just the individual parts, but the whole of him.

He had shadows around his eyes as dark as bruises, his beautiful grin had lost a little of its exuberance and there was the faintest tremor in his hands each time he lit a cigarette. 'Oh, but you're not all right, are you?' Rose exclaimed. She pushed away her plate, her food only picked at, so she could lift one of Danny's hands and hold it to her face. He let her, eyes watchful and wary. 'Please, won't you tell me what's wrong?'

'Nothing you need worry about, princess.'

'I'm not a princess. I don't break that easily.' The girl she'd been when she'd first jumped down from the train at King's Cross and set her hat at the first two GIs she'd found had grown up an awful lot. Rose could take whatever Danny had to give. She was sure of it.

'I'm just tired,' he said, when she wouldn't let go of his hand. 'The last couple of months, they've been intense.'

The thought of a tin box that could suddenly transport itself into the air always seemed fantastical to Rose but to climb into one night after night, to steal through dark skies, across the sea and over enemy territory took a foolhardy bravery that she couldn't comprehend.

'Don't you get scared? I would. I'd be so frightened,' she said, and he smiled faintly and held her hand instead of her holding his.

'The funny thing about fear is that a fella can find himself doing all kinds of crazy stuff to get a taste of it. Like going on the big rollercoaster at Coney Island even though you know you're going to lose your lunch,' Danny said and Rose nodded.

When she heard the whine of the siren and she started running for the nearest shelter, often caught up in a crowd, the ARP wardens shouting, sometimes she wanted to stop running and simply stand in the middle of the street, arms raised, fists clenched, and dare the bombs to find her. 'I guess I am a little crazy. A guy who's in full possession of his faculties isn't going to sign up for the Air Corps. You'd try your luck at a safe job in a nice, warm office.'

'You'd be miserable stuck in an office,' Rose said. Even sitting holding hands with her, he was restless. It wasn't just his foot tapping on the floor or how he absentmindedly stroked a spot on her wrist that seemed extraordinarily sensitive to his touch; even his skin seemed to hum as if the blood that flowed underneath was fizzing. 'You know you would.'

'If a crew survive twenty-five missions, then they're done,' Danny said quietly. 'They go back to the States and sell war bonds.'

Rose looked at the thin silver-coloured ring he'd put on her finger with no suggestion that it might mean anything more than a trick to fool a suspicious hotel landlady. 'How many missions have you completed?' She refused to look at him even when he took her chin between thumb and forefinger and tried to turn her to face him.

'Twenty-five,' he said. 'Twenty-five last week.'

Twenty-five successful missions meant he'd cheated death a staggering twenty-five times. He was alive, sitting next to her, solid and real. That was a good thing, and the purple spots under his eyes and his trembling hands told her that maybe not all of his crew had been as lucky.

'Your family must be thrilled that you'll be going home.' Rose tried to find a plucky smile. 'When do you ship back?'

'Wednesday.'

'That's nice. How long before you dock in New York?' She

stared down at the food she'd barely eaten. The flaccid suet sponge and the grey gristle on her plate made Rose feel bilious.

'No idea, because I told the big cheeses that they could ship me off home, but I'd just jump overboard and swim back to Blighty. That's what you guys call it, isn't it?'

Rose did look at Danny then, her eyes glassy, bottom lip quivering so she had to bite it to keep it still. 'Don't make jokes like that.'

'No joke. It takes time to train a pilot and the rookies that are showing up with their wings are useless,' Danny said hotly as if this wasn't the first time he'd presented this argument. 'I'll do more good in the air than back home selling war bonds.'

'Don't you care that you might die?'

'Of course I do.' He brushed her words away with an impatient hand. 'But I have to believe that every bomb we drop, every plane of theirs we take out, brings us a little bit closer to ending this damn war, pardon my French.'

'That's all very well, but you've done your bit. That should be enough.' There was no choice – she'd much rather have Danny safe with thousands of miles separating them than at an airbase a train ride away. Especially if he could climb into his stupid plane at that stupid airbase and never be seen again. 'No one would blame you for going home.'

'Don't paint me as some kind of hero. I'm not. Sure, I want to stick it to Jerry, but I tell you something, Rosie, I never feel half as alive as I do when I'm flying. It's a kick, a buzz. Ain't nothing else like it.'

Suddenly she was angry with him. That he could turn her heart over and right side up again simply because he thought it was such a wheeze to nuzzle up to death, bop it on the nose and dash away in the nick of time. 'Well, isn't that just *swell* for you.' Her American accent was Hollywood-ready. 'Don't you have any compassion for the people who are desperately waiting for you to come home safely?'

She meant his family in New York, whom she knew nothing about other than they lived in New York, but mostly she meant . . .

'Do you worry about me, then, princess?' They weren't holding hands any more but were knee-to-knee, nose-to-nose. Danny was looking straight at her as if he knew that there were many nights that she lay in bed next to Sylvia and counted the planes she heard overhead flying home and prayed that he was in one of them.

'No,' she said mutinously. 'I hardly think about you at all.'

'That's not fair when the only other thing that gives me that same kick as flying is when I'm kissing you,' Danny said and in the busy bar, not caring about the couple at the other table who'd been leaning in close so they didn't miss a single word, he kissed her.

It seemed to Rose as if he never stopped kissing her, though she supposed he must have at some point because they were back in the room. She'd been scared of ending up lying on the candlewick bedspread; now she couldn't think of anywhere on earth she'd rather be.

Kissing on a bed, pinned underneath him, her tweed skirt rucked up so high that she could feel the scratch of his wool trousers against the soft, untouched skin above her stocking tops, was an entirely new kind of terror.

His hand, which had been restlessly plucking at her blouse as if he couldn't bear the feel of cotton underneath his fingers, tugged it free of her skirt. The audacious slide of his palm against her ribs. Rose barely had time to gasp when his hand slid under her flimsy bra.

'No!' she said. Her hands, which had been helplessly fisted in the candlewick bedspread, clutched his wrist. 'No!'

He stopped kissing her and nuzzled a path down to her ear. 'No?'

'No,' she croaked. 'I don't know. This ... I wasn't ... I didn't ...'

'You did, Rose, you did.' Danny wasn't kissing her any more. His hands stopped touching her face, her breast so she felt the lack of them, then they were back on her, pinning her wrists above her head. 'You knew when I asked you to come away with me that we weren't going to spend the whole weekend holding hands. Didn't you?'

Of course she had. Those things that Sylvia had bought her were wrapped in a hankie and stuffed into a corner of her attaché case. She'd even read the instructions that came with the Volpar gels but the whole business had seemed so sordid it had been easier not to think about the mechanics of it all. Instead she'd thought about the heady feeling she got when Danny kissed her, when he was simply standing close to her.

'I've never ... I'm not ... I don't want you to think that I'm one of those girls,' she whispered, as if there might be someone with their ear pressed against the door to take down her words and use them against her. 'I couldn't bear it if you did.'

'You're not one of those girls. You're my girl.' There were times when he knew exactly what to say. 'Doesn't it feel good?'

If it felt so good then why was she so scared? Because for all the trappings she'd borrowed from Phyllis, Sylvia and Maggie, despite all the hard lessons she'd learnt since she'd been in London, there were an awful lot of times when she still felt like she hadn't grown up at all.

Also, it would hurt. Shirley had said so when she came back from her honeymoon in Southport. Not to Rose, but she'd whispered to Mother over tea that she'd 'barely been able to walk the Promenade and then Ian wanted to do it again. It was like sitting on razorblades.'

'How horrible! Why would Ian want you do anything that felt like sitting on razorblades?' They'd both looked at Rose sitting there with a piece of scone half raised to her mouth and Mother had sent her off to her room to read a nice, improving book.

'It will hurt,' Rose said, head turned so she could hide her blushing face in the pillow. 'It will hurt and I don't want to get into trouble.'

'It won't hurt,' Danny said and he was smiling and Rose didn't know why because she couldn't see that this was anything to smile about. 'And you won't get into trouble. I'll take good care of you. Look at me, Rosie.'

She stared up at Danny. His smile might have been soft and kind but she knew how easily it could turn into a sneer. Rose loved him with everything that she was but she still knew he wouldn't be careful with her; he'd break her heart if she gave it to him. Besides, it was all too soon. She'd seen him fifteen times, not including today, and most of those times they'd only snatched kisses in doorways.

You couldn't go from a few kisses when no one was looking to letting a man make love to you. 'I can't,' she said. 'I'm sorry.'

He let go of her wrists and rolled off her. His face tightened and a muscle popped in his cheek, but he didn't say a word. He sat on the side of the bed and pulled out a packet of cigarettes from his breast pocket.

'I've spoiled everything,' Rose said as she sat up and tried to tuck her blouse back in. She was sorry, sick to her stomach with it, but she also felt enormously relieved, as if she'd successfully evaded something ghastly like an exam or an unpleasant medical procedure.

'Don't be silly, you haven't spoiled anything,' Danny said rather mechanically, but he lit a cigarette for her and said that he'd nip out for five minutes if she wanted to freshen up and that she needn't worry. 'I'm not the sort of guy who'd force himself on a girl.'

After he left Rose discovered that someone had swapped Sylvia's peach Dupont silk negligee for Phyllis's lawn cotton nightdress that they'd nicknamed The Reverend Mother and she felt relieved all over again. There was absolutely no chance that Danny would be overcome by depraved lust at the sight of Rose swathed in the voluminous folds of Her Blessed Holiness.

Danny even grinned when he got back and saw Rose in bed, covers pulled all the way up to her chin. 'Lighten up, Rosie,' he said, which she couldn't do because she was still alone in a hotel room with a man.

He'd gone down to the bar to get his hip flask filled with cherry brandy that the proprietor fermented in his potting shed. It was the nicest grown-up drink that Rose had tried and Danny didn't mind that she drank most of it and Rose didn't mind too much when he took off boots and socks and stripped off his shirt. She did avert her eyes when he reached for his belt buckle and gulped down the last of the brandy when he slipped into bed next to her in shorts and vest.

They lay there for a little while, Rose trying to screw up courage to suggest that they put the lumpy bolster between them, but she couldn't quite muster the necessary amount of guts and actually the brandy had had quite a soporific effect on her.

'I'm so tired,' she murmured.

'Me too.' He grazed her cheek with the softest of kisses, then rolled away, turned off the bedside table lamp and whatever tension she'd still been clinging to slowly melted away.

Rose could hear Danny's steady breaths in the dark, feel the warm nearness of him, but now it felt comforting and she wouldn't even have minded if he'd put his arm around her, let her snuggle against him, but sleep was tugging at her.

She dreamed that she was swimming in the sea. Waves lapping about her as she floated lazily on her back, shoals of tiny fish nipping at her toes.

Rose never wanted to open her eyes, to wake up, but then the water turned from warm to cold and her eyes snapped open and fear meant she couldn't move, couldn't open her mouth to scream as Danny loomed large over her in the dark, covers pulled back, that ridiculous passion-killer of a nightdress not doing anything to kill his passion because it had been pushed up and he was yanking down her knickers with careless hands.

Rose tried to kick him away but his legs were on hers. 'What *are* you doing?' She had to squeeze the words out.

'I need you, Rosie. You know you need me too,' he said. She hardly understood the thick, slurred words. 'You know you do really.'

She would have jack-knifed off the bed if Danny hadn't been holding her down, forcing himself where she didn't want him. The wind stole right out of her so she couldn't even scream and had to bite down hard on her lip, but that tiny pain was no match for the terrible thing he was doing to her.

'Stop it,' she said. 'Stop it! Stop it! Stop it!'

His hand closed over her mouth as her hands beat down on his back.

Get off me! she wanted to say, scream it really, but the side of his hand was wedged into her mouth so Rose bit him. He snatched his hand away with a curse, but he didn't stop, even though she begged him to.

'Please, Danny. I don't want this. Not like this. Please.'

'It will only hurt this one time,' he said. 'Let's just get it over and done with.'

Then his hand was over her mouth again and Rose tried to fight. She really did. Hands clawing, scratching, punching at him but no matter that she used every ounce of strength she possessed, she was no match for the hard, heavy weight of him. He held her down and Rose had never felt so small and weak and useless as he lay on top of her and stabbed that thing of his into her again and again.

Now Rose knew what it meant to be ruined. She would never be right again after this. Could never imagine that the pain would go away and she'd feel like she used to.

'I love you, Rosie. I love you.' Danny was panting and just when she thought she'd got used to the pain, could breathe around it, he was moving in her faster, even harder and she didn't even want him to stop but to keep going until it was done. Over. Finished.

Then it ended with a choked cry and thank God, he was taking it out of her, splattering her stomach with his seed, then he let her go, got off her, so Rose could scrub at the mess he'd made with Phyllis's nightgown, which she was going to burn the first chance she got.

The bed shifted as Danny stood up. Rose heard the chink of china, a splash of water in the unfamiliar room, then his soft footsteps coming back to the bed, to stand over her.

'Go away,' she said.

'Please don't be like that, Rosie. Don't you love me any more?'

'No, I don't,' Rose said in a hard voice, but she found that she couldn't move. She was no longer sure that her body was hers – that it would do the things she asked of it.

'Poor baby. What a mess I've made of my beautiful girl.' It wasn't right that he could sound like that after what he'd done. He had a flannel in his hand, came towards her, eyes intent.

Rose managed to sit up and hold out an imperious hand. 'Give it to me,' she demanded. 'Turn your back. You're not to look at me any more.'

It was brave of her to talk like that now that she knew what he was capable of, but he nodded, and passed her the wet cloth, careful not to touch her. Rose waited until he was meekly staring at a muddy reproduction of *The Blue Boy* on the opposite wall before she slowly peeled back the nightdress.

She still hurt, smarted and stung terribly down there, but she hadn't expected the streaks of blood on her inner thighs. Some already dried to rust, some still fresh and red. She clumsily stood up to mop the blood away, scrub furiously at marks that wouldn't shift because they were bruises that hadn't had time to blossom. Then she supposed she was clean but she didn't feel it and she couldn't stop the tears that suddenly streamed down her cheeks. She sniffed, pinched her nose, but it was no good.

'Oh, princess, please don't cry.' Before she could tell Danny he wasn't to turn around, that she loathed him beyond all measure, he sat down on the edge of the bed. Pulled her stiff body towards him and kissed her forehead, her cheeks, as if he could stop every tear. 'Please don't.'

Rose didn't even struggle, but held herself very still. 'You've spoiled it all and I hate you now,' she hiccupped. 'I can't stand to be near you.'

'You don't really hate me, Rosie,' he promised. 'But you can't lead a guy on, let him kiss you, be as beautiful as you are and not expect him to take a few liberties.'

'That wasn't a few . . . '

'I said I wouldn't get you into trouble and I didn't. Next time, it will be better, I promise you,' Danny said, and he tried to stroke her hair, but she flinched away from him. She knew what those hands of his could do now.

'There will never be a next time,' Rose told him. 'Because there is no possible way *that* could ever get better. Even if I did lead you on, what you did, it was still wrong.'

'It's not wrong. We just started the honeymoon early, that's all,' he said and he was grinning now, even dared to nudge her as if Rose found it funny too.

'I don't know how we could have started the honeymoon early when we're not married. Not even engaged,' she reminded him, and she wanted to sound icy and dignified but she was still sniffling. 'I think I might have remembered if we'd got engaged, and even if we had, I'd still hate you. As a matter of fact, I don't want to have anything more to do with you.'

She got off the bed, her movements jerky and God, that pain in the heart of her, where he'd defiled her.

Rose turned her back on Danny, snatched up her clothes from where she'd draped them over the chair and started to get dressed, the nightgown shielding her from his gaze, though it was too late for that now.

Danny had seen her naked, he'd seen her utterly helpless and Rose thought that maybe that might be the worst thing of all.

'Rosie, you're being a brat,' he said cajolingly. 'Let's get back into bed. It's late. You're not going anywhere.'

Rose ignored him and as she buttoned up her blouse she felt a new resolve, a sense of certainty that she'd never had before. She would never let Danny, anyone, treat her like that again. As if her thoughts and feelings didn't matter. As if she didn't matter.

'I'm going back to London,' she said. 'I'm going home.'

'Don't be silly. It's half past one in the morning.'

'I don't care! I don't want to spend even one single second longer in your company.' Rose wished her words were bullets, but she eyed Danny warily as he rose from the bed.

'Rosie, sweetheart,' he drawled in that dark voice, which had done for her. 'Come on. Don't be like this.'

Later, she'd be rather proud that she didn't back away as he came towards her.

'If you come any closer, I swear to God, I'll scream the place down,' she warned him in a low voice that stopped Danny in his tracks and he stood there looking hurt and confused as if he were the injured party as Rose stuffed the last of her things in her case.

She'd be even prouder that when she took off the ring that he'd put on her finger she didn't throw it at him in a silly, meaningless act of petulance but placed it on the dressing table next to the chipped jug. Then she walked out of the room. Out of his life. Leaving all her childish hopes and dreams behind her.

20

Jane and Leo spent Saturday like tourists again. They took a boat from Westminster to Greenwich, then walked along the river until Leo realised that Jane was rigid with cold, too frozen to even shiver. 'I didn't really pack for winter in London,' she said and when Leo took her into a chain store and all but forced her into a sensible, padded coat, he thought that she might cry.

'What fresh hell is this?' she asked each time she caught sight of her reflection in a shop window and each time, she hit him on the arm when he laughed.

Leo had thought that pretending to be the people that they'd pretended to be in Vegas wouldn't work. That it was just trying to plug a gaping hole with wadded-up tissue paper, but both of them were so good at pretending that actually it worked just fine.

On Sunday, they lunched with Rose and George at Bluebird in Chelsea. Rose and George had been lunching there every other Sunday for years, so Lydia and Frank could have Sunday lunch with their family.

A steady procession of diners and staff, even an ancient and grizzled kitchen porter, furtively scurried over to pay tribute while George kept the three of them entertained with tales from past Sunday lunches. 'She was so fabulously drunk, wasn't she,

Rose? After she'd taken off most of her clothes, she then slid off her chair, very gracefully, and fell asleep under the table.'

Rose was in such an evidently good mood that Leo hoped to take advantage of it. But whenever he put down his cutlery, opened his mouth to start apologising, trying to explain, Jane laid a hand on his leg. Once she even kicked him, as if to say, *Not here. Not yet.*

Jane didn't kick him when Leo offered to get the bill, though Rose raised her eyebrows. 'Are you sure you can afford it?'

'Bad form, Rose,' George scolded.

'No such thing as a free lunch,' she replied, with a smile that was all lipstick and teeth and quintessentially Rose. 'Right, Leo?'

'Right,' he agreed. 'But if there's anything you need, you only have to say.'

'What else could I possibly need from you?' Rose asked and Jane gave him an encouraging smile, which was nice of her but not much practical help.

'I don't know.' He'd been really good, only had one lager with lunch, but now Leo wished he'd had more. 'Well, you . . . the thing is, I've been out with the maintenance crew a couple of times last week. Don't know if Mark mentioned it. He's down a few men and I thought that I could help out there like I used to if that's all right with you. I want to be useful while I'm here. Help out with anything you need doing. '

'I get the general drift,' Rose said and her eyebrows shot up again as the bill arrived and Leo peeled some notes off the Vegas rolls that he'd had changed into pounds.

It took a long time to leave the restaurant. So many people who wanted to waylay Rose. To take her hand, kiss her cheek, to share a story, as if Rose wouldn't be coming back, though she'd be back in a fortnight. Of course she would, Leo thought, as he watched her walk ahead of him and introduce Jane to the coat check girl. It was ludicrous to think that Rose wouldn't be here two Sundays from now. That he could go away again, come back a year, two years, even five years later, and Rose wouldn't be having Sunday lunch with George, every other week, at Bluebird. Even he as willed it, he knew it couldn't be true and for the first time since he'd got back Leo felt the loss of Rose, even though she wasn't yet gone.

'Goodness, Leo. I'd forgotten how you sulk when you don't get your own way,' Rose said crisply, when he walked through the door that George was holding open for him. 'Very well. I'm doing my first site visit of a new property tomorrow; you can tag along, if you want.'

The next morning, Jane waved Leo off to work, then took a taxi across London to Hatton Garden.

It had been a while but eventually she found the nondescript black door she was looking for and pressed the buzzer. Then she climbed up three flights of stairs to another door and another buzzer, which led to the one-room office of Solly Garfinkel, who paid the best prices in London for the baubles that rich men bought their women.

'Long time, no see,' he said to Jane by way of a greeting.

'About four years, isn't it?' she replied and now that they were done with the formal greetings, Solly leaned back in his big swivel chair.

'What have you got for me, then?'

One by one, on the piece of black velvet that Solly unrolled onto his messy desk, Jane placed her engagement ring, earrings, wedding tiara, a couple of cocktail rings, a bracelet and a prissy necklace Andrew had bought her strung with sapphire and pink diamond flowers that she'd never liked. Then Solly picked up his loupe and bent his head to scrutinise the stones.

They settled on three hundred thousand pounds for the lot, most of it for her art deco engagement ring. Usually Jane haggled,

Solly expected it, but this time she simply produced the certificates of authentication. Then she turned round while Solly opened the safe underneath the desk and when he told her that she could turn back, there were fifteen stacks of twenty-pound notes on the table.

It wasn't much, Jane thought, as she sat in the back of another cab with the money in a carrier bag that Solly had given her. Not for the three years she'd spent with Andrew when she'd turned down the opportunity to spend time with much richer men because she had her eye on long-term profits rather than short-term gains. Yes, there were lots of other gifts Jane could have sold if they weren't sitting in Andrew's Bay Area house, if Jackie hadn't already packaged them up and sent them to charity. But three hundred thousand pounds was not a good deal, especially as these were her prime years. Jane wasn't going to look much better than this.

The disquieting thoughts didn't stop until Jane was standing fifty metres below ground in a vault underneath a private bank in Knightsbridge with her safety deposit box waiting for her on a metal table.

Before she opened the box with an eight-digit pin code, Jane's heart always fluttered unpleasantly then started beating faster than it should. But when she opened the box it was just as she'd left it. An envelope containing her old birth certificate that Charles had managed to track down, her change-of-name papers. A couple of uncut diamonds that looked like tiny, dull pebbles. A few pieces of jewellery Solly didn't want, to which she'd add her tiara, because Solly had said that there wasn't much demand for tiaras.

And then there were the bundles of cash and a piece of paper with her running tally on it: six hundred and forty thousand pounds, give or take. Altogether she had just under a million in cash – not that a million went very far these days.

Charles would despair of her. He'd shake his head and sigh and say that her safety deposit box was no different to an old lady stuffing her life savings under her mattress, but Jane liked her assets where she could access them. Touch them. Know that they were solid and real.

As real as they'd been that Thursday evening long, long ago when Charles had got home from work and she'd presented him with that grubby wad of money. He didn't snatch it away for board and lodging, didn't ask where it had come from, didn't scream at her for wearing four twenty-pound notes down to almost pulp with her own sweat. He simply sat down and explained what he did for a living.

Charles was the only ethical investment banker in London. He took his clients' money and refused to put it to work anywhere that it might fund weaponry, drugs, child labour, sex trafficking; the list of amoral activities was endless, though Charles had laughed wryly and said that having principles narrowed his rate of return considerably.

He was the only person Jane had ever trusted. She gave him all her money, apart from those few ruined notes, and he doubled it, then doubled it again. She used it to replace the teeth that had been knocked out. To straighten and reshape the nose that had been broken but still looked like her mam's nose.

Jane touched her nose now. It didn't look like her mam's nose any more. It was her nose. But she didn't want to think about her mam, or Charles, or any of her ghosts.

She picked up one of the stacks and, just like that, the noise in her head stopped. This was her ultimate exit strategy. No matter how bad things got or how uncertain the future, if you had cash and lots of it, you'd always be able to escape at a moment's notice, to take care of yourself. And if she ever needed any more justification of why she did the things she did, it was the four twenty-pound notes in a white envelope. They were worn so thin that the silver security thread was about the only thing holding them together. There were still smears of blood on them.

The past held you back – you had to let it go, but it did you no good to erase it completely, Jane thought, as she packed everything away in the metal box. She still had what was left of her half of the Vegas money: just over seven thousand pounds, which she stuffed into her handbag for incidentals. Then she closed the lid. It made a satisfying clunk like a full stop. The jewellery was gone, the money banked; there was a neat line through Andrew's name. No point in regretting what might have been.

Her last appointment of the day was with her lawyer. Charles had introduced them when Jane had needed new documents and above all else, utter discretion. Mr Whipple operated within the confines of the law, but the confines of the law were full of shadows.

She was always scared she might bump into Charles, so she never saw Mr Whipple in his wood-panelled offices in Chancery Lane. They met in a hotel lobby, tucked themselves away in a quiet corner. Mr Whipple was tall and thin and grey ('like a character from a Dickens novel', Charles had said) and he drank milky tea and made notes in a crabbed hand in a leather-bound notebook.

Mr Whipple was also very encouraging. She and Leo hadn't signed a pre-nup and though Nevada was a community property state, that only applied to assets acquired after the marriage. It was doubtful that Leo and whatever shady lawyer he could afford would ever be able to track down Jane's safety deposit boxes or the deeds to her Primrose Hill garden flat or the New York apartment that she rented out (both of them goodbye gifts she'd negotiated from former lovers who no longer had any use for her), as they were owned by a company whose office was a

PO Box in the Cayman Islands. Mr Whipple had been quite adamant about that at the time.

He also assured Jane that unless Leo was named and specifically excluded from Rose's will, he had good grounds to make a claim on her estate. Even if he was cast out without a penny, there were always loopholes that Mr Whipple could wriggle through like a circus contortionist.

'But let's worry about that as and when,' he said smoothly. 'In the meantime, one hopes that Miss Beaumont continues to enjoy life for, say, at least another six months, do you think?'

Jane shrugged. 'Possibly. I'm not sure.'

'But you'll need to stay married until after probate has been granted. You can still contest the will up to six months after that, so that's something to keep in mind.'

'Hopefully it won't come to that, though,' Jane said. 'Having to contest the will. Rose absolutely dotes on Leo.'

Or she would, by the time Jane was done.

Yes, all in all, it had been a day profitably spent.

21

A week, then two, went by. They were already halfway through a grey, damp November.

Jane had joined the holistic gym around the corner and in the space of a day had made friends that she had coffee and pedicures and trips to Harvey Nichols with. Leo would never, ever be able to keep her in the style to which she'd long been accustomed but he went to the office every morning with Rose. There he'd meet up with Mark and spend the rest of the day with the maintenance crew.

The other guys, from the young apprentices to the seasoned pros who had been working for Rose for twenty, even thirty years had treated Leo with some scepticism at first because he was Rose's own personal black sheep. But it turned out that his plastering skills *were* still second to none and now that he didn't have a hangover each morning Leo's hands hardly shook at all, so they welcomed him into the fold and let him use the drill and the nail gun.

It was a routine and Leo couldn't remember the last time he'd had one of them. All of a sudden he had tangible goals: a freshly plastered wall all glossy and salmon-pink smooth. Skirting boards sanded down and waiting for primer. Dimmer switches installed.

Sinks unblocked. Bathrooms freshly grouted. All those things done in a day, when there had been weeks, *months*, that Leo hadn't been able to produce one decent painting.

It meant he could come home to Rose and have something to talk about that wasn't her decay or his failures. Every time he showed her a picture on his phone of an ancient panel of William Morris wallpaper revealed when they dismantled a cupboard, a fully working thirties Bakelite light switch or even the gimp mask that they'd found under one of her tenants' beds, it was another attempt at finding a way back to each other.

Maybe Rose was unbending slightly, because on a Saturday morning when even she didn't go into the office, she asked if he'd mind doing her a favour as they were having breakfast.

'Anything,' Leo said through a mouthful of porridge.

'I wouldn't be too eager,' said Lydia, who might have been unbending slightly too. 'Rose, weren't you saying something about needing a kidney?'

'Would that be a problem, Leo?' Rose was teasing him in a way that she hadn't done since the awful night he'd come home hammered. Leo was so relieved that he probably would have agreed to give her a kidney, not that his were in any great shape.

She wasn't after any of his vital organs, but wanted him to go to Leytonstone where some of her paintings were stored, to do an inventory. 'Take Jane with you,' Lydia said. 'Otherwise she'll go to another of those yoga classes where they turn the central heating up high.'

'It's meant to improve blood flow,' Jane said, because she'd joined them for breakfast that morning too. 'I have a class at eleven but I suppose I could give it a miss. I've never been to Leytonstone, so that might be quite an adventure.'

'Only someone who'd never been to Leytonstone would think that,' Rose muttered and Leo wished that Rose were with them when they got to High Street Kensington station and Jane confessed that she'd never been on a Tube train before.

She'd never been to a football match either. Or eaten at McDonald's (or Burger King for that matter), placed a bet on a horse, been to Scotland or Wales, or even Devon or Cornwall, and a multitude of other things that an ordinary person might have done in the course of their life.

'So, have you ever been to a supermarket?' They were in Rose's air-conditioned unit at the warehouse now. It was a fiddly business. Each artwork had to be unpacked, checked off against a master list on the iPad Rose had loaned Leo, then photographed and packed up again.

'Of course I have! I don't live a completely rarefied existence, darling.'

'Not a fancy organic supermarket, but a bog-standard supermarket with a budget range and a frozen food section.' There were only fifty or so paintings in storage; the rest of them were either in Kensington or on loan to various galleries or museums. They'd be finished in hour, which was just as well as he didn't think Jane liked Leytonstone very much or Rose's preference for English pop art.

'Does Waitrose count?' Jane asked and Leo was about to grudgingly concede that it did when he came across the painting and he felt his forehead grow immediately clammy, his skin prickle and his heart start to race as if he'd just snorted a line of pure, pharmaceutical-grade cocaine. Which was horribly and laughably appropriate given the circumstances in which he'd last seen the picture. God, he'd hoped never to see it again.

It was still in its simple wooden frame. An oil painting of a jagged cliff edge. Down below was the dark navy sea, the tide pulling away from shore and creating pools of turquoise topped with frilly waves. Painted in 1967 by Dame Laura Knight, who Rose had been introduced to just after the war. It had been one of Rose's favourite pieces. It had hung in her study in the house in Lullington Bay, then in her cluttered home office in Kensington, but after . . . well, she obviously couldn't bear to even look at it either.

'Darling! I said, does Waitrose count?'

'What?' Leo forced himself to turn round, to stop looking at the painting. Jane was standing behind him, holding the iPad. 'Right. We should stop mucking about and get on with this.'

She nodded, but seemed quite peeved that he didn't want to play any more.

Her peevishness gave way to anxious sidelong glances when they were back on the Tube. 'Darling, are you all right?' she asked, after every stop, because she was so used to him playing to the crowd that his silence had to be unnerving.

But there was nothing to say. Not just to Jane, but to Rose either. Leo understood that now he'd seen the painting again. Sometimes at night, over the years, he'd dreamed about that painting. Often he would be painting over it, destroying it, with thick strokes of dripping black paint, while Rose begged him to stop.

But his nightmares couldn't begin to live up to the bitter reality of oil on canvas.

When they got back to the house, Leo's mind was set. It was best for everyone, Rose mostly, if he just wasn't here.

'Darling? Are you sure you're all right? What do you want to do for lunch?' Leo was already halfway up the stairs. He paused to look down at Jane. Her beautiful face tilted towards him, like a flower seeking the sun. That suddenly didn't make sense either.

'What are you even doing here, Jane?' Leo asked her wearily and she looked affronted all over again, started to say something, but Leo turned away, took the stairs two at a time, so her words were lost.

All Leo needed to do was pick up the Vegas money and his

passport but instead he sat in his dressing room on the sagging Chesterfield he'd liberated from the house in Lullington Bay when Rose decided that it had long ago passed antique and was now simply ancient. He'd snagged the whisky decanter from the first-floor drawing room on his way up but hadn't actually started drinking yet as he could only handle so much self-loathing in one twenty-four-hour period.

He stood up. There was an antechamber off his dressing room – too small to be a room, too large to be a cupboard. Stored in there were his paintings. Leo didn't like to call them his art, because that made him sound like a wanker.

He flipped through the A2 mounted boards like he was flicking through a set of cards. Then he sat down in the middle of a circle he'd made of all the pictures that had never set the world alight. The only way to do that was to douse them with lighter fuel and strike a match. Make a bonfire and warm his hands on his broken dreams and failed ambition. That was what he'd do.

'Darling, please, won't you tell me what's wrong?' Jane was standing in the doorway. It felt as if their entire relationship had been spent with one or other of them loitering in a doorway, not willing to take those few steps that would bring the two of them closer. Then Jane took those few steps so she could sit down on the floor next to him and pick up the decanter.

'I haven't drunk any, if you've come to check up on me,' Leo told her. 'Not yet anyway.'

Jane put the decanter down, then leaned forward to peer at one of his sketches; a charcoal study of an old man in a betting shop. 'So, what is all this anyway?'

'My juvenilia,' Leo said. Jane looked at his work, her eyes narrowed and assessing, like she was in a jewellery shop with a man who'd just asked her if there was anything that she particularly fancied.

Leo had liked to think that his niche was nineties popular culture rendered in gritty black and white. Take That, *Buffy the Vampire Slayer* and Leonardo DiCaprio rendered in muddy watercolours to give them some gravitas. He'd assembled enough for an exhibition that he was going to call *Born in the Nineties*, but the dealers would barely look at them. That was when he could get through the door to see a dealer and only then because of Rose.

His technique was flawless. Everyone had said so. And even now, when he got a rare commission to draw someone's wife, usually with a freshly fucked glow, his technique was still flawless and OK, he wasn't going to faithfully record the fine spider-webbing of lines at the corners of their eyes or the faintest suggestion of sagging under their chins.

'So, what do you think, then? Does my art have any depth?' Leo tried to sound flippant.

'Well, I'm afraid it doesn't,' Jane said, as if she knew that, for once, she had to stick to the truth. 'Don't get me wrong, it's very *amusing* but it doesn't have any soul. But you already knew that, didn't you?'

Leo wanted to make a crack about her knowing the price of everything and the value of nothing but that would have been as clichéd as his shitty pictures. Jane's kindness was as illusory as his talent. It was just a façade when really she held herself as aloof and inviolate as a dictator. 'You wouldn't understand,' he said dully.

'Probably I wouldn't,' she agreed. 'But I know that we were joking about, having fun, and then you took one look at that painting, the one with the sea and the cliffs, and you shut down.' She took hold of his hand and entwined her cold fingers through his. 'Will you tell me about that painting? Why it upset you so much? You don't have to if you don't want to, but problem shared and all that, darling. Please . . . '

And Leo wasn't going to, but something about the way Jane held his hand and murmured wordlessly and encouragingly had him drawing a picture of himself at eighteen years old. He'd come to London, bag stuffed full of pencils and paints, head full of dreams and schemes, and he'd sit in Rose's home office when he wasn't at college and stare at the Laura Knight painting. In much the same way that he'd stared at it when he was a little boy and it hung in the house in Lullington Bay.

There was something about the picture; so different from the seascapes he'd painted on the beach during those long summers. The hard rock, the forbidding sea; he thought about what it would feel like to stand on the cliff-top and look down. It had called to him – a couple of times, he'd even sketched it – but the kind of art that brought glory and gallery shows wasn't pictures of the sea.

It was 1999. Everyone on his degree course at Central St Martin's was experimenting with video and performance and light installations. Drawing what you saw in front of you wasn't going to cut it.

The only thing that Leo was good at, as good as all his friends were with their transparent sculptures and interactive videos, was getting wasted. Art was about the whole lifestyle. You couldn't walk the streets of Soho without falling over a Young British Artist and if you hadn't got drunk with Damien Hirst, puked up outside the White Cube, done a couple of lines with a Turner Prize nominee, then you didn't get to call yourself an artist.

After his final degree show, when everyone else on his course had signed up with agents and had scholarships and prizes flung at them, they'd all suddenly found their work ethic. Leo had just found the bottom of another bottle.

'Take a year out,' Rose had said. 'Don't think about painting. Come back to it fresh.'

He could have travelled. Done Ibiza. Gone to Goa. He'd

stayed in London because that was where his friends were and if he still went drinking and clubbing and partying with them every night then he was still an artist.

Rose had threatened to cut him off a few times. 'Nobody likes a drunk, Leo,' she'd say to him when he'd stumble in saucer-eyed, after days of going MIA. 'They're too boring for words.' For all her worldliness, she hadn't imagined that he was getting his kicks with pills and powders. He had friends who would work through the night, chopping out a line each time they started to flag, but he wasn't working, just dancing, fucking and jabbering to anyone who'd listen about how he was going to be someone.

Every now and again he'd get the fear. Like the morning he'd woken up with chest pains and a heart galloping so fast that he'd sat in A&E for hours, until his heart had slowed to a brisk canter and he'd slunk away. Or when one of his friends was found dead in a Camberwell squat with the usual detritus around him: syringe, rubber hose, twists of paper like confetti.

It had scared him straight for a while. 'I just need to do something real,' he'd said to Rose. 'Stop messing around and start growing up.'

That was when Leo had begun to go out with the property maintenance crew. Painted and plastered, learned basic electrical and plumbing skills, even designed, recast and replaced a ceiling rose. He felt a certain sense of satisfaction at the end of each day but he still carried on drinking. Some mornings he was too hungover to go to work; the mornings became days, became weeks and he fell back into his old habits, his old crowd.

But Rose never gave up on him until Leo began to resent her too because she was the one who'd filled his head with nonsense. Made him hunger for a world away from Durham, away from the safe little life that his parents had wanted for him. She was so convinced of Leo's talent that Leo had also believed he was destined to be a great artist. When you'd spent most of your life expecting greatness, it was impossible to settle when greatness never came.

'Talent takes time,' Rose had said, when he tried to explain the thoughts that were crowding his head. 'A concert pianist doesn't simply sit down at a piano and begin to play. It takes practice and perseverance, day after day, for years. You have to be prepared to put the work in. Are you prepared, Leo?'

When he said he was because it was so hard to tell Rose she was wrong, she'd pulled yet more strings and got him a place on the MA programme at the Slade. As a gesture of faith, she'd given him the Laura Knight painting.

'This picture was given to me by someone I loved very much,' she'd said, her voice trembling slightly as if she still loved that person though he'd been dead for years now. 'But I know what it means to you and I want you to have it.'

Leo had been sucked in all over again. Touched by the faith that Rose still had in him. But he'd only lasted three months on the MA programme. Three months of being surrounded by people who were better and brighter than him and he could square it away by saying that he'd done it because he was angry with Rose for pushing him too hard all the bloody time, but maybe the simple truth was that he'd done it to get back at her. He'd sold the painting because he'd known there'd be no coming back from such a callous disregard for Rose's feelings, for the lover who was no longer at her side, and with what was left after he'd paid back his dealer, he'd got lost, got really, really lost.

A week later he'd woken up in hospital, his mother sitting in a chair looking as if she'd taken root. 'Leo,' she'd said mournfully. 'How could you? You nearly *died*. And you sold the painting. Rose is furious.'

He'd gone back to Kensington, before he was shipped off to rehab. Linda had stayed downstairs, more scared of Rose than he was. As Leo packed up his stuff, Rose had appeared in his bedroom doorway, as cold and as remote as the painting he'd betrayed her with.

'I can forgive you your laziness,' she'd said, as he'd zipped up his bag. 'Laugh some things off as youthful folly because we've all done awful, arrogant things when we were young, but to throw away everything I've given you . . . '

'You got the painting back, didn't you? Mum said that one of your art dealers—'

'I'm not talking about the painting,' Rose had snapped. 'Yes, well done, Leo, that hurt me more than you could possibly imagine, but I can't forgive you for squandering your talent. Turning your back on it, on all the opportunities you've had. I'm tired of waiting for you to grow up. Gosh, when I was your age, younger than you even, I seized every chance I had!'

'Yeah, yeah, I know. There was a war on,' he'd said in a bored voice. Rose had hardly ever talked about the war (though teenage Rose running away to London in her mother's fur coat was the stuff of family legend) but in that moment, with his head and bones aching, when even the effort of picking up his bag almost knocked him off his feet, he realised that he and Rose had never talked much about Rose. She'd never talked about the man who'd given her the painting, for example.

All of Rose's obsessive focus had been on him. She'd bolstered him up on her own dreams, not his, so it was no wonder he'd come crashing to the ground.

It was all Rose's fault.

'Yes, Leo, there was a war on,' she'd said coldly. 'It made us grow up fast. Taught us what was important, what was precious; something you've yet to learn. If you carry on as you are, then I doubt you ever will.'

'That's my decision,' he'd said sullenly, too much of a coward to lay the blame at her feet. 'It's up to me how I live my life, not you.'

'Just get out, Leo.' Rose had never shouted at him. She didn't need to. Her quiet voice, all emotion ruthlessly reined in, was as violent as a scream. 'Get out and don't bother coming back until you've made something of yourself and you have the guts to look me in the eye.'

She'd turned away then, as if watching him walk out of her life wasn't worth another second of her time. But he'd stood at the doorway, watched her walk down the corridor, stiff-backed, head held high, and the only thing that had felt real was how much he hated her.

Now, everything had turned full circle. He was back in Rose's house. Still hadn't grown up. Still hadn't made anything of himself, but one thing had changed. He didn't hate Rose any more – he never had. It had just been easier to hate Rose than himself.

'I care about Rose,' he told Jane, who for some reason was on her knees in front of him, her hands still in his. 'I wouldn't have come back if I didn't care. It's just – now I'm here . . . well, I can't make things right, because I can't be who she wants me to be. She'll never forgive me for that.' Leo cringed again. 'She'll never forgive me for selling the painting either.'

'I think Rose just wants you to be happy. That's all anyone wants for someone they love and she does love you.' Jane squeezed his hands even as Leo tried to pull free of her grip.

'If you're playing me . . . if this is still a game, some kind of con . . . '

'Don't,' she said and he realised that in all the time that he'd been talking, long enough that his voice was now hoarse, Jane hadn't taken her eyes off him. She'd listened to him in a way that made Leo think that normally she only pretended to listen to him. 'You and me, we're not important right now. This is about you and Rose. You *have* to find a way back to her.'

'I know.' Leo leaned forward so that his forehead rested

against Jane's and he was a little bit sweaty but she didn't even pull back. 'Don't think there's a map for that though, is there?'

'You must be honest with her.' Leo didn't altogether trust Jane and her pretty speeches, but he trusted the advice she was giving him now. 'Go back to Leytonstone and get the painting.'

'I can't even look at it,' Leo admitted. 'I've done so many things I'm ashamed of but that's the worst. That's my most shameful secret. I can't believe I even told you . . . '

'Darling, believe me, as secrets go that's not such a terrible one. There are people merrily getting on with their lives who have much, much worse secrets,' Jane said. She leaned in and brushed the hair away from Leo's face. 'Listen to me: just because you've done a bad thing doesn't make you a bad person.'

'Maybe I do bad things *because* I'm a bad person . . . '

Jane shook her head resolutely as if she was unequivocally right and Leo was in a world of wrong. 'In the short time I've known you, you've only done bad things when you're on drugs.' She looked up to the heavens. 'How can I put this politely? Drugs turn you into a raging arsehole, darling. It's so simple. Just stop doing drugs and give Rose the painting.'

'I can't give back what's already hers,' Leo pointed out doggedly.

'It's a symbol, darling.' Jane rocked back on her heels and took her hands off him. 'What am I going to do with you?'

22

April 1944

When Rose finally arrived at Montague Terrace after cadging a lift back to London on a coal train, she was relieved to find that only Maggie was home. Phyllis would gush over her and Rose couldn't stand to be gushed over right now and Sylvia would probably try to make light of it, say something scornful about Yanks and how they were only after one thing, but Maggie simply took in Rose's dishevelled appearance, the tear tracks and soot on her face, and said, 'You look like you need a drink.'

Rose would have given anything for a cup of tea but Maggie poured her out a tot of vodka. 'Don't sip it. One long swallow,' she ordered and Rose obeyed, then coughed and spluttered and her eyes smarted all over again but at last she felt as if she was back in her own body.

'I don't believe he cared for me at all,' she told Maggie. 'If he had, he wouldn't have ... ' She couldn't finish the sentence, couldn't put into words what Danny had done to her, but Maggie seemed to understand because she perched on the arm of the chair where Rose was sitting, glancing down at the bracelet of bruises that adorned each of Rose's wrists.

'Better to find out now, before you lost your heart,' she said.

'I'd already lost my heart,' Rose said.

Maggie kissed the top of Rose's head, murmured something in her own tongue and said, 'Little one, I forget how very young you are. You haven't lost your heart, only temporarily misplaced it. Now, go and have a bath,' she added as Rose opened her mouth to insist that she wasn't as young as she used to be.

At the moment she felt old and sad. Oh, she'd never felt this sad before. 'I can't have a bath,' was what she did say. 'Not on a Saturday. There's a war on.'

'I doubt the war will end just because you had a bath,' Maggie said. 'Would that it could!'

Rose longed to fill up the tub in their shared bathroom and sink underneath the water, but there *was* a war on so she filled the bath as far as the five-inch mark that Mr Bryce had painted on because he was a stickler for rules. Then she eased herself into the water and ruthlessly scrubbed herself clean. Tried to ignore the stinging pain between her legs, the angry marks on her thighs, tried not to think about anything until she heard a knock on the door.

'Rose? It's me,' Sylvia called. 'Can I come in?'

With a sigh, Rose heaved herself out of the water, to pad across the thin, torn linoleum and wrap herself in her dressing gown before she opened the door and peered out.

'Tea.' Sylvia shoved a steaming mug at Rose as she pushed her way into the bathroom. 'Thought I might as well have a bath if there's one going. Is it even a little bit hot?'

'Warmish,' Rose said as Sylvia peeled off her clothes because she wasn't at all prudish about that sort of thing but Rose still averted her eyes. 'I'll leave you to it, then.'

'You'll do no such thing,' Sylvia ordered as she got into the bath. 'Stay with me. Tell me how you are and don't fib. I always know when you're fibbing.'

Rose arranged herself on the edge of the tub and forced

herself to look at Sylvia, who wasn't making light of it at all; there was nothing but concern on her face. 'It hurt so terribly,' she whispered. 'He wouldn't stop, no matter how much I begged him to, and the worst of it is that it's all my own fault. He said I led him on and I did. I agreed to go away with him, after all.'

Sylvia pulled her legs into her chest and rested her chin on her knees. 'I can't agree with that. It seems to me to that all one has to do to lead a fellow on is to smile and say hello.' She fixed her limpid blue eyes on Rose. 'Every girl I know has had at least one absolutely beastly time of it with a man. They can be such animals but it's best not to dwell on it, Rosie. With the right man, it can actually feel quite nice. Better than nice. Quite, quite lovely.'

'I don't see how,' Rose said – she didn't even want to dance with a man ever again, never mind anything else. 'It was the most awful thing that's ever happened to me.'

'Oh, sweetie, if this is the most awful thing that's ever happened to you, then you don't know how lucky you are,' Sylvia said and she sounded so flat and hollow, so unlike Sylvia in that moment. But there was something so shuttered about Sylvia's usually cheery face that Rose knew not to prod. Then Sylvia lay back in the water and lifted one long, pale leg to inspect the red polish on her toes. 'At least tell me that he used a johnny, that he wasn't *that* thoughtless.'

Rose didn't think she capable of blushing any more but the sudden heat in her cheeks proved her wrong. 'I don't think he did.' She dropped her voice. 'His stuff was all over me.' Her voice dropped even lower. 'Inside me.'

'Damn him to hell.' Sylvia shut her eyes and sighed. 'Probably best not to worry about that until there's something to worry about.'

'But what if there is something to worry about?' Rose had been so intent on the act itself, the betrayal, that she hadn't thought there might be further consequences.

'You wouldn't be the first girl to get caught and one doesn't have to stay caught,' Sylvia said. 'I know a man who knows a man. Has a practice on Harley Street. It will be fine, darling, I promise. But if I ever see your Danny again, I'm going to wring his bloody neck.'

Maggie was of much the same opinion. It was only Phyllis who refused to condemn Danny. 'You mustn't be so hard on him,' she told Rose a week later as they were on the way to the butcher to collect their weekly meat ration. 'It rather sounds to me as if he was swept away on a tide of passion.'

'Honestly, Phyll, it wasn't passion. It was brute force,' Rose said, but Phyllis shook her head.

'My Brian was swept away by passion. Men simply can't help themselves.'

Danny hadn't been compelled to force himself on her, he'd chosen to. He'd waited until Rose was asleep to take what she'd already told him he couldn't have. But when a letter arrived from him the following Monday, Rose didn't rip it up unread. She thought about it, but curiosity got the better of her.

Inside was the ring he'd given her and a short letter.

Dearest Rosie

Are you still sore with me?

I know I acted like a dolt but I wanted you so much. The thing is that most girls have a rotten first time. It's best to get it out of the way as quickly as possible.

I wish you'd stayed so I could have made love to you over and over again. Showed you how good it could be. I hope you'll still let me. And I hope you don't hate me because I really do love my bratty, beautiful girl.

Say you still love me, Rosie. I'd hate to think that if the worst happened, I'd go to my grave unforgiven.

All my love

Danny

PS Please write back, if only to let met me know you're all right. Address at the top of the page is the local pub, so we don't have to worry about the army censors knowing our business.

If it was an apology, then it was a pretty shabby one, Rose thought and she resolved not to write back, to put the whole debacle behind her. Even Sylvia had told her it was time to stop mooning about. 'You must cheer up, sweetie. If I were some poor, lonely GI miles from home, I'd rather take my chances with Jerry than have to look at your miserable face all night.'

It did seem, though, as if there were fewer poor and lonely GIs at Rainbow Corner lately. There were still rumours that the invasion was imminent and that all leave was about to be cancelled, but Rose didn't want to hear them. Not just because it was unpatriotic to listen to idle gossip (though that had never stopped her before) but because it would be Danny leading the charge. In his plane where those searchlights and Stukas could pick him out and finish him off. So Rose supposed that despite what he'd done, in some small way, she still cared enough about Danny that she didn't want something terrible to happen to him.

She decided that she would write back to him, so Danny would know she bore him no ill will. And he should consider himself lucky that Rose was prepared to offer him that much.

Dear Danny

I don't hate you and of course I don't wish you any harm. But I can't forgive you for what you did so it's probably for the best if we break things off.

Please stay safe.

Rose

Danny refused to go down without a fight. He replied only a day later.

Come on, Rosie, give a guy a break. My old ma always said that you should never let the sun go down on a quarrel. Let's not keep fighting when we don't know what the future holds.

I just hope I get to hold you *in the future.*

All my love

Danny

It had been two weeks now since he'd taken Rose away. If this were just a silly lovers' tiff, she'd have given in, written back to him, wrapping her love and devotion around each letter, every punctuation mark. But now every time she thought about Danny, Rose would also think about that room, that bed and what he'd done to her on it, so it was best not to think of him at all. It was a blessed relief that her menses arrived the very next day so she didn't have to agonise over that as well, but she was still feeling dreadfully blue about the whole business when she bumped into Edward on the stairs at Rainbow Corner.

'Hello, stranger,' he said, and he smiled. 'How's the collecting coming along?'

Rose stared at him blankly. 'I'm sorry. What are we collecting for?'

Edward was still an unknown quantity; she'd barely thought of him at all these past few weeks, but there was nothing enigmatic or unambiguous about the way his jaw clenched. When he spoke, his voice had lost all its dark warmth. 'The refugees that are coming over from Europe. Forgive me if I'm mistaken, but I seem to distinctly remember you visiting the house in Kensington I'm getting ready for them. I also recall you writing a list of all the things they might need and volunteering to round up some toys for the children.'

It wasn't as if Rose had forgotten, not entirely. The refugees who might be arriving from Europe at some unspecified point in the future had been pushed to the furthest recesses of her mind and had stayed there, while she wallowed in her own self-pity. Thinking only of how unhappy she was, with no thought to anyone who might be suffering too.

'Oh,' she said. 'I was meaning to get round to that, but I haven't had a spare moment.'

'You haven't had time to ask even one person if they might spare some wool or an old jigsaw puzzle?' Each word was like a shard of ice. 'Not collected so much as a doll or board game?'

'Well, no, not yet,' Rose admitted in a hesitant voice. Nobody had been this cross with her since she left Durham and then it had been more disappointment than this cold anger that made Edward avert his eyes as if Rose was utterly loathsome to behold. 'I will, though. Right away. I promise. When are they arriving?'

'It doesn't matter.' Edward started to walk away before he'd even finished his sentence. But he'd only got as far as the first step before he turned. Rose shrank back; she'd only ever seen him look grave and kind and she hated the current harsh, forbidding set of his features.

'You really are a very careless, selfish girl,' he told her quietly. There was nothing Rose could say in her defence because it was true. She rarely thought of anyone but herself. 'These people, they've endured unspeakable horrors, risked their lives to come to a country where they know no one and *you* haven't had a chance to collect so much as an old spinning top.'

He carried on down the stairs and Rose rushed to the powder room and cried a little, because she didn't want people, especially Edward, to believe that she was that kind of girl, hardhearted and shallow.

Something had to change. She was sick of brooding about Danny – brooding wasn't going to change things, wasn't going to erase the memory of what he'd done to her. She kept reliving the memories of that night again and again and berating herself for not fighting back hard enough. It had to stop.

So Rose thought about the refugees instead and badgered everyone she knew for donations. Not only the girls at Rainbow Corner but Stan and Gladys at the café, who found a box of old comics at the back of the wardrobe in their daughter's room. Rose didn't suppose the refugees spoke English but they could cut out the pictures and stick them on the walls to make the house in Kensington look a little more jolly and welcoming.

In the end though, it was rather a motley assortment of ancient, battered toys hardly likely to cheer up any refugees fleeing from Occupied Europe. Rose even mooted the possibility of doing something with Shirley's limp blue taffeta – 'maybe if we cut it down to make a pretty dress for a little girl?' she suggested to Maggie.

Maggie stared at it, shuddered, then drawled, 'You don't think the refugees have already suffered enough?'

So the blue taffeta hung like a lonely shroud on the back of the bedroom door and it was Phyllis who came up trumps when she invited Rose home for the weekend. 'There's simply heaps of things in the attics for your refugees. Pa will never let anyone throw anything out.'

They travelled down to Norfolk late on Saturday afternoon in the cab of an army lorry. Part of Phyllis's family house had been requisitioned by the Army at the start of the war. 'Only the east wing, so we hardly notice they're there,' Phyllis explained, as they drove along winding country roads at breakneck speed lit only by the light of a full moon. A bomber's moon. 'To tell you the truth, the evacuees were far more trouble. They let off an indoor firework in the Long Gallery and blew a hole right through a Turner. After that, Mummy said that she'd only have girl evacuees and they had to come from good homes.'

'Are your people very top drawer, Phyllis?' Rose knew that Phyllis was an Hon, she'd even been presented at court before the war, but all this talk of wings and Long Galleries was rather daunting.

'Hardly! We're not aristocracy, only landed gentry.'

It wasn't even a little bit reassuring.

Neither was Phyllis's mother, Lady Carfax, who looked at Rose with icy regard as if she suspected Rose had dirty fingernails and all manner of slovenly habits. Despite her chilly demeanour, Lady Carfax gave Phyllis and Rose *carte blanche* to take whatever they wanted for the refugees.

On Sunday, fortified by a breakfast of egg and soldiers – a real egg laid by a chicken that very morning – Phyllis and Rose spent the morning battling cobwebs and opening packing crates in the attics. Their haul included several spiteful-looking Victorian dolls, two teddy bears who had seen better days, a doll's house complete with furniture, building blocks, a train-set, though half the track was missing, a stack of board games and a croquet set.

After a lunch of ham and leek pie, mostly leeks, they set off through the grounds to the stables, their destination the old barn where broken farm equipment, ancient lawnmowers and rusting pieces of metal that looked like medieval torture devices had been put out to grass. 'I don't think there's going to be anything here that the refugees might want,' Rose said glumly, as she peered inside a rotting cardboard box that contained some mildewed seed catalogues.

'There must be. Pa got a bit carried away when war was declared and ordered all sorts of things.' Phyllis scrambled over a barbaric contraption that looked like an old plough. 'He had this notion he'd train up all the spare men in the village into a lethal killing force in the event of a Nazi invasion, but they spend most of their time doing drill practice on the village green.'

Rose gingerly followed Phyllis into the furthest reaches of the barn, cursing when she caught her tweed skirt on a nail.

'Rose! Over here! You'll never guess what I've found!'

Still rolled up and wrapped in brown paper were ten canvas camp beds. Ten! There were also three Army & Navy crates absolutely chock-a-block with enamel mess tins and cups and cutlery, first aid kits and, improbably, several mosquito nets.

With the help of a young lad from the village who came up to do what he could in the gardens, they hauled their spoils into the yard to be packed in the same lorry that had brought them to Norfolk and would hopefully have enough room to take them back to London.

It was still light enough for a walk so Phyllis could show Rose the copse where she and her two elder brothers had built camps and picnicked when they were younger. The oldest, Anthony, had been stationed in Egypt, which they were all thankful for. 'He'd like to see more action but I think Mummy's quite pleased that he isn't,' Phyllis said as they sat on a fallen log. 'Teddy's in the Navy. I can't remember the last time we were all together. Isn't it odd that you take the everyday stuff for granted but that's what you miss most once it's gone?'

Rose had run away from her everyday stuff and she didn't miss it one bit. London was still enthralling and if she hadn't come to London, then she'd never have made it through the hallowed portals of Rainbow Corner. Never learned to jive. Never fallen in love. Fallen out of love. She'd never have become Rose Beaumont. 'I don't care for the bombs or rationing or always worrying that something dreadful might happen to the people I care about, but the other bits of the war are quite exciting. Don't you think?'

Phyllis gazed out at the long grass studded with pretty pale yellow oxlips. 'Well, without the war, I'd never have met you or Sylvia and Maggie.' She shook her head. 'I never got to be friends with the glamorous girls at school so that's rather thrilling.'

'Don't talk rot! You're just as glamorous as Sylvia or Maggie,'

Rose said stoutly, but Phyllis wasn't and that was why Rose loved her. She was kind and steady and had a soppy, romantic heart, which used to be a perfect match for Rose's. But it was here that Phyllis really belonged – among the wildflowers and the hedgerows, the sweet fresh air. 'Don't let's get maudlin. Didn't your Mrs Barnes say something about gingerbread? Come on, I'll race you back to the house!'

23

Three o'clock in the morning. Jane was wide awake and gritty-eyed. Leo might constantly complain that he couldn't sleep since he'd cut back on his drinking, but he was flat-out and gently snoring on the other side of the bed, one hand curled round their pillow chaperone.

The night stretched out before Jane. She tried a meditation exercise but it was hard to focus when all she could think about was Leo. But then she'd been worrying about Leo, as sleep remained just beyond her reach, ever since she'd taken his confession. Leo's problem was that he was too bloody fragile and Jane was an idiot not to have noticed that before.

Her other men might have hated Jane because she'd hurt their feelings, made them look foolish, bruised their pride, but that was normal collateral damage. More frequently, she'd been the one whose services had been brutally dispensed with.

But Leo . . . Jane wasn't a monster, or at least she didn't think she was, and she had no desire to break someone who couldn't put himself back together.

What am I going to do with you?

There was no point in lying there with her thoughts constantly circling back on themselves. So, carefully, because she didn't want to wake Leo, Jane slid out of bed and left the room.

It always gave Jane a thrill to glide through other people's homes in the dead of the night. She didn't rifle through drawers or poke her head into cupboards. She wasn't casing the joint or doing inventory but a house always gave up its secrets when you were the only one awake.

Jane knew what it was like to walk into a house and shiver and want to walk back out because the bad things that had happened were soaked into the walls, emitting invisible but toxic fumes. But Rose's house didn't feel like that at all. There was no terrible sense of foreboding when Jane walked into a room. Rose had been happy here.

She did a full sweep of the house, and then, just as she reached the top of the stairs, still not the least bit tired, she heard someone cry out. It wasn't loud but there was something so visceral about it that Jane's heart gave an emphatic warning thump.

The noise continued. It was coming from the far end of the corridor where Rose's rooms were and as Jane got closer the sound became words. 'Oh God! Good God!' It was the brittle cry of a frightened old woman.

There was no reply when Jane tapped on the door. It opened onto a sitting room, another set of double doors leading through to a bedroom. Jane didn't turn on the lights but called out, 'Rose? It's Jane. Are you all right?'

Rose cried out again, as if she couldn't even form words any more. And Jane had opened the door, made her presence known, so she was committed now. She turned on one of the lamps in the sitting room so she could see into the bedroom. Rose, her white nightgown rucked up, was slumped half-in, half-out of the bed. She seemed paralysed by the expectation that if she moved, reacted to the pain she was in with a jerk or a spasm, then the force might break the ghostly, pale limbs that Jane could see arranged in a haphazard fashion. Rose was no longer the calm, composed, utterly formidable woman Jane had encountered up until now.

'I was just coming up the stairs when I heard you,' Jane said, as if Rose at this moment cared why Jane had suddenly appeared. 'Are you in a lot of pain?'

Rose didn't speak or even turn her head, which was at an odd angle against the pillow.

'What a silly question, of course you're in a lot of pain,' Jane said, approaching the bed. Now she could see Rose's face and she looked so frightened that it made Jane feel frightened too. But they couldn't both be frightened. That wouldn't achieve anything. 'Were you trying to get out of bed? Do you need the loo? Or your pills?' Rose dipped her head once. 'Are they in the bathroom?' Another dip.

Jane tried to settle Rose first, carefully swinging her legs round, then cradling her head so she could move the pillows, smooth out the wrinkled undersheet as best she could. Rose had her bottom lip caught between her teeth; once she grunted and clutched hold of Jane's arm, then subsided. 'OK, you're safe now. I'm going to get your pills.'

She left the bathroom light on when she came back with tablets and a glass of water. 'I thought it would probably be the tramadol. Can you sit up a little?'

Rose couldn't but Jane adjusted the pillows again and put a careful arm around her shoulders, placed two tablets on her tongue, then held the glass to her lips. 'You're all right,' Jane said. She'd always been a good liar. 'Don't try to talk. Just concentrate on little breaths in and out.'

She sat on the edge of the bed and held Rose's hand, stroking the back of her knuckles to the rhythm of Rose's shaky breaths, which got steadier as the pain obviously receded. Rose's skin was thin and papery smooth, like vintage silk dresses that ripped too easily if you weren't careful with them.

Then Rose opened her eyes. 'That's better,' she said, as if she'd taken a sip of strong, restorative tea. 'I'm so silly. Usually I make sure that everything's on my bedside table before I go to sleep.'

'Do you normally wake up like that in the middle of the night?' Jane asked.

'Do you normally walk round other people's houses in the middle of the night?' Rose countered.

Jane held up her hands. 'You can frisk me to make sure I haven't stashed the family silver anywhere.' Rose was still too rumpled and trembling for her to be as intimidating as she was normally. 'Do you always wake up in that kind of pain?'

Rose folded her hands. 'Of course not. As I said, I usually have my tablets by my side but I'd been out with George and I was so tired when I got home, I must have skipped a dose.'

'It's been what, darling? Half an hour since you took those pills and you're still shaking. They should have done more than take the edge off by now. Maybe you should be on something stronger.'

'It's really none of your business.' Irascible old ladies really weren't in Jane's purview. Her own grandmother had died when Jane was six or seven. She'd seemed old because she was swollen and corroded from all the men and the booze and God knows what else, but it wasn't until Jane had got a little older, done the maths, that she'd realised Nana Jo had died in her forties. She hadn't been so bad as grandmothers went – she was a cheerful, functioning drunk who could throw some cereal into bowls and send them off to school – but when she died any semblance of normality went with her and all that was left was the greasy mark on the sofa where she'd sat day in and day out.

There had been a great-grandmother too, a white-haired lady

with a neat little garden and a neat little house in a neat little village a few miles away.

She'd gone there once, mainly to corral the little ones, while her mam hammered on the door, which was painted a sunny yellow. 'Granny Annie! Come out and meet the kiddies.'

Jane had stood there while the little ones rampaged through the neat garden. Her mam had told them to stop the once, but when Granny Annie was still a no-show, despite the demands to come out and give them a kiss, then demands to come out and give them some money, she'd laughed as they'd pulled up flowers and kicked dirt in each other's faces. Jane had sat on the wall and seen an anxious little face peering out of an upstairs window. Their eyes had met for a second, then the face disappeared behind the net curtains and a patrol car had turned up.

She'd picked up the littlest one and shoved him back in his pushchair, a cuff around the head from her mam all the thanks she got. 'Fucking move it,' she'd said and she was gone. Head down, she'd followed with the buggy and the three other kids, who jostled each other and jeered at the two policemen who'd got out of the car and stood there, arms folded.

Rose was nothing like Nana Jo or Granny Annie. 'You seem to know an awful lot about drugs, my dear,' she was saying now. 'Is that something you and Leo have in common?'

'Never touch them, but I've known a few people who have, and yours aren't working.' For a moment, she had another one of those pangs of something that might have been empathy for Leo. Now that she was in her right mind again, Rose was intractable and quite capable of withholding her forgiveness, and her fortune, no matter how much Leo might deserve them. 'Of course, it's none of my business, but I don't understand why you'd want to be in pain.'

'Of course I don't want to be in pain but neither do I want my mind fogged up with drugs. Then there'd suddenly be nurses and carers, strangers, traipsing all over my home.' Rose sounded petulant. 'Or worse, I'd become so enfeebled that they stick me in a hospice. Linda means well, but she wanted me to take a tour of a place out in the middle of Hertfordshire called Peaceful Meadows. Peaceful Meadows! Quite frankly, I'd rather blow my brains out with my grandfather's old shotgun.'

There wasn't much Jane could say to that so she sat there silently. Rose seemed exhausted by her own defiance, because she leaned back against the pillows and closed her eyes.

'Well, at least you're feeling more settled now,' Jane said as she stood up carefully so as not to disturb the older woman. 'You're right, it has to be your decision, but I can't simply ignore the fact that you're in pain and your drugs aren't working.'

'It's one bad night. Let's not get carried away.'

Jane had done her best and that was all she could do. If Rose woke up at the same time tomorrow night with the pain snapping at her, then it wasn't Jane's problem – except she'd made it her problem as soon as she'd opened the door to Rose's suite and now she needed to find a solution that would benefit all interested parties. It was a tricky one. Jane stepped into the bathroom to turn off the light and when she came out, she'd decided on a course of action.

'What I did tonight, well, that's about my limit, darling,' she said to Rose, who was carefully easing herself into a horizontal position. 'I'm really not cut out for bedpans or anything involving bodily fluids.'

They looked at each other for a long moment, the only light coming from the sitting room. It was hard to remember that thirty minutes ago Rose had been struck dumb and useless by pain when now she was smiling. It was a cagey smile, not anything you could trust.

'Well, I'm glad to hear that, because I'm not cut out for them either,' Rose said crisply. 'Also, your bedside manner leaves a lot to be desired.' She smiled again. 'How odd. I'd have thought that would have been one area you'd have excelled in.'

Rose's acidic response made what Jane had to say a little easier. She put her hands on her hips. 'If you keep being this vile, then I'd be well within my rights to smother you with one of your fancy hundred-quid cushions and put all of us out of our misery.'

Jane would have bet that not many people got to see Rose look shocked, her mouth and eyes three wide circles of surprise. She'd also lay even odds on the fact that not many people had ever rendered Rose speechless.

'I do understand, I really do. You're in pain. But it's pointless you suffering and making everyone around you suffer,' Jane said as she marched towards the door. Then she turned to look back at Rose, who was still sitting there, the very definition of aghast. 'Do what you have to do: phone your doctor, get a different prescription, whatever. But if you don't, then I'm calling Linda and she can come down to London and ship you off to Peaceful Meadows. It's your call, darling.'

As soon as he opened his eyes, Leo knew from the way sunlight slanted through the curtains that it was much later than seven-thirty, the time that Jane normally shook him awake before she left for her torturous hot yoga class. She was still fast asleep next to him, curled into a tight ball with only the top of her head visible.

When he dashed out of the house a few minutes later, Rose's car was thankfully still idling at the kerb.

'Another thirty seconds and you'd have had to walk,' Frank told Leo cheerfully as Leo slid into the back seat next to Rose.

She was looking out of the window at the little square and didn't acknowledge his presence in any way. Rose never looked pleased to see him, Leo was used to that, but cutting him entirely was something new. Yesterday he'd instigated an impromptu game of football until Mark had come back from the builders' yard and given them a bollocking. Maybe Rose had heard about that.

Leo glanced over at Rose, her face in profile. When you saw someone every day, you didn't notice them changing. But he'd only been back two weeks or so and the Rose that was fixed in Leo's mind was still much younger, much more vital than this Rose, so that every time he saw her, it was a shock. And every time he saw her, he was sure she was a little more faded than the day before.

'Rose?' he prompted as Frank pulled away from the kerb.

She half turned and flinched a little. 'Oh, it's you, Leo. I was a thousand miles away.' Even her smile was a little muted, something tugging down its corners. 'Overslept? I didn't think you'd gone out last night.'

He ignored the implication that he'd been too sauced to wake up on time. 'Jane didn't go to her yoga class so I had no one to poke and prod at me until I got out of bed. I really should set the alarm on my phone.'

'You really should,' Rose said sharply so Leo was immediately on his guard and guilty for all the things he'd done, even the things he hadn't done. 'Now about that girl, that Jane of yours.'

'She's not mine—'

'Unspeakably rude. She *threatened* me,' Rose muttered. 'You must keep her in line.'

'Marriage doesn't really work like that these days,' Leo said, like he was any expert. 'What do you mean, she *threatened* you?'

Rose sighed, an aggrieved little huff. 'I'll concede that talking of smothering me with one of my Neisha Crosland cushions might have been a joke, albeit in very poor taste, but there was nothing funny about wanting to call your mother so she could cart me off to a hospice.'

'Really? When did this all happen?'

Rose sniffed. 'That's not important. But I won't be spoken to like that, not in my own house.'

The Rose he used to know always rose above so magnificently, but this Rose wasn't rising so much as sinking. And then Leo got it. 'What number are you up to?' he asked. 'You said you were three when the pills kicked in, a six when they were wearing down. You're about a seven right now, aren't you?'

'Not a seven,' Rose insisted, but without any real vehemence.

Leo noted how carefully she was holding herself. 'Are you sure?'

'I took my tablets when I got up. I'm not due another dose for a good two hours yet,' Rose said, as Frank turned into Kensington High Street and straight into gridlock.

'If you're in pain, then take some more. You must have built up some tolerance by now, it's not like you're going to overdose.' There wasn't much Leo was an expert on but he knew his drugs. Did he ever. 'What are you on, anyway? Diamorphine? Oxycodone? Fentanyl?'

'Maybe you should have followed family tradition and become a doctor after all,' Rose muttered. 'You know an *awful* lot about prescription painkillers. I'm on tramadol. I'm nowhere near ready to start taking opiates.'

'Whatever, Rose! I bet the tramadol barely touch the sides.' Even when they'd been friends, there had always been some distance between them – not just Rose's age, her venerated status, but a certain aloof quality about her that seemed at odds with the modern world. So the tenor of this conversation made Leo feel as if he was crossing a line, one that was somehow more significant than all the lines he'd already crossed.

'Oh, Leo, what am I going to do with you?' Rose asked softly and she lifted her hand, her skin dry and thin, but still warm, to stroke his cheek. 'You never leave well enough alone.'

'You said you didn't want treatment because you'd rather enjoy what time you have left. How can you enjoy it if you're in pain? Don't try and deny it,' he added when Rose shook her head and took her hand away. 'Even you can't win this one, Rose. I wish you could, I really do, but you're not going to buy yourself more time by pretending it's not getting any worse. You're just hurting yourself.'

'I can take it,' Rose insisted and Leo wished that he'd inherited even a fraction of her stubbornness.

'But you don't have to. Get some drugs that work. Otherwise the pain will just drag you down, wear you out before you're ready.'

There was so much unfinished business between them. Reparations that he hadn't even begun to start paying.

'I don't want to go gaga,' Rose said quietly. 'I want to still be me. I like being me. Before . . . when you did drugs, it was to stop being you, to lose yourself. I'm not ready for that.'

'You won't lose yourself. You'll lose the pain,' Leo said and he hoped he was right, but then he'd never met anyone who took opiates for their intended medicinal purpose. 'Will you promise me that you'll see your doctor? Today, if possible. Because if you don't, then I'll have to let Jane loose on you again.'

Rose bristled all over again. 'That girl,' she said. 'There's something off about her, something I can't put my finger on. I give the two of you six months.'

'Really? I'm not sure if I give us six weeks,' Leo said. 'You know, she kind of reminds me of you a little bit.'

Pain all but forgotten, Rose turned a furious face on him. 'She is *nothing* like me.' She drew herself up. 'I expect an apology from her, Leo.'

That was a conversation Leo wasn't looking forward to. 'I'll see what I can do.' They inched onto the side street where Rose's offices were. 'We cool, then?'

'Coolish,' Rose decided, which was better than Leo had dared to hope for.

24

When Jane arrived back at the house that afternoon, Leo was already home from work, showered and sitting on the bed as if he was waiting for her. She'd been for lunch with some of the women from the gym, picking at salads and sipping mineral water in Harvey Nichols' Fifth Floor Café then trailing around the store aimlessly as none of them had any pressing engagements. Jane had forgotten how exhausting killing time was, so Leo was a welcome distraction.

'Hello, darling. I was going to say "hard day at the office?" but that would be a horrible cliché, wouldn't it?'

'Yeah, it would,' he agreed. Despite the greyness of November in London, the colourless skies, persistent drizzle, the nagging suspicion that they might never see the sun again, Leo didn't look grey any more. His tan had faded but his eyes were clear and Jane thought that maybe he was a little less jowly. 'Anyway, I spent most of today arguing with Rose about the merits of ceramic over porcelain tiles. It got quite heated at one stage. I thought she was going to hit me over the head with her first-choice tile.'

Jane unbuttoned her coat. 'I bet she said it was the only way to knock some sense into you.'

Leo grinned. Maybe it was because her day had been so deathly dull but Jane was pleased to see him. 'Pretty much. How did you know?'

'Educated guess, darling. So, is that why you're home early? Shall we—'

'Talking of threats of violence, though, what the hell did you say to Rose last night?'

There wasn't much spin Jane could put on it. Rose had obviously hit the highlights and now Jane had been cast as the bad cop and Leo was looking good in comparison, so she'd done him yet another favour.

'Did you really threaten her with asphyxiation and Green Pastures?'

'Peaceful Meadows, darling.' Jane was standing in front of Leo, with her legs crossed at the ankle, hands behind her back, eyes lowered and he was looking her up and down and side to side, one eyebrow quirked. Men were *so* predictable. 'I was tired. I haven't been sleeping well. I might have been the teensiest bit cranky.'

'Yeah, I get that, but the naughty schoolgirl act really isn't doing anything for me,' Leo said in a voice as dry as vodka. He stopped giving her the sultry once-over and folded his arms so he did look a little like an unimpressed headmaster. 'I'd be worried if it was.'

Jane longed to pout but forced herself to take it in good humour. 'I'll bear that in mind,' she said and sat down next to him. Then she remembered things that had happened last night that were nothing to do with her master plan. 'She was in a lot of pain. When I first went in, she couldn't even speak. Did she happen to mention that?'

'We had a long chat this morning about, you know, how she's coping, then she left work early to see her doctor.' For one moment, Leo's shoulders braced as if expecting a great weight to descend on them, then he brightened. 'Rose actually taking my advice *and* leaving work early? It must be a sign that the End of Days is fast approaching.'

Jane allowed herself to bask a little in the warm glow because everyone was winning. Rose would be on the good pills so she wouldn't be in so much pain and Leo had advanced his cause, which meant Jane's cause had also been advanced. 'Shall we go out for dinner? Dinner and a movie?' They did that quite frequently: dinner and a movie like they really were newlyweds desperate for each other's company.

'You have to apologise to Rose,' Leo said implacably. 'Say you're sorry and not one of those bullshit "I'm sorry if you were offended by something I said" apologies, a proper one.'

Jane did feel like a naughty schoolgirl when she stood in front of Rose later that same evening. Rose would have made a wonderful headmistress, autocratic and stately.

'I'm really sorry I threatened to suffocate you and have you dragged off to respite care,' she said, and George, who was sitting next to Rose on the sofa, gasped in shocked delight. Rose ignored him in favour of staring at Jane as if she'd been found in a compromising position behind the tennis courts with one of the lower groundsmen. 'It's no excuse, I know, but when I have trouble sleeping, it puts me in a filthy mood.'

'Very well, apology accepted,' Rose said and she nodded her head at Jane, as if she were dismissed. Jane had the urge to back away slowly, and not break eye contact with that cool blue gaze until Rose gave her permission to do so. Instead she stayed where she was.

'You're still upset with me, aren't you?' That much was obvious. She'd expected it, which was why she pulled out the card and the small bunch of violets, purchased from the flower seller on the corner of Kensington High Street, that she'd been hiding behind her back. 'I got you these as a peace offering.'

Rose gave the matter some thought. 'I've never cared much for violets,' she said. 'Used to know a woman who I'm sure used to bathe in Yardley's April Violets. I couldn't stand her.'

Jane had played enough people to know when she was the one being played. 'Well, I'll just be over here,' she said to Rose, who looked amused now, rather than affronted. Then she sat down next to Leo, who put his arm round her.

'Well, you gave it your best shot,' he whispered a little smugly. 'You think I never bought her flowers back in the day?'

But Leo's history with Rose was long and complicated. His apologies *would* take a lot more than a card and bunch of blooms, whereas Jane was allowed to make a couple of mistakes.

'I suppose that you were very kind and attentive before you threatened to smother me, dear,' Rose conceded with a cat-like smile. Jane suspected that her doctor had upgraded her pain pills and the new ones were giving her a serious case of the feelgoods. 'I was never as beautiful as you, not even in my prime, but you look so pretty when you're being contrite that I'm quite persuaded to forgive you.'

'Thank you,' Jane said and she couldn't resist the satisfaction of digging Leo in the ribs with her elbow. 'It will never happen again. Not the kindness, I mean the threats of GBH.'

'Even if you did do me in with one of my scatter cushions, one sorrowful look at the jury and I'm sure they'd let you get away with murder,' Rose said and as Jane let that sink in, tried to find a comeback, Lydia appeared in the doorway to announce that dinner was ready.

Rose's new drugs had taken immediate effect. She didn't quite skip down the stairs every morning, but she still managed to sweep regally out of the house on a cloud of Chanel N° 22.

Though when the drugs began to wear off, Rose's pain was sharper, less merciful. She was still a martinet about upholding the letter of the law and taking a dose exactly four hours apart, but in those long minutes spent waiting for the hour to strike, it seemed to Leo as if she was trying to find a new way to breathe.

She now left the office no later than four and stayed home most nights too, when before she'd been quite the social butterfly for someone on the wrong side of eighty. George would usually come round for dinner and sometimes Elaine from across the square or Gudrun would join them. Occasionally they'd even have a kitchen supper with Lydia and Frank, which Leo liked best of all because he could drink lager instead of wine and talk about football with Frank.

That wasn't to say the other dinners were dull. Rose took her tablets at six and by six-thirty she'd be halfway down a gin and tonic and on splendid form. Even after dinner, she'd still be sharp, eyes bright, smile wide as she kept the conversation humming along and Leo began to wonder if Rose could stay at a three on that entirely subjective and arbitrary pain scale for months if the doctor managed her drugs properly.

Rose was definitely at a three one evening a week into her new drug regimen when, after dinner, she asked Jane about their wedding. 'You didn't take even one picture?' she asked in disbelief. 'That's not the way to do things. Next, you'll be telling me you got married in jeans and a T-shirt.'

Jane looked quite affronted at the suggestion. 'I had a proper wedding dress,' Jane said indignantly. 'Vintage Dior. Had to lose an inch off my waist to get into it, but it was worth it.'

'I had the most gorgeous black satin cocktail dress I bought at Dior on a trip to Paris in nineteen forty-eight. Christian Dior actually came into the room while I was being fitted,' Rose said with a soft, wistful smile that Leo didn't think he'd ever seen before. 'Whenever I wore it, I felt like a queen.'

George sighed a little. 'Touched by the hand of Dior. You really should write your memoirs.' He clapped a hand over his mouth as he realised what he'd said, but Rose simply gave him a fond look.

'It's a bit late for that, I'm afraid,' she said. 'In fact, talking of dresses, I haven't even begun to sort out all my frocks. I was thinking of donating some of the fancier ones to the V&A and I've been meaning to ask you what the correct etiquette is, George, dear. Does one contact the museum pre-deceasing or just add a codicil to one's will?'

'Let's not talk about it now.' George's voice and all his features started to wobble. Jane, who was sitting next to him, patted his arm and murmured something in his ear that Leo couldn't catch, then she turned to Rose.

'George told us about the Claire McCardell dress you were wearing when you first met,' Jane said to Rose. 'Do you still have it?'

Fifteen minutes later, they'd decamped up to the attics on the third floor. Rose's attics weren't dusty crevices accessed through a trap door and a rickety ladder, lit by a single hanging bulb and with rotten floorboards so you had to watch where you put your feet. They were light and airy walk-through rooms with custom-built shelving and closets.

'Oh my goodness,' Jane exclaimed. She slowly turned full circle so she could take it all in. 'This is like being in the best vintage store in the world.'

'I've been putting off coming up here,' Rose said. As she cast her eyes over the nearest set of shelves, which were crammed full of folders and boxes all neatly labelled, her expression turned to dismay. 'Such a pity I won't live to see the paperless future I've read so much about it. I was rather looking forward to that. How many things I've accumulated! Then there's goodness knows what at Lullington Bay. Leo, I was hoping we could go down during the next week or so. Now would you be a dear and get me a chair, please?'

Once Rose and George were installed in a pair of matching Eames lounge chairs, she had Leo and Jane hunt for her Claire McCardell dress. They rifled through garment bags and discovered opera jackets, evening coats, cocktails gowns until eventually Leo found what Rose was looking for and placed it reverently in her lap.

'This one's like an old friend. I bought it in New York in nineteen forty-six,' Rose said of the navy blue dress with red polka dots and shawl collar that they'd already heard about from George. 'You can't begin to imagine what New York was like after all those years of rationing. You could walk into any store and buy whatever you liked. You just pointed at it, paid for it and walked out with it – I'd forgotten what that was like.'

Jane stopped with a garment bag half unzipped so she could look at Rose as if she were crazy. 'Did they ration *clothes* during the war? Why would they do that?'

'Good God.' Now it was Rose's turn to look appalled. 'Don't they teach you young people anything in schools today? Of course clothes were rationed.'

'I knew food was rationed,' Jane said, though she sounded uncertain. 'But I don't think we learnt about clothes rationing at school. It *was* decades ago.'

'Thank you for making me feel positively ancient,' Rose snapped.

'I think the pills are wearing off,' Leo mouthed at Jane, who was biting hard on her bottom lip, so Leo had a split-second recall of doing just that in Vegas when he had her pressed up against the wall of their hotel room. They all lapsed into silence, which lasted a whole two minutes, long enough for Leo to mentally scroll through an album of images – all of them with Jane half-naked underneath him, even as she crouched to take down boxes of shoes from a bottom shelf, still smelling of blackcurrants.

Then she suddenly stood up. 'It's fine if you don't want to talk about it but . . . you could buy knickers during the war, couldn't you?' Jane was usually very adept at picking up social cues, at knowing when to leave something well alone, but not tonight, apparently. 'Please tell me that they didn't ration knickers?'

'And bras and stockings!' Rose smiled at the scandalised look on Jane's face. 'That's when you could actually find them in the shops. The food rationing wasn't so terrible – after I moved to London I even put on weight – but I did mind not being able to buy a nice frock whenever I wanted one.'

'How did you put on weight if there was food rationing?'

'Because every night I'd stuff my face with doughnuts at the American Red Cross Club at Piccadilly Circus. To this day, if you left me alone with a plate of doughnuts, I could have them wrapped in a napkin and in my handbag within three seconds.'

It dragged up a half-buried memory. 'Mum mentioned that place. Something about you running away in Great-Grandma's fur coat. You nicked two of Grandma's best dresses too.'

'Oh, I wouldn't say nicked. Borrowed without asking,' Rose said and she should have been fading steadily now, but she suddenly seemed ready for adventure; if Leo had decided that they should head out into the cold November night to find somewhere to dance the chill away, Rose looked as if she would be the first to lead the charge.

'You never talk about the war,' George said. 'We talk about everything else.'

'Don't I? How odd. I think about it all the time lately.' Rose stretched out one leg and gingerly rotated her ankle, then the other. 'Anyway, no one wants to hear some old coot wittering on about her glory days.'

'Well, I do, darling, especially if it involves you having romantic intrigues with strapping GIs,' Jane said. 'It sounds like something out of a film.'

'Oh, I'm sure you'd find it very boring,' Rose demurred.

'Well, considering that Jane didn't even know clothes were rationed, I'm sure she'd find it educational,' Leo said, easily stepping out of range of Jane's arm, which was poised to strike. 'What? Even I knew about clothes rationing and I used to sleep through history lessons.'

'Unless it's too painful to talk about,' George said and Rose placed her hand over his as if there was nothing so painful they couldn't talk about it. 'If it hurts too much to remember.'

'Maybe once it did, but now it's rather lovely to remember Rainbow Corner.' Her voice was full of longing. 'It was the most marvellous place. When it opened, they threw away the key because they said their doors would always be open for any American servicemen who needed a place to go. Not just GIs – Rainbow Corner never turned me away either.'

25

May 1944

The refugees arrived on a sunny day at the end of May.

Rose hadn't seen Edward at Rainbow Corner since he'd reprimanded her on the stairs but she'd sent word via Mickey Flynn and two men turned up at Montague Terrace to collect the teetering piles of donations stacked up in the hall.

Edward had sent a note back with Mickey.

Dear Rose

You really have gone above and beyond anything I expected. Did you break into a NAAFI warehouse, by any chance?

Please accept my apologies for being so unnecessarily harsh when I saw you last. I had wanted to apologise in person but have been called away from London these last few weeks.

I do hope that you might be able to come to the Kensington house on Thursday at 3? I'm sure you'll be a lot more welcoming to some weary travellers, especially the little ones, than I could be.

Please do try to come.

Fondest regards

Edward

That Thursday, with a teddy bear knitted from wool repurposed from her old school jumper and her pockets stuffed with chocolate, Rose arrived at the house in Kensington.

Since she'd been there last, the front door had been repainted a cheery cherry red. Rose rang the bell then waited long moments before the door opened and Edward appeared. He'd discarded his uniform jacket and the top two buttons of his shirt were undone, sleeves rolled up.

'Oh, it's you.' He frowned. 'Sorry. I didn't mean to sound so abrupt.'

Rose clutched the paper bag she was holding tighter to her chest. 'Are they not here, then?'

Edward ran a hand through his fair hair, which was rumpled as if he'd been running his hands through it all afternoon. 'They are, but, well . . . you'd better come in.'

She didn't want to – he looked so discombobulated – but she stepped past him into the hall. The walls gleamed fresh and white. The smell of new paint caught at the back of Rose's throat as she moved towards the front room, but Edward took her arm.

'Just to warn you – they're not a pretty sight,' he said quietly. 'Try not to be alarmed.'

Then he ushered her into the room. Rose held her breath as she glanced timidly around. The place had been transformed: pristine white walls in here too, the rotting floorboards replaced, sanded and polished, even the fireplace tiles had been cleaned, the grate blackened.

Then she saw them in the corners, at the edges, where the shadows congregated, and it was just as well Edward had warned her so she had time to bite down her shocked gasp.

There were six – no, seven of them; ghosts hugging the walls, watching her with wary faces. Two men and two women, who could have been eighteen or eighty, and three children. Their skin, as pale yellow as the pretty oxlips that had fluttered in the breeze as she'd sat in the copse with Phyllis, was stretched tight over protruding bones and if a draught drifted in through a gap in the newly restored windows, they might topple like skittles.

When Edward put a hand on her shoulder Rose nearly screamed, but she managed to bite that down too and let him push her forward.

'This is Rose,' he said. 'She's come to say hello.'

'Do they speak English?' she whispered, though her voice sounded loud and shrill in the suffocating stillness of the room.

'I don't know,' he whispered back, as if he felt as helpless as she did.

One of the children, a little girl with mousy hair in two spindly plaits, was nearest. Rose had always hated it when grown-ups loomed over her so she crouched down. 'Hello,' she said. 'I'm so pleased that you're finally here.' She smiled. The girl stared back at Rose.

'My friends and I have been busy finding you all sorts of things to play with,' she said because her gabble was better than silence. Inspired, she delved into the paper bag she'd placed on the floor and pulled out the misshapen bottle-green bear she'd knitted. 'I made you a new friend in case you had to leave some of your old ones behind.'

She held it up for inspection. Maggie had donated two jet beads for eyes and Rose had sewn on a smile with a scrap of red felt. 'He's called Bill. Bill the bear. He's ever so cuddly. Here, why don't you see for yourself?'

There was still no response.

'I have other things too.' Rose smiled at each of the children in turn. 'Do you like chocolate?'

She pulled a handful of Hershey bars from her pocket. In no time at all, the chocolate was snatched away by hungry little hands.

Rose's mother had said, frequently, that good manners meant making other people feel comfortable no matter the circumstances, so once the children had retreated to a corner, where they sat on the floor and sniffed the chocolate as if they weren't sure whether it was real, she straightened up and walked over to one of the women.

The closer she got, the less the woman looked like a haunted apparition. She was wearing a ragged black coat, thin brown hair falling in her face as she looked at Rose with suspicion. It would be so much easier to leave, simply run away from the house and these broken people.

It was much harder, maybe the hardest thing she'd ever had to do, to hold out her hand and say, 'I'm Rose. It's lovely to meet you.'

The woman looked at Rose's hand, then her gaze travelled upwards to the hopeful expression on Rose's face. Rose tried to smile welcomingly, though she wasn't sure she'd succeeded because the woman suddenly bowed her head and started to cry.

'Oh, please don't. I never meant to upset you,' Rose said and it was easier even than running away to put her arms around the woman and hold her as she sobbed, her head resting on Rose's shoulder. She was so thin that Rose was scared she might shatter. Beneath the thin coat, she could feel each of the knobs of her spine, her ribs like spillikins. 'Everything will be all right. You're safe now. Edward will see to that.'

Edward stepped forward then, proffered his handkerchief and the woman allowed herself to be led to an ancient overstuffed armchair where she sat down and blew her nose. 'Thank you,' she said in an accented voice. 'Thank you. Thank you. Thank you.'

Her tears unlocked the others from their inertia and soon all the adults were seated on the chairs that Edward had managed to rustle up from somewhere. Rose was still holding the woman's hand and the little girl with plaits, clutching Bill the bear as if she'd never let him go, had climbed onto her lap while Edward went to the kitchen to make tea.

They drank black tea, as Edward's connections hadn't stretched to obtaining any milk, and ate stale buns, though no one seemed to mind. They didn't mind sleeping on camp beds either or not having much in the way of furniture. As Edward and Rose showed them around the house, they exclaimed over each new discovery – from light bulbs to running water to a playroom on the second floor with Rose's spoils displayed on the shelves.

Rose didn't know where they'd come from or what horrors they'd escaped, but whatever their circumstances, they really didn't need to keep saying thank you. It was the very least she could have done and she'd only done that to take her mind off Danny. These seven lost souls, and the hundreds of thousands of others just like them, were the reason he climbed into his plane night after night. Danny's treatment of her had been cruel and selfish but even cruel and selfish Danny had been prepared to risk his life twenty-five times over to save people he'd never met, from countries that he'd only seen in an atlas. If Danny could do that, then Rose could have done so much more than the odd assortment of bric-a-brac she'd scrounged up.

'I'll keep hunting things out for them,' she told Edward when he walked her to Kensington High Street to catch the bus. 'Those poor people. And the tinies! What happened to them?'

'They've spent the last two years hiding in a cellar but . . . never mind about the finer details. They're Jewish. They were lucky to have spent the last two years in a cellar.'

Rose glanced up at Edward. His voice was flat, toneless, but his face was even tighter than when he'd told her off for being selfish. 'They were lucky you heard about them, that you brought them here.'

He shrugged. 'Seven lucky ones. Thousands upon thousands of not so lucky ones.'

'Do you think they'll be any more of them arriving?'

'No.' It was unequivocal. 'Not until this whole ugly business is finished.'

'So, it will be finished soon? I know that we're not meant to talk about it on account that one of us might be a spy but if you were an enemy agent then you wouldn't be smuggling Jewish refugees out of Europe. And I'm definitely not an enemy agent,' she exclaimed, because a Nazi official would only have to give her a stern look and an '*Achtung!*' and she'd spill every single secret she knew.

'Oh, Rose!' It wasn't one of Edward's slow, serious smiles but a grin that scrubbed away the troubled expression he'd worn all afternoon. 'If you really are a Nazi spy, then you're a very good one. Anyway, you're at Rainbow Corner most nights – I'm sure you have a better idea of what's happening than even Winston himself.'

Rose giggled. 'I'm sure I don't.' They'd reached her bus stop. 'But, well, it feels like something big is about to happen. Maybe this time when people say that the war will be over by Christmas, it might actually be true.'

The number nine bus stopped, but Rose made no move to board. There'd be another one along soon. She wanted to spend just a little longer with Edward. He didn't treat her as just another pretty girl but as if she had some substance to her.

'I'm not sure it will be over by Christmas,' he said. 'But I am sure that things will probably get worse before they get better.'

'I don't see how,' Rose groused, as she fished in her purse for the thruppence fare. 'Unless they start rationing water and fresh air and the Nazis drop bombs morning, noon and night.'

'What an alarming thought.' Edward smiled again. 'Would you mind awfully coming back next Thursday? You don't have to bring anything, just yourself, and if they're feeling a little stronger and the weather's nice, maybe you could take the children to the park.'

'Of course. And I'll bring Phyllis. Most of the things I found came from Phyllis and she's awfully good at making people feel at home.'

'By all means bring Phyllis and when you have a free night, I'd like to take you out to say thank you. Have you ever been to The Ritz?'

Just hearing the name of that place made Rose's heart flutter. 'You don't have to do that. I'm glad that I could do something for them. I want to help.'

'And I want to take you to dinner as long as you promise not to order the Tournedos Rossini again. You can bring your Phyllis too, if you like.'

Rose did like, because having dinner alone with a man, especially somewhere terribly expensive and grand, might give him the wrong idea. Then there was the whole ghastly situation with Danny, but that was far too complicated to explain, especially when she could see another bus bearing down on her. 'That would be nice,' she said.

'All these notes through Mickey Flynn are ridiculous. Are you on the telephone?' Edward asked as the bus came to the stop.

'Only at work.' Rose jumped on board. The bus was pulling away so there was no time to debate the consequences of giving Edward her number. 'Gerrard 7531, but you'll have to pretend that it's a national emergency. I'm not allowed personal calls.'

26

Sometimes Jane thought her adult life could be measured out in the number of dreary dinners she'd sat through. Making small talk with the person on her left. Thinking desperately of something to say to bring the person on her right out of their shell. Picking her way through food that contained ingredients she'd never heard of and couldn't even pronounce anyway.

Tonight was going to be a dull dinner with two of Rose's business advisers. Not like the dinners they'd been having lately, when it was just the three of them and George. After dinner they'd retire to Rose's sitting room and she'd tell them stories about Rainbow Corner and as she talked, Jane could see glimpses of that girl who'd danced until three in the morning.

It was all coming together nicely. Rose was on the good drugs and seeing Leo in a fonder, kinder light. Leo had a new sense of purpose and even if he didn't trust Jane, he was grateful. She'd much rather have someone's gratitude than their trust.

Anyway, what was one more dreary dinner, Jane thought, as she stepped into her heels. She hadn't worn heels in weeks and was a little wobbly as she turned and checked her reflection in the bathroom mirror. Rose had insisted quite sharply last night that standards had been allowed to slip and that she expected then to dress for dinner.

At least George would be there and Leo had promised to keep her entertained. 'We'll play a drinking game,' he'd said that morning when they were walking down to breakfast. 'We both have to take a sip every time someone mentions the housing bubble.'

'Or talks about affordable housing for essential workers,' Jane had suggested and they'd texted each other back and forth all day with rules for their game, though Leo's last text had been a plea to stop him drinking after one glass of wine. *Then I'll switch to water. Can't have you taking advantage of me if I get drunk.*

He was quite hung up on the idea of Jane taking advantage of him and she knew that if she dispensed with the pillows down the centre of the bed, he'd quite happily lie back and think of England. Not that Jane was going to, but just thinking of the look on Leo's face if she did made her smirk as she started walking down the stairs. She heard a ring on the bell, saw Anna the maid scurry to answer it, then two men walked through the door and Jane froze. Literally froze. As if she'd suddenly been turned to ice and was frightened to take a step in case she shattered. He looked up and it wasn't a trick of the light.

It was Charles, all colour drained from his face, so he looked like a negative image, a picture that hadn't been developed.

With her hand suddenly clutching her thumping heart, Jane wondered if Charles had looked like that when she left him. When he found the note she'd written on the kitchen counter, along with her keys.

Now Charles was waiting for her as Jane walked slowly down the stairs, like she'd planned her entrance, but she hadn't. It was all she could do to put one foot in front of the other.

Anna was still waiting to take Charles's coat. The younger man he'd come in with was waiting too, but all Jane could see was Charles. He was older. His hair was greyer, receding; there were lines around his eyes, his mouth, that hadn't been there before. She had to steel herself to meet his anger and disappointment, but instead he smiled as if nothing delighted him more than to come face to face with her again.

'Jane, how lovely you look,' he said, as she reached the bottom step. His eyes swept over her high-maintenance hair, the little black dress, and the heels that she'd learned to walk in while she was under his care. 'It really has been far too long.'

'It has,' she agreed and another five steps took her close enough that her hands were in his and his lips brushed against one cheek, then the other, an inconsequential greeting between old friends. The first time he'd ever touched her. How odd that there was nothing terrifying about Charles's hands; they held Jane steady even though she was sure that Charles could feel the frantic quiver that shot through her. The whole thing was unbearable. Jane smiled and pulled her hands away and glanced at the younger man waiting patiently in the wings. 'And who's this, darling?'

Charles hadn't liked it when she'd started calling people darling. 'It's so horribly contrived,' he'd complain, but now he continued to smile and took her hand once more as if seeing her again was so wonderful that he didn't want anything to spoil it.

'Jane, this is Fergus, Rose's right-hand man and a good friend of mine,' Charles said as she shook hands with the tall man in his thirties with a shock of bright red hair and the air of a gangly teenager.

'Jane, Leo's told me so much about you but I didn't know you knew Charles too,' Fergus said with a bright smile and a gentle handshake. 'I'm never sure if it's comforting or terrifying that the world is so small. How do you two know each other?'

Charles had always introduced her as his niece. There was

something more respectable about a niece rather than a god-daughter or the daughter of an old friend.

'We go way back,' Jane said and Charles nodded. 'So far back that I can't even remember how we met, can you?'

Charles wouldn't give away her secrets, or maybe he'd planned to but Lydia arrived to usher them into the drawing room. 'I'm afraid Ms Beaumont is delayed,' she said. Jane had never heard her sound so formal. 'And we're still waiting on Mr Hurst.'

It was thirty absolutely-fucking-agonising minutes of clutching a glass of white wine and perching on the arm of a chair while they talked brightly about the weather, why the council had dug up Kensington High Street yet again, then moved on to possible plans for Christmas.

Jane had cultivated the art of being witty and unstudied but that didn't mean much when she was sitting across from Charles, who'd witnessed her learning her trade. She felt like a wind-up doll whose mechanism was malfunctioning and when Fergus started talking about the Bank of England base rate, it was a relief not to have to contribute anything.

It was an even bigger relief when Leo walked in. For a moment, Jane wasn't sure that it was Leo. He wasn't wearing a crumpled T-shirt and baggy jeans, but a suit. Leo didn't do suits, except apparently he did: a slim-cut, navy blue suit with a black shirt. He rubbed his hands together nervously and smiled. 'Fergus! Great to see you again. You must be Charles? No, don't get up. I'm Leo, Rose's great-nephew. Sorry to keep you waiting. Can I top you up?'

Leo had also been to a barber. The bleached ends had been shorn off and he now had a short back and sides with enough hair left on top that he could run his fingers through it as he was doing now while he chatted to Fergus and Charles about a job the maintenance crew had been working on that morning.

'He swore he didn't know how the flat had got flooded but then we discovered all his clothes had been cut into tiny pieces and eventually he admitted that he'd cheated on his girlfriend and she'd let herself in while he was at work and left all the taps running.' He quirked an eyebrow at Jane. 'Don't be getting any ideas.'

She'd seen Leo every day and every night for over a month now, but she'd stopped seeing him, so she hadn't noticed that his face was leaner, pared down, his shirt no longer straining against his belly. He seemed to take up more space now that there was a little less of him, Jane thought as she watched Leo snag a footstool and sit down so he could talk to Fergus about some new Arsenal midfielder who wasn't living up to the promise of his twenty-five-million-pound transfer deal.

Leo glanced over to where Jane was still perched on the arm of a chair. 'God, I'd forgotten how well you scrub up,' he said. She'd had better, more elegant compliments but they'd lacked Leo's sincerity. When Leo bothered to make the effort, he could be so sweet. Suddenly, Jane wanted to pretend that she was a proper wife and that Leo had meant it when he promised to love, honour and protect her. Tonight, she needed his protection.

Lydia appeared in the doorway to announce that Rose was waiting for them in the dining room and when Leo got his feet, Jane tucked her arm in his and gave it a little squeeze as they walked through.

'You look really good,' Jane said slightly incredulously, which made Leo wonder if he'd really looked *that* bad before. 'Positively svelte. Just how much hard labour have you been doing, darling?'

'I think it's because I've cut down on the booze,' Leo told her. 'If I'm not hammered then I don't get a craving for a doner kebab with all the trimmings once they've called last orders.'

'Yuck.' Jane grimaced. 'I fear for your arteries.'

Rose was seated at the head of the table, George leaning over her to show her something on his phone. Like Jane, she was dressed all in black. It might have been the effect of the candles on the table, the dimmed uplighters on the wall, but Leo was sure there was a yellowing tinge to her face lately that even her red lipstick and the discreet glimmer of diamonds couldn't mask. Leo noticed that Rose wasn't getting up to greet Fergus and Charles. That was a first. She'd been fine this morning, but now she must feel . . . not fine.

Rose hadn't lost her autocratic edge, though. She directed them all to their places. Charles on her right, Jane seated next to him. Leo on her left, Fergus alongside him, George at the other end of the table. He didn't exactly know who Charles was, only that he was some kind of investment whizz and that Rose trusted him with her portfolios, so he had to be good people, because Rose hardly trusted anyone. Then he heard Charles say to Rose, 'Actually, Jane and I are old friends. Though it's been a while, hasn't it?'

Being an old friend of Jane's could mean anything: fund manager, distant relative, lover. It was impossible to tell, only that she nodded her head briefly, tersely even, then stared down at her place setting and wouldn't look at Charles, while he stole tiny, furtive glances at Jane when he thought that nobody would notice in the bustle of shaking out napkins and Frank, drafted in for the evening as butler, bringing in the wine.

Dinner parties had never been Leo's speed, but somewhere between the bread and the soup he started to enjoy himself. Fergus was Rose's heir apparent, charming, amenable but with an iron-coated backbone, much like Rose herself. He also seemed to love the bricks and mortar, the houses, the *homes,* which made up the core of the business as much as Rose did.

'You were going to tell me about the place on Powis Square,'

Fergus said to Rose after the wine had been poured, and she was suddenly at her sparkling best as she embarked on a long, funny story about renting out a house in Notting Hill in the seventies to a rock star and his wife with a granny annexe for the rock star's boyfriend and *his* wife.

Then George talked about how he'd worked at Seditionaries, Malcolm McLaren and Vivienne Westwood's shop on the King's Road, and that early on in their friendship he'd taken Rose to see the Sex Pistols play on a boat.

'Lovely boys,' Rose deadpanned, as Fergus coughed into his napkin and Leo thought he might actually cry he was laughing so hard. 'And I only got gobbed on once before the whole affair was shut down by the police. Really, I've been to worse parties.'

Jane and Charles were the only ones who weren't laughing. She sat silent, teeth worrying at her bottom lip, a deep furrow between her eyebrows. Charles couldn't take his eyes off her.

Neither could Leo, for that matter.

'So, Leo, what do you do?' Charles had torn his gaze away from Jane. 'I know you've been overseas for a few years but I was wondering what your plans were now you're back in London.'

'He's an artist,' Jane said quickly, as if she dared anyone to contradict her. 'Portraits mostly.'

It wasn't even the anticipation of Rose's disapproving sniff that made Leo admit the truth. 'I'm barely that. I'm between commissions, though to be honest, sometimes there have been whole years between commissions.' That was the thing with not drinking. It made you confront some hard, ugly truths. 'These last few weeks I've been going out with the property maintenance team. Swapped my pastels for matt white emulsion, you know.'

Of course his ambitions amounted to doing more with his life than sanding down skirting boards, but then Leo was staring down the wrong side of his thirties and he didn't exactly know what his ambitions were any more.

They talked shop for the rest of dinner: Leo, Fergus and Rose, Charles and George chiming in with the odd comment and Leo couldn't remember the last time he'd been this fired up as he pleaded the case for doing something fancy with the keystone and springers on their latest renovation project in Westbourne Grove.

He was also saying 'we', when he wasn't part of 'we', but a disinterested third party. Except he *was* interested, especially when Rose talked about her employees' right-to-buy-scheme.

'When this company started it was solely to house refugees coming from Europe at the end of the war,' she said, which Leo hadn't known. 'Kensington was on the wrong side of the Park, as we used to say. You could buy up huge swaths of bomb-damaged property very cheaply. There were refugees, soldiers suddenly without work, who needed jobs. They got a decent wage and for a heavily reduced rent they lived in the properties they renovated. Back then, we all needed a sense of purpose, the belief that everything we'd fought for hadn't been in vain.

'I still believe that if people are prepared to work hard, then they should have a decent wage and somewhere they can afford to live,' Rose stopped and smiled wryly. Maybe she was having a good day after all. 'Goodness, I think it's time I climbed down from my soapbox.'

'I like the view from up there,' Fergus said and Leo couldn't help but feel a little pang of something. Not jealousy, not entirely, but maybe regret that it was Fergus who shared Rose's passion, her vision and not Leo, or Alistair, or one of their cousins, so she could keep her legacy in the family. 'You should be very proud of the right-to-buy scheme. Actually, Leo, if you're interested,

I've got a property development company from Denmark coming in who are thinking of setting up a similar scheme. They specialise in carbon-neutral developments. Might be interesting, if you'd like to sit in. I remember we had quite a heated discussion about the challenges of being eco-friendly when renovating listed buildings.'

'Did you?' Rose sounded quite surprised. Then she stared pointedly at Leo's elbows, which were resting on the table.

Leo stopped slouching and sat up straight. 'Oh, I'm just an unemployed artist doing a bit of decorating on the side. You'd be much better off taking someone who knows what they're talking about.'

'Don't be so down on yourself.' Jane had finally roused herself from her funk. 'If you feel that passionately about the way people live, then get involved. Because it's important, isn't it? Everyone should have a home. Somewhere that they feel safe.'

It was odd to hear Jane speak with such conviction too. Also, she hadn't called anyone 'darling' for at least an hour. Leo wanted to ask Jane where she felt safe, but the conversation had already turned to Charles who was apparently an ethical investment banker, which sounded like an oxymoron to Leo.

Lydia had excelled herself with pudding – a chocolate fondant liberally laced with brandy – and after dinner, when they were lingering over coffee, Rose smiled at Leo; a smile shot through with warmth, maybe even approval. It had been a long, long time since he'd earned a smile like that from Rose.

The evening was a success, however you qualified it. Leo no longer felt as if he were being allowed to stay up late with the grown-ups as a special treat. He even saw Fergus and Charles out with a firm handshake apiece. 'It was a pleasure to meet you,' Charles said and sounded like he meant it

Leo wondered what Charles's story was. What he was to Jane. He didn't seem the type to indiscriminately shower his ethically invested funds on a woman. Maybe he was feeling a tinge of jealousy about that too as he walked back into the dining room for the debrief.

But George and Jane were crouched down in front of Rose, who was still sitting at the head of the table, her head bowed, hands clawing at nothing and making a horrific, rattling sound as she tried to gasp for air.

All of a sudden, the evening wasn't a success at all.

27

June–September 1944

On June seventh they woke up to the news that the Second Front had started. The Allied Forces had landed on the beaches in Normandy.

Rainbow Corner, not surprisingly, was deserted. The hostesses holed up around the big radiogram in the billiard room, and in between news reports they took it in turns to describe how wonderful their lives would be once the war was over. How they'd never have to eat tripe or bathe in five inches of lukewarm water ever again. It was impossible not to feel optimistic.

If only they'd known that there were still fresh horrors to come.

On the Saturday afternoon, a week after D-Day, Rose was walking to the butchers' for their Sunday meat when she heard a rumble above her, like a motorbike engine about to cut out. She looked up to see a tiny plane, its tail on fire.

The rumble became a roar became an eerie whistle and then . . . silence. Rose watched the flaming plane glide gracefully out of sight behind the buildings, then an almighty bang and she dropped to the ground, grazing her knees, as she covered her head with her hands.

All weekend and for weeks after that, the V1s, the doodlebugs, came.

If they were at home, they were meant to go to the shelter when they heard the siren, but the two nearest shelters were in Queen Square and at Holborn Tube station and, as Sylvia said, 'Chances are we'd be dead before we got there. Anyway, if a bomb has your name on it, then it will find you.' So, they usually stayed in their beds, though Mr Bryce kept threatening to report them to the ARP warden.

It wasn't the noise of the V1s that frightened Rose. Though sometimes at night their roar was so close that she swore they scraped their roof as they flew overhead. What terrified her most was the quiet, deathly hush before the rocket dropped, already locked onto its target. It was unbearable – but somehow she had to bear it.

Even her mother telephoned the café and begged her to come home. 'You won't have to join the Land Girls, darling. We just want you to be safe.'

For the first time since she got to London, part of Rose wanted to go back to Durham, but London was her home now. Her girls were her family, the little ones in the house in Kensington, Paul, Hélène and Thérèse, they all needed her – Edward was relying on her to look after them.

So she couldn't go home but she promised her mother that she'd write every day and go straight to a shelter whenever she heard the siren. Yes, even if she was in the middle of the lunchtime rush. Promise.

June became July and July brought storms and Rainbow Corner was full of new recruits and reservists, callow youths still wet behind the ears who trod on her feet and held her all wrong and still the bombs came night after night. London was bloody and blackened and bowed and Rose wondered if she'd ever grow accustomed to the dread that now lodged like heavy stones in the pit of her stomach. The dread made Rose miss Edward, who'd disappeared somewhere official, because he was always calm and steady even when all around was chaos.

Despite everything, Rose found herself missing Danny, too, in a strange way. Or rather, she missed the love that she'd used to feel for him; that ravenous love that couldn't be sated by the little he gave her in return. It had made her feel so alive. But you couldn't spend your life mourning a love that had been unrequited then so ruthlessly abused. Rose's bruises had faded away, though not the memory of what Danny had done to her, but still she needed to know that he was alive. She had sent several letters to the address he'd given her, the pub, but no reply ever came from him, so she began to fear the worst. She tried to be hopeful but sometimes hope felt as scarce as oranges.

She never wanted to see him again, but she didn't wish him dead or even injured. 'Or maybe a little bit injured,' she said to Sylvia, after yet another day without even one line from Danny hastily scribbled on a postcard. 'I wouldn't mind if he lost a finger or got wounded by some shrapnel.'

The end of August, summer diminished, Paris was liberated and how they all cheered when they heard that glorious news. London picked herself up too, dusted off her skirts and was daring to dream again. Rose was even starting to look forward to her birthday because they'd all been saving their sugar rations and Mickey had promised her three eggs – enough for Maggie to make her a splendid birthday cake.

Then Edward came back.

There was a note waiting for her on the first Sunday in September when she went over to Kensington. The children solemnly handed her the envelope with as much ceremony as if it had come from Buckingham Palace via a bewigged equerry.

Dear Rose

I'd be delighted if you would be my guest for dinner at The Ritz on Friday, September 8th, 10.30 pm. If you would like, please bring your friend, Phyllis.

Fondest regards

Edward

Rose asked Phyllis to come with her to The Ritz, but Phyllis refused. 'I'm not promising anything, you understand,' she said, 'but that's the night before your eighteenth birthday and Maggie, Sylvia and I have plans for that evening that don't involve you.'

They always arranged birthday surprises for each other. For Sylvia's, Maggie had wangled her a pass to attend a recording of *American Eagle in Britain* at the BBC and Sylvia had ended up dancing down a corridor with Fred Astaire himself. They'd managed to get a tiny bottle of Chanel N°5 and seats in a box to see Ivor Novello in *The Dancing Years* at the Adelphi for Phyllis's birthday. Maggie's surprise had been much harder because she gave so little away but Rose had procured two bottles of vodka from a Pole working on the houses in Kensington and Sylvia had come by two yards of black silk so Maggie could make herself a dress. Having dinner with Edward would give the girls ample time to put the finishing touches to Rose's birthday surprises, which she hoped would include a new frock and lipstick as her Tru-Color red was all but a distant memory.

The three of them saw her off from outside Rainbow Corner. Phyllis dabbed Rose's wrists with a few precious drops of Chanel N°5, while Sylvia warned Rose not to drink too much.

'You know what happened last time,' she said, her blue eyes gleaming. 'He'll think you're a dreadful lush.'

'But have a lovely time, Rosie,' Phyllis said. 'And don't do anything I wouldn't do!'

Sylvia turned to Phyllis with a look of confusion. 'But Phyllis, sweetie, you never do anything,' she drawled and Phyllis squawked in outrage and pretended to throttle Sylvia as Maggie laughed at their antics.

'You'd better go,' she told Rose, who was laughing too. 'You'll be late.'

Rose *was* late but Edward was still waiting outside The Ritz for her, as if he'd known she was horribly nervous about having to go inside on her own. He was in his uniform, which always looked so crisp, so beautifully cut that Rose wondered if he'd had his tailors run it up for him, and he tipped his cap in greeting when he saw Rose hurrying towards him. He was taller, less stooped, than she remembered him.

'Hello,' he said, and she'd also forgotten how welcoming his smile was, so all of a sudden she wasn't nervous about how shiny her black crêpe de Chine had become or that she might make an awful faux pas with the cutlery. 'You look quite, quite lovely.'

Rose was sure she didn't. She'd run out of powder and the hurried walk down Piccadilly must have made her face all red. She waved his compliment away. 'Have you been back long?'

'A week,' he said, tucking his cap under his arm and offering Rose his other arm as the doorman ushered them inside. When the door closed behind them, muffling the sounds of the night, it was as if the world outside had ceased to exist.

They followed a solemn waiter across a vast dining room. It was all Rose could do not to gawp like a halfwit at the garlands of chandeliers that lit the huge room, their glow reflected in the mirrors, the gleam of silver and the sparkle of crystal on the tables they passed. The friezes painted onto the gilt-edged wall panels were like the pictures in art books she used to look at in the school library. Women in pre-war furs and satin and silk shimmered too. It was like suddenly finding herself in a beautiful dream.

She sat down on the plump red velvet chair that had been pulled out for her. 'This is exactly how I imagined the court of Louis the Sixteenth before the French Revolution.'

Edward smiled. 'Do you think if we listen very carefully we might hear the roar of angry peasants come to take us to the guillotine?'

'Oh, they wouldn't take me, not once I'd explained that I was just a simple worker,' Rose said and maybe she was being a little cheeky but it was worth it to make Edward laugh. Otherwise he looked so serious. 'Can you tell me where you've been and what you've been doing or is it absolutely top secret?'

'If I told you, then the angry peasants would be replaced by military policeman who'd take us away and lock us up.' He signalled to a waiter who was keen to present them with menus. 'Now, you're to tell me, if you could have absolutely anything, what would you like to eat?'

Rose took a moment to think about roast chicken and Cook's special stuffing with prunes and apricots. She thought about trifle. She thought about a proper breakfast: fried eggs, plump sausages, crisp bacon and field mushrooms. She thought about all of those things and then she thought about the one dish she wanted more than anything. 'Welsh rarebit,' she decided. 'Made with lots and lots of cheese and swimming in Worcester sauce.'

'Then that's what you shall have,' Edward said. He called the waiter over. 'We'll both have Welsh rarebit liberally doused in Worcester sauce. Two Bellinis for an aperitif, then a bottle of Merlot. The nineteen thirty-seven if you have any left.'

The waiter seemed to think that cheese on toast was a perfectly acceptable thing to order at The Ritz and it was then that Rose thought that it might be her favourite place in the world, or maybe it was when their Bellinis arrived and she made the happy discovery that champagne was quite delicious when it was mixed with peach juice, even if it was a scandalous waste of a good peach.

She and Edward talked about the refugees, though they weren't the refugees any more. They were Hélène, Thérèse and Paul, who loved playing their own raucous version of croquet and would run up to hug Rose when she popped round every Thursday and Sunday afternoon, even as their hands crept into her pockets in the hunt for chocolate. They were Madeleine and Gisèle, who spent most of their time digging and weeding and hoeing in the garden even when it was pouring with rain simply because they loved being outside after so long cooped up below ground. And they were Yves and Jacques, who always insisted on walking Rose to the bus stop and had come round to Montague Terrace once to try to do something about the plumbing because the pipes made a death rattle every time one of the girls turned on a tap.

Rose asked Edward about his plans for the house next door, which was almost habitable again, even if there was no one to live in it. Though surely, now that the Allies were gaining ground in Europe, it would be easier for people who wanted to leave.

'We'll see,' Edward said, as the waiter placed a small silver bowl in front of Rose. For pudding she'd asked for strawberries and ice cream and because she hadn't cared much for the Merlot, Edward had insisted she have another Bellini. 'Let's talk of brighter things.' He glanced at his watch. 'There's still half an hour to go, but Happy Birthday.'

'How did you know?' Rose asked.

'A little bird told me,' Edward said. Rose supposed that the little bird was Sylvia, or Mickey Flynn, who probably made a note of that sort of thing. 'I hope you don't mind, I got you a little something to say thank you for—'

'You don't have to thank me,' Rose said forcefully enough that Edward raised his eyebrows. 'I was happy to do it.'

'Look, you might as well know I've lost the receipt and I'm sure I can't take it back, so you're leaving me in quite a bind.' He reached into the inner pocket of his jacket and pulled out a small grey leather box. It glided over the smooth white linen of the tablecloth towards Rose and it would be churlish not to take it and . . .

'Oh! I couldn't possibly accept this,' Rose gasped as she stared down at the two diamond clips nestled in yellow velvet. 'I really couldn't.'

'Did I mention that I've mislaid the receipt?' He was so sweet, which made it all the harder.

'You don't understand.' Rose had been dreading this. Sylvia had told her to keep her mouth shut but Phyllis said that it was a pretty lowdown trick to play on a fellow if you let him take you out to dinner when your heart wasn't really in it. 'It's just . . . well, I'd hate for you to get the wrong idea. There's another man. There *was* another man. It didn't end well.'

Edward, though he was still sitting there, drinking his Merlot, smoking a cigarette, had suddenly withdrawn from her without so much as leaning back in his chair. 'Oh. I'm sorry. My condolences.'

'No, you don't understand. He's not dead.' It was hard to stumble across the right words, even though Rose had been thinking of little else but how to phrase this speech ever since she'd received Edward's note. 'He's a bomber pilot. He was meant to go back to the States to sell war bonds but he wanted to stay and fight,' she added a little defensively.

Edward had only just crushed out his cigarette but he lit another one. 'How commendable of him,' he said in that same toneless voice. Rose didn't think that she'd led him on, though as Sylvia had said, men always accused one of leading them on and agreeing to have dinner with Edward might have given him the idea that Rose was keen. Even though they hardly knew each other and he was much older than her. It was hard to say how much older, but he was at least thirty. At the *very* least.

'The thing is, I haven't heard from him in ages. Not since before the invasion and though I don't have feelings for him any longer, not kind feelings anyway, I was hoping, I know it's a lot to ask, but if you might make some enquiries. To see if he's safe.'

Edward barely even blinked as Rose reached into her little evening bag and pulled out the scrap of paper on which she'd written Danny's details. It wasn't much. Just his name, though she wasn't sure how to spell his surname, where he was stationed, and that his people lived in New York. But Rose knew so much more about Danny than just these few scant facts written on the back of an envelope. After what he'd done to her, she knew the secret heart of him and though it might not be a good heart, a true heart, she needed to know it was still beating.

'What's the name of his squadron? What's his rank? There are three United States Air Force stations in Cambridgeshire, might you be more specific? Where do you send his letters when you write to him?'

Rose couldn't answer any of the questions that Edward all but barked at her because she didn't know the answers. Not because they'd had some fly-by-night encounter but because there was that whole business of Danny using the local pub as a postbox to outwit the army censors. Surely that had to be against regulations and Danny could get into trouble if his CO found out? What silly things people did when they thought they were in love, but Edward wouldn't understand. He was too buttoned-up, too serious, to let himself fall in love.

'It doesn't matter,' Rose said. She held out her hand for the piece of paper. 'I'm sorry to have bothered you.'

Edward tucked the paper away in his pocket. 'I'm not promising anything but I'll see what I can do.'

The gilt and the chandeliers, even the diamond clips in front of her had lost their sparkle, the bubbles in her champagne no longer fizzing on her tongue. Rose stared down at her melting ice cream. She heard Edward sigh, then she heard nothing but the unholy bang that rocked the room, made the chandeliers shake as the hallowed space of The Ritz was breached.

There were screams and Rose pushed back her chair. Then there was another bang, as if a hundred doodlebugs had suddenly exploded in one huge blast right outside the windows, and she gasped.

'Get down, you little fool!' Edward pulled Rose under the table, his body covering hers, shielding her from the horrors outside.

'Oh God, what is it? Why didn't they sound the siren? I can't bear it,' she whispered, the argument already forgotten because *this* was what had ruined the evening. The bloody war. It ruined everything. 'I can't stand it.'

'Yes, you can. You have to be brave,' Edward said and he took Rose's hand, squeezed her fluttering fingers until she was still and in that moment she felt safe. Nothing could get to her because Edward simply wouldn't allow it.

She pressed her cheek against his chest, felt the buttons on his jacket dig into her, and she matched her breaths to his, slow and steady, until she felt her heart stop racing, let calm sink in and when the siren finally began to wail, five minutes after the first explosion, she was angry that it broke the spell.

They were led to The Ritz's bomb shelter, a restaurant, La Popote, in the basement with a funny mural on the wall. Edward ordered more champagne and insisted Rose drink it all because she was so pale. There was a band playing, people dancing, laughing, greeting friends – and suddenly waiting it out until the All Clear became a fabulous party. Edward even danced with her – he insisted on a slow, sedate waltz though they were playing a foxtrot and he stepped on her feet a couple of times, but the sheer selflessness of Edward asking her to dance because he knew that she wanted to meant more to Rose than the diamond clips that she'd scooped up from the table on their way out of the much grander restaurant upstairs.

It was ages before the All Clear sounded. They left The Ritz just after two. Even at the best of times, it was hard to find a taxi. Tonight it proved impossible.

'I'll walk you home,' Edward said and Rose didn't feel the least inclined to argue. Tonight's bombs had scared the wits right out of her, though when they crossed over Shaftesbury Avenue they met a policeman coming the other way who said that there hadn't been any bombs. 'Word from on high is that it was a gas line explosion, sir,' he'd said.

That would have explained why there'd been no siren, no warning, just those two almighty bangs as if the heavens had wanted to show just how furious they were at the destruction they were forced to look down upon every day and every night.

'I think the war will be over soon,' Rose told Edward as they walked along New Oxford Street. 'The doodlebugs haven't been doodling much and I can't believe that the Germans aren't as sick of all this as we are.'

'You should be careful what you wish for,' Edward muttered obliquely. 'You're shivering. You should have said you were cold. Take my jacket.'

He draped it over her shoulders so she could smell the faintest hint of his aftershave, something subtle and smoky, and then they didn't talk at all. Rose's feet were aching and she was so tired that it seemed pointless to even go to bed, only to have to wake up again almost as soon as she'd fallen asleep.

Though when she did wake up, it would be her birthday and there'd be all sorts of treats. Even Shirley, who seemed quite over her snit about Rose making off with her dresses, had sent her a large, intriguing parcel. It was enough to make Rose quicken her steps and then, as they reached Theobald's Road and her bed was only three minutes away, they were forced to come to a stop. The street was littered with broken glass from the shop windows that had blown out. There were huge lumps of masonry and twisted hunks of metal lying in the road, where this morning there'd been buses, trams and taxis, people hurrying to get to work.

Neither of them said anything, because there wasn't much to say. Besides, it was heavy going. The nearer they got to Montague Terrace, the thicker the air became, heavy with dust and smoke, so that Rose and Edward had to pull out their handkerchiefs and hold them over their mouths. Edward called to her, but his words were swallowed up by the fug.

The closer Rose got to home, the greater the devastation. No shops, no houses left. They'd been torn up and replaced by charred, still-smoking mountains of debris and Rose had to weave this way and that to fight her way through the mess, but she knew that when she got to their corner everything would be all right. She'd already come through the eye of the storm, where the damage was at its greatest, and maybe they might have some broken windows . . . it wouldn't surprise her if the roof had come clean off, but she'd soon find the others. They must have gone to the shelter. Not even Sylvia could have slept through this. 'You took your time,' she would say and they'd laugh when Rose told them she'd been to The Ritz only to dine on cheese on toast.

Edward called out to her again, but he was far, far behind her and she was almost home. Just round the corner. The dust was clearing. There! She was through the worst of it.

At the top of Montague Terrace a cordon had been set up, and as she struggled nearer, Rose saw it was manned by an ARP warden. The dust and smoke weren't so bad now but tiny blackened pieces of debris were floating from the sky like confetti and

Rose shivered again. Everything was going to be all right. She was almost home, but when she swallowed, all she could taste was fear and soot.

'You can't go through,' the ARP warden shouted at her, though Rose was sure that her legs would refuse to take another step. 'Gas line explosion.'

'How bad is it?' Edward had caught up. 'The young lady lives on this street, you see.'

'You can't go through,' the warden repeated. 'No one's allowed through.'

'Rose! Come back!'

She was running, dodging past the warden who shouted at her to stop and she did stop because she'd rounded the corner onto her street. Her dear little street. It was strewn with broken bricks and shattered glass and the terrible dust was so thick, coating her clothes, Rose sucked it in with every ragged breath. It was impossible to see where she was going when her eyes were streaming but still she pressed on.

'Oh God, oh God, oh God,' she heard herself chant as she stumbled over bricks and rubble,.

This was the heart of the explosion. Not like the damage she was used to when one could still see the shell of the home you once knew. Her home was no longer there. It was simply *gone*. No more. Disappeared. Not here. Here was now a crater where their entire terrace had once stood, as if the earth had swallowed all the houses up whole, then spat out the joists and jambs as if they were bones. There was a gaping hole in her world.

'Rose! Come back to the cordon. It's not safe.' Edward came up behind her, panting.

She whirled round. 'My girls! Where are my girls?'

He put an arm around her shaking shoulders. 'Let's go and find out.'

'Miss, you listen to your bloke.' The ARP warden, his sooty

face creased with concern, wasn't shouting any more. 'The WRVS has set up a canteen in the church hall on Bloomsbury Way. You go and have a nice cup of tea and a bun and sort yourself out. We need to keep this area clear to let the Civil Defence boys do their job.'

'My friends . . . ' She couldn't say any more than that, but pointed to the hole. 'My house is in there. My friends were in the house. You see, normally they'd go out dancing, but it's my birthday tomorrow, well, I suppose it's today now and they came home early to plan my surprises. They're all right, aren't they?'

The warden took her hand. 'If you go to the WRVS canteen, they'll have set up an IIP. They'll know what to do.'

Rose might even have let herself be led to the draughty church hall, but then she saw the look the two men shared, the swift shake of the warden's head.

'No!' She wrenched free of them, sprang forward. All this time, she'd been staring blindly at the hole that stretched two streets back and it was only now that she looked down at what was left of the pavement.

On the ground were six stained beige blankets, shrouding what lay beneath. Next to them there was a straw hamper, the kind you might pack full of sandwiches and fruit and bottles of pop for a picnic. Rose couldn't imagine what it was doing there and then she remembered Sylvia telling her about the time she'd passed a street half an hour after a doodlebug had dropped from the sky. There'd been a young ambulance worker crying as she collected chunks of flesh ('I'm sure one of them was a tiny foot, it was the most gruesome thing I'd ever seen, I felt like crying too') wrapping them in newspaper and placing them in a basket.

'Is that them? Is that my girls? Is it? Is it?' How could it be them? If it was, that would mean that Sylvia had left her. That she'd never see her or Phyllis or Maggie again. Even miserable

Mr Bryce and the two sisters who lived in the ground floor flat and worked at the library on Chancery Lane. They'd all vanished and weren't coming back. No goodbye, no note. She'd waved her girls off outside Rainbow Corner, too excited about her birthday treats and dinner at The Ritz to make that last 'Cheerio. Don't wait up!' have any real meaning.

'Rose. Darling Rose.' Edward's voice caught. 'Don't do that. Darling, please don't.'

She was on her knees and hammering the ground with fists that were quickly bloodied. Demanding that the earth, which had taken her girls, return them safe and sound.

'I want them back right now! Do you hear me? You bring them back to me!'

'If I could, I would. I'd do anything for you.' Edward was on his knees too, arms holding her immobile so she couldn't do any more damage. His big body covered hers and he clung to her tightly as if he could suck all the pain out of her and carry it around with him day after day so she wouldn't have to bear the burden.

But he couldn't. No one could. The pain was hers and hers alone.

28

When Rose was able to breathe again, when her lips were no longer blue, she'd forbidden Leo from calling her doctor and refused to even countenance sending for an ambulance.

She had, eventually after much persuasion, permitted Leo to carry her upstairs. Jane and Lydia followed at a respectable distance to allow her some semblance of dignity and so they could pretend not to hear Rose make an awful gasp every time Leo had to shift her in his arms.

After Rose was settled, they'd sent Lydia to bed and Jane had stayed. They'd barely spoken. Jane's face was white, her carefully applied make-up suddenly garish. In the end, Leo had sent her to bed too. She'd obeyed without even a token protest and Leo had spent the rest of the night sitting with Rose, who slept in painful fits and starts.

Leo supposed that he must have dozed off in the armchair because the arrival of Lydia with a breakfast tray closely followed by a man who he assumed was Rose's doctor made his eyes snap open. He stretched out his legs, felt his right calf begin to cramp up.

'Really, what a fuss about nothing,' said a crisp voice from the bed. Rose was sitting up. She looked better than she had last night but as there'd been five long minutes when Leo thought that Rose might suffocate from lack of oxygen, better was a relative concept.

I should never have come back, Leo thought as he staggered to the kitchen. He didn't have the bottle or the balls to handle this situation, which was only going to get worse.

Then again, maybe he should never have left in the first place.

Jane was in the kitchen, between him and the coffee pot. She was wearing jeans and an old black jumper that she must have found in his chest of drawers. Her hair was tangled, her face still sleep-creased.

'You must be desperate for some coffee, darling,' she said. 'Black, right?'

'As black as it will go.' He hauled himself up on one of the wooden stools and leaned his elbows on the breakfast bar as she poured coffee into two mugs. Jane handed one to him, kept one for herself and took a sip. He waited for her to say something, but she was silent. As if she was the one waiting for him.

'We've all been kidding ourselves, Rose included, that this was under control,' Leo finally admitted. He looked up at the halogen spotlights set into the kitchen ceiling as if he'd find salvation in their soft glow. 'That she could carry on the way she was for months and months.'

'Last night might have been just a one-off.' Jane frowned. 'Though I've noticed that she hasn't had much of an appetite lately.'

'This isn't a game any more, Jane. You know that, don't you?' Leo asked baldly, because ever since last night he'd had this sick feeling of dread like the end of the world was well and truly nigh. Whatever Jane was up to, he didn't want to play. 'You can't be here, in Rose's home, if you're only . . . '

'What? Only what?' She was no longer pale but red-faced and

surely even Jane couldn't flush on demand. 'I said that I'd help you, darling, and that still stands.'

'Why? I've told you already that there isn't going to be some big payday.'

Even though her face seemed to be regaining its ability to show emotion, it was still hard to get a read on what Jane was thinking, especially when she turned away to gaze out of the window. 'Whatever else we may or may not be to each other, I thought we were friends, and as a friend I want to be here for you.'

Jane seemed different this morning. Her head was bowed, the graceful line of her shoulders slumped, her posture forlorn. Leo stood up and walked over to her. He thought about smoothing down a stray lock of her hair but didn't. 'So that Charles – is he gay, then?' It wasn't what he was going to say. Not the right time or place, but there it was. He'd said it.

Jane's shoulders twitched. 'Oh . . . Charles . . . he's not anything, I don't think. Not gay, not straight, he's just not interested.' She turned round and Leo hadn't realised how close he'd got. One step closer and they'd be nose to nose but before he could move back because he didn't want Jane to think he was crowding her, she put a hand on his arm, her fingers cool on his tired skin. 'Look, I'm not everything that you think I am. And I'm not always on the make. I'd like to stay, but only if you want me to.'

And when she put it like that, Leo didn't have to think twice about it. 'I do.'

She smiled faintly. 'But I don't want to get stuck playing bad cop any more.'

'You won't,' Leo said firmly. It was all getting painfully serious again. There'd be time enough for that later. He dreaded the thought of *later*, so he banished it with a sly smile. 'Though I can't promise not to use you as a human shield to deflect the blast from one of Rose's glares.'

'That I'll allow,' Jane decided then she stepped past him to pull herself up on a stool.

They hadn't even finished their coffee when Lydia rang down on the house phone and asked them to come up to Rose's suite.

Rose was ensconced on the sofa in her sitting room, as if she were just resting between social engagements. 'I thought it best if you had an update while Dr Howard was here. I do so hate having to repeat myself.'

Dr Howard was incongruously perched on a footstool, but he stood up so he could shake hands. He was barely taller than Jane and as sleek and dark and dapper as an otter.

'So important to have family around at times like this,' he murmured. Leo wondered if he ever had occasion to raise his voice. 'Ms Beaumont has agreed to have a nurse administer an injection three times a day for more effective pain relief, though we did talk about a cannula . . .'

'No, Gerard, *you* talked about a cannula,' Rose reminded him. From the repressed, rigid look on Lydia's face, Rose had been reminding Dr Howard of quite a few things this morning. 'And I told you in no uncertain times that it would only get in my way.'

The doctor sank back down onto the footstool. He didn't look quite so calm and capable as he had when Leo had met him earlier. Rose had obviously been testing his bedside manner to breaking point. 'Now, Ms Beaumont, we've talked about this. This is the time to start thinking about what all our options are. Whether we can make some modifications here to make you more comfortable or—'

'Don't use the royal we with me, young man,' Rose said grandly and Leo knew that they had to allow her this: to put up a good fight, shake a fist at death and all that. He'd start panicking when she stopped fighting. 'I admit that maybe I've been overdoing things a little, but I'll take the weekend to regroup. I'll be fine by Monday and tomorrow we'll go down to Lullington Bay. I'll be sitting in the car, that's not going to be tiring.' Rose sighed. 'Such a shame that the roses won't be out. You promise that we'll go tomorrow, Leo, no excuses?'

He promised, hand on his heart, then they left Rose to get some rest. Leo and Jane saw Dr Howard out. He held a hand apiece for an uncomfortably long count and made a murmured speech about how strong Rose was and that her generation was full of Blitz spirit and that they didn't make them like that any more.

'It's always darkest before the dawn,' he concluded, just before Leo shut the front door behind him.

'Do you think he's practised that in front of a mirror?' Leo asked Jane. 'Worked really hard to get the sincerity *just* right?'

'I think he probably used an acting coach,' Jane said with a sniff and even though they might only be pretending to be a united front, it was still much better than having to do this on his own.

After lunch, Lydia asked Jane to take a cup of tea up to Rose. The older woman hadn't left her rooms all morning and when Jane went in she found her sitting in a chair by the picture window in her bedroom that led out onto a pretty wrought iron balcony.

'I can't stand being cooped up all day. I want to go outside,' Rose said, her eyes still fixed on the bleak winter landscape outside.

'You do? Are you feeling better, then?'

'I'm not suggesting dinner and a show.' This was why Jane was never particularly keen on being left alone with Rose. Rose was so sharp, so bright, and Jane had always been a creature of shadows. 'I simply want to go and sit in the square.'

'But, darling, it's freezing and—'

'I wasn't asking your permission but my silly old legs won't do what I want today so I need your help.' Rose threw her hands up in frustration. 'Don't ever get old. There's not much to recommend it.'

'Of course I'll help. You should be able to go out if you want to,' Jane said, because she remembered what it was like not to be able to do what you wanted to do, when you wanted to do it. Even now, there were times when her freedom still felt like a novelty. Like some delicate bauble that could get smashed underfoot if she didn't look after it carefully.

So, if Rose wanted to go and sit in the square even though the cold would penetrate bones that Dr Howard had implied this morning were starting to get eaten away by the cancer, then Jane wasn't going to refuse her request.

'I'll get Leo,' she said.

Leo carried Rose down the stairs again, even though she said she could walk. Frank brought the car round as near to the back door as he could, then drove the few yards around the corner to the locked gate that led into the tiny square. Then, leaning heavily on Jane, Rose made her way to a wooden bench tucked into a tiny arbour created by the trees, which, over the years, had curved around the seat.

Rose was wearing a ragged fur coat they'd unearthed in the attics a week or so ago. 'My mother's funeral fur,' she'd said. Lydia had insisted on gloves and a scarf, Leo was despatched back to the car to fetch the travel rug, then Rose asked him to go to her office and fetch some files.

'I had planned to pop in this morning, there were a few things I wanted to look at over the weekend,' she said to Jane, as if she needed to suddenly justify her actions. 'But I'm definitely going to the office on Monday morning. There's no question about it.'

'Of course there isn't,' Jane agreed as she tried hard not to shiver, even though Lydia had forced her to wear a hat too. Leo had grinned delightedly as he pulled a grey woollen beanie, unearthed from one of his bottomless drawers, onto her head. 'Well, it's no tiara,' he'd said.

There was something different about Leo these last few days. It wasn't just the new haircut and the way he suddenly looked different, all devastating angles and cheekbones. Despite everything, he seemed happier, stronger, more his own person.

She'd been so worried about breaking him that she hadn't thought to worry about herself, which was a first. But now, after last night, after Charles . . .

'Did I tell you about the refugees?'

She turned to look at Rose, who'd also been lost in her own thoughts. 'No, I don't think so.'

'I used to visit them on my Thursday afternoons, which I had off from the café. It felt like the least I could do. All of them were so weak at first, but the children recovered very quickly and we'd come out here, though it was covered in piles of rubble, and play croquet. Just over there.' Jane still wasn't sure who Rose was talking about as the other woman pointed at a flowerbed where viburnum shrubs bloomed improbably pink in the fading afternoon light. 'Madeleine and Gisèle had turned the back garden into a vegetable patch and Yves and Jacques were helping to renovate the house next door. It was very important for them to feel that they were repaying Edward in some small way, though I don't think he felt the same way.'

'You've never mentioned Edward before . . .'

'Haven't I? How odd! Most of the time I played with the little ones. Paul, Hélène and Thérèse, who some twenty years later would give birth to our Lydia.'

'Really? You've known her long enough that you used to change her nappies?'

'I have never changed a nappy in my life,' Rose said with a little of that imperiousness which Jane aspired to. 'One has to have some standards.'

'I have to say, no disrespect to Lydia, but she's terribly bossy to someone who's known her since she was a snot-nosed little brat.'

'You noticed that too.' Rose allowed herself a small, dry smile. 'So, this square, the house, it's been my home for practically my entire life.'

'I never had a home, just places that I lived in for a while,' Jane said. She was raw enough today that she was sick of having to watch everything she said. 'Home is where you feel safe, right? The only thing that makes me feel even a little bit safe is money. Once you have enough of it, you can do anything, go anywhere, be anyone you like. No one can stop you.'

'You're not there yet, then?'

Jane shook her head. 'I have no idea how much it will take. Five million? Ten million? A *billion*?' She turned back to Rose, who was lucid again and looking at Jane as if she were some curiosity behind glass in a museum. 'Does your money make you feel safe?'

'I never really cared about the money. Oh, it's nice to have and yes, it does cushion you a little, but there are some things even money can't protect you from,' Rose said and Jane didn't know if she meant the way her body was breaking down or if she was talking about something in the past because Rose was getting that faraway look again. 'I've always felt safest when I'm with the people I love. I've loved very well, not always wisely, and this house and the house at Lullington Bay are associated with some of the people that I loved so very much. That's why they're my safe places.'

After everything that had happened to her, there was no possibility that Jane was capable of love, but she was capable of kindness, even when there was nothing in it for her. Everyone deserved to feel safe – especially at their end. 'I'll make sure you stay here. No hospice. I promise. Whatever happens.'

'Thank you,' Rose said and then she took Jane's hand and through their gloved fingers gripped her with a strength Jane hadn't thought possible. 'This last week or so, I see my loved ones all around me. At night, when I can't sleep, I can see them in the walls.'

Rose might be getting that misty, unfocused look again but her voice was clear, so it was hard to know how to respond. 'Oh, well ... it's probably just the new drugs you're on, darling.'

'No, I think they're waiting for me. I thought I had more time than this. I would love to have a little bit more time. There are still so many loose ends to tie up.' Rose placed her other hand over their clasped fingers. 'Still, I don't think I'll have to bother with Christmas cards this year. Having to write them out was always such a bore.'

It was a relief that they were back to being flippant. 'You probably won't have to bother with buying Christmas presents either.'

'Or eat Brussels sprouts. Never could stand them. They were the one thing that was in plentiful supply during the war.'

'They're not so bad if you take off all the outer leaves and fry them with bacon,' Jane said and Rose wasn't so far gone that she couldn't give her an incredulous look. 'Sometimes – not often, I admit it – I cook. Last year, before I met Leo of course, I cooked Christmas dinner for my boyfriend's family.' Jane laughed as she remembered it. 'They didn't really understand the concept of Christmas dinner. Kept saying it was too soon after Thanksgiving to have turkey again,' she told Rose. 'Jackie, Andrew's mother, said that next year she'd give me her baked ham recipe and I could make that instead. I dodged a bullet there. Are you too cold, darling? Shall we go in now?'

Rose was staring at her incredulously again. 'Gosh, you really are an odd duck,' she said as if she were seventy years younger and she wasn't talking to Jane but one of those ghosts of hers that lived in the walls.

Then, thank God, Leo was coming through the gate. 'I hope you two aren't talking about me,' he said cheerfully. 'Frank gave me a lift to the office. I've got everything you asked for and Liddy says it's too cold and you have to come in now.'

29

September 1944

Rose sat on a wooden chair clutching a mug of tea that tasted faintly of Brussels sprouts as a lady from the WRVS asked her questions, each one punctuated with the word 'dear'.

'Do you have an address for Phyllis Carfax's next of kin, dear?'

'Do you know when Magda Novotny arrived in England? Is that the correct spelling of her surname, dear?'

'Is it Sylvia or Sylvie, dear?'

'Do you have your rent book, dear?'

Then she sent Rose off to the other end of the church hall to talk to an Information Officer. There were more questions, forms to be filled in, a card handed over with the address of the mortuary because Maggie – they kept calling her Magda even though she was Maggie – didn't have any relatives to identify her body.

'You can't expect her to do that,' Edward said harshly. 'She's barely eighteen.'

Rose was glad Edward knew the truth about her age so that she didn't have to lie to him too. She was fed up with lying. 'I don't mind,' she said. 'I couldn't bear the thought of Maggie . . . I want to do it.'

They got a lift to the New Middlesex Hospital from one of the ambulance crews and waited in a corridor until nine o'clock when the mortuary office opened. Rose handed over the card and they were sent back outside to wait.

'I'm so late for work,' she said to Edward. 'And I still need to go home to change.'

She kept forgetting that there was no home to go back to, no clothes to change into, no one to yell at her to make them a cup of tea too.

'It doesn't matter,' Edward said. His fair hair was soot-blackened. There was also soot and brick dust all over his uniform and his cap had got lost in the mêlée. Edward was very important so he probably needed to go to work too even though it was a Saturday, but he shook his head when Rose pointed that out. 'None of that matters today.'

Eventually Rose's name was called by a young woman in a tweed suit who led them down several flights of stairs, then through a labyrinthine maze of passages until they came to the door with a handmade sign pinned to it: MORTUARY.

The woman was talking to her. 'I'll try to make this as quick and painless as possible, but it was a very concentrated explosion. You need to prepare yourself.'

Rose tilted her chin and straightened her shoulders. 'I'm absolutely fine,' she insisted, but was glad of Edward's hand resting on the small of her back as she walked through the door.

The room reminded her of the science laboratory at her old school. The same jars and phials arranged on shelves. There was even a blackboard and the peculiarly prickly yet flat smell of chemicals, but her school science lab had never had a large trolley in the middle of the room with a shrouded body on it.

Except it was too small to be a body and Rose stalled, but Edward flexed his fingers and pushed her forward on unsteady feet.

Then she stopped. 'It looks too little to be Maggie . . . '

The woman consulted her clipboard. 'Maggie? Magda Novotny?'

'We call her Maggie. Called her Maggie.' Rose gestured at the covered figure. 'She wasn't as tall as me, but she was bigger than that.'

She heard Edward suck in a breath. The woman stared fixedly at the papers in front of her. 'It was a very concentrated explosion,' she repeated. She looked at Rose and raised her eyebrows. Rose stared back at her. 'That is to say, not all the bodies are, um . . . intact.'

Rose thought of the wicker hamper sitting on what was left of the pavement. Thought again of Sylvia telling her about the tiny foot and couldn't prevent one sob escaping. She clamped her hand over her mouth.

'Darling Rose, you don't have to do this,' Edward said, his hands coming up to rest on her shoulders, his fingers hard against her bones as if he was trying to pour his strength into her. 'You don't have to be so brave.'

'I don't think I'm being very brave.' She took a deep breath now. Remembered all the tiny kindnesses that Maggie had done her. All the mending, all those delicious things she'd miraculously produced from their tiny stove, all the good advice that she hadn't taken. This was her only chance to repay them. 'I'm ready.'

The woman approached the table and gingerly took a corner of the sheet between thumb and forefinger so she could slowly peel it back to show just half of Maggie's face.

There was her dark wavy hair, imperious nose, but her lips weren't curved into the tiny smile she usually wore, and her eye was taped shut. Rose crept nearer and just peeking beneath the edge of the sheet she saw something red and livid and raw that made her turn away so she could press her face against Edward's shirt. He felt warm and solid.

'Darling, is it Maggie?'

'Yes,' she mumbled against filthy khaki cotton. 'Can we go now?'

They retraced their steps, signed more forms, and only then were they were free to leave. To open the big double doors out onto a world that hurried by, quite unaware that something terrible had happened.

Rose clung to the railings that thronged the building. 'I feel as if I should be crying but I can't.'

'I don't think you have to cry if you don't feel like it,' Edward said. She still had his jacket around her shoulders and he fumbled in one of the pockets for his cigarette case and lighter. 'It's the shock. It can play funny tricks on one.'

'I should go to work now. Mrs Fisher is always telling me off for being late.' Rose took the cigarette that Edward proffered. 'I don't want to get the sack.'

But she didn't go to work. Instead they walked. To Regent's Park, past the zoo all boarded up, through the Rose Garden and around the lake.

She and Edward counted the sandbags as they walked past Broadcasting House, stared at the paltry goods on display along Oxford Street, then worked their way through Mayfair until they arrived at his building.

It was a mansion block overlooking Green Park. 'Very convenient to have Fortnum and Mason as my corner shop,' he joked heavily as Rose followed him up the marble stairs to his flat on the fourth floor. There was a lift but apparently it had been out of order for weeks.

Edward ushered her into the living room, which was quiet and uncluttered, apart from the crammed bookshelves and the art on the walls. Art that that didn't look like proper things like people or animals or landscapes.

Rose sat on a chesterfield, the tan leather worn in places because Edward was rich and the rich didn't seem to make such a fuss about things that were worn out, and watched him pour brandy into two tumblers.

'I don't much like brandy,' she said.

'You're in shock and you're going to drink it,' he said and he handed her the glass and sat down next to her.

Rose took a cautious sip. She supposed it was meant to taste warm and mellow but it was harsh in her mouth, though she liked the way she could feel it scorching a path down to her belly. 'Do you think it took a long time? Do you think they suffered? That they lay there, in pain and frightened, waiting for someone to come and help them?'

Edward moved his hand nearer to where hers rested on the seat but didn't touch her. 'I think it was instantaneous. That they were all asleep and never woke up.'

'*Was* it a faulty gas line though?' That was another thing worrying at her. 'If it was, why was the ARP warden there? Why was the place suddenly swarming with all those men in suits as we walked to the church hall?'

He shrugged helplessly. 'I don't know, Rose. I'm sure, whether it was a gas line explosion or something else, that they simply used the protocols already in place.'

She wasn't satisfied with that either. 'They shouldn't have even been there. We always go out dancing on Friday night after the Rainbow, always. They came home because it was my birthday today and I nagged Maggie about making me a birthday cake because we had enough sugar and eggs. What if it was the gas line? What if it was our oven? What if you hadn't asked me to dinner? What if—?'

'For God's sake, Rose.' Edward drained the contents of his glass in an angry swallow. 'You weren't there, they were. There is no rhyme or reason to it. Haven't you learned that by now?'

'I only agreed to have dinner with you because I wanted to go to The Ritz and to ask you to help me find Danny.' Rose didn't know why she was doing this. Just because she felt numb was no reason to make Edward furious enough for both of them. 'I was being selfish and spoiled. Worse, I've been rewarded for being selfish and spoiled because I'm sitting here drinking brandy and generally being alive and they're dead. Well, I don't call that fair!'

'Will you just *shut up*?' Edward sounded as if he were in agony. As if he'd lain there with the dead and dying and waited in vain for someone to rescue him but when Rose turned to him, to apologise, she saw the damp track of tears on his face and before she could say anything, he reached for her.

She never expected Edward to kiss her.

Never expected that she would kiss him back.

Finally she felt something: that she was truly alive and in a body that moved and twisted and turned underneath someone else because Edward was so greedy. He demanded everything that she possibly had left to give and Rose gave gladly.

She'd never felt like this when Danny had kissed her. This mad, unrestrained urge that made her kiss Edward with a messy, graceless mouth and slide her hands under his shirt so she could scrabble and scratch at his back, all that warm skin just begging for her touch.

It was lust. Carnal lust. Debased. Immoral. All those words that Rose had never really understood until now on Edward's sofa as she writhed and moaned and gasped as he did absolutely maddening things to her with his mouth and fingers that Danny had never done.

Then Edward was inside her, hands still working on her, kissing her until the only thing Rose knew for certain was that she'd never felt this wonderful before. That Edward, of all people, could make her come completely undone and she hadn't even slipped off her shoes or unhooked her dress. That should have been enough to make her feel terrible but it didn't, not until Edward suddenly gripped her wrists and came into her with one last ferocious thrust. 'I love you!' The words were wrenched out of him. 'How I love you!'

'Oh God! Get off of me!' She shoved at his immobile weight, pounded at the shoulders that she'd been clutching only moments before. 'Get off me!'

Edward reared back so suddenly that he landed on the floor with a thud and such a dumbfounded expression that it almost made Rose laugh. But there was nothing to laugh about when his seed was trickling down her thighs and her dress was rucked up to her hips and her friends were dead.

'Rose?' Edward was sitting on the floor and he'd been her ballast today, her sandbag, but now he looked just as lost as she was. She'd ripped the buttons off his shirt, they were scattered like loose change on the rug, and she could see the curve of his shoulder, the knobs of his collarbones, his skin so pale and vulnerable that it made her want to cry. 'I know my timing's terrible, worse than terrible, but you must know that I love you. I think I've loved you from the first moment I saw you.'

He was flushed from their exertions and Rose was sure that if she looked closely enough she'd see the blood rushing through his veins, his heart beating to keep the blood pumping. Unless your heart had been blown right out of you and picked up by an ambulance worker and stuffed in a wicker hamper.

Edward must have taken her silence for encouragement, though Rose couldn't imagine why. He cleared his throat and tried to smile. 'I know that right now you feel as if you might never be happy again, but you won't always feel that way.'

'I don't want to be happy,' she said. 'I have no right to be happy.'

'But you do and, if you let me, I'd like to try . . . I love you.'

Rose stood up so she could look down at Edward sitting on the floor, clumsy and diminished. 'Well, I don't love you,' she said. 'I could never love you.'

30

How could they have known when Jane and Leo flanked Rose on her slow, slow walk back to the house that it would be the last time she went outside?

The next day, Sunday, Rose was too tired to go to Lullington Bay. On Monday morning, she said that she'd go to the office after lunch but she didn't. Nor Tuesday either and so for the rest of the week, and the week after that, the office came to her. Fergus would pop round in the mornings for an hour and Leo would stop by after lunch with papers, plans, paint and tile samples and leave not with a series of instructions that had to be followed to the letter but with Rose saying, 'Just do what you think best, dear. Talk to Fergus if you're not sure.'

Each day brought a new development, a new symptom of decline that drew Rose's end ever closer: the first day she didn't come downstairs, the untouched breakfast tray, the call to Jane on the house phone to ask for help in shuffling from sofa to bathroom. George still came round for dinner and Rose would talk about Rainbow Corner but she was starting to repeat herself.

Yet, Rose was still unmistakably Rose. Still had all her marbles and could still change her will while she was of sound mind. Add a codicil that granted a favourable bequest to her troubled but much adored great-nephew. But Jane had other problems that were weighing far heavier on her.

She turned up at Charles's office at the end of the first week of December. He worked out of three interlinking rooms on the ground floor of a Georgian townhouse near the American Embassy, though this late on a Friday afternoon it was just Charles and his personal assistant, her understated beauty understated even further by heavy black-framed glasses and an unflatteringly tight updo.

Charles didn't run the kind of business that catered for walk-ins, but the woman didn't even ask if Jane had an appointment. She rang through to Charles, then showed Jane through the middle room stuffed full of filing cabinets and into his inner sanctum.

He didn't seem surprised by Jane's sudden visit. Why would he, when he knew enough to destroy her? With little effort, Charles could easily dismantle the shiny life Jane had built because it often seemed to her that it was held together by hair-spray, sugar-free chewing gum and oh yes, a web of lies. Instead he simply said, 'Hello. I was hoping we might see each other again.'

He walked around his desk and gestured at one of two black leather club chairs. Asked Jane if she wanted something to drink. Then they sat and had a perfectly friendly conversation about Rose and about the bloody weather again and all the time Charles looked at her with sad eyes and Jane was sure that only under extreme interrogation, maybe even waterboarding, would he admit how he really felt about her. Even then he'd say something so typically Charles-like: 'I could never be angry with you. I'm just a little disappointed.'

She couldn't put it off any longer. 'I came here because I need to talk to you.'

Jane's hands were sweating, so she tucked them against her sides. She'd never apologised to anyone before. But then, she'd never stuck around long enough to say sorry. Once her crimes had been discovered, she was already gone. Anyway, an apology was really an admission of guilt and Jane had nothing to feel guilty about – that was what she'd always told herself. The decisions she made, the havoc she sometimes wrought on other people, were beyond her control.

And in some ways they were. Every punch, every slap, every kick, every other ...... cruelty that had been inflicted on her had made her what she was, but Charles had been her salvation. He'd all but killed her with kindness and Jane had let herself conveniently forget that, but being back in London had brought constant reminders of him, of how she'd hurt him when he hadn't deserved to be hurt. So, for some reason that she couldn't, wouldn't, analyse, she wanted, no, *needed* to make amends with Charles.

Jane took a steadying breath. 'I wanted to tell you that when I left ... before I left, I should have ... ' God, it was hard, but Charles was already shaking his head.

'We don't have to do this, you and I,' he said softly but firmly and Jane should have been relieved – that his part of her slate was wiped clean. But she could feel panic rising up in her.

'We do. I do. I never thanked you for saving my life, because that's what you did.' Her words were pitched so low, throat throbbing and prickling as if the tears weren't far off.

Charles got up from his chair to kneel at her feet and asked, 'May I?'

Jane held out her hands and Charles took them and Jane wondered what might have happened, how different her life might have been, if she'd have let Charles take her hands all those years ago. Now she clung to his touch, his never-wavering touch. Lowered her head because she couldn't bear to look at him, to see anything even approaching pity in his eyes, then she felt his lips ghost against her knuckles so briefly that she might even have simply imagined it.

'I don't deserve that much credit,' Charles said, after Jane had freed herself and he was sitting in his chair, their hands by their sides again. 'When you got on that train you saved your own life and Jane, I think you must have realised, long before I did, that once you were saved we couldn't carry on as we were.'

They'd carried on as they were for two years, Charles still trying to mould her, to shape her life along the narrow lines of his own ordered existence, so who could blame her for starting to resist? To chafe against the bit? She liked Charles. Maybe in her own broken way, she'd even tried to love him, but that didn't mean she had to stay with him.

Rafe was young and handsome in a slick, Eurotrashy sort of way and he'd looked at Jane like he couldn't even believe that he was lucky enough to breathe the same air as her.

They'd met over the garden fence. Rafe had friends who lived next door and made Charles as angry as Jane had ever seen him with their raucous parties that went on all night and their guests who would never speak but roar in loud confident voices and throw up in the street. But Rafe wasn't like that. He was quiet, adoring and very persistent. And his parents were very, very rich. They'd even paid Jane off with a flat in Primrose Hill when it looked like she was going to become a permanent fixture, but that was a year further down the line.

To start with, it had been a whirlwind courtship conducted during daylight hours when Charles was at work and Jane was left to her own devices; Charles probably thought that she was arranging flowers and looking for recipes and all the other little tasks that made up her continued quest for self-improvement. Instead she was taken to Cowdray Park to sip champagne and watch Rafe play polo. Flown to Paris for lunch. Bought her first diamond. And all she had to do in return was thank Rafe with a kiss that meant more to him than the diamond did to her.

Leaving Charles wasn't a decision Jane had taken lightly, but she'd taken it all the same. She had form and at least this time she left a note in the unformed, ugly scrawl that was one of the few things she couldn't improve on. *Thanks for all that you did*, the note had said. Maybe she should have enlarged on that theme, spun it out over several sheets of Charles's finest linen bond paper, but it still came down to those six words to encompass how he'd saved her.

'I'm sorry about how I left. I want you to know that.' And she'd said it now and she couldn't believe it was that easy. Maybe she'd start saying sorry more often now.

'You left on a Friday,' Charles said, his gaze fixed somewhere beyond Jane. 'It was June. It was so sunny, hot, and you'd mentioned getting out of London, that you'd only seen the sea once. I'd left work early, booked two rooms at a place in Brighton and thought that we might drive down there that evening. As soon as I opened the door, before I even saw your note, I knew you'd gone.'

It turned out that it wasn't that easy. It wasn't easy at all. 'Charles, please . . . '

'We couldn't have carried on as we were, but were you not happy? Was it something I did? Something I said? Did I give you a reason not to trust me?' Charles still wouldn't look at her and his tone, his endless unbearable questions weren't relentless, but resigned, rehearsed as if he'd lain awake reliving the moment when he'd come home to find her gone. And still he continued. 'What was so special about that boy – because I did know about him, you weren't as good at covering your tracks as you thought you were. Two years we spent together and then you left me six words on a piece of paper, Jane. I thought I was worth more than that.'

Jane covered her face with her icy cold hands. 'I can't help what I am, Charles. I did a bad thing to you, I know, but that doesn't make me a bad person.'

'That's an excuse, it's not a reason,' Charles said gently and it was that gentleness that threatened to break her, make the sobs rise up.

Six words weren't enough. Sorry wasn't enough. She owed him some kind of explanation. 'You see, with you, I wasn't scared any more but I still didn't feel safe,' Jane said haltingly. 'I still felt as if the world could crash down on top of me at any second and I thought that if I had money, if I was with someone who had lots of money, more money than you, then it would cushion the blow. Money gives you security. It makes you bombproof, I've always thought that, though lately I wonder how true that is.'

'Nobody is bombproof,' Charles said. 'Everyone can be hurt no matter how much money they have.'

'And I hurt you and I am so very sorry, Charles ... I don't what else to say but sorry. Don't know how to make that word mean everything it should.' She was starting to sound pleading, tearful. 'You have to believe me.'

'I do. It's all right. Apology accepted,' Charles said hurriedly as if he couldn't stand to hear another word, but Jane wasn't done. She'd come this far and now she had no choice but to doggedly trudge on.

'There's something else. The first night ... you must have wondered ... I mean I had blood on me ... my clothes, my hands and you never even ... you didn't ... ' It was an ungainly rush of words vomiting out of her, both of them in disbelief that she was saying this. Going there.

'Jane, please stop now,' Charles whispered. 'I can't do this.'

'But I have to.' She hardly recognised her own voice, the manic, desperate, *lost* cadence to it. 'Because I also wondered about you. When you gave me the knife that first night and you told me to sleep with it so I'd feel safe. I need to know what happened to you.'

'I can't. You can't expect me to . . . '

'But . . . '

'I'm not brave like you. Please, Jane, if you ever cared anything for me, you will drop this.'

Jane held out her hands towards him, imploringly, but Charles shook his head and his face, his kind, gentle face, was on the brink of collapse, so she dropped it.

'You're right,' she said. 'Let's not do this any more.'

Charles nodded. He crossed one knee over the other, found a smile.

'So, Rose was telling me that you've been helping her go through her attics and that you found a whole collection of taxidermy that she has absolutely no memory of buying.'

They had another perfectly lovely chat, though that made Jane want to cry too, then Charles walked her out. 'By the way,' he said, just before she left, one foot already over the threshold. 'I liked your Leo. I liked him a lot.'

It was raining outside. Pouring. Heavy and biblical. Jane didn't have an umbrella. Didn't want to take a taxi. She felt . . . didn't even know how she felt, but as she walked she wondered if she was crying or if it was just the rain on her face. By the time she reached Kensington, she'd decided that there was no point in feeling guilty any more. It was easy when your feelings didn't run that deep in the first place. She couldn't help that there was something missing, something in her internal wiring not properly connected. Not her fault at all.

As soon as she opened the front door, Jane could tell that something was wrong. The house could speak volumes and it was silently screaming at her.

Jane took the stairs two at a time. Once she was past the first floor, she could hear a raspy sort of shouting, which got louder as she ran up the last flight of stairs and down the corridor to Rose's sitting room.

Lydia, Agnieska, one of the agency nurses who came to give Rose her injection, and Leo, with a stricken look on his face, were standing there as Rose shouted at him.

'It's you! You've done this to me! I was fine until you came back. Why did you come back?'

'Rose, you know why I came back.' He choked on every word. 'Because I care about you.'

'You care about my money. Well, you're not getting a penny!'

Rose was locked in a grotesque, hunched crouch as she tried to lift herself off the sofa. But worse was the look on her face. Like a terrified, cornered animal, wild and yet caged.

Jane had to say something to stop Rose looking like that. 'That's not true, darling. Leo's here because he wanted to make things right with you.'

Rose turned accusing eyes on Jane standing in the doorway. 'You! Who *are* you? The two of you are in cahoots with each other. You're trying to finish me off. You're poisoning me!'

And for the finale she struggled to her feet, and then crumpled with a startled cry, ending up on her knees as they all rushed forwards.

It felt like a long time before Agnieska had finished checking over a now compliant, placid Rose, no bones broken, no harm done, except for Rose's panting breaths.

Rose suddenly sank back and for one heart-skipping moment Jane thought that she'd gone. Then her eyes opened. 'I hate you all,' she said petulantly. 'Leave me alone. Get out!'

'Enough, Rose,' Lydia said calmly. 'You don't hate us and no one is here to hurt you.'

'I'm all alone.' Rose's voice quavered. 'I don't have a friend left in the world.'

'Don't be silly, Rose.' Jane didn't know how Lydia could sound so steady. 'I'll make some cocoa, and sit with you while you drink it. Shall we do that?'

Rose nodded meekly and Agnieska said she'd stay and get Rose into bed.

'Come with me, you two.' Lydia bustled Leo and Jane out of the room. They followed her down the stairs and through to the kitchen.

Leo sniffed and rubbed the back of his hands across his eyes. 'I came back because you asked me,' he said as if Lydia needed convincing too. 'I couldn't leave things as they were between us. Haven't I done enough now to prove that to you?'

'I know that and she knows that too,' Lydia said as she turned to put the kettle on. 'I expect it's the drugs and whatnot, but she's not good. Not good at all. I don't know how much longer we can go on like this.'

'But she's been steady these last two weeks,' Jane ventured. 'Now that she's not going to the office and rushing all over London.'

'Yeah, she's been a bit more like her old self,' Leo added and he shot Jane a grateful smile and she tried to smile back but her face wouldn't work.

Lydia turned round, her expression resolute. 'I have to call your mother, Leo. Rose is adamant that she doesn't want her to come down but she has to know.'

'Um, should I? Do you want me to call her?' he asked uncertainly as if he was volunteering for open-heart surgery without any anaesthetic because he didn't want to cause a fuss.

'I'll do it,' Lydia said and she stroked her hand down Leo's cheek. In that moment, Jane supposed that she really had forgiven him. 'I want you to go to Lullington Bay and fetch some of Rose's things. We wrote out a list the other day.'

'Yeah, of course. Tomorrow.' Leo looked through the open door. 'I'll do it tomorrow.'

'No, do it now. Take Jane with you.' Lydia started rooting in the drawer next to her and eventually pulled out a set of car keys. 'You can take my little Nissan.' Then she opened her kitchen diary and took out a piece of paper. 'I think everything's in a trunk in her bedroom. Call me if you have any trouble.'

'But we can't go now. It's late,' Leo protested.

'It's not even six-thirty.' She thrust a piece of paper at Jane who had no choice but to take it. 'You should be there and back in four hours.'

Jane tugged on Leo's sleeve because he didn't seem inclined to move. 'But you will call us if, you know . . . '

'Of course I will. Well, don't just stand there. Go!'

They went.

31

London 1944–1945

Although it was against the rules, when Rose turned up at Rainbow Corner late that Saturday afternoon after she'd left Edward's flat, shell-shocked and shaking, the other girls made a cosy den for her in the Where Am I? room. Rose stayed there for three days, which passed in a blur of staring at the walls, endless cups of tea and people popping in to tell Rose how sorry they were.

She was also visited there by one of the grandest of the American Red Cross ladies, whose sister was married to someone very high up at the War Office, almost as high as Winston Churchill himself. The woman sat on the bed next to Rose, took her hand and whispered in Rose's ear that it hadn't been a gas line explosion but a bomb like nothing anyone had seen before. A V2, Hitler's 'vengeance rocket', his secret weapon, which had always been something of a national joke as they'd all speculated on what old Adolf would pull out for his final act.

Soon the room was needed again for GIs who were too inebriated to make it to their billets and Rose moved into the house in Kensington. She slept in a back bedroom on one of the camp beds donated by Phyllis, which smelt of paraffin wax. It was there that the items salvaged from Montague Terrace were delivered. 'You're a very lucky girl,' a man from the Civil Defence Squad said as the wardrobe and drawers were hefted up the stairs. 'Still got most of your clothes in here. That's more than a lot of people have, you know.'

Sylvia's crocodile skin attaché case had also been saved, and wrapped in a torn, dirty sheet, torn and dirty itself, was Shirley's limp blue taffeta dress. It had been hanging on the back of the bedroom door and had stayed there even when the door was blown into a back garden three streets away.

Shirley's pale blue taffeta might well outlive them all, Rose thought, and it was oddly comforting to walk around in her dead friends' clothes. Still having part of them, even if it was just things, meant Rose had something to pass on to the people who were left behind.

After Maggie's funeral, her émigré friends invited Rose to the wake in a tiny basement bar in Bayswater. Rose sat and drank vodka with them and they told her what little they knew about Maggie. She'd studied art at the Prague School; her father had taught philosophy at the university. When Hitler had invaded the Sudetenland in 1938, Maggie had dyed her hair blonde and got to Paris on false papers. She'd run far and fast from the Nazis but they'd still got her in the end.

There was a redheaded woman who'd known Maggie in Prague and had worked with her at the BBC who didn't say a word while everyone else talked about Maggie. But when Rose gave her Maggie's beaten copper wrist cuff and the handkerchief she'd embroidered, though Rose really wanted to keep them for herself, the woman kissed Rose on the lips, then stood up and walked away.

Next was Sylvia's funeral. Sylvia's people were from Hoxton, where Mickey Flynn said even he wouldn't go after dark. Rose knew Sylvia wasn't top drawer. She'd mentioned a kindly uncle 'who lifted me out of the gutter as kindly uncles are wont to do' but that was with a wink and a nudge so Rose had decided that, strictly speaking, he hadn't been an uncle at all.

What was left of Sylvia was put in a mahogany coffin and carried by a horse-drawn hearse, black feather plumes dancing in the breeze. Propped up against the coffin was a floral tribute, *RIP Our Syl*, spelt out in white chrysanthemums. It was the flowers that nearly did for Rose but Sylvia wouldn't have wanted her to cry. 'Chin up, darling,' she'd have said. 'What a waste of mascara.'

There was nothing special about a funeral procession, not these days, but as they made painfully slow progress along the New North Road towards the church, people stopped, took off their hats and bowed their heads as Sylvia passed.

'She'd have got a kick out of this,' Rose said to Mickey but he said that Sylvia would have much preferred to have her ashes scattered over the dancefloor of the Embassy Club than buried in the graveyard of St John the Baptist church.

The wake was at the George and Vulture on Pitfield Street. Rose and Mickey sat in the corner surrounded by a press of people all having a whale of a time, until the crowd suddenly parted to let through a middle-aged man and woman. The man had a big red angry face and had taken off his jacket and rolled up his shirtsleeves to show meaty forearms covered in crude tattoos. By contrast, his wife was so thin that her shoulders looked like coat hangers in her black dress,

'You knew our girl? Our Syl?' the man demanded and Rose wanted to shrink back but Mickey gave her hand a warning squeeze and she nodded.

'Yes.' She couldn't make her voice any louder than a whisper. 'She was . . . I . . . ' It was impossible to sum up what Sylvia, lovely, lithe, larger-than-life Sylvia, had meant to her. 'She was my friend. My very dear friend.'

Rose was hauled out of her chair and paraded around the

room. Introduced to uncles and aunts and cousins and friends of the family as 'one of our Syl's friends from Up West.' They all shook her hand and a woman even bobbed as if Rose were one of the young princesses. But when Rose gave Sylvia's parents their daughter's gold locket and powder compact, her mother made an awful noise, a keening, that made all the hairs on the back of Rose's neck stand up. Mrs Crapper suddenly clasped her hand over her heart and was then swallowed up by a gaggle of female relatives who spirited her away and Rose was left with her husband, who looked even bigger and redder and angrier.

'I'm sorry,' she said in the same hoarse whisper. 'I just thought you might like to have them. I didn't mean . . . '

His face suddenly crumpled like a paper bag crushed in a careless fist. 'Syl, she always said you were like a little sister to her.' Tears streamed down his bulbous cheeks. Rose watched aghast, tears spilling unchecked down her own face too, as the huge brute of a man was brought to his knees. He went down hard and when Rose crouched down to make sure he was all right, he seized her hand in a punishing grip. 'You're family now,' he said as if he dared Rose to defy him. 'If you ever need anything . . . anything. You get yourself down to Hoxton and ask for Henry Crapper.'

There was only Phyllis's funeral left but Rose wasn't allowed the time off work. 'We're sorry about your friends, of course we are, but it's not like they were family,' Mrs Fisher told her. 'Besides, there's nothing like a bit of hard work to take your mind off things.'

The day before the funeral, as arranged, Lady Carfax walked into the café as if she were walking into Claridge's. She sat at a table surrounded by market traders and office workers and sipped tea from a chipped mug as she waited for Rose to finish washing up.

Rose would never have expected Lady Carfax to take hold of

her reddened hands and not let go. It seemed entire lifetimes ago that she'd gone down to Norfolk with Phyllis and Lady Carfax had been an austere chilly presence looking down her patrician nose at Rose. Now she'd aged ten years in the preceding months.

'The last time you saw her, was she happy?' she asked.

Rose thought of Phyllis standing outside Rainbow Corner with Maggie and Sylvia, waving Rose off with her wide, toothy smile.

'She was very happy,' she said as fervently as she could. 'And they said . . . that . . . she . . . they wouldn't have . . . they were asleep when the bomb went off. They wouldn't have woken up. Wouldn't have felt a thing.'

Rose had to believe that death had been swift and merciful.

She hadn't been able to find anything of Phyllis's so Rose gave Lady Carfax the little gold and pearl brooch her parents had given her for her sixteenth birthday. She'd never found it quite so hard to lie before. 'Phyllis always wore this,' she said. 'She'd want you to have it.'

'You expect to lose your sons in a war,' Lady Carfax said heavily. 'That would have been easier, I think. But not Phyllis. Not my little girl.'

Then she'd left to accompany her little girl's broken body back home so she could be buried in the family plot in the local churchyard.

There was just one more visitor. Mr Winthrop surprised Rose late the next afternoon as she was putting chairs on tables so she could mop the floor and though Mrs Fisher sighed and muttered about docking Rose's pay, she let her leave early so she could take her father to the Lyons on Tottenham Court Road.

'Enough now, Rosemary,' he'd said sharply after they'd had a pot of tea and two scones and she'd refused all his entreaties. 'Enough of this nonsense. You're coming back to Durham with me. You'll be safer there.'

Safe didn't mean anything any more.

Rose doubted that their ghosts would follow her back to Durham so she had to stay in London and walk down the streets she'd walked with her girls. Eat in the same cafés, dance in the same clubs. Keep them close, otherwise she'd lose sight of them.

'Daddy, you have to accept that I'm staying here,' she said, as she'd been saying for the last hour. She didn't belong in Durham any more than her father belonged in London with his country tweed suit and his country manners. 'There are people here who need me.'

'I'm not sure that Mother will let me in if I come home without you,' he said. Then he held Rose for a count of three and kissed her forehead as he'd used to do when she was little before he hurried off to catch his train.

But London wasn't just home to her ghosts; it was home to Rainbow Corner. Rose sleepwalked her way through each day as if she were only pretending to live. Oh, she brushed her hair and teeth, washed up and took orders, ate breakfast, lunch and dinner and all the time it was as if she were playing a part. But for three hours every night, on the dancefloor at Rainbow Corner, she could almost find her way back to the silly, careless girl she'd once been. Could feel something other than the sadness that coated her bones and encased her heart.

There was another way to feel something, though.

On the nights when Rose left Rainbow Corner and knew that she wouldn't be able to sleep, her feet would carry her to Mayfair. To Edward's flat.

Of course they'd seen each other often since that terrible night and the terrible day that followed. She was living in one of his houses after all and he'd been one of the silent mourners when they'd buried Maggie and Sylvia. Edward had even caught the bus back with her and Mickey Flynn after Sylvia's wake when

Rose hadn't been able to say a word because she knew that if she opened her mouth, she'd choke on her tears.

Mickey had got off the bus at Piccadilly Circus but Edward and Rose had continued on to Kensington. They hadn't been alone together since the afternoon in his flat and it should have been terribly awkward, but somehow it wasn't.

Edward was far too much of a gentleman to even mention it, but despite what had happened, Rose was still comforted and calmed by his presence. In a peculiar sort of a way, she supposed that she did love him. No, not love, but she was incredibly fond of him.

'It's not that I don't love you,' she'd suddenly blurted out right there on the top deck of the number nine bus. 'It's just I can't. Not any more. Everyone I love gets taken away from me so it's probably for the best if I don't love anyone.'

'Rose … ' Edward had said and he didn't sound the least bit angry with her. 'Oh, Rose, what am I to do with you?'

'You can be my friend,' Rose had told him. It wasn't the right word but it would have to do. 'You really are the best man I know and I couldn't bear it if we weren't friends.'

They didn't speak for the rest of the journey but Edward had taken Rose's hand and she was glad of it.

But on the nights that she went to his flat in Mayfair, it wasn't to speak, but to feel. Rose knew that it was wrong to be happy for those hours when he took her to his bed, but she couldn't do without it. She did everything that he asked of her: to touch him, take him in her mouth, to kneel on his bedroom rug on her hands and knees so he could have her like that and she did it all, because everything he did to her felt so good.

Then afterwards, they would barely talk but held hands again as Edward walked Rose all the way back to Kensington. He'd see her to the front door, tip his hat then disappear into the shadows of the dim-out.

32

It took a long time to get out of London. Leo hadn't had to negotiate the snarly rush hour in years and Jane couldn't fathom out the SatNav so kept stabbing at random buttons until Leo snapped at her to stop. Then she snapped at Leo for snapping at her.

When they finally made it onto the motorway, they were immediately stuck in traffic. Jane sighed then twisted round to look out of the back window as if she expected to see Lydia in a car behind frantically signalling them to turn round.

Leo wished that he still smoked. And he wished for the hundredth time that he'd stayed down and out in Las Vegas. He might have hated himself when he got the call to say that Rose had gone, but at least he wouldn't have had to listen when she . . .

'Leo, Rose didn't mean what she said.' Jane's hand covered his where it rested on the gear stick. 'She's in a lot of pain and she's all muddled up with the drugs.'

He took a steadying breath. 'I shouldn't have come back.'

Jane tightened her grip on his hand, even as he indicated, then changed lanes. 'Yes, you should have. There's no question about it.'

'I don't see that I've been much use.' He hated when he got like this, elbow-deep inside himself. Usually the only way out was to get lost. 'I don't get absolved of my sins just because I've spent a few weeks plastering and painting old houses.'

'You've done a lot more than that,' Jane said. 'You've listened to her stories and you've made her laugh. She's been able to rely on you, lean on you.' She tightened her fingers again. 'Leo, you must realise that Rose adores you. She doesn't do a very good job of hiding it.'

Leo looked over at Jane. Her hair was loose and hanging in sodden rats' tails. She must have been out in the rain for hours. She looked anxious, especially when they talked about Rose, but she seemed softer too. She was still beautiful, but he'd got used to that. 'While we're on the subject, Rose likes you too.'

'Well . . . maybe.' Jane plucked at her seatbelt. 'Mostly I've stayed for Lydia's cooking. I'm surprised I can still do this up.'

'Stop fishing. You know you're hot, even with a few extra kilos,' Leo told her, because she was and his mood lightened as she hissed and took her hand off his so she could punch him lightly on the arm.

'Not *kilos*. Maybe a couple of pounds. Is a pound more than a kilo? I can never remember.' She was able to pull a face now. 'Two pounds to a kilo, right?'

'Yeah, give or take.' The atmosphere had shifted along with the traffic, which was now moving slowly but steadily. Leo missed the feel of Jane's hand resting on his.

'Have you thought about what you're going to do when this is all over?' she asked. 'Will you go back to the States?'

'I don't know,' he said, because it was something that he tried not to think about. When this was all over it meant that Rose would be gone. Besides, in a strange sort of way, he was enjoying this limbo. He'd left his bad habits behind and, so far, he'd managed not acquire any new ones. 'I've never been big on forward planning. What about you? Do you think that there's even an outside chance that you might get back with Mr Ex?'

Jane shook her head just the once. 'Oh God, no. That ship has well and truly sailed.' Leo thought that he might have veered into dangerous territory, but then she smiled. 'You know, I wish I had gone back to him sometimes. It would have been simpler. Less confusing.'

'You didn't love him? Not really, did you?'

Jane glanced over at him, her expression ancient and unfathomable. 'No, of course I didn't.' She suddenly grinned, all teeth and gums. 'God, being stuck in this car is like being trapped in a Confessional.'

Leo wanted to ask Jane if she'd ever been in love, but deep down he already knew the answer. So many things he wanted to ask her, to tell her, but it was best to stay silent. They'd cleared the motorway now, driving along unlit country lanes and though Leo had thought they'd be hopelessly lost, he realised that he knew the way. He'd always know the way to Lullington Bay.

He saw the narrow turning just in time and swung right. All he had to do was say 'Lullington Bay' in his head and in the time it took there was another turning, the trees parted and he could see the shadowy outline of the house.

'So, talking of love lost and all that, who did Rose end up with after the war?' Jane said. 'Was it Danny, who I have to say sounds like a wrong 'un, or . . . '

'I'll tell you later,' Leo promised. The rumble of the tyres on the gravel drive sounded like coming home. He remembered falling off his bike after attempting a wheelie and landing face-down on the same gravel and Rose and his mother picking tiny pieces of it from his skin with tweezers, promising him an ice cream if he managed not to cry. 'This is Lullington Bay.'

He wished that they were here on a summer's day when the

sun shone down on the sandstone and glinted off the gabled roof. The house stood high on the cliffs, which undulated gently down to sand dunes they'd raced across to get to the beach. It had always felt as if the sea was taunting them as they made the trek from the house laden with towels, picnic baskets, buckets and spades, his mother yelling at Leo to slow down before he broke his neck.

They got out of the car and crunched towards the front door. 'I thought it was a cottage.' Jane sounded a little put out. 'I didn't think it would be this big.'

'It was the old manor house but it burned down in the nineteen-hundreds so they rebuilt it in the Arts and Crafts style,' Leo told her. 'Caused a hell of a row at the time. Come on, we'll go round the back.'

There were light sensors that snapped on every few metres and the familiar shapes of the garden came into view. The rose bushes, a new one planted each year; the vegetable patch; the herb garden by the back door, covered in netting to protect it from the neighbourhood cats; and the patio with the wrought iron table and chairs where they used to eat their meals when they weren't on the beach.

'We spent every summer here.' It didn't even matter whether Jane was listening, he just wanted to say the words out loud, make the hazy memories a little brighter, a little more defined. 'It's such a sad cliché, isn't it? To say that the summers were longer when we were kids but it felt that way. Our aunts, uncles and all our cousins would come down too so there was always a huge gang of us. Sometimes we'd walk along the shoreline until we came to a little kiosk that sold ice cream with real honeycomb studded through it and we'd round up the kids from the village to come back to our beach so we could play hide and seek in the dunes. I used to live for the summer holidays.'

'My summer holidays weren't really like that,' Jane offered, though she didn't say what her summer holidays had been like. 'Sounds nice, though.'

'Yeah, like something out of Enid Blyton,' Leo said with a sneer to counteract the dreamy tone that had crept into his voice.

'Never really had much time for Enid Blyton either,' Jane said and Leo found it impossible to imagine what she'd been like as a child. 'So, did you ever learn how to jimmy a window during your endless summers here or have you got a key?'

There was no full-time staff at the house, but lodgers; Victoria and Katy, who taught English at the University of Sussex. The house was in darkness so they were obviously out playing bridge or attending a reading of Virginia Woolf's *Selected Works* in nearby Alfriston or whatever it was that English professors of a certain age did at gone eight on a Friday night.

There was always a key hidden in the little wooden house on top of the bird table and the alarm code was his grandparents' old telephone number but it still felt like they were intruding as Leo turned on lights and led Jane through the kitchen and down the hall. The parquet floor and the panelled walls gleamed dully and Leo could still smell beeswax and the faintest lingering trace of the perfume Rose wore, though Lydia said that Rose had hardly come down at all this past summer.

'It has that lived-in feeling, not at all like the place in Kensington,' Jane said, running her hand along the carved banister as they walked up the stairs. 'This, this . . . feels like home.'

'Rose used to spend most of her time down here. Ages ago. Before I was born.'

'Oh? Why did she move back to London?' Jane asked and the answer wasn't a happy one but before he could tell her, he felt his phone vibrate.

It was Lydia. As stoic and as calm as she'd been when he was going to pieces in front of her, over the phone now her voice was stilted like she was holding back tears. Dr Howard had been over and was adamant that Rose should be on a morphine pump and Rose hadn't even argued. 'I'm expecting him back any moment now. He was quite shocked at how much she'd deteriorated from when he saw her this morning. Anyway, how are you getting on? Have you found everything? What do you mean, you've only just got there? Let me speak to Jane.'

While Jane spoke to Lydia, he guided her up the stairs towards Rose's room where you could look out of the windows at the big blue outside where sky met sea. When he was little, he'd lie here with Rose in the early evening when it was still too light outside to sleep and she'd read to him. And when he still refused to go to sleep, they'd stare out at the horizon with her big binoculars to see if they could spot any pirate ships.

She wasn't even dead yet but he could already feel her ghost in this house.

'I'll just see if it's in there.' He was standing idle in the middle of the room as Jane, still on the phone, walked over to the big walnut wardrobe and unlocked the door. Another intrusion. She clamped the phone between shoulder and ear as she began to move the hangers to one side, stopping to unzip garment bags. Then she stiffened and Leo felt the answering shiver trip down his spine. 'I've found it. I'll get the trunk and we'll head back.'

Leo could see Jane's shoulders shake; she raised a hand to touch her face. Then she took down the garment bag and when she turned round her face was bright, blank.

'There's a trunk under the bed. Cream with black leather straps, Rose's initials stamped on it,' she told him and Leo obediently dropped to his knees, peered under the bed and hauled it out.

'What's in the bag?' he asked.

‘A dress.’ Jane stared at her feet. Her shoulders shook again. ‘A limp, pale blue taffeta dress.’

Her voice cracked a little and she stood with head bowed for a few moments until she could raise her head and give Leo another one of those glittering, empty smiles that promised everything and delivered absolutely nothing.

‘Are you all right?’

‘I’m fine. Are *you* all right?’

‘No, not really.’

Jane nodded. ‘Lydia says everything else is in the trunk. We don’t need to open it. Let’s just go.’

It was a small trunk but it needed both of them to push and tug it carefully down the stairs. It *had* seemed small but it was too big to get in the boot of Lydia’s little car and in the end they managed to get it on the back seat, but only by pushing the front seats so far forward that they had to drive back to London with their knees almost touching their chins.

When they got back to Kensington, Rose was still asleep. Agnieska was sitting by her bed and knitting. ‘I’m staying the night. Miss Beaumont is fine. Didn’t even wake when I took her blood pressure.’ She nodded approvingly. ‘The sleep will do her good.’

‘It’s not like a good night’s sleep is going to suddenly cure her cancer,’ Leo grumbled as they reached their rooms. ‘Maybe I should sit up with her.’

‘Maybe you shouldn’t,’ Jane said because he looked ashen with exhaustion. ‘Not tonight. Who knows what tomorrow might bring?’

Leo traced a pattern on the floor with his toe. ‘We should try and get some sleep, then.’

He just stood there, not moving, until Jane pulled him into the room and shut the door. All of Leo’s newfound assurance had vanished and he looked . . . untethered. It really had been such a horrible day. 'I'm not even a little bit tired.' she said. 'Would you mind if we stayed up and chatted for a little bit . . . if you want to, that is?'

'You mean, what the young people call hanging out?' Leo sat down on the bed and toed off his sneakers. 'Sometimes I think you learned to speak in the early nineteen-hundreds.'

He was scowling again, which was hardly surprising.

'Shall I tell you a secret? It's guaranteed to cheer you up.' Jane didn't mean *that* kind of secret but Leo obviously thought she did because he nodded, his sudden smile a millimetre away from a leer.

'Yeah, go on then. Give it your best shot.'

Jane struck a pose; hand on hip, leg bent. 'In Hertford, Hereford and Hampshire, hurricanes hardly ever happen.'

Leo looked at her as if she was talking in tongues. 'What?'

'The rain in Spain stays mainly on the plain,' she elaborated and when Leo shook his head and gave her a tiny, amused, almost pitying smile like he thought she'd completely lost the plot, she threw up her hands in exasperation. 'Audrey Hepburn, darling! *My Fair Lady*, which I must have seen at least fifty times,' Jane went into the bathroom. 'That's how I learned to speak proper.'

'Really? How did you speak before then?'

'Improperly. Mostly through a series of grunts and hand gestures.'

Leo laughed, even though not a word of it was a lie. 'I bet your first words were a beautifully constructed sentence in perfect RP.'

Jane was already taking off her make-up but she made sure to meet his gaze as he leaned against the doorjamb so she could arch an eyebrow at him. She hadn't been able to do *that* in a long, long time. She was too scared to subject the delicate skin around her mouth and eyes to anyone but the man she saw in

New York who did her fillers and injectables. Maybe, as the feeling returned to her face, it would make her feel other things that she'd hidden away for so long that she thought they were truly dead and buried. 'Hardly, darling.' She managed to sound as artless and artful as ever.

'Haven't we moved past that whole "darling" crap?' Leo edged into the bathroom, closed the lid on the loo and sat down. 'You called me Leo in the car. Don't even try to deny it.'

'So I did.' Jane concentrated on easing off every last scrap of make-up. Maybe it was the hours spent listening to Rose tell her stories, take stock of her life, pulling and picking at the threads, tracing them back to that first stitch. Or seeing Charles again, which had upset her, unsettled her, made her remember too much, but Jane wanted to tell someone her stories too. But there would be consequences . . .

'Leo,' she said deliberately, lingering over the two syllables. 'Tell me more about the summers at Lullington Bay.'

'What shall I tell you?' he asked.

'Everything,' Jane said.

So Leo told her about being allowed to stay up late and lighting bonfires on the beach and toasting marshmallows while Rose told them stories about America. Of drive-ins and cowboys and driving out to the desert to watch rockets fly into space and a hundred other things that she knew would enthral two little boys.

While Jane's face was soaking in cream from a pot of magical ingredients that cost over a hundred pounds, they sat cross-legged on the bed and he told her how he'd lie on the floor of the sitting room at Lullington Bay with Rose's art books spread out before him and copy the pictures while Rose looked on approvingly. That she hadn't been quite so approving when he got older and would get drunk on cider with the lads from the village and then slope off with one of their sisters to the little lane behind the pub.

'She didn't say much but you know what Rose is like. She can say plenty with just one look,' Leo said and he pursed his lips, flared his nostrils and narrowed his eyes but still didn't come close to approximating Rose's disapproval. 'She'd leave condoms under my pillow. They had to be from Rose. No way were they from my mum.'

'No, I can't imagine your mother going into a chemist to ask for a packet of Durex's finest,' Jane said. The thought of Linda, handbag clutched tightly in front of her, looking furtively about to make sure that none of the Rotary Club wives had spotted her, made Jane giggle and then she noticed that Leo wasn't laughing along. 'Oh, darling ... Leo, don't. Please don't.'

He was crying. Jane hated seeing people cry. Depending on the person, she could be sympathetic, stroking their hair and cooing platitudes, but now when she reached out a hand to gently touch Leo's shorn head, it was different. Leo was different. Oh God, *she* was different. How had that happened?

'You have all these happy memories of Rose,' she told him softly. 'That's a lot more than some people have.'

He didn't say anything but covered his face with his hands as he must have done when he was a little boy who liked to look for pirate ships and stay up late to toast marshmallows.

It was pure instinct to raise herself up on her knees and shuffle closer so she could put her arms around him, kiss the top of his bent head. 'Please don't cry, Leo. You'll start me off too.'

He mumbled something but it was unintelligible through the sobs he was failing to hold back.

'Come on. You have to stay strong for a little longer,' she said and he took a couple of deep breaths and when he raised his head, Jane wished he hadn't because he didn't even bother to try to hide his vulnerability.

'I'm going to miss her,' he whispered. 'I wish I'd become

someone she could be proud of instead of wasting all these years fucking about. She had all this faith in me and I blew it.'

'That doesn't matter. You've shown Rose who you could be and now you owe it to her to become that person.'

Jane was still holding him, foreheads almost touching. It felt very intimate, comforting someone. Not entirely unpleasant either.

'It's not that easy to become someone else, though, is it?' Leo said quietly.

Jane couldn't help but smile. 'Oh, it's much easier than you think,' she said. At that moment she was simply desperate to tell him her story, almost as much as she wanted to wipe the haunted look off his face.

It was easier, safer, to close the tiny gap that separated them and kiss him.

She kissed the next sob right out of his mouth and she kept on kissing him until Leo got the message that it was all right to kiss her back. He still looked like he might cry but that was only because Jane pulled back from him and peeled off her jumper and unclipped her bra. She was used to men looking like they might cry when she took her clothes off.

Leo stared at her face fixedly as if it was a superhuman effort of will not to stare at her breasts instead. 'Why? Why now? I mean, Vegas doesn't count, we were both hammered.'

Jane shrugged and his eyes did drift down to her breasts then. She'd have been insulted if they hadn't. 'Because I want to and because I think we both need to get out of our heads in a way that doesn't involve artificial stimulants.'

'I can't even tell if you're playing me any more,' Leo muttered, even though Jane wasn't. At least she didn't think she was, but before she could contradict him he held up his hands. 'Just so we're clear, I'm allowed to touch, aren't I? You're not going to smack me again?'

'Only if that's what turns you on, darling,' she drawled and this might just have been about trying to put him out of his misery but the way Leo kept looking at her with hooded eyes, his tongue caught between his teeth, made Jane wonder if she was really doing this out of the goodness of her heart. 'Come here and kiss me.'

Leo's kisses tasted of all the sweet things Jane had ever known: champagne and red velvet cake and pink spun sugar from the fair. She did smack him when he shaped her breasts and whispered, 'I thought you said we weren't going to do anything that involved any artificial stimulants,' because they were all her. No implants. Just the fat sucked out of her arse to plump up what had barely been there. She was still mostly bones and edges and hard lines, but it seemed as if her flesh spilled voluptuously into Leo's reverent hands. He said he'd never felt anything so soft as her breasts and thighs and the tiny bulge of her belly as he rubbed his cheek against it.

Jane couldn't help but laugh even though sex was never a laughing matter. 'You're tickling me,' she whispered.

'Sorry,' he whispered back, although only the moon glinting through the window was witness to the two of them sprawled on the bed.

'It's all right, it's a good kind of tickling,' she said and Leo, even as he had his hands full of her, gave her a suspicious, fearful look as if could actually hear the cogs whirring in her brain.

'Oh no,' he murmured fiercely. 'Don't even think it, Jane.'

'But now I've thought it, I can't unthink it,' she reasoned. 'Are you ticklish? I bet you are.'

Leo tried to hold her back with kisses but her hands were already skimming down his back, tugging his T-shirt out of the way to trace figures of eight with the tips of her fingers.

He squirmed away from her, but Jane let her touch dance against his rib cage and then under his arms. Leo was helpless as a baby as she sought out his secrets. Jane watched incredulously as he giggled and moaned and begged her to stop when she ran her fingertips along the soft skin of his forearms.

'I think you needed to laugh even more than you needed to get laid,' she said as he batted her hands away and lay back panting. It was true. He was always joking, always smiling, but he never really laughed.

'There's not been much to laugh about lately. And actually, now you mention it, I don't think I've ever seen you laugh. Not properly.'

Then it was Leo who comforted her, although Jane wasn't crying but wearing the same neutral expression that seemed to take an awful lot of effort these days. But still, Leo drew her closer so he could kiss the shadows away from her face.

Maybe sentimentality was contagious but it seemed to Jane that Leo healed every inch of her that he touched, his mouth a warm, wet, insistent thing as he travelled down her body. She wasn't so damaged or broken that she had to fake it (not all the time) and Leo was good at this. Really good, she thought, her eyes rolling back in her head, as he draped her legs over his shoulders and feasted on her.

It was no wonder all those women, all those other men's wives, had been so hot for him when he was so clever with his hands and his mouth, so generous with his attentions, so pleased that Jane was pleased with him that he let her go once and then twice, though strictly speaking it was his turn now. She twisted under him as he fucked her with his fingers and at the same time his tongue kept stroking over her again and again and again.

'No. Stop. Stop,' she said when she could speak again and it didn't take much effort to coax him up the bed because he was so hard and needy for her. He sighed in relief when she grasped his cock in her hands and began to rub it gently.

'You're so pretty, Leo,' she purred, her cheek brushing against his prick. 'Is this all for me?'

'You don't have to do that,' he said, reaching out for her, but Jane pulled away and stuck her tongue out at him.

'I want to do this,' Jane insisted. 'You just lie back and think of England.'

In the end, he gave up, and let her do God's work. Jane had certain smarts in this department too, had always got rave reviews, and she wasn't surprised that the things she did, both of them naked now, made him buck his hips and beg her to fuck him.

She'd barely got started, had only just lowered herself onto him, when he came undone. Coming and crying under her and she didn't despise him for being weak. This time, Jane understood. She stayed where she was, her flesh fluttering all around him as she licked his tears away.

'Come on, Leo, this was meant to make you happy,' she sighed. 'Why are you so scared to get happy?'

'I don't know,' he said. Then he looked up at her. His face was still damp but he smiled. It was a shaky, watery smile but it was exactly what Jane wanted to see. 'I don't usually come that quickly. Honestly. You can call some of my exes and they'll tell you I could go all night. Then they'll tell you that I'm insatiable.'

'Darling, I'd already figured that out all by myself,' Jane said. Leo did laugh then and he was still half hard inside her, and got even harder when she dragged his hands up to her breasts.

'Seriously though, are these real? They feel real.'

'Oh!' She gasped as he worked one nipple between thumb and forefinger, pulled the other one into the wet heat of his mouth so she could hardly think. 'I'm not sure that any of me is real,' Jane said, though she hadn't meant to.

'This . . . right now, this is real,' Leo said and he sat up, his chest, skin so warm, flush to hers so he could kiss her again.

It was the first time Jane had told a man exactly what she liked, instead of pretending that everything they did was fine with her. Leo was very biddable. He gripped her wrists, held them tight behind her back because she needed that tiny hint of pain, as his mouth worked her breasts again, licking, tugging, sucking and eventually, to reward his efforts, Jane rose above him and slowly, inch by inch, took him inside her again. She wondered if Leo felt as if he was plunging underwater into oceans warmed by the sun too.

Then he seemed to instinctively know that a hint wasn't going to be enough and he flipped them so he was on top, Jane underneath and he rode her like that. His hips snapping against hers, her legs wrapped tight around him and she was almost *there*, needed one more deep thrust, one more filthy word whispered in her ear. She was straining towards something just out of reach, just beyond her grasp.

'It's all right,' Leo said. 'I've got you,' and he pushed her over the edge.

33

May 1945

Every day the papers listed the foreign towns and cities, a sea away, which had been reclaimed by the Allied forces. It was hard to reconcile the pictures of women in headscarves, small children waving flags, all cheering as the tanks rumbled past, as a decent exchange for what had been lost.

When they liberated the concentration camps, those terrible places with ugly names, even Rose was shocked out of the torpor that had settled around her like a fine mist of perfume. She sat in a cinema with her hand to her mouth as she watched the newsreels. Impossible to believe that the sepulchral mountains of parchment-white skin and bones could have once been people. But they had been, and there was a collective disbelief that any one person, never mind whole nations, could be so evil.

It would have been easier to pretend that it hadn't happened, but Rose danced with men at Rainbow Corner who'd seen it first-hand. They were different from the other men who'd passed through on their way back home. There was a haunted quality to them; a certain desperation in the way they held Rose just a little too tightly.

Back in Kensington, Yves had put his fist through a wall in sheer helpless rage and Madeleine cried all the time. She cried as she peeled potatoes, tended her beloved vegetable patches and scrubbed the kitchen floor. She even cried in front of Edward when he visited, which he did quite often. He always arrived with something – flowers, a toy, once a bottle of red wine – and the sweetest, softest smile for Rose as if he were remembering the kisses they'd last shared, of touching every inch of her body. But on the day the papers were full of the liberation of Auschwitz and Madeleine was crying as she laid the table, he took Madeleine in his arms and kissed the top of her head.

'They won't get away with this,' he told Madeleine in a clenched voice. 'I promise you that.'

They hid the papers in the coal bucket so the little ones wouldn't see but when Thérèse woke up screaming three times in the night, Rose retrieved the newspapers and burnt them.

But there was so little time to mourn when there was so much to celebrate. The bombs had stopped falling and one Monday night at the end of April the blackout officially ended. The next day the papers reported that Hitler had committed suicide and suddenly, when it had been a grim reality for so long that Rose couldn't imagine life without it, the end of the war was inevitable.

It took just over a week and then it all stopped. Rose was at work and doing battle with the urn, which was on its last legs, when the BBC announced that the war was over. Everyone stopped talking. Even the anaemic sausages in the pan stopped spitting. 'Can it really be true?' someone asked and then everyone cheered and a young lad leapt over the counter and tried to kiss Rose but she stamped on his foot. Mr Fisher was so swept up in the moment that he declared that tea and buns were on the house.

Rose had never seen anyone quite so tight-lipped and furious as Gladys Fisher as she watched her husband give away free buns to all and sundry. Then, while she was still reeling from the shock, he closed the café and opened the bottle of sherry he'd hidden away for that very day, that very moment. The pair of them got quite tipsy as they waltzed around the tables and chairs, and they told Rose to go home and that she could have tomorrow off too.

Tuesday, May the eighth, VE Day. All of them, the little ones as well, walked into town. Madeleine was still crying but she said that they were joyful tears and Yves and Jacques bought red, white and blue hats from a hawker standing outside the Royal Albert Hall and red, white and blue ribbons that the girls tied in their hair. They walked through Hyde Park and everyone they passed smiled and said hello and 'isn't it wonderful news?'

They joined the crowds outside Buckingham Palace but they were packed in like sardines and a policeman said that the King and Queen wouldn't appear for hours and Rose was so worried that the children would get crushed that they ended up walking home and sat by the Round Pond in Kensington Gardens to eat their sandwiches.

'I don't want to go back,' Gisèle said in her heavily accented English to Rose as they made their way back to the house, the children dragging their heels and complaining that they were tired. 'This isn't home, but home isn't home either.'

For Rose, home was Rainbow Corner; it was her anchor, her lodestone, but that night, as soon as she walked through the doors, she was gathered up and spilled back out onto the pavement.

She found herself arm in arm with a pair of sailors marching through the heaving streets to Trafalgar Square. There were flags everywhere, the lights blazing defiantly after all those years of darkness, and people, so many people. Clinging to lampposts, splashing through the fountains, on top of the stately lions that had kept guard throughout the war. Rose joined the end of a massive conga line and she laughed and cheered and sang 'Pack

Up Your Troubles' and made a good show of it, a newspaper man even took her photo, but she wondered why she had to pretend to be happy. Surely she should have simply *been* happy?

Later, as she walked towards Mayfair, she wondered if the triumph was worth all that they'd sacrificed? Maybe that was why victory felt like the end of a deathly dull party that had dragged on for far too long and now one was walking home through cold, empty streets knowing that there was no food in the larder, no money left to feed the meter.

But she wasn't walking home. She was going to Edward. There was every chance that he might be out drinking brandy and smoking cigars with his Whitehall buddies in a gentlemen's club, but he'd never yet let her down.

So Rose wasn't at all surprised to hear his footsteps coming towards her when she knocked on his door. She didn't think he'd been home long because he was still in his uniform, jacket unbuttoned, and he had that soft look he often had when he'd been drinking. 'I was hoping to see you tonight,' he said and she stood there and delighted in the tremble in her legs, the way she suddenly found it hard to breathe.

Some nights, as soon as he closed the door behind her, Edward would tell her to take her clothes off in that precise, proper voice of his and he'd stand there and watch her as she made herself naked for him, but tonight he simply took her hand and led her to the sofa. 'I have a bottle of champagne I've been saving – will you have a glass?'

Rose fussed with her hair, tugged down her skirt and fidgeted while Edward was in the kitchen. Her hand shook slightly as she took a whisky tumbler from him that was almost full to the brim.

'I'm afraid my champagne glasses were yet another casualty of war,' he said as he sat down next to her. He was so serious tonight and Rose was all wrong-footed because usually, by now, he'd have kissed her at least.

Still, he watched her sip champagne as hungrily as he would kiss her. Despite all the things they'd done, Rose felt inexplicably shy. She was blushing as she put the glass down. 'I thought the end of the war would mean something,' she said at last. 'That it would make everything better, but it hasn't. Not at all.'

'Well, it's not quite over yet. There's still the war in the Far East.'

'But that's the Far East – it's awfully far away, otherwise they'd call it the Near East.'

They both smiled and the tension eased enough that Rose could toe off her shoes and tuck her legs up underneath her. She wasn't nervous now, but relaxed into Edward's intent gaze because he'd told her so many times that he loved to look at her. Not that he loved her, she didn't think he'd ever say that again, not now she'd explained matters, but it was comforting to know that on the outside she was still the same girl, fresh off the train, that he'd first met all those months ago at Rainbow Corner.

'I'm glad you're here. Well, I'm always glad when you're here but there was something I wanted to tell you in person, not by letter,' Edward said casually as he removed his cufflinks and placed them on the end table. 'I'm afraid I have to go away.'

'Where are you going? You won't be gone long, will you?' Everyone had left her, but not Edward. He was meant to be constant. He was meant to be here whenever she needed him.

'I'm going to Germany,' he said and instantly, her world hollowed out.

'Why on earth would you want to go *there*?' Rose turned to look at Edward but, for once, he refused to meet her eye.

'I have to tell you something,' he said woodenly though it couldn't be worse than him going to Germany, to be among those people. 'It might come as a shock.'

'What? What do you have to tell me?' she demanded.

He shrank back from her slightly. 'I'm Jewish.' He actually

flinched then as if he expected Rose to strike him, or turn away from him in disgust, though she had absolutely no inclination to do either of those things. 'Or rather my mother is – was – so according to Judaic law and well, Hitler, that makes me Jewish too.'

The relief made Rose quite lightheaded. 'Is that it? Goodness, for a moment you had me worried. Anyway, I thought your mother was American.'

'Rose.' Edward slowly shook his head, fought back a smile. 'The two things aren't mutually exclusive. Officially, her family left Russia in the middle of the last century to further their business interests. Unofficially they came to America to escape persecution. They did very well for themselves. My grandmother married a banker and somewhere along the way her history, her religion, the family that had been left behind in the shtetls, got erased. It's rather curious really – I've never set foot in a synagogue, quite happily eaten bacon and done whatever I pleased on the Sabbath, but lately being Jewish seems terribly important.'

Now Rose could understand why he'd spent all that money on buying up houses for what turned out to be seven Jewish refugees. But she couldn't understand why he'd want to leave her to go to *Germany* where those *bastards* had tried to wipe his people out of existence. 'I think going there would be a dreadful mistake,' she said and she took his hand and tried to put everything she couldn't say into the way she laced her fingers through his. 'I don't see how it would achieve anything. The war is over now.'

Edward disentangled their fingers, but didn't let go of her hand. 'I was a lawyer before the war and I shall become a lawyer again. I'm going to find the people who were responsible for the concentration camps, for all that suffering, and make them confess their crimes. Put them on trial. Bear witness for their victims. They have to be held accountable.'

'Edward, they're not people! They're animals.'

'No! They are people. If we think of them as animals then we allow them to abrogate all responsibility for what they did. We forgive them for just blindly following orders.' Even though he was keeping it tightly wound like cotton on a reel, Rose could feel his anger. 'Justice must be served.'

Rose knew, with a dull, resigned certainty, that when he came back, he wouldn't be the same. He'd be fundamentally altered. She could bear to lose Edward – her sweet, serious Edward – too. The thought made her ache. 'I wish there were a way I could change your mind.'

Edward patted her arm to signal that he couldn't take her wishes into account. 'While I'm gone, I need you to do something for me,' he said. 'Quite a lot of things actually.'

'Watering your plants and forwarding your post?' Rose frowned. 'Don't you have someone who comes in to do that for you?'

'Nothing like that. We have all those empty houses in Kensington and no one to live in them and there are all those people with nowhere to go. I'm going to send them to you,' Edward said as if that was a perfectly sensible plan. 'You'll need to sort out their papers, rustle up some British relatives who'll sponsor them, oversee work on the houses, furnish them. Then you'll have to find jobs for the ones who are able to work, but even the ones who can't, they still get a roof over their heads. They'll all have somewhere to call home.'

'I can't do that!' There were a hundred, a thousand reasons why she couldn't. Rose started with the most obvious one. 'I haven't got time. There's my job—'

'Rose, you're wasted in that café. You should be doing more with your life than mopping floors and peeling carrots.'

'You can't just magic paint and long-lost relatives out of thin air.' The war hadn't even been over for a day and Rose knew that when she went to the shops in the morning, the shelves wouldn't suddenly be crammed with all the things that had slowly disappeared. 'I tried to buy a packet of hairpins and the shopkeeper looked at me as if I'd asked to buy the Crown Jewels.'

Edward was unmoved. 'Money won't be a problem. My lawyer and my man of business will help. You can even put Mickey Flynn on the payroll if you have to.'

'But, Edward, I can't!' She rose up on her knees so she could look him in the eyes. He looked steadily back at her, and then reached out to smooth back the one errant lock of her hair that would never stay pinned and rolled. 'No one would take me seriously. I'm just a girl.'

'You're the only person I trust to do it.' He sighed. 'Besides, once you've set your heart on something, it's impossible to say no to you.'

'That's simply not true,' Rose said because all people ever did was say no to her.

'Let me remind you.' Edward stood up, walked over to his desk by the window and opened one of the drawers. 'I didn't want to give this to you before ... You tried to put a brave face on it but I know you've been sad, so dreadfully sad, and I didn't want to add to your burden.'

He held out a sheet of paper but Rose made no move to take it from him. She didn't think she could bear even an ounce more unhappiness.

'You asked me to find out what had happened to your ... friend?' Edward prompted.

Rose shrugged. She already knew what had happened to her friends. If she could get through an hour without thinking of the three of them, then it was a good hour until she remembered she had no business feeling good and she felt wretched all over again. 'What?'

'Your Danny,' Edward said. Oh, *that* friend. Rose had long

made her peace with the complicated, conflicted loss of Danny because it didn't begin to compare to the agonising pain of her girls being snatched from her. But when Edward held out the paper to her again, she shook her head. Once she saw the words, black on white, then it was real.

'Just tell me,' she implored. 'Do it gently.'

'Sergeant Daniel de Franco, Aircraft Maintenance Division. A successful bombing crew are only as good as their ground staff but your Danny was never a pilot. He's now back in Newport, Massachusetts where he has a wife and two children.' He paused and made sure to hold her gaze. 'I know it sounds rich coming from me, but I am sorry, Rose.'

It should have been a shock; in a way it was, but it also made utter sense. Now, with only seconds to parse this new information, it was so obvious, so hidden in plain sight, that Rose felt like the biggest fool. It had just been a game to him to win her heart, her slavish and dogged devotion, and for what? One lousy night in a hotel in Henley-on-Thames.

As she so often did these days, Rose thought about what her girls would have said if they'd known. Maggie wouldn't even have feigned surprise. Phyllis would have been indignant and angry on Rose's behalf and Sylvia – Sylvia would have laughed and laughed as Rose was doing now. She laughed until the tears streamed down her cheeks. 'Well,' she spluttered. 'Well . . . at least he's not dead, I suppose. That's something.'

The worst thing about thinking Danny dead was that it hadn't really mattered, not just because of what he'd done to her but because she didn't have the room to mourn him too. Even the good memories – his beautiful face, the sound of his voice and the way she'd felt when he'd kissed her – were faint and indistinct.

And then there was Edward, her Edward, because Rose realised in that moment that she thought of him as hers. She'd known him now for twice as long as she'd known Danny. Had spent hours and hours with him. So many hours that if she squashed them all together, they added up to days, even weeks. Not just the hours that they spent in the dark, his body teaching her body new shapes and patterns . . .

'I knew this would upset you,' he said and he peered anxiously at Rose as she sat on his sofa still shaking with mirth at the utter idiocy of it all, trying to mop up the tears with the back of her hands. 'You're quite hysterical.'

'I'm not. I'm just stupid! I'm so stupid I can hardly stand it.'

Edward must have thought she was a lost cause because he left the room but returned almost immediately with a handkerchief and a glass of water. He sat down, dipped the white linen square in the water and began to dab her face with it. 'You're not stupid. You're the bravest, loveliest, sweetest person I've ever known,' he told her softly.

Rose stilled instantly under his soothing touch. 'I'm not any of those things.'

'You're also very young and you've been through so much already.' The handkerchief was discarded but he continued to stroke her tear-streaked face with his hands, tilting her chin so she was bathed in the glow of the lamplight. She'd never been this naked in front of him. Not even when she was actually naked. 'I was wrong to ask you to—'

'No, you weren't.' She rested her hands on top of his as they cupped her cheeks. 'I want to do it. It works both ways, Edward – this finding it impossible to say no. Anything you want me to do, just ask and you know that I'll say yes.'

'Anything?'

'Anything.'

34

Leo was awake when Jane came out of the bathroom next morning. He was sitting on the side of the bed in his shorts looking very sure of himself. He smiled when he saw her. 'I've decided that I'm going to get through today without crying,' he announced.

Jane paused in the doorway. 'Let's not get carried away. Until lunchtime maybe, darling?'

'I've also decided that you're not to call me darling any more.' He stood up and stretched.

Jane had only had her touch to guide her last night, but now she could see he had muscles and hollows where before he'd been soft and doughy. 'I call everyone darling,' she said absently.

'I'm not everyone,' Leo said and that had to be a precursor to a talk about where they were going and what they were going to do when they got there, but he just scratched his head and padded to the bathroom. 'I won't be long. Are you going downstairs? Could you stick the kettle on ... or actually, I should probably check, see if there's any change ... '

'We'd know by now,' Jane said. 'If there was anything to know.'

Rose had slept through the night, Lydia told her in awed tones, as if Rose were a usually fretful baby.

Neta, who'd arrived for the day shift, was with Rose when they took the trunk up to her room. Today was very, very different because Rose was lying flat in bed, waiting for Neta to arrange the mound of pillows to her liking, a silk scarf covering her hair. Maybe Jane hadn't noticed her gradual decline, had never seen Rose in her prime, but suddenly, in the space of twenty-four hours, she looked as if she was dying.

Her skin was yellow now rather than simply having a yellowish tinge and her skin hung on her bones as if she were slowly deflating. Rose's eyes were closed, her breathing uneven like a record jumping and one hand plucked at her belly, which was distended enough to be visible even under the bedclothes.

'Let's make you comfy, Ms Beaumont,' Neta said and Jane was pleased that there was still that thin veneer of dignity in place.

Rose slowly opened her eyes as Neta asked her to lean forward. She closed them again as the pillows were placed behind her as if even that tiny kindness caused her undue suffering.

Once a pillow had been placed underneath Rose's feet for ominous reasons that Neta said they didn't need to know about, the nurse folded her hands and backed out of the room. 'I'll be with Miss Liddy if you need me.'

Jane and Leo looked at each other and she wondered if he knew how helpless she felt. Then he touched her arm as he walked to the bed, just a simple brush of his fingers, but it signified something had changed between them. Jane pulled up a chair alongside his.

'So, we went to Lullington Bay, got the things you wanted,' he said and Rose's eyes opened.

'Did I ever tell you about my friend Mickey Flynn?' Even her voice was different today, barely more than a croak. 'He used to say that I owed him so many favours that I'd have to live to be a hundred before I finished paying them off. Do you think he'll take an IOU?'

'I'm sure he will, darling,' Jane said. 'Though he's probably forgotten by now.'

'Forgetting is easy. It's remembering that's hard. One wants to remember only the good times but the bad times have a way of staying with you too.'

She lapsed into silence. Leo glanced at Jane, his eyebrows raised, because neither of them knew if these were her last profound words or just jumbled thoughts brought on by the morphine that was being administered by a pump on the other side of the bed, which cheerfully whirred as it went about its business.

They sat there. Jane listened to the pump and stared out at the naked treetops she could see from the window. She really wished she'd brought up a cup of tea and a magazine to flick through. Weeks ago, Jane had had a hazy notion that because Rose was old and had cancer she'd go to bed one night and simply not wake up. She hadn't expected that death might involve long stretches of sitting around, waiting, having to pretend that you were lost in thought when actually you were quite bored.

'Did you get my things?' Rose asked and Leo gave a little start as if he'd been dozing.

'Yeah, I already said. Everything on the list.'

'How is Lullington Bay? My roses?'

'The garden looked beautiful,' Leo said, though the garden had been a shadowy cluster of trees and bushes when they'd visited. 'The house was exactly as I remembered it.'

Rose smiled and the rigidity of her limbs eased as Leo talked about Lullington Bay; of those endless days on the beach and sunburned, sticky nights. The stray cat they'd taken in and called Mr Bobbins, who'd turned out to be a Mrs Bobbins and had given birth to a litter of kittens in Rose's bed.

Leo talked, his voice hoarse, until Dr Howard arrived. For Rose to open her eyes and dare to admit that the pain was 'quite bad', was something else that was very, very different.

They went down to the kitchen, where Lydia was in the middle of a baking frenzy. Gingerbread, scones, shortbread, a fruitcake 'but only sultanas. Rose hates dried fruit. Always used to say that mixed peel and chopped dates ruined a perfectly good sponge.'

Neither Jane or Leo needed to point out that it had been days, maybe even weeks, since Rose had eaten anything as substantial as a piece of cake, because there were so many things that didn't need to be said any more.

Though Dr Howard had lots to say when he came into the kitchen twenty minutes later.

He talked about Rose's kidneys most of all. About how they were in danger of shutting down and that if Rose would agree to a catheter, she could be put on a rapid drip.

'If Rose doesn't want it, I'm not sure I could persuade her,' Leo said.

'Someone will have to make decisions for her if she's not capable of making them for herself,' Dr Howard said. Today he didn't even attempt to be smooth and dapper. 'That's going to happen sooner rather than later.'

'But she's not like she was yesterday,' Leo said, as they walked the doctor out. 'So that has to be a good sign, doesn't it?'

'A temporary respite, I fear. There will come a time when you might decide that it's best for Ms Beaumont to keep her sedated until she passes.'

'But she wouldn't be hurting, would she?' Jane asked, because she couldn't imagine how awful it would be for Rose to be trapped between worlds, with nothing but the pain to keep her here. 'How much morphine can you prescribe without her overdosing?'

'I'm not a punitive man.' The doctor paused as he put on his hat – he was one of those men who still wore an old-fashioned trilby. 'I don't believe in unnecessary suffering and sometimes if the drugs do their work before the body fails, well, then it can be a blessing.'

When he was gone, Leo sat down heavily on the bottom step of the stairs. 'Fuck.' He rubbed his face with the heels of his hands, but when he took them away, his eyes were dry. 'Fucking hell. I don't know if I can do this.'

Jane stroked her fingers through his hair as she stepped past him. 'This is why you came back. To do what's best for Rose, so yes, you can.'

Rose slept for the entire day and when Agnieska arrived to take over from Neta, Leo and Jane gave up their vigil. They still hadn't talked about what had happened the night before. Leo wasn't going to mention it first. Not a chance in hell. Because if he did, then Jane would laugh it off, call him darling, become flippant rather than admit that she was perilously close to actual real feelings and emotions. But it turned out neither of them needed to say anything.

Jane stroked her hand slowly and deliberately against Leo as she walked past him into his bedroom. Without thinking, he immediately had her pressed up against the wall, soft where he was suddenly painfully and achingly hard. It was a clumsy dance to the bed where they spent the night rediscovering the taste and texture of each other. Leo supposed he should have felt guilty that he and Jane had picked now, this moment, to stumble towards something that resembled happiness, but he didn't. It could have been another strategy, another feint in Jane's master plan, but Leo needed to lose himself for hours and hours that all bled into each other and Jane had the means.

Afterwards, Jane fell asleep before Leo did. Sleep didn't

smooth away the strains of the day, because she wasn't still. Her eyelids twitched as if she was dreaming hard, her teeth worried at her bottom lip as she shifted first one way, then the other. Leo watched until he couldn't bear to watch any more. She'd kept the true heart of herself locked away and watching her now felt like an intrusion; as if he were reading her private papers, rifling through her drawers. In the end, he retrieved the pillows that they'd tossed on the floor and placed them in the middle of the bed again, so they were separate, apart, and then it was easy to fall asleep.

It was past eleven the next day when Neta came into the kitchen to tell them that Rose was awake and asking for them. 'Did you go to Lullington Bay?' Rose asked as soon as they walked into the room. 'How were my roses?'

Leo took a step back, but Jane pushed him forward. He could do this. He had no other choice. 'Your roses are fine. Beautiful. No greenfly on them.'

'Good.' Despite sleeping for almost twenty-four hours, Rose's eyes were bloodshot. She had another gaily-patterned scarf tied around her head, which made a mockery of her sunken cheeks and parched lips. 'Where are my things? Did you come across a small wooden box?'

Leo squatted down and opened the trunk. Inside were bundles of letters, some yellowed with age like Rose, others tissue-thin and edged with blue and red airmail chevrons. There was a small rosewood box that Leo passed to Jane who passed it to Rose. Her fingers fumbled with the catch, then stirred up the collection of books of matches, cocktail sticks, menus from nightclubs and restaurants. At the bottom was a small, tattered piece of cardboard with a photo stuck on it.

'It really happened. I was really there,' she said, as she tried to close her fingers around it.

Jane reached over and plucked it out of the box, then held it up so Leo could see it. It was a membership card for Rainbow Corner. Staring back at them was a teenage Rose; hair elaborately rolled, her smile dark with lipstick. 'Gosh, darling, you look like a movie star.'

'Hedy Lamarr.' Rose crooked her fingers. 'Where are the photos? They're in a album.'

Leo carefully rifled through old birthday cards and theatre programmes until he unearthed a dark green leather-bound book. Rose took it with a tiny sigh, but before she opened it she patted the bed beside her.

'Come here so you can both see,' she said and once Jane was settled precariously so she wouldn't jostle Rose and Leo was on his knees, elbows resting on the edge of the bed, Rose started flicking through the book.

There was Rose as a tiny baby swathed in an enormous frilly christening gown. School photos: gap-toothed and freckled. Then a sullen teenage Rose on a seafront, arms folded, chin tucked down, a ferocious frown on her face. She looked, though it pained Leo to admit it, a lot like he had during his own sullen, teen years. And then . . .

'Oh! You're in London now!' Jane said gleefully, as they looked at Rose standing in Trafalgar Square with another girl, skirts hiked up, legs in a showgirl pose, flanking a short man with a pencil moustache, a sharp suit and an ingratiating smile. 'Who are you with?'

'That's Mickey Flynn, the old reprobate.' Rose's croak couldn't disguise her delight. 'I don't know who she is. Mickey's lady friends would come and go. Go, mostly.'

Leo perched on the other side of the bed and watched the two women, their heads together, as Jane exclaimed at Rose all gussied up in her finest and posing for the camera.

They came to a Christmas celebration: a spindly, sparsely

decorated tree in the background, three children kneeling in front of the adults who were arranged on and around a sofa. Rose tried to trace each face but her fingers wouldn't obey her. 'My other family. This used to be the lounge downstairs and that's Yves, Jacques, Madeleine not crying for once, Gisèle and that's Thérèse and Hélène on either side of little Paul. Nineteen forty-five. That was a hard Christmas. But Phyllis's mother sent us a chicken and a plum cake. Every year until she died. She was far more terrifying than I ever was.'

'I doubt that.' Leo rolled his eyes. 'You're next-level terrifying, Rose.'

Rose managed to snort. 'If I were feeling better, you'd get a clip round the ear for that.'

Leo had been worried that this would be too much for Rose when even opening her eyes the day before had been a Herculean task, but this morning Rose was happy, or what passed for happy when she was so close to the end. Jane also seemed happy to pore over someone else's family photographs because she didn't have any of her own. Whether her parents were really dead or not didn't matter. She'd still chosen not to have a family.

Leo hadn't had too many family photo ops over the last few years either. He was just a blurry face in other people's photos.

Who's the drunk-looking dude?

Oh, a friend of a friend. Can't remember his name but later that night he puked in the swimming pool.

Leo shook his head, turned his attention to the photo that Rose and Jane were looking at. 'Who's *that* blonde girl?' He tried to sound eager and interested. 'She looks all kinds of fun.'

'It's Sylvia. My honorary big sister.'

Leo leaned over to stare at the laughing girl in black and white, hands on her hips, head thrown back, but Rose was already turning to the next page, then she said with quiet satisfaction, 'Ah, there we all are.'

She pointed to each of them in turn: Phyllis, who looked earnest and slightly anxious; next to her was Maggie, her angular face wreathed in smoke from the cigarette she was clutching in her right hand and Sylvia and Rose with their arms around each other. All of them smiling, all of them wearing the same red lipstick in the hand-tinted photograph.

'It's your girls, Rose,' Jane said, as if she wanted to jump into the picture with them.

In all the time he'd known her, Rose had never been one for sentimentality, but with Jane's help she took the photo out of the album and rested it on her chest, over her heart. 'I had no photos of them. They were all lost, but one of my old friends from Rainbow Corner found this, years after the war, and sent it to me.'

'I'm so glad we fetched it for you,' Jane breathed. Rose smiled at her and Leo felt as if he was intruding. Then Jane stroked his hand where it rested on the bed and he belonged.

'Have you got pictures of the four of you after the war?' Leo asked.

'I'd love to see what you all looked like in the fifties when you could get *really* glammed up,' Jane added but Rose turned her head away.

'There was no "after the war",' she said quietly. 'There was a bomb. Direct hit. They lay in pieces in the street.'

Jane gripped Leo's hand tight enough that he wanted to whimper. 'When you talked about them . . . I never thought they'd died,' Jane said so bitterly that even Rose looked startled.

'Of course they died. It was obvious.'

'Not to me.'

'Jane! It's not like Rose did it on purpose,' Leo said with a glance at Rose who was lying with her eyes closed, picture still pinned to her heart. He frowned, inched closer, then straightened up and took a shaky breath. His eyes met Jane's, as if to say, *It's all right, she's still here.*

Jane was instantly contrite. 'Darling, I'm sorry that you had so little time with them.'

'I think she's asleep,' Leo said. 'We should go.'

They left the album on Rose's pillow so it was within reach and were just unpacking the trunk, placing each little box stuffed with memories on the wheeled table that fitted snugly over the bed, when Rose opened her eyes again.

'I'm not sleeping.' Rose raised her head and trembled with the effort it took. 'You couldn't possibly understand how fleeting it all was. That suddenly the people you loved, were just gone. You'd say, "Night, night," then the next morning they'd disappeared. Their time card had been stamped. And the tragedy of it all is that they never finished being who they were meant to be.'

When Jane popped in to see Rose a day later, the picture of her Rainbow Corner girls was in a silver frame on her bedside table.

Leo had gone out somewhere with George. Rose had refused to see George for three days running and they'd found him on the back step with Lydia, crying as he tried to light a cigarette. 'George, I've got to go and see a man about a dog. I could do with some company,' Leo had said and Jane had watched them walk down the mews, Leo's arm round George's shoulders. She was sure that they were only going to go as far as the nearest pub, but if Leo came back drunk, Jane would forgive him this once.

As it was, she could hardly refuse to sit with Rose. She wanted to, though, because it was painful to sit and watch someone you'd grown quite fond of deteriorate in front of you.

Jane sat in an armchair she'd placed as far away from the bed as she dared and leafed through fashion magazines, but more often than not she'd gaze around the room, out of the window, anywhere but at Rose who mostly slept now. Sleep was meant to be peaceful, a reprieve from the part you played during the day, but Rose was anything but peaceful.

Her panting breaths sounded painful, the whimpers far worse, her face contorted into a rictus grimace though Neta said that soon, Rose would stop fighting. 'Rose will know when she's ready,' she'd told Lydia and Jane. Neta was very zen.

Jane knew that she should have come up with a different plan. All the weeks in this house with these people had got to her. She wasn't the glittering creature that she'd striven so hard to become but she wasn't the girl hiding under the bed either. She was stuck somewhere between the two of them and the only time that she was really happy lately was when she was with Leo. Then she didn't have to think at all. Just feel. His fingers, his mouth, his cock all doing such wonderful things to her that she actually began to imagine what the future might hold for both of them if they decided to make a go of it. Though you could plead the fifth on any thoughts you had when you were coasting a post-orgasm high.

Instead of holding something back, Jane had given Leo and Rose everything that she was capable of giving, which might not be that much but when it was time to walk away she'd leave that best part of her behind. Then that little voice, more insistent by the day, reminded Jane that she didn't have to walk away. But how could she stay? The person that Leo was becoming deserved so much better.

Then Rose jolted back to consciousness with a pained, surprised cry. She lay there, not moving, eyes darting wildly around the room.

Jane stood up and walked over to the bed. She poured Rose some water from the jug, then gestured at the beaker. 'Will you drink something, darling?'

Rose had hardly had anything to drink for two days now, but there was a box of foam lollipops sitting on the over-table. Jane dipped one in the water and stroked it over Rose's chapped lips. Rose latched onto the lollipop, feebly sucked on it and she was back in her own body, back in the room.

'Are you sure you won't have a drink? I could go downstairs and get some ice.'

'Hurts to swallow.' Rose's voice had shrunk down to a rasp. 'Hurts to talk.' She bit her battered lip. 'I don't know what to do with myself.'

Jane sat down on the bed, careful not to jar the other woman, and took Rose's now-mottled hand. 'Darling, Leo will be back soon and if you're ready, then you should go.'

'Not yet,' Rose said, and when Jane found a packet of straws nestling among the packets of sterile gauze and syringes in the bathroom, she took some water. Not much, and Jane didn't know why she was the one doing this. She was the five-minute wife passing through. But then again, right now, with Leo gone and Lydia frantically cooking things that Rose wasn't going to eat, she was the only one available to do it.

Jane racked her brains for any films she'd seen with similar scenes. Maybe something with Bette Davis? 'Is there anything you wanted to do? Someone you wanted to say goodbye to that you haven't?'

'No. Everyone's already trooped through.'

'What about, say, Danny?' Jane asked, because she was sure that Danny had been Rose's one true love. Not that she suddenly believed in true love, but younger Rose had believed in it. 'When did you last hear from him?'

'Danny?' It looked as if Rose was having trouble placing the name though she was a little less groggy, maybe a tiny bit more comfortable since she'd managed to sip some water and Jane had rearranged her pillows. 'Not since the war.'

Jane picked up the iPad. 'I could try and track him down. See if he's still alive. There's this thing called Facebook that . . .'

'I do know what Facebook is. I'm not dead yet.' Rose sounded peevish but then she smiled. 'Danny. He was just a boy. A silly, selfish boy, but all the boys back then were going off to fight and it made them seem like men. Not like Leo. I don't think he'll ever really grow up.'

'He's trying to, darling. That has to count for something.' Jane wondered where Leo was. He'd been gone ages and she was really missing him –not just because it was so very hard dealing with Rose all by herself. 'That boyish thing is all part of his charm.'

'Will you stay with him after . . . ?'

Jane smoothed her thumb against the back of Rose's hand. 'I haven't really thought about after,' she said carefully.

'I'd like you to. Not for ever. I know you're not a forever sort, but I worry about what will happen to him. He has a tendency to go off the rails.' Even in her weakened state, Rose was still able to look a little shifty, though it could have been a trick of the watery light of the afternoon. 'Will you promise to stay until he's out of the woods?'

'Of course I will.' Jane didn't have to think twice about it, which was odd. Normally a promise she made was a promise that had been strategised, negotiated, sometimes even notarised.

'Good.' Rose sank carefully back on the pillows. 'At least, I'm not angry with him any more. I am glad he came home.'

'Rose, darling, do you think you could tell him that?' Jane gave Rose's hand a little squeeze. 'I know he talks a good game, but really, he's so soft-hearted and he's so sorry about letting you down. About all those stupid, thoughtless things he did years ago.'

'Deathbed absolution?' Rose asked with a weak smile. 'How Catholic.'

'Just forgiveness because you love him,' Jane said, because Rose did. How could she not?

'It wasn't meant to be like this.' Jane could see the fatigue creeping over Rose again. 'Champagne, pills, a suite at the Savoy with a riverside view. That was how I was going to go. I didn't plan to linger.'

'Still not too late, if you fancy toddling down the stairs, darling.'

She was only half-joking, but suddenly Rose was gripping her hand with a puny strength. 'When I'm ready, you'll be here, won't you?'

'Darling, I'm not going anywhere. We'll make sure that you won't be on your own.'

'It has to be you. You're strong. I'll need you to be strong enough for the both of us,' Rose said.

'I don't know that I'm *that* strong,' Jane demurred as Rose's eyes, suddenly all too focused, bored into her.

'You are. Like I was. I think that we're both quite similar. Neither of us afraid to face our futures head-on.'

'Oh Rose, darling, no. You . . . ' Jane swallowed. 'When you came to London, you were running towards something. All I've ever done is run away.'

'But you won't run away now, will you?' Rose asked. 'You'll be here when I need you.'

'I'll be here,' Jane said and she would be. Leo would need her too.

She was doing that thing again: being selfless. Nothing good ever came of that.

35

February 1946

The bombs no longer dropped. There were no more beautiful boys dying in foreign fields, but the end of the war still felt like a gigantic let-down. There was still rubble and rationing. The loss of what had been still ate away at Rose if she stayed still for long enough, so she made sure to always stay in motion.

It helped that she was kept busy with the refugees that Edward kept sending her. Often, she went to Dover to meet them off the boat. Then, once they were back in London, it was an endless trudge of endless queues. Everyone needed ration books and work permits and identity cards.

Thankfully, Mickey Flynn could perform miracles: anything from obtaining milk tokens to having a telephone installed in the house in Kensington at a day's notice. Lady Carfax also knew all sorts of muckety mucks, even a couple of lords, which was terribly useful when it came to cutting through red tape.

Then there were Maggie's old friends, who were happy to offer their services whenever Rose needed a translator. Even Henry Crapper, Sylvia's father, though he said he had no truck with a bunch of foreigners turning up and thinking they were entitled to housing and food ahead of folk who were born here, found Rose her sponsors.

'It strikes me as singularly odd that so many residents of Hoxton have long-lost Jewish relatives but have immense trouble recalling their names,' Mr Costello from the Aliens Department of the Home Office had told Rose crossly.

He'd also said, a little less crossly, that his staff quaked in fear when Rose turned up promptly at nine on the first Monday of every month and refused to budge until she'd got her forms stamped and signed off. She was prepared to stay there all day, on a hard-backed chair that one of the secretaries would grudgingly find for her, with her knitting.

He said that the clacking of my needles drove them all to distraction, Rose wrote to Edward. *In future, I'm to ask for him personally and he'll see me within the half-hour. I think that's what one would call a palpable success!*

Edward was constantly in her thoughts. Not least because he was always sending her people who were relying on Rose to give them some semblance of the normal life that they'd hardly dared to dream about when they were in the camps.

And Edward wrote her letters. Not just lists of names and dates of birth and countries of origin of the people she was to meet off boats and trains, but surprisingly funny, sweet letters. She couldn't imagine that he found much to amuse him when he'd been to those places with the awful names that she still stumbled over when she tried to say them out loud. When he'd spoken to the people who'd lived there, though it was hardly living. People who'd seen their loved ones shot, starved, sent off to the gas chambers. Then sat in the same room as the men and women who'd perpetrated these crimes.

With so much going on, Rose only turned up at Rainbow Corner at seven-thirty, six nights a week, because it was a deeply ingrained habit and she could get chocolate and cigarettes from the GIs to trade for more useful things. Rose often wondered how long Rainbow Corner would stay open – there had been rumours of its demise swirling around ever since VJ Day. Then, one wet, squally day in January when Rose arrived for her shift, she found a small huddle of girls in front of the noticeboard in the cloakroom.

She stood on tiptoe so she could see the edict over the heads in front of her. Rainbow Corner was closing.

'Oh, well. We all knew it was on the cards.'

'It's so soon. Only two weeks,' one of the other girls said. Rose didn't know her name. There were so many new girls these days.

Most of the women who'd been here when she'd started, who'd looked after her, lent her hairpins, taught her how to fight off the advances of over-amorous soldiers, were long gone. Not just dead but dispersed too; back to villages and towns to rebuild their lives. Some had sailed to America to be reunited with the men who had wooed them at Rainbow Corner. The American Red Cross had even organised War Bride Orientation Classes.

With Rainbow Corner closed, it would leave Rose more time for her work, her lost souls. But on the last night of Rainbow Corner, as Rose dressed in her trusty black crêpe de Chine, which she'd sworn she'd never wear again but necessity had made a liar of her, she was surprised to feel a little frisson of excitement.

So be it. She'd say goodbye to Rainbow Corner on the dance-floor in the arms of the handsomest GI she could find. She'd eat those misshapen sugar-sprinkled doughnuts for the last time and wash them down with Coca-Cola.

All those things about Rainbow Corner that Rose had taken for granted, she'd celebrate tonight. And she'd try not to see her ghosts, but she knew that Phyllis, Maggie and Sylvia would be there with her, in her heart, angels at her shoulder. She'd dance for them. Raise a glass and toast their memory.

First she had to get into the bloody place. The crowds were twenty deep on Shaftesbury Avenue and there was only one policeman on the door valiantly trying to beat them back.

Rose slipped round the back, down the steps that led to the basement and hammered with her fists on the kitchen door until one of the bus boys let her in.

It was pandemonium as soon as she left the steamy bustle of the kitchen for Dunker's Den. Rose had to swim through a heaving sea of khaki to reach the stairs and employ her elbows to climb up them. At one point she even had to aim a sharp kick at the ankles of a cocky airman who took advantage of the scrum to goose her.

'Rosie! Over here!' There was a gaggle of girls behind the reception desk. Dora, Jean and Peggy, back from Lowestoft. On the way to the ballroom, they picked up more stragglers.

For this one night, when there wasn't room to do anything more than shuffle to the music, they were happy to find a corner and share their stories. The drunken midshipman who'd thrown up all over Peggy's suede dancing shoes. The time Nancy had sneaked her little sister in for a stack of pancakes and she'd ended up getting engaged to a GI instead. The awful month when even Mickey Flynn couldn't get any stockings and they'd all painted tea on their legs, which had run in dirty rivulets in the sultry heat of the ballroom.

Rose laughed until her ribs ached. Posed for pictures. Swapped addresses even as she made a note to buttonhole one of the American Red Cross higher-ups to find out what they planned to do with the chairs and tables. All those plates and mugs. Curtains. The list was endless.

'We should at least *try* and dance,' someone said. 'We'll never have the chance again.'

It was a simple matter to find a man who wanted to spin a girl in his arms, not that there was any room for spinning

When the band stopped playing, the crowd howled their disapproval. 'What's happening?' Rose asked, craning her neck to see some of the grander American Red Cross ladies walk on stage, followed by . . . 'It's some great-and-goods!' she called out to the girls. 'Anthony Eden. Gosh! It's Eleanor Roosevelt. She's awfully ducky!'

She was that girl tonight. Little wide-eyed Rosemary Winthrop in love with London, and Rainbow Corner was the city's frantically beating heart.

There were speeches. 'This club, I think, proved that we can work together,' Eleanor Roosevelt said, as Dora wiped her eyes and Peggy sniffed. 'More than eighty per cent of the volunteers here were British and they worked with our American staff and made this club what it was and what it will always be in the hearts of our servicemen: a wonderful success!'

Rose clapped until her hands were sore, cheered until her throat was hoarse and still she refused to believe that it was coming to an end. That this would be the last time she'd stand here on this spot where she'd truly come of age. That she would never smell the mingled scent of Lucky Strikes, Brylcreem, wet wool and sweat again. Perhaps if she refused to leave, sat down on the dancefloor if she really had to, Rainbow Corner would stay open.

She wasn't the only one who felt the same. 'I'm not going,' Jean said. 'Not until they drag me out.'

The others agreed and though the American Red Cross ladies bobbed through the crowd in their dark grey uniforms and tried to cajole people towards the doors, they stood firm.

'One of the girls in the office said that they'd lost the original key and had a frantic scramble this afternoon to get a new one cut,' Jean said.

'They're not going to actually lock the door,' Rose scoffed. 'Rainbow Corner's always open. It's just a closing ceremony. Not a proper closing and none of us are to budge from this spot. They can't *force* us to leave.'

So, they stayed put. Not just Rose and her friends, but every man and woman who had managed to gain entrance.

Some of the Americans began to sing and they all quickly took up the chant of

'*We shall not, we shall not be moved.*

We shall not, we shall not be moved.

Just like a tree that's standing by the water, we shall not be moved.'

Suddenly they heard the mournful notes of the trumpet getting nearer and nearer, the haunting tune of 'Auld Lang Syne' echoing in their ears. The trumpet player had stepped off the stage and was moving across the floor, people following in his wake. That was how Rose left Rainbow Corner for the last time, as part of a huge, hungry surge that poured out of the club and onto the street where thousands of people were still congregated.

Those multitudes raised their voices in song.

'*Should old acquaintance be forgot and never brought to mind?*

Should old acquaintance be forgot, and auld lang syne.'

Rose didn't know how she could be one of those thousands but feel so alone.

'Rosie! Rosie, my darling! Up here!'

Rose brushed an impatient hand across her cheek and looked up to see Mickey Flynn hanging from a lamppost.

'Rosie! Come up! Hey, Yank, give a girl a hand, will you?'

Before Rose had even decided if she wanted to climb a lamppost so all and sundry could see up her dress, she was hoisted into to the air. Some foggy memory of how to climb a tree, a lost art from her childhood, surfaced and she slowly inched up the pole until Mickey hauled her the last foot or so and she stood with him on the junction box.

They were high, high, *high* above the masses. So high that

another girl and her fellow had found a spot to hang just below them. Mickey had made a special effort tonight – his silk tie bore the stars and stripes but his usual snaky grin was drooping at the corners.

'What's the matter, Mickey? Heartbroken that your supply of American cigarettes will dry up?' she asked him with a laugh.

'Oh, I wouldn't say that, Rosie. Where there's still a GI, there's a way.' He looked down at the crowds. Even though it was a cold, goosepimply February night, there were so many people collected below them, their heat all rising, that Rose could feel her black dress sticking to her. 'Look at them all. This is our piece of history, this is. They'll write books and make movies about this place. No one will forget Rainbow Corner.'

'Of course they won't,' Rose agreed. 'Anyway, I keep telling everyone: they're not *really* closing the place down. I'm sure Eleanor Roosevelt decided she wanted to visit and they felt as if they had to put on a show for her. We'll all feel pretty silly tomorrow.'

'Maybe you're right.' Mickey didn't sound convinced and Rose was just about to tell him all the reasons why Rainbow Corner couldn't close when a shout rang out from below them.

She had a bird's eye view of the front of Rainbow Corner and though she couldn't hear the door being shut or the key being turned in the lock, she saw it and she felt it in her heart.

Oh, how she felt it!

Rose started to cry, because it was really and truly over. Whatever else she'd lost, and she'd lost so much, she'd always had Rainbow Corner. Known that she could walk through those doors and never be turned away. Now they'd shut those double doors, locked them up tight and she had nothing left to lose.

'Don't cry, Rosie, my darling,' Mickey said but she couldn't stop.

She'd spent so long trying to be brave and strong and it had been easy because there was always a place she could go to forget all her troubles.

'What will I do now? Where will I go? Who'll have me?' She wasn't even talking to Mickey but had lifted up her streaming eyes to the heavens.

Rose started to shimmy down the lamppost, sweaty hands making her slide down too far and too fast so the couple below her had to wriggle down too before she sent them flying.

Mickey called out to her just before her feet hit the pavement, but she turned, tripped away, down this street and that street, until she found a quiet courtyard and could sink down, head in her hands, and weep for all that was gone.

She didn't know how long she cried but when she stopped, sniffling rather than sobbing now, Rose realised that she wasn't aching from the pain of it all, but rather because she was sitting in the kerb on a cold February night and her coat was still hanging up in the cloakroom at Rainbow Corner. Fat lot of good it was going to do her in there. She shivered and looked up to see Edward standing at the mouth of the alley.

It was such a shock to see him that for a moment she mistook him for one of her ghosts. In the same way that every platinum blonde might be Sylvia, every slender, dark girl could be Maggie and the sound of a plummy, breathy voice always made Rose look round to see if it were Phyllis back from the dead. But her ghosts were just ghosts and Edward was walking towards her now, a tentative smile on his face.

'I saw you nearly break your neck climbing down that lamppost,' he said, as if the memory wasn't a happy one. 'Then I saw how upset you were and I didn't want to intrude. If I am . . .'

'You're not intruding. Not at all,' Rose said and she patted the space beside her as if it were a soft, inviting couch and not hard, unyielding pavement. 'You can pull up a pew, if you want.'

The thought of Edward watching her cry, or howl to be more accurate, made Rose bristle a little, but not that much. He'd already seen the very best and the most dreadful worst of her, but he was still here, sitting down next to her, trying to place his coat over her shoulders.

'There's no point in both of us being cold,' Rose said, but she let Edward put his arm around her so she could nestle against him. 'Goodness, you startled me appearing out of the shadows like that but now I think about it, I'm not surprised you're here.'

'I thought about raising a glass to dear old Rainbow Corner in some dreary German beer hall, but I couldn't bear to miss saying goodbye, so here I am.'

'But you're going back there again?'

'Yes.' He sighed. 'I have to. You see, it's not—'

'You once said it was impossible to say no to me, so I'm asking you to not go back to Germany. To stay here. With me.' She stared at his rigid profile. A little muscle in his left eyelid pulsed when she clutched hold of his knee. He had ever such bony knees. 'Please, Edward. Everyone leaves me and they don't come back. I hate it.'

He shook his head. 'I have to see it through. Don't you understand? I'd rather be anywhere but there.' Rose slipped out from under his arm so she could hold him. She kissed his forehead, his temples, took his face in her frozen hands so she could press her lips to his.

'Is it awful?' she whispered.

Edward shook his head again as if he had no adequate words. 'I would say that it's unimaginable, but that would be a lie, because it did happen. That's why it's important to bear witness. To shout from the rooftops until everyone knows.'

Rose began to cry again, though she felt that she had no right to cry when her suffering was unimportant, infinitesimal compared to what others had gone through. 'I'm sorry,' she said.

'I'm sorry too. Please don't cry any more.' He turned his head so he could kiss her hands. 'Shall I tell you something that will make you smile?'

She didn't think anything could make her smile but now that Edward was here, being so tender and now so playful, when he hadn't let himself be either of those things before, Rose could only think of how much she'd missed him. 'You can give it the old college try.'

He gave her a sudden wicked smile. 'Earlier I popped into my club and a man from the Home Office felt the need to cross the bar expressly to tell me, and this is a direct quote, "that girl of yours is a damn bloody nuisance".'

Rose gurgled with laughter. 'It wasn't my Mr Costello, was it?'

'Probably your Mr Costello's boss.'

'I hope you told him that the Home Office and the acres of red tape they expect one to wade through are a damn bloody nuisance too!'

'I did nothing of the sort.' He pulled away from her hands. 'Rose, it's far, far too cold and we're far too well brought up to sit in the gutter like this.'

Edward stood up and held out his hand. Rose let him pull her to her feet. 'There were just so many people and when they shut the doors of Rainbow Corner, I felt so sad. Like nothing good was ever going to happen again. I feel wicked for saying this, but I miss the war. In a way, it was glorious, wasn't it? Wasn't it?'

She'd lived with the uncertainty of war for so long and now every day was the same. Life seemed smaller. The good times weren't harder, faster, brighter compared to the bad times, which no longer plumbed the depth of despair and depravity. Without the highs and the lows, Rose felt adrift, as if she were merely treading water, the horizon never getting any nearer or further away. So yes, she rather missed the war.

'It made heroes of us all, didn't it?' Edward said, as he linked his arm through hers and led her out of the alley. 'Whether we deserved it or not.'

Edward, in his quiet way, was a hero. He'd saved lives, rescued widows and orphans and even now, when other men were hanging up their uniforms, he was avenging the people whose lives he couldn't save.

'I'm not much of a heroine,' Rose said. 'Not when I ran away to London for excitement and glamour and because I didn't want to be a Land Girl and wear corduroy knickerbockers.'

'You've had heroic moments. We all have,' Edward said emphatically and maybe he was right. Maybe they all were heroes in their own small way.

They'd come out onto Piccadilly now where the crowds were drifting away, rushing to catch last trains and buses back to the suburbs. 'Can we go somewhere?' she asked, because she didn't want her last memory of Rainbow Corner to be streaked with tears and she didn't want to go back to Edward's flat. Not yet. 'Somewhere that we can dance.'

'And drink champagne. The American Bar at The Savoy seems appropriate. Let's find a taxi.'

There were no taxis. 'Anyone would think there was a war on!' Rose said as they walked along Coventry Street. 'It will be odd when all the GIs finally go home not to hear an American accent any more. You don't sound remotely American.'

'I've lived here since I was eight so any accent I did have was thrashed out of me at prep school,' Edward said. They were holding hands now and Rose was wearing his coat because it was easier to wear it than argue over whether she should wear it. 'I'll have to go back to New York for a while once this business in Germany is over.'

Rose came to a halt in the middle of the street. 'You said that you'd come back after Germany. To me. You didn't say you were going away again.'

He stared at the hand that she'd been holding as if he couldn't quite understand why she'd let go. 'You see . . . well. I thought – that is, I hoped you'd come with me.'

'But there's too much to do here. There are all these people turning up and none of them are fit for work. They need somewhere to stay and food and warm clothes. How am I meant to go to New York?' she demanded and she didn't know why she was thinking of reasons, excuses, obstacles to stop her, but then someone else had promised her the world and that promise had been as empty as his heart.

Edward stepped back from Rose. 'It would be easy enough to take on an assistant for you but if you're set on staying here then I won't try to change your mind,' he said stiffly. 'I was mistaken. Forgive me.'

That was the other thing that Rose missed about the war. How it simplified everything into yes or no, black or white, dance or sit this one out. Everything was so much more complicated now. There were no handy little pamphlets from the government to tell you what you had to do. Rose couldn't tell Edward that she loved him, but she knew that she wanted to be with him for as long as he'd have her.

'Haven't you realised by now that I often say things that I don't really mean?' she asked him. 'If you could bear to be around someone like that, then I would still quite like to go to the American Bar with you, and maybe New York,' she persevered and Edward wasn't looking quite so boot-faced as he had done. He even held out his hand for Rose to take. 'I did hear a rumour that there's no rationing in America. That you can just walk into a store and they allow you to buy whatever you want. I can't even countenance such a thing.'

'Probably a cruel rumour. I'm sure they have to ration some things, otherwise it would just be bad form.' Edward still sounded a little wooden. 'Also, when we get back from New York, I'm going to buy another house. Would you like to live by the sea, Rose?'

'Perhaps,' she said but she wasn't going to allow herself to say any more than that. First he had to go away again and then come back. Then there might be a trip to New York and only then would she think about whether she wanted to live by the sea.

'I think it would be lovely to have a little cottage somewhere in Sussex or Kent. To be in the country, but also to be near to the sea.' He shot her a sidelong glance. 'When I'm in my barren hotel room in Nuremberg, reading witness statements, I close my eyes and think of the two of us sitting in an English country garden, with apple trees and rose bushes in every colour you could think of. I can hear birdsong and beneath that, the sound of waves lapping against the shore. There has to be a garden like that somewhere in England, surely?'

Edward smiled at her bashfully as if he hadn't meant to say that much but Rose was pleased that he had. They were walking past Charing Cross station now. Soon they'd reach The Savoy.

'I missed you,' she said. 'I'm so glad you came back.'

36

'I missed you,' Rose said to Leo the next morning. 'I'm so glad you came back.'

'I missed you too, Rose.' He ever so gently lifted the hand that didn't have the cannula carved into it and kissed her wrist right where her pulse must have once beat out a frantic rhythm. It was faint and thready now. She smelt of something slightly over-ripe, like flowers a day away from drooping decay. 'I wanted us to be friends again.'

She smiled. Awkwardly patted his cheek. 'I missed you so much. Promise that you won't go away again.'

'I won't.' Guilt gnawed at him. That was why he was doing penance now at her bedside, had done the entire nightshift, because yesterday he'd been a no-show. Yesterday had been terrible. Probably not as terrible as it had been for Jane, left to sit with Rose for hours and who'd left Rose's bedroom looking as if she'd narrowly avoided a collision with a ten-ton truck, but still pretty bad.

Rose was in the weeds now. Weeks had become days and the days were shrinking down to hours. Hours that he'd wasted going to Leytonstone and back with George on a day when Leyton Orient were playing at home. They'd sat on the Tube and George had suddenly said, 'We agreed that when she got to the end, she wouldn't see me. Said it would be too cruel for both of us. But the end has come too soon and I haven't had a chance to say goodbye to her.'

Then George had cried again and even though the train was stuffed full of men, testosterone thick around them, Leo had taken George's hand and dared any of them to call him out.

But when they'd got to the art storage facility, the woman on the desk had refused to let Leo in without two forms of ID and signed permission. She didn't care that Leo was on a clock.

He'd shouted at her. He'd sworn at her. Then he'd wept as George gently pushed him to one side and said, 'My dear boy, stop causing such a commotion. I can sign us both in,' because if Leo had stopped to think about it, then of course George was Rose's designated curator.

The painting was propped up against the bedroom wall but now, no matter that it symbolised the gulf between them closing up, Leo couldn't give it back to Rose. The cliff-edge, the dark sea – it was too prescient. He wanted to cry again.

Maybe it was being off the booze and pills. He wasn't numb any more, but having to feel everything.

There was a gentle tap at the door. Agnieska, about to finish the night shift, and Neta, about to start the day shift, were here to reload the pump, check Rose's blood pressure and temperature, change the bed linen and 'make Ms Beaumont a little more comfortable'.

It was a hackneyed old cliché but there was a certain truth to 'live fast, die young, leave a beautiful corpse', thought Leo as he left the room, though he wasn't sure he qualified. Apart from the living fast. God, he'd done that.

'Morning, darling.' Jane was slowly negotiating the stairs with a laden tray. 'I thought you'd be ready for breakfast.'

She reached him and set the tray down on the occasional

table that had been placed outside Rose's suite along with two armchairs and they breakfasted together. There was a tense moment when Jane told him off for leaving crumbs in the butter, but he found comfort in the mundane. 'God, now I feel bad about enjoying a piece of toast and marmalade and a pot of tea that's been left to stew for just long enough.'

Jane paused with her knife in the raspberry jam. 'I don't know how I feel any more,' she said, holding up a piece of Lydia's sourdough toast as evidence. 'I'm eating my feelings instead.'

'Morning.' They both turned to greet Dr Howard, who opened the door to Rose's suite just wide enough that he could slide through, then shut it behind him. As if there were all sorts of arcane rituals going on inside.

'Was she awake?' Jane's voice dropped to a whisper as if anything louder might penetrate the walls.

'Not for long, but she said she'd missed me and she was glad I was back.' God, he was on the verge of tears *again*. 'I can't even tell you what that means.' He let his voice drop even lower. 'Even if she goes today, I had that moment.'

Jane took his hand, her fingers smeared with jam, and Leo lifted it to his lips, as he'd done with Rose, and kissed Jane's knuckles. Jane's skin was tea-warmed and pulsing with life. 'She talked a lot yesterday,' she said. 'About the past, mostly, but she said that when she was ready, she wanted us both there. Said she was so pleased that you'd come home then too.'

Jane was a consummate liar. Leo was sure that you could hook her up to all sorts of devices and she'd never give herself away. But Rose had told him the exact same thing, so they couldn't both be lying. 'Look, this thing between us, I know it's complicated, but I'm glad you stuck around. Not sure how I'd have coped if you weren't here.'

'You'd have coped just fine,' Jane said. Now *that* was a lie and they both knew it. 'Darling, any chance of having my hand back so I can drink my tea *and* eat my toast at the same time?'

'So you'd rather eat breakfast than hold my hand?' he asked Jane, because that little thrum between them had started to vibrate again. 'God, you're a heartless wretch.'

She pouted. 'I'm not, darling. I'm just very hungry.'

He dropped her hand. 'There. You can have it back, then.'

'Let me finish my toast and then you can hold it again,' she promised, like she wasn't his wife but a beautiful girl he was flirting with in a bar.

If they stayed married for fifty years, had breakfast together every morning, would he inevitably take Jane for granted or would he always flirt with her like she was a beautiful girl he'd just met in a bar? It was worth thinking about.

'As long as you wipe the jam and butter off your fingers first,' he told her with a grin. 'You're kind of sticky.'

'So I am,' Jane agreed and she sucked the offending fingers into her mouth, smiled round them when he raised his eyebrows and—

'God! Stop it! Stop it! Stop it!'

The frightened, mewling voice was loud enough to breach the walls.

Leo froze in an agony of indecision. Should they go in? Would they see something they shouldn't see? Would it be compromising Rose's dignity? So many reasons to sit there and do nothing . . .

Then a reedy, high-pitched wail that had both of them bolting into the room where Rose was propped up between Neta and Agnieska, stalled on her journey to the bathroom. Static white hair fell into a face that was distorted in pain, hands clutching at nothing, while even the good Dr Howard looked on helplessly.

*

It took all five of them to get Rose back into bed when every movement, every touch, even the displacement of air against her skin, made her moan.

When Rose had regained some kind of control over her own treacherous body and wasn't making those awful sounds any more, Jane steeled herself to approach the bed and take Rose's hands. 'Darling, you're all right. Everything's going to be all right.'

'I'm not,' Rose insisted. 'Do something. Make it go away. Stop it! Stop it! Stop it!'

She had to be ready now. So why was she struggling so hard?

'Give her something,' Jane barked at the doctor. 'She shouldn't be in this much pain.'

Leo came in on the chorus. 'Yeah. Do it.'

Dr Howard nodded. 'If you're sure?'

He was looking straight at Leo, who held his gaze and nodded back. 'Absolutely sure.' Then he turned to look at Rose, though her head was lowered and she was chanting, 'Stop it! Stop it! Stop it!' under her breath, like a mantra.

Jane watched as the doctor directed Neta to inject something straight into the cannula in the back of Rose's hand. It seemed to take a long, long time before Rose quietened, then dozed and Neta could rearrange her pillows and pull the covers up around Rose as she slept.

Jane still had this horrid fear that Rose could feel all the pain and torment but was trapped behind a drug-induced haze and couldn't tell them.

But still they all pretended that Rose was simply sleeping, though Dr Howard said that her kidneys were shutting down now. 'If there's any change, call me,' he murmured before he left. 'It could be hours, it could be days.'

He'd been saying that for what felt like weeks. Death didn't keep to a schedule. As soon as he'd padded down the stairs, Leo turned to Jane and she held out her arms so he could fall into them. 'We will get through this, Leo,' she told him sharply. 'Because Rose needs us and we don't want to let her down.'

'Don't go all tough love on me,' he groused, but he kissed her cheek and at least he was still up to making jokes, even if they weren't good jokes.

The vigil continued. Neta was banished to the kitchen but came up every hour, along with Lydia who brought tea and sandwiches, or tea and cake, or simply just tea, to check on Rose.

Rose slept on, mouth open as her body tried to release the toxins that her kidneys couldn't. Her wheezing added to the ambient noise from the bed, the pump and the beeps from the game on Leo's phone, which was annoying, but Jane couldn't summon up the energy to tell him that it was annoying. It was exhausting watching someone die.

Eventually, she went downstairs for dinner, then stood shivering outside the kitchen door as she and Lydia shared a glass of wine and Lydia smoked a cigarette, blowing the smoke out of one side of her mouth like a wisecracking heroine from a black and white movie.

Then Jane rushed back upstairs, terrified that Rose would have gone in her absence. That the gasps would have got fewer and fewer, then simply stopped. No deathbed confessions. No final words. That she would just go.

But she still wasn't ready. Katya had replaced Neta. And Agnieska had replaced Katya. Jane had told Leo to go to bed and catch a few hours' sleep but he was sprawled in the chair next to hers, breathing heavily, and occasionally he'd drop off long enough to snore so loudly that he woke himself up again with a startled cry of, 'I wasn't asleep.'

Each time it happened, Jane laughed. Leo laughed too when he told her that he didn't want the last thing that Rose ever heard to be Jane crunching her way through a bag of kettle chips.

They took turns to moisten Rose's lips with the foam lollipops dipped in iced water. They'd even played I-Spy at one point but now Agnieska had been in to do her checks and report that Rose's blood pressure was low but her pulse was steady and Leo was asleep. Not even snoring now, but curled up as much as he could in the chair and it was only Jane left.

It was very lonely. Jane wondered why the Germans with their strange portmanteau words didn't have a phrase to describe the bleak mood that settled around you between three and five a.m. when you and the dying were the only ones left awake.

'Rose?' she whispered, because Rose's eyes were open and fixed on her. 'Are you all right?'

'I'm ready. Everyone is waiting for me but I can't go . . . '

'Why not?' Jane wondered if this was a strange dream. She ran a series of checks, even pinched herself, but, no, it was just her luck to still be awake. 'Darling, we've talked about this. You don't need to stay if you're ready, you can go.'

'I can't.' It was only because the room was so still that Jane could make out the words. 'I'm stuck.'

'Can you see a light? Can you move towards it?' For God's sake, what was she talking about? There was no light. No heaven. No hell. Nothing.

'Help me. I can *not* go on. No. Stop it! Stop it! Stop it!'

'It's all right, darling. I'm here.'

'You said you'd help me when the times comes. Now. *It's now.*'

Jane hadn't realised that that was what she was agreeing to when she'd promised Rose she'd be there at the end. Or maybe she had, because Jane wasn't agonising over what she should or should not do. She was already glancing around the lamp-lit room to see what she could use to speed Rose on her way. A cushion seemed the best option but what if Rose wasn't truly ready? What if she struggled? Fought it? So it wouldn't be helping. It would be something else, something that Jane wasn't sure that she could do.

But this was what Rose wanted. What she'd planned. 'The champagne and pills? Do you want that, Rose? Can you swallow?'

'Stop it! Stop it! Stop it! Stop it! Oh please. Please. Stop it.'

If Rose was stuck then she wasn't going anywhere and Jane could slip out of the room and creep silently through the house. She smoked one of Lydia's cigarettes as she calmly selected a bottle of champagne from the huge wine fridge, a 2002 Dom Ruinart, not the most expensive, but probably the nicest. Then she went back to Rose's room, to the bathroom where the nurses, even Dr Howard, had got sloppy, and took a packet of pills from the green drug safe, which had been left unlocked.

It was to her credit that she did think about fleeing into the night, thought about it again, then walked back into Rose's room.

'Where have you been?' Leo asked hoarsely. He wasn't meant to be awake. 'Champagne? Really?'

'It's for Rose, isn't it, darling?'

Rose's eyes were open but she was muttering indistinctly and looked frightened. She was determined to make this as hard as possible.

'It's a nice gesture but if she can't swallow water, then how is she going to sip champagne?'

Jane had been wondering that too. About how she was going to get three or four, even five or six temazepam into Rose without a struggle. It was the struggle that she was most worried about. But now that Leo was awake, that was something else to worry about too.

One thing at a time. She ignored Leo as she circled the bed, then perched on the other side to him and took Rose's hand. 'Darling, do you still want to go?'

There was nothing but muttering, which made no sense. Jane wondered why it was so hard to die, though she already knew the answer, when Rose said very clearly, 'I want to go. I can't bear it any more. Help me. Now.'

Leo sucked in a breath. 'Just close your eyes and go to sleep.' He was wobbling. Tears not far off. 'You can go. It's all right.'

'Darling, she doesn't need your permission, she needs help. My help. Rose and I talked about this. I promised her.'

Rose lay there, eyes flickering between them. 'Do it,' she said. 'Help me.'

'You can't. She can't, Rose,' Leo said pleadingly. 'It's wrong.'

'But you heard what the doctor said the other day about . . .' About terminally ill cancer patients being given enough of the good drugs that they didn't have to suffer through the final ravages. How could she say that with Rose here?

Instead she grabbed Leo by the sleeve of his jumper and yanked him into the corner. 'Shut up!' she hissed at him. 'If I don't do this, then she'll spend a day, maybe three or four days, even a week, in pain. In fucking agony, Leo. She's going to die anyway.'

'You don't know that. She could go in the next hour and then you'd have her death on your conscience when it needn't be.' He tried to cup her face but Jane wrenched her head back.

She was all right as long as he didn't touch her. 'Darling, it's not like I have that much of a conscience for it to be an issue.' Jane made her words sound as sharp and as hard as she could. Like a diamond.

It was true, after all. It was why Rose had wanted her to stay. Maybe death dogging your heels gave you clarity, Jane wasn't sure. All that she knew was that Rose could see beneath all the gloss, all the gilt-edging, all the *bullshit*, to the sordid truth of what she really was.

If Rose needed an executioner, then Jane was her girl.

'It's the right thing to do,' she told Leo, who wasn't trying to hold her any more, but looking at her with revulsion, which she deserved. She'd earned it. 'Rose has lived her life exactly as she wanted to. She gets to choose how and when she's done with it. You have to respect that.'

'You don't even know her!' Leo said sullenly as he sat and watched her pop the tablets out of the blister pack.

'But Rose knows me.' Jane looked at the pills in her hand then at Rose, who was watching her. Not alert, but present. 'Rose, darling, do you think you could swallow these pills?'

'Of course she can't!' Leo sounded like he was close to exploding. 'Fucking hell, I'm never going to forgive you for this.'

'It's not about you, Leo,' Jane said distractedly. 'Rose? Can you take one of the pills?'

She wanted Rose to reach out a hand, take the pills and pop them in her mouth. That way it would be entirely Rose's doing. It would be her hand. Jane would be one step removed.

'I can't. Help me.'

She could mash the pills into powder, mix them with champagne, cradle the back of Rose's hand and tip the mixture down her throat. Jane could do that. How many times had she done that when she was cajoling Rose into taking some water? 'I'm going to dissolve them into the champagne and then you just need to have a little drink.'

Leo didn't say anything, maybe because he was kissing Rose's forehead, stroking back her limp strands of hair, while they watched Jane attempt to mash four pills between two teaspoons. She did a lousy job of it. Then she opened the champagne with a pop that sounded inappropriately jubilant and poured a little into the tumbler with the crushed pills and stirred it around. Soon the chalky debris soaked up the champagne and turned into a claggy white paste.

She could spoon that into Rose. There was a very thin line

between helping someone with their last wish and killing them – even if you were killing them with your kindness.

She had promised Rose but lately Jane had stopped making promises that she couldn't keep. 'All right,' she whispered. She picked up the tumbler and the spoon and took the four steps to the bed. 'I'm going to put this in your mouth, darling, and then give you a little champagne to wash it down.'

Rose blinked, then nodded. At least, Jane thought it was a nod. Maybe she just wanted it to be. 'Rose, darling? I have to be certain it's what you want.'

'Do it.' Rose mouthed the words rather than said them out loud. 'Now. Please.'

'Are you sure?' Leo asked. 'You can't let go by yourself?'

'Do it.'

'Go on, then.' Leo said and this time, when Jane caught his eye, he nodded.

Jane glanced down at the contents of the tumbler, then scraped some of the paste onto the spoon. It was going to take about five spoonfuls before it was all gone. Five times she had to spoon the mixture into Rose's mouth. Five times she had to tilt her head and make her drink. Five times. Five times was too many times. Five steps too far – even for Jane.

She turned away; let the spoon drop to the floor. 'I'm so sorry, I can't. I just can't.'

'It's OK,' Leo said. He pressed another kiss to Rose's furrowed forehead. 'I can. I'll do it.'

37

Lullington Bay, 1974

It was a beautiful September evening, summer determined to outstay its welcome. They sat in the garden, which was a glorious riot of colour and scent, though the roses, which they added to every year, had blossomed in June and were now long gone.

Still there were flowers enough that bees fat with pollen could lazily dance among the petals. Birds circled overhead and if Rose listened carefully, she could hear the faint lap of the sea.

On other days, they'd dragged deckchairs through the garden and across the dunes to the beach, but it was all Edward could do to manage the short walk from the house to the little shaded spot in the garden where they liked to sit.

He only had a couple of weeks left, though neither of them knew that. He was scheduled for surgery mid-October – they'd already started planning Christmas in Palm Springs.

But no matter where they were – and by now Rose thought they must have gone round the world at least twice – at six o'clock it was time for a drink.

On birthdays and special occasions they had Bellinis, but this evening it was a gin and tonic. Rose swirled the ice in her glass, glanced around the garden, then at Edward, his face in profile, and felt entirely at peace. She was where she was happiest and with the one person who made her happier still.

'I do love you, Edward.' It was the simplest of truths, but she'd never said it before. Hadn't even realised. Her love for him had crept up on her slowly, permeated right down to her marrow, and she was so used to it living there that she'd never thought to give it a name. 'I've loved you for such a long time and I've never once told you.'

He turned his head and smiled at her. She often reminded him that he was a cradle snatcher – 'you're much, much older than I am' – but now it was as if the years and the disease in him had vanished and she could see him as he'd been on the night Rainbow Corner closed. When he'd danced with her at The Savoy and kept apologising for treading on her feet. He still was a dreadful toe-stepper.

'I love you too, my darling girl,' he said, as naturally and as easily as if he said it all the time, though he hadn't, not since that night when she'd thrown his 'I love you' back in his face.

Maybe it was also why he'd never asked her to marry him, not that Rose minded. It was a measure of just how much her parents had adored Edward that they'd never held it against him either. Then again, marriage wasn't something they discussed. Neither were children. Or the exact nature of his war work.

There were so many things unsaid between the two of them, but in the end that didn't matter. Just that you said what was really important at least once.

'I'm going to tell you that I love you every day now,' she decided. 'Sometimes even twice, or three times.'

'We are a pair of silly old fools, aren't we?' Edward sighed and then Rose got up out of her chair and draped herself very gently across his lap so she could kiss him.

His skin was warm underneath her lips and hands and she sat there with his arms around her, listening to the sound of the sea. She could have happily stayed like that for ever.

38

Leo picked up the spoon from the carpet, took the glass from Jane, and walked to the bathroom, where he washed both of them slowly and carefully.

He didn't know why Jane had bothered going to all that trouble. There was liquid morphine in handy phials just sitting there. It wasn't as if Rose was going to toddle in here under her own steam and none of the expensive agency nurses knew about his history with drugs.

Leo took two of the phials, picked up a syringe and tore off its sterile packaging. Then he went back into the bedroom.

At first he didn't see Rose. All he could see was a singed and yellowed limp pale blue dress laid out in front of her, one of her hands resting on the bodice.

And there was Jane, arm around Rose, gently spooning her.

In that moment, Leo loved Jane. He could tell she was scared to get too close to Rose and that sweet-sickly smell of rotting lilies. Scared to touch Rose – not because she didn't want to hurt her, but because maybe death was catching, but she did it all the same.

Leo sat down on the bed. He plunged the syringe through the plastic seal of the first phial, then the second. Tap, check for air bubbles, release. Some things you never forgot.

'There's no need to be scared, darling,' Jane said and Leo didn't know if she was talking to him or Rose who was so still, only her lips moving as she took in little sips of air.

'Are you sure you want to do this?' Leo asked.

Rose didn't answer at first. Then her fingers, resting over the heart of the charred dress, lifted. 'I've had such a lovely time,' she said, and she closed her eyes. 'It's been wonderful, it really has, but I have to get back to my friends now.'

It was simple, in the end. He lay down so he was facing Rose, but looking at Jane, who looked back at him, steady and sure. Then Leo slid the syringe into the cannula. Rose took two more laboured breaths, breathed in again and then no more.

Leo wished he could say that in that moment he felt Rose's soul leave her body, but he didn't. His hand rested on top of Rose and Jane's hand rested on top of his.

After a while, though Leo couldn't say exactly how long, there was a tap at the door. 'Can I come in?' asked Agnieska.

'Just a minute,' Jane called out as Leo curled his fingers round Rose's wrist, her skin cooling, but not cold. Flesh pliable, but also resistant.

'She's gone,' he said. Rose looked like a blurred copy of herself. She was without animation; that magnificent, restless spirit. Without life. Lifeless. He didn't want this to be the way he remembered her and he pulled his hand free and got off the bed. Walked to the door. Opened it. 'She's gone,' he said again. 'Can you go and wake Lydia, then call the doctor?'

'I'm sorry for your loss.' Agnieska didn't even peer in through the open door but hurriedly walked away.

Leo couldn't look at Jane or at the bed. He went into the bathroom and splashed his face and hands with cold water and by the time he was done, Lydia was there in a lilac dressing gown, face creased, crying.

'Oh, my dear. My Rose,' Lydia sobbed, her arms tight around her midriff.

Leo wondered if Jane had died too because she was so still but as Agnieska approached the bed, she rolled away from the body and stood up. Lydia walked into her arms and Jane rocked her, shushed her, but refused to look at Leo.

Suddenly Agnieska's mobile rang and when Leo heard the opening bars of *Carmina Burana* blast out, he laughed. He was sure that Rose would have laughed too, though she'd have pretended to be very cross. If there was an afterlife, then it was just the right kind of portentous fanfare to announce Rose's arrival at the Pearly Gates.

Agnieska looked affronted. 'Dr Howard's on the doorstep and there's no one to let him in,' she said huffily.

Everything went very smoothly after that. Leo waited outside while Agnieska and the doctor did whatever they had to do. Then the door opened and Leo was ready.

'Can I have a word?' he said and he took Dr Howard into the bathroom and picked up the empty phials. 'I have to tell you something. I—'

Dr Howard, three-piece-suited and booted though it was barely six in the morning, held up a hand to stop Leo. 'I've already signed the death certificate. There shouldn't be any need for a post-mortem. Not when I saw her yesterday and, well, this was expected.'

'But I—'

'Just be thankful that you were with Rose at the end. I'm sure that was an immense comfort to her.' The doctor shifted his case to the other hand. 'I've left you a form to hand in when you register the death. The undertakers will be able to assist you with everything else.' He sounded as if he was reciting lines. 'Please call me if you need to, but as far as I'm concerned it's all in order, Leo.'

It felt as if his world was teetering on the very edge of chaos. 'But . . . Don't . . . Are you sure?'

'Absolutely sure. I'll see myself out.' Leo watched Dr Howard walk through the other room, past the body, then paused in the doorway. 'I'm so sorry for your loss. Rose . . . Ms Beaumont, she really was an incredible woman. I will miss her more than I can say.'

Agnieska came in to pack up the medical equipment and Leo went downstairs to the kitchen where Lydia, still in her dressing gown, still sniffling, was sitting at the breakfast bar. Frank hovered anxiously. 'I've called the undertakers,' he said. 'What else can I do?'

There was nothing else to do but drink tea, smoke all of Lydia's cigarettes, though she was still maintaining that she only smoked socially as she had ever since Leo had known her, and then, with heavy sighs and heavy feet, she and Leo went back upstairs.

Neither of them looked at the bed. Lydia marched straight into the dressing room and he followed her blindly.

'Rose left specific instructions. Didn't want an open casket. There's a dress she wanted to be . . . ' Lydia couldn't get the next word out. Leo rested his hands on her quaking shoulders. 'No, I'm all right. Do you think I should change her now?'

'No,' Leo said, because Lydia couldn't manage by herself and he couldn't help her. Rose wouldn't have wanted that. 'We'll give the dress to the undertakers.'

'But her hair . . . she'd hate not to have her hair done.' Lydia turned round and buried her face in Leo's chest and as he closed his arms around her, she shook with the force of her sobs.

'We'll ask her hairdresser if they can send someone to the funeral parlour. It will be fine, Liddy,' Leo said. Somehow he knew the right things to say without having to think about it.

The undertakers arrived. They parked their black private ambulance outside the front door, because he wasn't having Rose sneaked out round the back. Lydia, Frank and Leo watched the body (covered by a white sheet because he wasn't having Rose zipped into a black body bag either) wheeled out, then driven around the square that she'd loved so much.

It was seven-thirty now. How could it only be seven-thirty? 'I need to go and register the death,' he said, but it would be another two hours before he could do that, so he wandered back to the kitchen with Frank and Lydia, the three of them in a state of limbo. Not shock but an uncertainty because Rose had gone and she'd dictated the rhythms of their day and without her, they weren't sure what to do.

Lydia put the kettle on but Frank said, 'No more bloody tea. Let's have a proper drink.'

Leo waited for Jane to say, 'Champagne, darling. It's what Rose would have wanted,' and it was then he realised Jane wasn't there.

'Where's Jane?' he asked.

'Jane? She's around, isn't she?' As Lydia was staring at the tea bags and milk as if she had no earthly clue what to do with them, Leo wasn't surprised that she had no recollection of when she'd last seen Jane.

'Probably gone back to bed,' Frank said. 'When my mum passed on, my dad slept for the best part of a week.'

Jane wasn't in any of the downstairs rooms. He didn't go back into Rose's room but stood in the doorway and that was enough to see that Jane wasn't there.

He walked into his room – no, *their* room. It was empty. There was a towel draped over the back of a chair. Her phone and handbag was dumped on the bed, so she couldn't have gone far. But Leo couldn't say exactly where she had gone to until he heard her crying.

He'd never heard crying like it. As if the sobs were being torn out of her against her will. As if she was locked in a battle with her own grief.

'Jane? Where are you?'

There was a moment of silence and then came another one of those pitiful cries, more dreadful than anything he'd heard from Rose, from under the bed.

He crouched down. She was curled into a ball, hair in her face, hands clutched in her hair.

'What are you doing under there? Come out.'

Jane didn't say anything and Leo thought about pushing the bed back, but he didn't want to disturb the little cocoon that she'd made so instead he stretched out full length on the floor.

'I know it's awful about Rose,' he said. 'I can't even deal with how awful it is, but she was in terrible pain and now she's not. You made the right call.'

'Shut up,' she said thickly. 'Shut up. Don't be nice to me. I don't deserve it. I'm disgusting. I'm a monster. The absolute worst.'

'No, you're not,' Leo said, because she wasn't. She was a lot of things, but she wasn't a bad person. He knew bad people and Jane didn't even come close.

'Oh, Leo, I'm sorry. I'm so sorry.'

'You've got to nothing to be sorry about.'

'You don't know the half of it.' Her voice was raw from crying for so long in the dark. 'I was meant to do it. It's why Rose wanted me there at the end. She knew me. She'd been around, she knew everything.'

'Not everything. Just because she was old didn't make her some great all-seeing, omnipotent being. Alice Neel was her favourite artist. That's not someone who knows everything.'

*

'She knew what I was really like without me having to say a single word.'

Leo still hadn't shifted the bed, dragged her out and exposed her to the light. He was just lying there, looking at her with concern instead of condemnation. That was about to change.

'What are you really like?' he asked and God, she couldn't tamp it down any longer. It was leaking out; knocking down the walls she'd so carefully constructed.

'You've always had a life, Leo. Even if you pretend that you don't care about your parents, your brother, you have a family; you have roots. You have history. You're part of something.

'But before I came to London, I didn't have a life. Hardly even had a name. I barely existed. I crept round the edges. I was nothing. Less than nothing. And I still feel like . . . a ghost. There's nothing anchoring me down. I feel like I could blow away.'

Back then, she wasn't aware of things like day and night or what the seasons were. The days had no rhythm.

Sometimes, earlier on, she'd gone to school but only when Nana Jo was alive, and after she'd died she didn't even have the haven of school for a few hours.

She learned quickly that it was better to be ignored, to keep out of sight, even if it meant going hungry. Her brothers and sisters fought for approval, attention, though approval never came and attention rarely led to anything good. How quickly they'd even turn on each other, because there was no honour among thieves, so she'd hidden herself away from them too.

Jane had heard all about the 'deserving poor'. She'd been at dinner parties with politicians, intellectuals, do-gooders with a rosy view of the decent working classes bettering themselves through education and honest toil, but she'd come from the undeserving poor. An underclass despised and feared by the other families on the estate.

Their part of the estate was where the council had shoved the great unwashed and unwanted. ASBO Alley, they called it, the one desolate road where no one, not even the police, would visit after dark. Sometimes, to get away, she'd walk across the estate to the library. Not to read – it wouldn't have occurred to her that there was anything for her in the tiny black letters that crawled across the pages – but the library was warm and next door was a shop where her family hadn't been banned and she knew the blind spot where she could stuff a sausage roll down her track-suit top and the lady on the till wouldn't see.

There were lots of bad times. Each time her mother brought home a new man, each one worse than the last. Meaner. Harder. More demanding. Dreadful times when she found herself cornered by one of them but there were worse times even than that. Like just before benefits day when there was nothing to eat, nothing to put on account, no booze, no pills, no puff, no powder and that was when tempers got ugly. There'd be screaming. Things and bones would get broken. One time her mother had taken a swing at one of her sisters, who'd ducked so her mother had ended up putting her fist right through the wall.

Staying tucked away in one of the damp bedrooms was a good way to not get noticed but crawling under the bed was better – scooched right up against the mildewed wall so she couldn't be yanked out unless the bed was lifted up. It had been lifted up that day when her mother had dragged herself upstairs on ulcerated legs.

'You! Shift your arse to Fat Alan. Get me something on tick.'

The only kindness her mother ever showed her was not sending her off to Fat Alan to get something on tick, unless she'd exhausted every other possibility.

She'd walked the ten minutes to Fat Alan's house on the nicer bit of the estate. It hadn't occurred to her to say no. Saying no was as unimaginable as being invited into one of the nice houses she passed with their cladding and their satellite dishes; some of the really fancy ones even had hanging baskets and flowerbeds.

Fat Alan's house didn't have flowerbeds. Just two cars and a white van parked on the drive and that wasn't good news. Sometimes Fat Alan would force her down onto her knees as soon as he shut the door behind her. Ram himself down her throat so hard that she'd choke and her nose would be pressed against the stinking raw folds of his pendulous gut, but when Fat Alan had other men there . . . it was the worst of all the worse times. She'd blank out, pretend she was under the bed, until it was over, until they were done with her and she could leave with a wrap of something worth no more than twenty quid.

'Who the fuck is it?' Fat Alan shouted when she knocked on the door.

'Sally sent me,' she said and she heard him laugh before she saw the big unformed mass of him through the frosted panel.

He opened the door. She walked in. Kept her head down, stared at his trainers, felt his pudgy hand clutching the back of her neck and she let him push her down, saw his other hand delving into his tracksuit bottoms and then there was a sharp knock on the door. Two sharp knocks. Pause. Two sharp knocks. Pause.

'Fuck's sake,' Fat Alan had shouted at the unseen caller. 'Give me a minute.'

He frogmarched her down the hall. For one heart-stopping moment, they passed the lounge where the sound of music, heavy beats, thudded through the door, but he kept going until they came to the kitchen.

'Don't fucking move,' he said and shut the door.

The dog was in there. It was a huge Alsatian called Killer. Fat Alan treated the dog like he treated everything else, but the dog didn't take it quietly. It snarled and snapped, growled and barked. Once it had bitten her when Fat Alan had made her put her hand in its mouth.

Now the dog sat there, ears alert, staring at her. She looked everywhere but at the dog. At the empty bottles, cans and take-away containers. Then she looked at the table. There were bags and bags of pills and powders because Fat Alan knew that she was the only person he could leave in there with strict instructions not to fucking move and she wouldn't fucking move.

Then she saw the money. A huge roll of notes secured with a rubber band. That much money didn't even look real, not when she'd hardly seen a twenty-pound note before, not hundreds upon hundreds of them, and perhaps that was why she picked it up; just to see if it was real.

She hadn't imagined that money would actually weigh something. That there'd be so much of it that she could hardly close her hand around it.

The dog just sat there and watched her, like he couldn't quite believe it either.

She didn't know how long she stood there, holding the money. Not even thinking about what it could buy because that was too much to process. Then Fat Alan was in the doorway.

'What the fuck are you doing?' He didn't shout. Didn't need to. 'Taking my fucking money, like a thieving bitch? Give me one good reason why I shouldn't slit you from ear to ear?'

There were no good reasons. Not one. He walked over. She watched him get closer. She wasn't scared. Not really. More resigned, accepting that this was what was coming to her. Then she saw the knife. It was just an ordinary knife. In an ordinary home, ordinary people would use it to chop up vegetables. She picked it up and he laughed, like it was funny. He said something to her, she didn't hear what, because she shoved the knife at him, into him. It wasn't easy. It didn't just slide in like all his blubber was butter. She had to drive the knife in. Really smash it into him.

Then she took her hand away. The knife stayed where it was. Inches deep.

'What the fuck did you do that for?' He didn't sound angry, but curious.

'I don't know,' she said.

'Do you know what I'm going to do to you?'

'No.'

'I'm gonna take the knife and I'm gonna shove it in your cunt and up your arse and then I'm going to make some more holes in you and then I'm going to get my friends to fuck each one. We'll fuck you to death,' he'd said, like that was a nice way to spend the afternoon. 'That's what I'm going to fucking do.'

She'd pulled the knife out then. There wasn't any blood until she did that and then there was, so much of it, and he gave one surprised bellow and that was when the fear grabbed hold of her so she slammed the knife in and it was much easier this time to stab it through all that fat, all those rotten layers. Push. Pull. Push. Pull. Push. And he must have fought back, but she couldn't remember that, though later she discovered that she was covered in bruises and, to this day, she still didn't have any sensation in the little finger and ring finger on her left hand. But back then, he slipped on the blood and landed with a dull thud and a roar and she heard a someone coming down the hall and she left the knife stuck in him and the back door was unlocked and she launched herself through it.

She ran. Could hear barking and the dog, Killer, was coming after her. No, not after her but running with her because he hated Fat Alan as much as she did and at last he was free too.

She kept on running, running, running beyond the confines of the estate, running until she hit the main road and pulled off her tracksuit top because it was covered in blood and threw it over a hedge then she ran until she got to the big supermarket and she slowed down and despite what she'd done, she was back to nothing and she could slip unseen onto a bus that was headed to the station amid a crowd of old ladies with shopping trollies and smokers' coughs.

Then she hid and waited until the train pulled into the platform. She got on the train. Found a seat and hunched herself up as small as she could and she stayed like that until the ticket collector came round and asked for her ticket and she pretended to ignore him. But he wouldn't go away and then she saw that she was still holding all that money and that she could use some of it to buy a ticket but she didn't need to, because someone said, 'It's all right. I'll pay for her ticket,' and that was when she met Charles.

She was crying again, the tears slipping out along with her confession. The burden she'd carried on her back all these years ... it had weighed her down. Crippled her. Made her hard. But even now, she didn't feel sorry. She wasn't ashamed of what she'd done. If she hadn't killed Fat Alan, then she wouldn't have been able to kill the shadow that she'd been. But the thing about shadows was that they had a way of reappearing whenever it got dark.

'That's it,' Jane said. 'That's who I am. You know what I'm really like now.'

She waited for Leo to look at her as if he couldn't bear to look at her. Waited for him to turn away from her. To hate her. To pull her out from under the bed.

But he was still lying on the floor, eyes fixed on her face. Then he stretched out his arm and she flinched away from him. 'Jane, please,' he said. Those two words gave nothing away. 'I've lost loads of weight but I'm still too big to be able to get under the bed with you.'

'You're never as funny as you think you are,' she told him, though somehow he'd managed to crack a smile from her frozen face. 'You can't hide behind a joke for ever.'

'Yeah, I'm starting to get that,' Leo said and he stretched out his arm again and this time she let him take hold of her hand. 'It's all right. Everything's going to be all right. You have to trust me on that.'

Leo didn't say anything else. He held her hand and stroked her knuckles over and over again, while she cried. Even once she'd managed to stop crying, he didn't let go and Jane hoped that maybe they could stay like that for ever.

Epilogue

Lullington Bay

In the end, they both chose not to be fucked up.

Though Leo never realised how hard it would be to love someone who didn't believe in love.

Still, he's fiercely glad of his love, though he never expected it to feel so sentimental, like a cheesy love song playing on the radio and leaking out of an open window on a sunny day.

His love for Jane – and he winces even as he forms the thought – makes him want to be a better man. He can't imagine that he'll ever do drugs again. Not now that he knows what he knows. He's only faltered once and that was one almighty alcohol-fuelled bender the night that Jane confessed her crimes. Her other crimes. The man that she'd jilted, not the other way round. The long con she'd been planning. Waiting it out so she could get a decent alimony payment from Rose's estate.

Leo had gone and got so drunk, he could hardly see straight. He'd come back, vomited on Rose's roses and ended up comatose on the kitchen floor.

Jane had been furious. 'If you promise that you'll never get like this again, then I promise that I'll never keep another secret from you. You have to promise, Leo. I can't be strong enough for both of us. I can't do that any more.'

Leo had promised because a world without Jane in it would be cold and lonely and a quick slide back into dirty old habits. But Jane tilts his world by one hundred and eighty degrees and she's usually right about everything, apart from the times when she's spectacularly wrong.

Just as he builds houses, he's building a life for the two of them. He wants to give Jane the things she's never had, the kind of things that don't cost money.

Now that it's summer at Lullington Bay, on the weekends he fills the house with people. George, of course, and Lydia and Frank who are renovating a guesthouse down the coast in Brighton; Mark and his family; Fergus and his wife and their three redheaded, freckle-faced little girls. Leo even invited his parents down, although that was two days of awkward silences, barbed remarks, passive-aggressive comments and one enormous row over Sunday lunch between him and his mother, while Jane and his father made their excuses and walked to the village pub, even though it was pissing down with rain, where they bonded over a mutual love of Ealing comedies and sticky toffee pudding.

Now he Skypes his mother every Sunday afternoon and she knits coats for the two Staffie-cross puppies he and Jane found in a layby the time they went to see a man in Hayward's Heath about some reclaimed timber.

'But they have to stay downstairs, Leo,' Jane had said the first night but she was always the one who got up to comfort them when they began to whimper and howl. Now they sleep in a basket next to their bed.

It's almost a family. It's ties that bind them together.

Leo's still a gambling man, a risk taker. Jane might not know what love is but if he loves her hard enough and well enough, eventually even Jane has to give in. He's counting on it.

He's put everything he has on red and he's waiting for the wheel to stop spinning.

It's easy, the easiest thing in the world, to love Leo.

He's actually very loveable. Not in some sweet, saccharine way that involves date nights and flowers bought from petrol stations on a Friday evening. Or necklaces and cuddly toys that spell out 'I love you'. That's not their way.

But love isn't something Jane takes lightly. There'd been a time when she'd found it ridiculously easy to say 'I love you' because it wasn't true, but when you thought it might be the greatest truth you'd ever told, it was very, very hard. Besides, once you'd told someone that you loved them and really, really meant it, you'd shown your entire hand and Jane has always played her cards close to her chest.

For a long time after Rose's death, it felt like Jane was holding her breath and she only let it out when Rose's will could no longer be contested. When she told her lawyer, Mr Whipple, that she didn't want a divorce. When Leo sat down with Charles, Rose's executor, and said he wanted his inheritance placed in a trust, that he could manage on the salary he draws as what Rose stipulated in her will as an Executive Without a Briefcase. 'You give me access to all that money and I might go off the rails,' Leo had said. 'I really don't want to go off the rails.'

With Leo's salary and the interest Jane earns on the investments that Charles makes for her, they're comfortable. They have a comfortable life. Sometimes what you think you want doesn't come close to what you really need.

Jane needs Leo now he's the best version of himself. He uses his time wisely: working with Mark on converting an old art deco council block in Stoke Newington into homes for essential workers. Spends one day a week shadowing an architect and is forever taking meetings with people from the Tate Modern about an exhibition he's curating of British Pop Art, mostly culled from Rose's art collection.

During the week they live in the little mews house in Kensington. Jane helps George pack up Rose's house and takes classes, studies anatomy and makes notes as she trains to become a yoga instructor, then on Friday afternoon, they head down to Sussex.

Lullington Bay is invariably full of people but Jane prefers it when it's just her and Leo and their two silly dogs. They have a kitchen disco on Friday nights and Leo gets up early to go down to the beach and paint the sea. Jane like the pictures he paints on overcast days the best.

Mostly Jane lives for those long nights in Lullington Bay when she lies in bed in Leo's arms, her hand over his heart. In those moments, she finally knows what safe feels like. Underneath the steady cadence of his breathing, she can hear the faint lap of the sea against the shore and it echoes in her head like the words she still hasn't found the courage to say.

I love you, I love you, I love you.

Coda

Rose is back on the dancefloor of Rainbow Corner, with the smell of brilliantine and sweat-soaked rayon catching at the back of her throat. The band plays on, ever on and on, light from the chandeliers glinting off the brass section as Rose is dipped and twirled and spun round.

Everyone she loves is here. Reunited with her girls, her precious, precious girls. Sylvia, as beautiful and brilliant as ever, brushes past in the arms of a strapping GI. Phyllis waves each time Rose glides by, shouts something out that's lost in the beat of the music and Maggie's sitting with a drink in her hand and her smile is no longer a dark, secret thing.

Sometimes she thinks she sees Danny. Men she danced with. Girls who gave her hankies, spare change, a shoulder to cry on. Gosh, even Shirley is here, absolutely splendid in her pale blue taffeta. But Rose only has eyes for Edward, who's holding her in his arms and he hasn't once stepped on her feet.

She's going to stay here for ever. Because Rainbow Corner never closes. They never turn anyone away.

When they opened the doors of Rainbow Corner, they threw away the key.

Sarra Manning is an author and journalist. She is currently literary editor for *Red* magazine and has written for the *Guardian*, *ELLE*, *Grazia* and *You* magazine. She is the author of several bestselling young adult novels, including *Guitar Girl*, the *Diary of a Crush* trilogy and *Adorkable*. *After the Last Dance* is her fifth adult novel. Sarra lives in North London with her Staffordshire bull terrier, Miss Betsy, and prides herself on her unique ability to accessorise.

Author Note

I have tried to be a stickler for accuracy in the historical sections of this novel. However, for the sake of dramatic licence: although the first V2 rockets were launched at London on 8th September, they didn't fall on Holborn but Chiswick, killing three people, and Epping with no casualties.

'Someday they'll write stories about this place': How I came to fall in love with Rainbow Corner

I don't know if it's because I read Noel Streatfeild's *When the Siren Wailed* at an impressionable age but I've always been fascinated with what life was like for the people of Britain during World War Two. I've devoured countless novels, diaries and non-fiction about the Home Front and imagined that some day I would write a novel set in London during those tense, turbulent times.

Then, a few years ago, I was watching a documentary series, *The Making of Modern Britain*, and saw a five-minute segment on a place called Rainbow Corner. It was a social club run by the American Red Cross which opened at the end of 1942 and was a place where American servicemen could go for a small slice of Americana.

I couldn't believe that in all my reading I'd never heard of Rainbow Corner. For years I'd worked on Orange Street, the other side of Leicester Square from where Rainbow Corner had once stood on the corner of Shaftesbury Avenue and Denman Street. I'd walked past that very spot a hundred times and on Fridays I'd often gone to the New Piccadilly Café on Denman Street for a lunchtime fry-up.

Rainbow Corner sparked something in me. I imagined a teenage girl watching a Pathé newsreel in a cinema far away from London and being just as transfixed by Rainbow Corner as I was some seventy years later. How her whole life would feel as if it were monochrome, drab and dreary until she stepped through the doors of Rainbow Corner and saw the whole world explode with colour, glamour and possibility.

I started plotting a novel about the girl in that cinema desperate to run away to London and began to research Rainbow Corner in earnest.

When America entered the Second World War in 1942 and American servicemen were stationed in Britain, they discovered a country battered by a brutal Nazi bombing campaign, strict food, petrol and clothing rationing and unfriendly natives. 'Overpaid, oversexed and over here' was how the British described the GIs, as the Americans were known, an abbreviation of 'Government Issue' because everything from their uniforms to their toilet roll was supplied by the US government.

The American Red Cross were charged with the task of providing their servicemen with a taste of all the things they missed from back home. There were the famous Clubmobiles that welcomed the US troops at the docks and travelled to their bases, even following them to France after the invasion, to serve them coffee and doughnuts.

There were also clubs for American servicemen, mostly in London, and the largest, most legendary one was Rainbow Corner. Originally a famous restaurant called Del Monico's and an adjoining Lyons Corner House, Rainbow Corner was created as a Little America for all those GIs thousands of miles away from home.

I didn't have to make up any of the details about Rainbow Corner in *After the Last Dance* because Rainbow Corner really was that magical place. It had two dining rooms, a snack bar (Dunker's Den) in the basement and, as far as I know, it was the first place in Britain to stock Coca-Cola. They held boxing and wrestling matches, and dances five nights a week where English hostesses like Rose, Sylvia, Maggie and Phyllis would jive with the soldiers. Even the Where Am I? room really existed.

Rainbow Corner was a place where GIs could get their hair cut in the American style, their shoes shined, their cigarette lighters filled. Glenn Miller, Ed Murrow, Fred Astaire and countless other celebrities came to entertain the troops and when it opened on a foggy night in November 1942, they really did throw away the key as a symbolic gesture that for as long as US troops were fighting in Europe, Rainbow Corner would never turn any of them away.

One of my most prized Rainbow Corner finds was a yellowed and musty copy of *Picture Post* magazine from April 1944 with a four-page story on the club, complete with photographs that I pored over. I scoured accounts from the women who worked there. I even tracked down an obscure 1946 film, *I Live on Grosvenor Square*, because the director had recreated the Rainbow Corner basement snack bar on a film set in Welwyn.

My magic a-ha moment was when I discovered that Pathé had put their news archive online. There was a newsreel showing volunteers at Rainbow Corner helping GIs to wrap Christmas presents to be sent back home and a newsreel of the night that Rainbow Corner closed in February 1946.

Hearing Eleanor Roosevelt speak the exact same words that I later transcribed for *After the Last Dance*, seeing the hordes of people standing out on the street as they finally locked those doors struck a chord deep in my heart and I truly understood what a special place Rainbow Corner had been for all the men and women that had visited.

Many months later, when I was writing the chapter where Rainbow Corner closes, I watched the newsreel again. This time, I scoured the footage for Rose, for Mickey Flynn, for Edward, because they'd become as real to me as Rainbow

Corner and when I heard Eleanor Roosevelt talk once again about its legacy, tears streamed down my cheeks. And I'm a stony-hearted non-crier.

After Rainbow Corner closed, they put up a plaque at the site in 1949:

THIS PLAQUE IS PLACED HERE AS A TRIBUTE TO ALL RANKS OF THE UNITED STATES SERVICES WHO KNEW THE ORIGINAL 'RAINBOW CORNER'.

But in 1959 the Del Monico restaurant (and the plaque) was demolished to create a faceless office building.

Now, it's as if it never existed, but I think that the spirit of Rainbow Corner still survives. All of us yearn for somewhere that will never turn us away, that will always be open when we need a haven, a magical place where we can be our best selves.

Sarra Manning, London, 2015

Turn the page for an exclusive
extract from Sarra Manning's new novel,

The Echo of Your Last Goodbye

From the author of *After the Last Dance* comes this exquisite love story that moves from the 1930s to the present day and back again. Bold, thrilling and full of secrets and drama, this tale about the healing power of love will steal your heart.

HIGHGATE – HOUSES

from £900 FREEHOLD

The best of town and country guaranteed for the discerning home buyer! Moments from Highgate Tube station and delightful woodland.

SEMI-DETACHED house
with space for a garage.

TWO reception rooms, **FOUR** bedrooms,
BATH and KITCHEN.

ALL ELECTRIC!
LIGHTING, HEATING, HOT WATER!

Free conveyance and no road charges.

G. A. SHAW, ***Master Builders &***
Sole Proprietors

Telephone: BARNET 3745

PRIVATE SALE

FOUR BEDROOM HOUSE, HIGHGATE £POA

SEMI-DETACHED PROPERTY IN NEED OF COMPLETE RENOVATION AND MODERNISATION.

◆ Two reception rooms ◆ Four bedrooms
◆ Kitchen ◆ Bathroom ◆ WC
◆ Large south west-facing garden.

Two minutes' walk from Highgate Tube station. Both Highgate Woods and Queens Woods are moments away as are the vibrant cafes and boutiques of Highgate Village.

Applications are invited for purchase of this property, which has been priced considerably below its market value to take into account the work and expense required to turn this house into a delightful family home. Private buyers only, no property developers.

For further instructions apply in writing to Messrs Flintlock & Harding, Solicitors, 91 Devonshire Square, Mayfair, London, W1.

Chapter One

January 1936

The King is dead.

As Libby travelled across the city, the London she could see from the top deck of the 24 was draped in black, and when she got off the bus at Victoria Station the swirl of travellers and businessmen was sombre and muted and she was pleased of it. For these few days, until the funeral had passed, London, England, the whole damn Empire, matched the dark mood that she'd carried round with her these past few months. Now, no one would dare to tell her to cheer up. To will away her troubles with a smile.

She hurried across the road, breath curling in the air like little puffs of dragon smoke, which made her think of funeral pyres. Her destination was a small hotel down a side street. Libby was ushered inside by the doorman, a black armband bisecting the smart navy blue of his military style coat.

Libby paused in the doorway and looked around the lobby, which was as gloomy as the solemn streets outside. It was a cold, grey day, not a single shaft of sunlight shining through the windows to chase away the shadows. Uncomfortable-looking high-backed armchairs arranged around tables didn't tempt one to linger. Even the ferns drooping in the big brass pots added to the air of general despondency and gloom.

There were two men sitting in the darkest, furthest corner and as Libby squinted in their general direction, one of them caught her eye and stood up.

Despite the solemnity of the days since the King had passed, Mickey Flynn hadn't thought to adjust his swagger, his cocky grin or exchange one of his famously lurid silk neckties for a shade more fitting.

'Libby, my darling,' he greeted her, brushing his lips against the cheek she proffered. 'Why the long face? Has someone died?'

'Oh, Mickey,' she admonished him. 'That's in very poor taste, even for you.'

Mickey ducked his head. 'Now why would a fellow like me be weeping over the death of an English king?' he asked, exaggerating his brogue so he sounded as if he were fresh off the boat, when Libby knew full well that he'd been born and bred in Kilburn.

'Because someone's still dead and that's always sad,' she said as she let Mickey take her case and guide her to a table near to the window, quite some distance away from the corner where he'd been sitting. 'It doesn't feel right not having a king.'

'There's your fellow Edward, isn't there?' Mickey sounded as if he were already bored with talking about it and though Libby had plenty to say about the former Prince of Wales, about how nice it would be to have a young king on the throne, one who seemed simpatico with the plight of the working man (and the working woman for that matter), she simply shrugged.

Mickey tilted his head. 'You're looking awfully peaky since the last time I saw you, my darling.'

The last time Mickey had seen Libby had been on a glorious September day. Then, he'd toasted her health and happiness and, along with the rest of their friends, he'd waved her and Freddie off a few hundred yards from this very spot as they'd boarded The Golden Arrow, the boat train to Paris, still in their wedding clothes. It wasn't even six months ago, but it seemed to Libby that she'd lived through several lifetimes since then, aged a hundred years.

Instead of the pretty, laughing woman with orange blossom threaded through her red hair who'd leaned out of the train window to shout, 'We'll send you a postcard. Each and every one of you! We promise!' in her place was a thin, pale woman whose hair had faded, the gleam gone from her green eyes. Libby hardly recognised the reflection that stared back at her in the glass each morning so she'd taken to avoiding mirrors and no longer lingered in front of shop windows.

'That's not a very gentlemanly thing to say, Mickey.' Libby fixed him with what Freddie had always called her basilisk stare – he insisted that it made him feel as if he'd died a thousand deaths – but Mickey was uncowed and waved her words away with a brush of his pudgy fingers.

'Never been much of a gentleman, you know that.' He leaned forward. 'This isn't going to be too much for you, is it?' He glanced over his shoulder at the dark corner from where he'd emerged, but the man he'd left behind was still sitting there, an indistinct figure hidden by a copy of *The Times*. 'You'd really be helping your good friend Mickey Flynn out of a bind. Got one girl on her way to Hastings with a Lord of the Realm and another on her way to Harrogate to meet up with the heir to a biscuit dynasty, not that you heard it from me. It's Christmas, that does it, Libby, my peach. January's always my busiest month. Must be something in the bread sauce . . . '

Libby had forgotten how much Mickey liked the sound of his own voice. 'I'm much better now,' she said firmly. 'Quite able to manage a weekend in Brighton.' Now it was her turn to nod her head in the direction of the dark corner. 'What's he like?'

'Salt of the earth,' Mickey assured her. 'A diamond among men.'

'Oh, Mickey, please stop it. We both know you've never so much as crossed the Irish Sea, never mind kissed the Blarney Stone. I'm going to spend two days with a man I don't know, two nights with him in a hotel room. So, tell me what he's really like. No fibbing.'

Mickey straightened his tie then wiped the oily smile off his face as if he'd taken a damp rag to it. 'Very stiff, very proper. Ex-Army, made his money in the motor trade, but not a toff. Wife's been keeping company with the younger brother of his business partner. Messy business all round his solicitor said, but our Mr Watkins has agreed to do the decent thing and give her grounds to divorce *him*, poor bastard that he is.'

'Isn't it funny that when it comes to divorce, it's the man who always decides to do the decent thing?' Libby noted with a contemptuous sniff. 'If I were Mr Watkins, I'd bury the bitch.'

'You'll have to mind your language!' Mickey said sharply and hurriedly because the mysterious yet upstanding Mr Watkins had unfolded himself from the chair and was walking towards them. 'I told him you were a teacher. Widowed. Respectable. Now, quickly, let's get this squared away. We agreed twenty pounds, didn't we?'

'Thirty,' Libby snapped, though they'd actually agreed on twenty five, but Mickey had to be getting fifty and she was the one who'd have to spend two days with a stiff, proper man with an axe to grind. 'Thirty or I'm catching the first bus back to Hampstead.'

There wasn't much Mickey could do about it but nod unhappily and discreetly tuck the money into Libby's coat pocket as Mr Watkins was now bearing down on them. 'The Brighton train leaves in twenty minutes,' he said brusquely as if to chivvy them along, though Libby rarely caught a train without a hurried dash down the platform to the accompaniment of the guard's whistle and a cacophony of slamming doors.

Mickey made the introductions. Libby kept her face still and slightly wistful as befitted a respectable widowed teacher, though she wanted to smile when Mickey called her Marigold, the nickname they'd agreed on. He said he had flower names for all his girls and Marigold wasn't as ridiculous as a little tart like Sylvia becoming a Primrose, but still she had to press her lips together.

'Hugo Watkins,' Mickey said and Libby shook his hand, which clasped hers in a grip one shade away from punishing. 'From the moment you leave this hotel, you need to play the part of the besotted couple. Just imagine that one of the King's Proctor's lackeys is trailing you at all times. And remember to sign the hotel register as Mr and Mrs Watkins and it's not enough to have the maid come in in the morning and catch you happy as larks in bed together. You'll need to be seen having dinner in the hotel restaurant this evening; tip well—'

'I do believe that we've already covered this in some detail.' Mr Watkins spat out the words as if they were pieces of rotten apple. 'We mustn't miss the train.'

He set off for the door, without waiting to see if Libby was following him. She quickly stood up, though everything in her wanted to stay, to not hurry after this terse, bitter stranger.

Then she wished she hadn't stood up at all, because the dull ache in her side, which was a constant these days, transformed itself into a sharp tugging sensation and she gasped.

'I wouldn't worry about it,' Mickey advised, mistaking her pain for trepidation as he walked with her to the door where the odious Mr Watkins was pointedly looking at his watch. 'Two days of sea air will put the roses back in your cheeks, my darling.'

Mr Watkins didn't offer to take Libby's case but he did hold the door open for her, even as he held his body stiff and bristling so there wasn't the remotest possibility that Libby might brush against him.

He didn't say anything either, though when Mickey called after them, 'Don't forget to take off your wedding ring, Marigold!' Libby heard his contemptuous snort.

*

Mr Watkins didn't speak to Libby for the entire journey to Brighton.

Indeed, Libby wouldn't have been surprised if he'd deposited her in a third class carriage and hurried away to the loftier climes of first class. He didn't, though there were a lot of other things he failed to do. Such as ask Libby if she minded sitting with her back to the engine or if she needed help putting her suitcase on to the luggage rack, earning him the censorious disapproval of an elderly gentleman whose splendid handlebar moustache quivered in outrage at Watkin's cavalier attitude to women. 'Chap's an out-and-out bounder,' he muttered to Libby as he hefted the case for her but unfortunately he left the train at Clapham Junction.

Then it was just the two of them, Mr Watkins fulminating from behind his *Times*, though Libby was sure that he must have read it from cover to cover several times.

Libby had borrowed a couple of Angela Thirkell novels from the library but she couldn't settle to reading. She wrote a list in her diary of things she needed to do on Monday when this hellish weekend would be over and then she took out Freddie's letter, though she'd reread it at least a hundred times. Committed every word to memory.

It's impossible to love you the way you wish to be loved.

I don't believe that I've ever managed to give you one single moment of the true, pure happiness that you deserve.

If only I were a better man, but I'm not and you always knew that, Libby.

She might have reread the letter a hundred times, but still each word felt as if it had been seared into her flesh. They were the words of a liar. The confession of a coward. And the worse thing of all was that she still loved Freddie, even as she hated him. Libby thrust the letter away, stuffed it back between the pages of her diary, and pressed a hand to her belly.

At one point, as they were approaching Hayward's Heath and each jolt of the train along the tracks seemed to sharpen the pain on her right side, Libby glanced up to see that Mr Watkins had lowered *The Times*, so his gaze could flicker over her. He caught Libby's eye then and made not the slightest attempt to hide his distaste, as if she were a cheap tart that Mickey had found hanging about Shepherd's Market.

Then they were in Brighton. Back in the day, Libby would visit the town twice, sometimes three times a year, to do a run. Occasionally at The Theatre Royal but more usually at The Gaiety before it was turned into a cinema, like so many theatres before and since. Always, but always, the company would take rooms at a ghastly boarding house in Kemptown, sleeping six to a room and three to a bed, though usually there wasn't much sleeping but staying up to all hours playing gin rummy for ha'pennies and drinking cherry brandy out of the toothbrush tumbler.

Libby had forgotten about the viciousness of the Brighton wind whipping in from the sea, as she and Mr Watkins stood outside the station and looked down the long, long road that led down to the front. Libby turned up the fur collar of her astrakhan coat and glanced hopefully towards the tram stop and the one cab that idled on the station forecourt.

'We'll walk,' Mr Watkins decided. 'It's not far.' Then he set off, not even bothering to check with Libby that she wanted to walk, which she didn't. She was wearing such silly shoes, three-bar snakeskin pumps with cotton reel heels because all her other shoes needed mending and when she lifted up her suitcase, she winced at the corresponding throb of pain in her side.

But she'd be damned if she'd give Mr Watkins the satisfaction of thinking that she really was some cheap, whiny tart, so Libby trudged through the drizzle and the fierce wind down the long road that was much longer than she remembered. Halfway down, when she still couldn't so much as glimpse the sea, because all she could see in front of her was a murky greyness so it was impossible to distinguish between sky and water, the wind picked up. Now she had to keep tight hold of her hat with one hand, her case with the other, bobbing around people walking towards her, their heads down, their steps brisk, and that terrible wound tightened and pulled so now it felt like the very worst, most agonising kind of stitch.

It was all too soon. She'd only been back in England since mid-December and was meant to be resting, but idling in bed all day didn't pay the bills. To take her mind off the pain, Libby stared at Mr Watkin's stiff black-coated back and cursed him silently but fluently.

You unutterable bloody bastard. Stinking son of a whore. Pox-ridden son of a bitch.

He suddenly whirled round as if she'd hurled the epithets out loud. 'Don't dawdle,' he barked at her.

Oh, you fucking bastard! You bloody bugger . . .

It was the anger, the fire of rebellion in her belly, that kept Libby going, even once they reached the seafront and the wind all but flattened her against the buildings. Then, at last, they were at the hotel, rising up through the murk like a gothic wedding cake, a door held upon for her by a uniformed commissionaire as Mr Watkins sailed in before her, then stalked over to the Reception Desk.

Libby gratefully relinquished her case to the porter and with pained, hobbling steps caught up with Watkins, took hold of his sleeve and tucked her arm in his.

Though she'd already thought him impossibly stiff, he stiffened even further at her touch. 'We're meant to be in love,' she reminded him. 'Maybe not love, but as if a weekend in a hotel together isn't an ordeal by fire.'

'Very well,' he muttered and he continued his path to the Reception Desk, with Libby on his arm as if they'd suddenly become attached and he didn't have the first idea about how to shake her free.

As they were taken to their room by the porter, the lift creaking alarmingly between floors, Libby decided that she would have to find it within herself to be gay and charming. When she really set her mind to being gay and charming there were very few people who failed to succumb. Mr Watkins might present her biggest challenge to date, but they couldn't spend two whole days together with him either silent or snapping at her.

They were shown to a large, rather nice room on the fifth floor with sea views and its own bathroom, which was thrilling. No bundling into one's robe and thundering down the corridor in fear and dread of bumping into another guest. Libby smiled approvingly when Watkins tipped the porter half a crown and as the young boy shut the door quietly behind him as he left, she made her smile bigger and brighter.

It was wasted on Watkins. He turned away from Libby to stare out of the window at the rainlashed view. He hadn't even taken off his hat and coat. 'This needn't be awful, spending time together like this,' she said to his shoulders, which tightened as she spoke. 'It's only two days. That isn't such a long time, not really. We might as well make the best of it, don't you agree?'

At first, Libby thought that he hadn't heard, though she'd spoken clearly enough. She sighed, put a tentative hand to her side where the pain ebbed and flowed and was just thinking of the drubbing she'd give Mickey when she got back to town, when Watkins turned round.

Then Libby wished he hadn't, because those glances he'd given her before, as disdainful as they had been, were nothing compared to the contempt that contorted his face now.

'Just how do you suggest that I make the best of this damned ugly business?' he demanded. 'If you have any ideas then I'd love to hear them.'

'It's two days,' Libby repeated with less conviction this time. 'Forty-eight hours. They'll be over in a flash.'

'Two days for you, maybe. Twenty bloody years for me gone down the drain and all I get to show for it is a weekend in a hotel with some floozy . . . ' He stopped then, for which Libby was grateful, though she'd been called much worse before. Watkins looked disgusted, repulsed, though she wasn't sure if she was the cause or just a symptom.

The funny thing was that this wasn't even going to be the worst two days of her life. She'd had far worse times than this – days when her despair had meant that every second felt like a minute, every minute dragged by like an hour – but still Libby didn't relish the prospect of having to deal with the furious Watkins for any longer than she had to.

'I'm not a floozy,' she said mildly, because there was absolutely no point in antagonising the man any further.

'And I'd bet a pound to a penny that your name isn't Marigold and you're not an impoverished widow either,' he said and sprang towards Libby. She reared back in alarm, but Watkins didn't so much as touch her. Instead he walked past her to the door and then he was gone and she was glad of it.

Libby sank down on the bed and oh God, she didn't even want to think about how the bed would feature in her bravura performance tomorrow morning when the maid brought in tea and saw her and Mr Watkins tucked up together as if they'd spent the night hours in the throes of passion. Instead she hung her head and breathed through and around the pain until it receded enough that she could get up and slowly, so very slowly, take off her coat and hat, then slip off her shoes.

It gave Libby no small amount of satisfaction to stuff her damp shoes with pages torn out of Watkin's copy of *The Times* and then she decided to run a bath. She'd have much rather had a shower; the last time she'd had a shower was when she'd been in California five years ago, but now that the pain was past, she felt so tired, her legs trembling, that she didn't want to stand for any longer than she could help it.

Soon enough Libby was sinking into the water, head lolling back, arms on either side of the tub, her eyes closed. She didn't know how long she lay there, occasionally easing up the plug with one foot, so she could let in more hot water, but it was so blissful to simply do nothing. To free her mind from worry.

Then she opened her eyes, glanced down, and the calm was shattered. She always tried not to look at the scar because then she'd wonder again and again, the thoughts chasing around in her head like panicked hens, what they'd done to her in that hospital in Paris because now she felt so empty. A husk. As if they hadn't just taken away what was left of the baby but every other part of her too.

True, her heart was still intact, beating away though she often wished that they'd taken that away too. Her heart had always been a useless thing. Leading her such a dance, making a fool of her, persuading her that she was in love time after time . . .

Now Libby had nothing to show for all that love but a jagged, puckered scar across her belly. The raw red skin itched and Libby put her hand between her legs then held it up to see her fingers streaked with blood. Oh, not again.

There'd been so much blood; thick, viscous, clotted with clumps. Libby had had to waddle into the hospital with one of the hotel towels between her legs. Freddie, his face muddy with shock, had clung to her arm, though he was meant to be the one who was holding her up. It had been a Catholic hospital but the nuns had been so cruel to Libby because she'd left her wedding ring on the bureau back at the hotel and they thought she was a whore.

It made Libby quite light-headed to remember, though when she put her hand between her legs again, her fingers came away clean and the pain was ebbing, on the wane.

Suddenly there was a rap on the door. 'What *are* you doing in there?'

It was Watkins. At least she'd managed to forget about him for the last hour. 'I'll be out soon,' Libby tried to say but the effort it would take was too much when she needed every ounce of strength that she possessed to brace her hands on the lip of the bath and heave herself out of the water.

Climbing out of the tub was like trying to scale a mountain but finally Libby was standing on the bathmat, legs shaky, fingers fumbling as she wrapped a towel around her.

Another peremptory knock on the door. 'Please come out. You're being so childish. I need to talk to you.'

Libby pulled a face, even that made her head swim, as if she were in a dream, pitching forward. 'I'm not decent.' It was nothing more than a whisper.

'I can't hear you!'

Oh go away, you hateful man.

Libby took a faltering step towards the door and then she really was pitching forward, not falling, but floating, floating, floating . . .

Libby drifted in the hinterland between sleep and wakefulness. Sometimes Freddie's face was all she could see. How she'd missed the soft, tender look in his eyes when it was just the two of them and the rest of the world could go hang. Other times, she was conscious of being jostled and dragged, another man's face in front of her, creased with concern, then two young woman in white caps, black dresses, like the nuns, their voices anxious but muted as if they were speaking from another room.

Then Libby was awake, in bed, the covers pulled up to her chin. 'Ah, she's back with us,' said a voice and Libby turned her head to see a man, white-haired, well-fed, with a bulbous red nose. Likes a drink, she thought to herself, as he patted her shoulder. 'You gave your husband quite a fright, Mrs Watkins.'

'I'm not . . . ' She wasn't Mrs Watkins. She was Mrs Morton. Then she remembered that really she'd only been Freddie's wife for a few short months, weeks really, and then he'd left her. And now she was in this room, in this ghastly situation, helping another man leave his wife. She turned her head to see Watkins on the other side of the bed.

She'd been too cowed by his contempt to have a proper look at him before, but now she could see that he had dark hair greying at the temples and swept back from a patrician face, dark blue eyes, full mouth. He rather looked like Freddie but his features were broader and there was a weariness to him; a jaded quality that Freddie had yet to acquire. 'I feel much better now. Did I faint? I never faint.'

'No more hot baths for you,' the doctor ordered jovially then he chivvied Watkins from the room so he could take Libby's temperature and pulse and it seemed a pity to waste the services of a doctor, when one was at hand. So when he asked her if she was still feeling peculiar, she nodded.

'I lost a baby last November. In Paris. I had to have an operation and ever since then I've had these episodes where I feel quite queer,' she explained haltingly, then she described the agonising stitch in her side, the intermittent bleeding, how sometimes she feel so tired, so despondent, she could hardly drag herself from her bed.

The doctor perched on the side of the bed, had a cursory glance at the scar marring her belly, then patted her hand. 'These things happen,' he said in the same jovial tone. 'How far along were you?'

'About six months, but I thought . . . I hoped, that there . . . I'd still be able to have a baby.' Libby shut her eyes and sniffed. 'At the hospital, they never really explained and my French isn't that good. There was a letter but I can't find it and you see . . . '

'I do see, my dear. Judging from the mess they made of stitching you back up and the symptoms you're presenting with, there can be no doubt that it was a hysterectomy. But that's the Frogs for you, far too melodramatic for their own good. Knew a French chap once, the type of fellow to take a sledgehammer to crack a walnut. How old are you?'

Usually, Libby told people that she was twenty seven – she'd always been able to pass as younger – so it was hard to remember to tell the truth. 'Thirty-two,' she admitted.

'You had left it rather late to start a family.' Libby was starting to hate the doctor with his glib pronouncements and air of a man who was long overdue for a stiff drink and his dinner. 'Still, best not to dwell on it. I have a sister who never had children. She breeds poodles and seems happy enough.'

'I've never liked poodles,' Libby said as there was a soft knock on the door and Watkins came back into the room.

'Maybe gardening, then,' the doctor said, rising to his feet and shaking out the creases in his trousers. 'I imagine you're probably anaemic. You need building up, my dear. Two spoonfuls of cod liver oil twice a day. A glass of milk stout every evening and if I were you, young man, I'd make sure your good wife has steak once a week.'

'Well . . . I . . . that is . . . ' Watkins was wrong-footed and stuttering, so different from how he'd been before. Libby wondered if she shouldn't faint more often.

'Can't afford steak?' The doctor looked around the hotel room in disbelief. 'Liver, then. You'll be as right as rain in no time.' All the while, he was putting stethoscope, thermometer and notebook back in his bag. 'Aspirin for the pain, if you must.'

Then he stood there for one awkward, uncertain moment until realisation dawned on Watkin's face. 'I'll see you out.' He walked the doctor to the door, where they had a brief, hushed conversation before money exchanged hands.

Libby arranged the pillows behind her and when Watkins turned from the door she was sitting up, hands neatly clasped together. Someone – she fervently hoped that it was one of the two maids she'd glimpsed during her funny turn – had dressed her in the oyster silk nightgown that had been part of her trousseau: the only item in her trousseau, because she'd hardly been a blushing, nervous virgin on her wedding night. But how fitting in a grim, horrible way that she'd planned to wear it tonight.

She was surprised at how calm she felt. 'I really don't know what you must think of me,' Libby said as she wondered exactly what information about her condition the doctor had shared with this man pretending to be her husband. She decided that she didn't much care. After this weekend, she'd never have to see Watkins again. 'I generally don't make a habit of swooning.'

'It wasn't a swoon, it was a dead faint,' Watkins said. His voice was much softer, kinder now that he wasn't spitting words at her like they were bullets. 'What I said to you, how I behaved, it was unforgiveable.'

'Either way, it's forgiven,' Libby said and she meant it. Not just because her forgiveness might prolong this new accord between them but because she knew exactly how it felt when the person you loved hadn't cared one jot for the 'til death do us part' portion of their marriage vows.

It felt like the end of the world.

'Shall we start again, you and I?' he asked her, as he came to sit on the bed, in the same spot that the doctor had recently vacated. Not that Libby was alarmed. She liked to think that she could spot a wrong 'un a mile away and only a wrong 'un, an absolute cad, the very lowest of the low, would take advantage of a woman who'd been in a dead faint not half an hour ago. 'Is your name really Marigold?'

'It's really not.' There didn't seem much point to the pretence any more. 'It's Elizabeth. Libby, my friends call me.'

'Hugo,' he said, holding out his hand for her to shake. 'Pleased to meet you.'